DESTINY'S WAR

MARIE BILODEAU

DESTINY'S WAR

MARIE BILODEAU

Destiny's War
Copyright © 2013 Marie Bilodeau

ISBN 978-1-7771381-3-4

DEDICATION

To Karen Henderson (née Force. How cool is that?). For believing.

Litras

Elsa

ACKNOWLEDGEMENTS

This third book in the *Destiny* series represents my sixth published book. With each new book, I'm more grateful than ever for the team that makes it all happen.

The team at Dragon Moon Press deserves to be lavished with cookies and cream: Gabrielle Harbowy, for helping to forge the vision and editing thoroughly, Gwen Gades, publisher supreme, and Kari Ann Anderson, for another wonderful cover AND extra art this time!

I'd get nowhere without the support of my family. First off, special thanks to my mythical "Roomy," a.k.a. ElfPony, a.k.a. Kerri Elizabeth Gerow, my long-suffering roommate and biggest supporter. My team is always willing to put up with my whining/cheering/destroying of worlds. I love them all for it: Jessica Torrance, Katherine Gallant, Karen Henderson. My brother, Jean-François Bilodeau, who likes to distract me with bad movies, which I enjoy. My honourary brothers, Martin Gallant and Dave Henderson. Thanks to my mom, Suzanne Desjardins, for always listening. Thanks to my dad, Gilles Bilodeau and my stepmom, Nicole Caouette.

I've met many wonderful people since *Destiny's Fall* was published and one in particular provided the right words to turn this book into reality. Thanks to Karen Dudley for being my writing coach (whether she realized it or not) and wonderful friend.

I would be remiss not to thank the friends who have managed to inspire, whether they know it or not: Rob Uhrig, Sarah Parkinson, Nicole Lavigne, Brian Grassie, Mary Pletsch, Dylan Blacquiere, Megan and Ian Postin, Vicki Gerow and the entire Torrance and Gerow clans. Special thanks to Kathryn Hunt, Ruthanne Edward and Sean Zio, for whispered words and inspirations.

Thanks to my colleagues, Sarah Watts-Rynard, Shawn Watson, Emily Arrowsmith and Amin Rawjani. I'm sure they deal with more insanity than I care to acknowledge.

And of course thanks to my writing group, the East Block Irregulars, for continuous wisdom, inspiration and motivation: Derek Künsken, Matt Moore, Hayden and Liz Trenholm, Peter Atwood, Geoff Gander, Agnes Cadieux, as well as Kate Campbell-Moore and Mavourneen Mooney.

CHAPTER 1

IN A SMALL section of the red-hued sky, stars melted into each other for about five of Mirial's seconds before engaging in a slow rotation. Green tinges danced around its edges and stitched stars back into the sky, in a perfect circle of light.

Layela Delamores, Keeper of Mirial, looked up from the tiny symbols etched on the wall of the temple, her breath catching in her throat at the sight. Her fingers still grazed the stone, now more smooth than coarse. She absent-mindedly ran her fingers over the Three Fates, surrounding the once brilliant sun of Mirial.

Her mouth opened and closed twice, trying to wrap around words she didn't fully understand. She took a deep breath. The circle was steady in the sky, Mirial's greeting a whisper on the air around her.

Maybe no one else had seen it yet. Maybe no one stared and pleaded with the stars as much as she did. She didn't have much time and, despite waiting for this day for ten years, there was much to be done. Selenor, the temple caretaker, stood near her, mumbling as great lasers cut into the stone of the temple, between the stabilizing ropes.

It would be moved to a ship, soon. They would all be moved to a ship.

The urgency crashed into her and she walked out, Selenor too absorbed to notice her departure. Loran, her captain of the guards, fell in line with her at the entrance. Layela passed the three pillars of the Three Fates, which guarded Mirial and all of the known universe. Loran wisely kept any questions to herself.

Layela had to find Ardin. She had to make sure he knew; that their small fleet was ready.

She waffled between excitement and dread.

The Seeders had finally returned. Mirial would perish.

And they would finally be free.

***

They entered the palace minutes later, Layela catching only glimpses of the tunnel as she walked. Mirial coaxed speed in her, sighing insistently in her mind.

The tunnel entrance, at least, was mostly composed of ether for now, which meant she seemed to be the only one able to see it. Someone else would have surely said something, otherwise. She wanted this controlled. Mirialers were not prone to panic, but the thought of losing their planet, their sun and their entire star system had already resulted in more than one incident since she'd announced the Seeders' plans, ten years ago. The more in control she seemed, the better for everyone.

Children ran across her path, unattended. So many Mirialers had taken her invitation to move into the palace with her that it brimmed with laughter and conversation.

Once their own star had faded and life proved more difficult to uphold, gathering all of the remaining citizens of Mirial closer together had only made sense. Some life support equipment was adapted to provide heat for their gardens, extra light for plants and to ward off people's depression, and a few animals, even, so they could enjoy fresh milk and eggs, a luxury not afforded to Mirial in well over a generation.

Some ether creatures walked nearby, joining them from all over the universe to bid Mirial a final goodbye, and Layela paused to watch them for a moment. All colours, different body shapes, some so ethereal that only she could perceive them…they all depended on the First Star for their survival. They all depended on her to ensure that the ether passed from one star to the next.

Over the past ten years, Layela had absorbed every piece of lore about the First Star that she could find…which had proved to be very little. The First Star was cloaked in more mythology than fact, and whatever knowledge remained of it lay with the silent Seeders, who worked away at forging a star so distant it wasn't yet a pinprick in their sky. It would not be, until well past their lifetimes.

The one thing she had come to understand, not from the texts or stories but from Mirial herself, was that the First Star would not survive the transfer of ether.

Mirial's whispers became more insistent.

A Zoorsa stepped in front of Layela. He was young, probably a teenager, she guessed. His pearlized olive skin reflected the sunset, and his eyes were slit like a feline's. Layela didn't know much about the Zoorsa, save that they were not normally a spacefaring race. She did her best to hide her surprise to even see one on Mirial. Loran stood near her on her right, her stance alert.

"Good evening," Layela said, trying to remember if a proper title existed for his people.

The Zoorsa stared at her, his eyes wide with recognition or fear. She was never really sure with the ether creatures. "Um, good evening, Keeper." He lowered his head in an awkward bow.

"It is a pleasure to see your people on Mirial," Layela said, fighting the urge to brush him off. She didn't want to be remembered as the Keeper who ignored the need of the ether races. So much of what she had set in place was for their survival, after all.

"I came by myself, to witness for my people." He swallowed and looked back up, almost looking her in the eye, but focusing somewhere near her nose instead.

"That's good to hear, Mr…"

"Oh! Hoast. My name is Hoast. Keeper! My name is Hoast, Keeper."

Layela struggled not to laugh. "Hoast. It's great to meet you. Thank you for coming."

"Of course, Keeper." He hesitated as though he had something else to ask. Mirial's practically screamed in her mind, now. Soon, the tunnel would be revealed to everyone, and they had to be leave. Farewells, long coming, would still feel hasty. And so many ether creatures like this Zoorsa also had to evacuate, lest they be swept up in Mirial's demise.

She forced her smile to stay plastered on her face, despite the growing feeling of urgency.

"It was lovely meeting you, Hoast."

He held up his hand, and Loran took a step forward. Layela held one hand up to stop her, the other to accept the offering. Hoast opened his fist and a flower fell from it. "This is...this is a flower that a friend of mine grew. I think she'd want you to have it."

He met her eyes for a second and then mumbled something and scampered away. Layela sighed and put the flower in her pocket. Every ether creature seemed to want to offer her a gift or ask for a favour. The ether creatures had been begging and pleading with her, worried about losing their lifeline to the ether. She had put as many worries to rest as she could, and was certain the Seeders would see to the survival of the ether races.

Mirial danced in the back of her mind, the tired star sighing more quietly, preparing herself for a final rest she desperately craved.

The First Star offered her Keeper no more comfort than Layela could offer everyone else.

***

The research and experimental shipyard was attached to the palace, with a docking shipyard further away, to ensure the safety of the inhabitants of the palace. *Not that anyone really cares about invading Mirial, now.*

The past ten years had been quiet. A tentative peace had been struck with Solaria, who obviously didn't see Mirial as a threat. At least they had ensured safety for any ether creatures seeking asylum. Solaria had never quite brought itself around to shutting down its gassing chambers over the past decades, a fact that didn't escape Layela's attention or worry.

The stones of the palace turned to metal as she entered the newer shipyards. She could hear some shouted orders and a drill started up. The stench of metal fatigue filled the shipyard.

She turned a corner and spotted Ardin talking to Biolt, his head engineer. The two were staring intently at a piece of metal. Layela softened into a smile, even though her heavy heart weighed it down. Ardin didn't spot her coming, too intent on his conversation. Layela walked slowly, letting his sight burn itself into her memory. She always did, now, as though she expected to lose him at any moment. She had caught him doing the same to her, and figured he felt the same.

He grew more handsome with each passing year. His bearing was still proud, although she was well aware of how difficult it was to hide the pain in his shoulder, which tugged at his back and folded him in the evenings, when it was just the two of them in their chamber.

His hair was still auburn, though it was a tinge darker now. He still wore it long and in a ponytail. She was glad for that—the simple reminder of life before Mirial, so many years ago.

She came too close, and his shoulders stooped slightly. She stopped and gave him time to adjust and recover.

Once he straightened again, she approached him, broadening her smile. He always let her approach, as though he feared he couldn't stop himself from gathering her in his arms if he was the one to breach the gap. That might kill him.

He should have left her, years ago, like she'd pleaded him to. But she was more glad than ever that he'd decided to stay with her, shunning the chance at another life on another planet or traveling the stars with his sister.

Her hand was on his lower back before he looked up and grinned. Mirial practically danced in her mind, now. The tunnel would be visible, soon. She wanted to lock gaze with Ardin and ignore what would soon happen, but instead of grabbing the moment, she let it float by her as any other moment. Their last normal moment on the planet where they had created so many wonderful memories.

"We think we've figured out how to improve the exterior shell of our M-23 shuttles."

She fought back her growing sense of urgency. A final normal, everyday conversation. Possibly for a long time.

"Oh?"

"A different metal mix, by just a fraction of a percent, and we should see a huge improvement in sturdiness."

Layela looked at the worn piece of metal in Biolt's hand. "Is that the, um, improvement?" She got another grin from Ardin.

"Nope. Failed test. But each failed test gets Biolt closer to the answer."

Biolt flushed red and mumbled something about ion qualities before walking back towards his computer.

Ardin focused on Layela. "Are you done for the day?"

She nodded. "We're ready." Before she could continue, Ardin exclaimed.

"Agreed!" He glanced back to Biolt. "I think we're done here, too. The sun is pretty much set, so how about we go for a walk?" He grabbed her hand and tugged her out. The warmth mixed with the tang of dark ether made his grasp uncomfortable, but she didn't let go. She hadn't for ten years, and neither had he.

But soon, that shouldn't be an issue, either.

Whatever vegetation had regrown since Layela had stepped up as Keeper was long gone. The landscape rose in bumps and rocks, dry earth reflecting the low moon, which hung large and bright on the horizon. The ground was hard under Layela's feet. It always made her feel as if she walked on a tombstone.

It's time to let Mirial rest.

Layela clung to the ether and encouraged Mirial to encircle the opening tunnel, to let it be visible to all of those on Mirial. She smiled to Ardin and leaned in for a quick kiss, pulling back before she hurt him too much.

She whispered the words, afraid she would choke on them. "They're finally coming."

Ardin looked at her, his confusion vanishing as he followed her gaze up into the skies, where the circle of light, now tinged with muted green light, danced into sight.

He squeezed her hand. She glanced sideways at him, a huge smile on his face. She looked back to the circle and returned the squeeze.

CHAPTER 2

THE AIR DANCED around her, a flutter of petals and children's laughter. She leaned back, the wooden bench creaking. The sunlight jumped in her eyes as she leaned forward again, elbows on knees.

Despite her aching back and the hunger somersaulting in her stomach, Avienne Malavant couldn't peel herself away from the park. The fresh air smelled of spring, her favourite season. It had been years since she'd seen a spring, and on this planet it was particularly charming.

She rested her arm on the back of the bench, letting her hand dangle. The wind played with wisps of her red hair. In the park, the children dispersed for dinner, small hands falling into larger hands. Laughter followed behind them.

Not one larger hand amongst them belonged to Rose, the woman who had taken her niece to safety, ten long years ago. And not one child teased recognition from her. No auburn hair like her brother's, no differently coloured eyes, no strong cheekbones reminiscent of Layela's.

There were millions of planets, more than a hundred of which were colonized, and those were just the ones that made it on maps. Beyond that, hundreds of moons held large, flourishing colonies. She was certain many others existed that a Mirialer like Rose might choose. And there were also thousands of ships travelling the length of Solaria and beyond: small ships, freight ships, colony ships and behemoths that carried the equivalent of a large planet in population.

And she was looking for someone who didn't want to be found. Someone who knew how to survive, and who had vowed never to be caught. Rose had enough money to keep going for a while, and she could always get some work repairing shuttles if she needed more. They were fine, Avienne suspected, but still, she had promised her brother ten years ago that she would keep looking. Even if she hadn't promised Ardin, she would still have continued to look. Family was everything.

The park stood empty around her, even the swings refusing to move in the breeze. Avienne stood up and stretched.

Her comm unit flashed to life with a message.

- ETD 1H -

She took a quick puff of oxygen—the air was a bit too thin on this planet for her liking; she was used to a much richer, if artificial, atmosphere.

"Time to go," she mumbled to herself and turned to leave the park, re-entering the quiet cobbled city street. The buildings were magnificent—all produced from local stone, which gleamed in the light of the planet's dual suns.

A shadow caught her attention, darkening the ground to her right. Someone had come up fast behind her. Letting her instincts take over, Avienne whipped around, knife in hand.

A familiar orange-tinted face was before her, sharp teeth parting the lips in a smile.

"Avienne Malavant, well met again."

Avienne hesitated for a split second before sheathing her knives. There was no mistaking the Kilita. Her toothy grin seemed silly, but Avienne spotted the careful, confident stance and the cunning in her eyes.

"Litras," Avienne cocked her head sideways. "Looking as young as ever."

Litras' grin widened. "Kilita take a long time to age."

"Oh? Do they all jump as high as you and fly invisible ships?" Avienne's hand twitched for the feel of a knife. Litras shrugged.

"We all do what we have to do. But I didn't just come here for a little reunion. I intercepted something that I thought might be of interest to you."

Avienne sighed. "All right. I'll bite, oh mysterious Kilita. What, pray tell, is of such interest that you reappear in my life?"

Kilita tipped her head sideways. "Giving up drinking made you cranky. I told you some things just aren't that important."

Avienne furrowed her brow. How did she even know? She had promised the Fates she would give it up if they saved her brother, more than a decade ago. Avienne knew enough of a good thing to know when not to chance screwing it up. When Litras had left, she had given Avienne a bottle and told her that some promises didn't matter that much…

"Kilita are telephatic," Avienne said bluntly. Of course they were. She always assumed ether creatures' special abilities were only triggered when they touched something or someone, but that might not be the case for Litras.

"Well, if you are telepathic, you can guess what I'm thinking right now?" Avienne visualized Litras being torn limb from limb, pulverized, powdered, and served as a drink. Which she enjoyed greatly.

"I don't think I need to be telepathic to figure out what you're thinking, Avienne."

Avienne imagined herself downing a whole pitcher of powdered Litras. *Read my mind, will you!*

"Then I suppose you don't want to know what I found out about your niece."

Avienne's thought bubble burst. "What? What do you know about Ardice? Is she okay?"

"I honestly don't know," Litras said. "But Rose is being held in a detention centre on the Solarian colony on Olte."

Avienne resumed walking, practically running towards her ship. "That's a moon in the Carmel system, right?"

Litras, with her shorter legs, jogged along beside her. Avienne slowed her stride a bit.

"How did you find out?"

Litras shrugged. "I read someone's mind."

"You're a pest, but at least an informative one. Shall we take your ship or mine?"

"Yours is more spacey."

"If that's a pun, it's a bad one. All right, let's go. Should take us just over a day to reach the moon through the Stollar tunnels. They're expensive to travel on, but our best bet."

Litras just nodded and kept up as Avienne broke into a full run.

It had been ten years. Ten long, uneventful years since Rose had taken Ardice off the *Destiny II* and sworn to protect her at all cost.

She hoped the price hadn't been too high for Rose, but she hoped even more that Ardice had not paid any price at all.

***

Avienne stormed onto the bridge to find only her second-in-command, Gobran Kipso, sitting at the engineering station. Gobran had lost his daughter and his eyesight in their final confrontation with Solaria. He had adapted to the lost vision thanks to his memory and his keen sense of hearing, but the loss of his daughter had left him old before his time. In his mid-seventies, he looked as frail as an eighty-year-old man. But his mind was still sharp and he knew the ship better than anyone else, so Avienne didn't question his right to remain in her service, even though she offered him a nice retirement from time to time.

He always refused.

"Captain," he said. She wasn't sure how he identified the crew so easily—if it was how they walked, smelled, or if he had bought an implant to see heat waves. Even the contractors they took in to fix the ship or help with big shuttle shipments only required one introduction, and Gobran would never mistake them for anyone else.

She never asked him how he did it, because she didn't really care. As long as he kept being as good as he was, she'd keep him on as her second in command.

"Gobran, get Jaru and Patros up here." He pressed a few buttons and sent out the notice.

Three crew members were all she needed. She'd never belonged to a big crew, and she found them a waste of time and resources. They could accomplish just as much being only four. Well, maybe not quite as much. A dedicated engineer would have been nice, but it had proved impossible to find a good and trustworthy one. The best ones all worked for Solaria military, since they paid the most, and you didn't necessarily want the bad ones touching your engine.

The lift door opened and Jaru and Patros stepped onto the bridge. Jaru slipped quickly to his station, looking as he always had except for a bit less hair and a bit more of a tremor in his hands. Of course, maybe if he drank less coffee he would probably tremble less.

Patros headed to the navigation station, before spotting Litras and staring at her with a raised eyebrow. Avienne smiled at him. The Slont's skin was blue, although much paler than when she had first met him. His dark blue hair tousled to his shoulders. He'd long given up on keeping it trimmed.

Avienne took a deep breath.

"You all remember Litras?" she said, more for Gobran's benefit. She wasn't certain he had heard the Kilita, since he'd mentioned nothing.

Patros nodded and Jaru looked up momentarily from the data feed before returning his attention to it. Gobran's face didn't betray any surprise.

"Jaru, can you access Olte's records and get a list of current detainees?"

Jaru nodded and his fingers flew on the control panel. "Got it."

Avienne waited while he scanned the list. He paused and looked up. "Who am I looking for?"

"Rose Delamores."

Patros sucked in his breath. Avienne forced herself to keep her eyes on Jaru. She didn't want to meet Patros' eyes and see the question that would be lingering there.

What had happened to Ardice?

"Nothing," Jaru said. Avienne was elated and crushed at once. She had always imagined that she would catch a glimpse of Ardice at a park, or a school, even. Young Ardice would turn to her and her eyes, one twilight blue and the other sea green, would catch Avienne's for a moment. There would be a flicker of recognition, but they would not exchange any words.

Then she would join her group of friends and laugh as she walked home, where Rose would be waiting for her with a warm meal. Her laughter would be like Avienne's, wild and free.

Litras scattered her daydream. "She wouldn't use her real name, of course. Especially not Delamores, in case someone's looking. But she's there, trust me."

Avienne looked at her questioningly. "Trust you?"

"Did we not fight in battles together? Did I not help your brother save you from the slave camps?"

Patros joined Avienne. "We barely know anything about you."

"Yes, and I was escaping fine when you showed up half naked, thank you very much," Avienne chimed in.

"Say I'm wrong. What do you have to lose by checking it out?"

Avienne turned to Patros. His eyes creased just a bit at the corners, and she had her answer. A decade in the wide emptiness of space was a long time to learn how to read someone down to the simplest expression.

"All right. Let's do this, and then we bring a shipment to Mirial. They probably have some shuttles ready for us to go re-sell. Gobran, get us out of here."

Patros exchanged another quick glance with Avienne before going to his post. Avienne turned to Litras.

"Are you still just as useless in a ship?"

The Kilita looked wounded. "I was getting pretty good, wasn't I?"

Avienne grinned. She didn't think she could trust the Kilita, but blood and bones, she liked her.

"Just sit over there where you won't hurt anyone, especially yourself."

Litras flashed her teeth before taking a seat, looking enthusiastically towards the viewport.

"What about your ship?" Avienne asked as she sat at tactical. She'd long given up on the captain's chair. It had always felt strange to her, and besides, she couldn't shoot guns from there.

"Oh, it'll be fine."

"Right." Avienne checked weapons and defensive measures. The *Dessicate* was an old and worn ship, but she came with well-sharpened teeth. Ardin had offered Avienne newer ships from Mirial's slowly forming fleet, but she had grown fond of her old ship. And no one ever took her for a threat, which proved a nice advantage.

"There's something else, too," Litras said.

"Oh?"

"The timing is a bit…worrisome."

Avienne nodded. That, she had already thought of. The timing *was* worrisome, for Rose to show up in a detention facility now, with the new First Star so soon to ignite.

For ten years they had kept the secret of Ardice's survival, to keep knowledge of her away from the Seeders and buy her freedom from becoming Keeper of the new star. Buy her freedom, and Layela's, and Ardin's.

And Avienne's. She had already lost more than a decade for Mirial.

They had planned to seek Ardice once they were free of Mirial. Not before. Especially not *right* before, when the whole flow of ether was about to change.

So close, and yet…

Avienne ran another check on her weapons, just in case.

CHAPTER 3

LAYELA'S EXCITEMENT TUMBLED into queasiness. The throne room of Mirial buzzed with energy. Every Mirialer seemed to be here, summoned by their Keeper to join her in welcoming the Seeders. Ardin stood not far from her, looking just as excited, beaming with anticipation. The Seeders' arrival meant that the new First Star was ready for ignition, to take over supplying the universe with life-giving ether. Mirial had done her duty, and its nearly empty engines would be allowed to finally rest.

Over the last decade Layela had combed the library of Mirial, but she had found no reference to a changeover of First Stars. Maybe this was the first time it ever happened, or maybe the recorded histories and lore didn't stretch quite far enough. Much from the libraries of Mirial had been lost during the Great Darkness more than thirty years ago. That information might just no longer be available or known to any Mirialer.

She thought of her old court advisor, Gresko Listan, and wished he were here. He would have loved these proceedings and the formality of it all. He would have advised her endlessly and practiced protocol with her. She smiled.

I'll make you proud, Gresko.

Loran Natwar stood to the left of the throne, wearing her guard uniform. A few other uniformed guards, selected by Loran herself, stood near the throne to add to the importance of the occasion. It brought weight to the ceremony. Her guards rarely wore their uniforms, since they worked in the mud alongside their Keeper.

With Mirial's ether about to stop flowing, its planet would no longer be protected by it. The atmosphere would be ripped away, the blast from the sun would then rip the planet to pieces.

Layela swallowed hard and forced herself to smile. She reminded herself over and over again: *We will soon all be free.*

This would be the last official proceeding in the palace, which would remain behind on Mirial, to be destroyed in a wave of dust or to survive on a broken rock. The temple, gateway to Mirial herself, would come with them. Layela wasn't certain how the new Keeper would communicate with the new First Star, but leaving behind their only link to the First Star had seemed foolish. It had already been laser-cut according to fine-tuned architectural schematics, then transported aboard the *Lady Mirial.*

Nor could she fathom leaving behind her last remaining connection to her sister: the Temple that essentially served as her tombstone.

Layela looked around the room, seeing mostly smiling faces. The buzz was electric, and laughter drifted in the air. When Layela had first announced to the Mirialers that a new First Star would soon be active and Mirial would retire, she had feared morose faces and rebellion from her proud people. But the promise made by the Seeders, of a new planet filled with vegetation and life, protected by a strong First Star, had reanimated many a broken spirit. They suddenly had something to strive for, aside from trying to rebuild a planet orbiting a broken and failing sun.

Children were born, as Mirialers once again planned for a future that was not just an impossible dream. They had embraced Layela's call to help restore the buildings, and many had taken her invitation to move into the palace with her and Ardin. Whatever veil had existed between her and her people, it had lifted with the failing sun. She had not left them, and so they trusted her, their last hope in a dwindling world.

A few children sniffled in the back. Even the newborns were here today, swaddled in their parents' arms. Layela knew all of them well. She had been there at every birth, introduced every child to Mirial, welcomed every new life with ether.

Layela waved at some of the children, who waved back enthusiastically.

She wore a simple dress to welcome the Seeders, the best one in her small wardrobe. Its silk traveled from greens to blues, the colours of Mirial, lined with some gold highlights, like Mirial's sun.

The room filled with light, green and blue hues dancing across the white stone of the throne room, illuminating ancient frescos and highlighting every man, woman and child. Warmth spread across the room and cut the evening chill. Every speck of light gathered in the centre before the throne. Loran stiffened but held her place, not stepping directly in front of Layela.

A Seeder appeared before Layela. Tall and lanky, hovering a bit over the ground, its skin shone gray and light all at once. She assumed it was the same Seeder they had visited previously, although she'd only ever met the one and so couldn't swear to it.

Its voice flowed from barely moving lips, floating on the air around all of them, a whisper that landed directly into the ear and could not be ignored or misheard.

"Greetings, Keeper of the First Star." He lowered his head in respect. Layela smiled and opened her arms in greeting.

"Greetings, Seeder. Welcome to Mirial. You and your people are welcome here."

The Seeder waited a few moments before speaking again. Layela wished she could read their body language better.

"We have come to tell you, as promised long ago, that the new First Star is ready for the ether and colonization. Mirial's services are no longer required, although we welcome you to continue as Keeper of the new star."

The room grew still around her, and time stretched into eternity. She wished she could reach out and take Ardin's hand. She wished she could turn and meet his gaze, but she knew he would not be looking at her. They had spoken about this at length. They had planned and rehearsed in the dead of night, whispering to each other across the darkness.

The words flowed from her lips like life-giving water.

"Thank you, Seeder. Your offer is heard and appreciated. But, as I have no heir, it would be wiser to select another Keeper. One whose blood can long maintain the First Star and help it grow to its full potential."

The Seeder lowered its head slightly. Layela hoped it was acknowledgment.

"Very well," its voice floated around her. "You speak with wisdom, Keeper of Mirial. Your duties will end with Mirial's end, and the new First Star shall select its own Keeper."

Grief tugged at Layela's heart at the thought of Mirial's passing. She had longed for this place, then hated it. She had betrayed it, then cherished it. She had lost a sister here, buried her best friend, felt the treachery of her own blood. She had kissed Ardin for the first time here, learned to love him more deeply, had almost lost him. A piece of her would always stay with Mirial. Here, she had tried to become more than she was, for her sister, for herself, for her daughter.

Ardice.

She would see her soon. She just had to hold on for a bit longer, without speaking of her. Without revealing her longings and fears to anyone but Ardin, who shared them so deeply words were not necessary.

The silence stretched, and Layela interrupted it.

"Thank you, Seeder. As my final duty as Keeper, I would like to see my people safely to their new home."

"Of course, Keeper of Mirial. You know the way. We will await you by end of day tomorrow. Mirial will then end its long journey."

The Seeder vanished in another ray of light, and Layela stood before her people. Silence lay heavily in the room.

She had imagined this moment a thousand times. Laughter, hope, relief…

But looking around at the faces of her people, Layela knew none of them felt that way anymore than she did.

"We'll begin boarding the ships before noon tomorrow," Layela said, her whisper smothered by the silence.

"If you will join me tomorrow morning at the temple, we will bid farewell to Mirial."

***

Layela watched the stars vanish from the sky as Mirial's weak sun swept in the dawn. Neither she nor Ardin had spoken a word or slept all night. They no longer shared a bed since her ether tended to hurt Ardin, but they still slept as closely as they could—on either end of their large bedroom.

She had stayed awake, listening to him twist and turn. After a while, they were both looking out the windows, waiting for the weak sun to rise and illuminate the dead landscape of Mirial.

Mirial had fought hard, lived a good long life, and now she was old and dying, suffering under the lack of rain and sun, dry as a bone, empty and shrivelled. Her death wouldn't just be a release for Layela and her family, but for Mirial, too.

So many had tried to maintain her and keep her, and each time she had paid a greater price. It was time to let her go.

Layela turned to Ardin. "I think I'll take a walk before heading to the temple."

"See you there," he whispered, his eyes piercing the darkness. She blew him a kiss and held on to the hope that she would be able to hold him again by the end of the day. She hoped the dark ether would be removed from him; she knew hers, at least, would be gone.

She tucked away the uncertainty about whether the wards set by her brother a decade ago would outlast Mirial's death; the fear that Ardin would die within days once they were free. She tucked her fear far away into herself, so that it would not impede her steps or stop her entirely.

Even if they fail, perhaps the new First Star's ether won't hurt him. Perhaps his darkness will be healed, too.

She sighed. There was nothing they could do but move forward and hope the Three Fates favoured them this day.

She dressed in her travel clothes. Pants, shirt, coat—nothing remarkable. Today was a journey, and by the end of it, she would no longer be Keeper of Mirial. She would simply be Layela Delamores. Wife. Mother. And she would find her daughter again, if it meant turning the entire universe upside down.

Layela walked the grounds in silence. Little wildlife remained on Mirial save some lizards and bugs that had survived the Great Darkness. There were no thriving populations to leave behind to perish in the aftermath of their sun's death.

She walked up the hill to where the Berganda gardens once bloomed. The broken half wall that kept them safe from the elements still stood, dead vines clinging to the broken brick. All of the vegetation had paid the price when Layela had failed to save Mirial. When, in her eagerness to save Ardin and stop the dark ether, she had doomed the planet.

Layela placed a hand on one of the dead plants, a booknot, sentient while it lived. It was cold, without even a spark of ether or life. Layela withdrew her hand and crouched, touching the dead, crumbling earth. There was nothing here, either. No trace of the Berganda who had been born here, or of the ones who had died.

She almost reached out to Elsa, Josmere's firstborn, leading her sisters on a world faraway, but she resisted the urge. Elsa had precious little ether left and she was old for a Berganda now. Layela did not want to weaken her further with her own selfish need to reach out to someone who would understand her pain.

She suddenly realized that she had not paid attention to last night's sunset. There would never be another sunset on Mirial, and she couldn't quite recall the hues reflected in the atmosphere. She remembered the large moon, Mirial's moon, which she would never see in the sky again.

By the time she reached the temple, her heart and feet were heavy. The Mirialers had already gathered. They parted to let her through, to access the heart of the temple, a place they had never before been allowed.

They shuffled in silence behind her. The great trees still reached up towards a sky that no longer gave enough light to keep them alive, their branches long turned gray and ashen.

Layela stood by the altar with her back to her people. She needed a moment before she could turn to face them. Ardin was here, she knew, feeling the pull of the dark ether on her. Loran would be here, and Biolt, and Selenor…they would all be waiting for her to give them the hope and encouragement they so craved. To provide the right words of farewell.

Layela picked up the knife at the altar, blood from her and her siblings encrusted on its hilt and blade. She placed it in her belt, not intending to leave it behind. She had never cleaned it, and had never let anyone else do so. She remembered Yoma's final sacrifice and wish.

Yoma will be gone. The caresses she felt when sad or afraid, the spirit that stubbornly clung to Mirial, would be gone. Would she lose her eye, too? Her green eye that reminded her of Yoma? The half of her face, if she covered her blue eye, that still reflected Yoma back at her in the mirror?

She clung to the sides of the altar, feeling dizzy, waves of grief threatening to sweep her away. Her hands felt warmth where they touched the stone altar.

I will always be with you, Layela. Mirial is old and in pain. It's time to let us go. Think of Josmere's children.

Layela closed her eyes. "I know," she whispered. Mirial washed over her, trying to soothe her, but no longer having the strength to do more than remind Layela how weak the great star had become.

Yoma said no more and Layela clutched to the altar, feeling her strength grow as the inevitable became necessity. Mirial had done much good in her time, but the ether creatures needed a strong, healthy First Star.

She opened her eyes and took a deep breath, looking at the great mural etched into the wall behind the altar. It recorded everything about the First Star, instructions for the Keeper on the star's workings. She wondered which symbol showed the star's end.

She turned around. Every eye rested on her. She let her gaze capture every single one before speaking. She had planned it all, from start to finish. It was going to be an inspiring speech, filled with historical references and poetic sentiment. But when she opened her mouth, different, unplanned words tumbled out.

"Mirial is so proud of you," Layela said, allowing the tears to run unchecked down her cheeks. "Mirial has seen you all face such challenges and triumph over them. When you were in darkness, you strove to reach her light again and again. You stuck by each other, as only Mirialers can do. You believed in Mirial, in her light, and in her power to change the world. Not just this world, but every world, the whole universe."

She took a deep breath and let her echo fall away. The sun's rays found their way into the temple and lit every corner, ousted every shadow. Mirial was bidding them farewell, glistening in each of their tears. Layela let the warmth fall on her, too, and smiled.

"Mirial is proud of you, and so am I. Your new world will be wonderful, and the new First Star will gain strength from you. It will grow by your care, by all of your care, not just by the new Keeper's." She swallowed hard. "Remember that. The First Star needs all of you. So be good to each other, and be kind to one another. Mirial will always be with you. Never doubt that."

The light intensified in the temple and Layela watched as each pair of eyes closed and let that familiar warmth fill them for a last time. She wondered if the new First Star would feel the same, or if each ether-producing star was made unique through experience and care. The light dimmed and eyes reopened and focused on her again.

"Mirial bade you all farewell. It's time to go. You'll see this temple again—Selenor's team is ready to transport it to the *Lady Mirial.* You have your ship assignments—we'll see you on the new planet."

At this point, Layela had always imagined applause and cheering. But it didn't happen. There was only silence, and no movement to exit the temple.

Then Loran moved in front of Layela, staying on the other side of the small river that separated her people from the altar. She brought up her hand and saluted Layela with her fist, in the old salute of Mirial. She then walked out, but another Mirialer followed, and another, and another. They each came one at a time, every woman, man and child, every Mirialer who had stood with her or against her, who had fought for Mirial during the Great Darkness or fought to return here after being exiled for almost two decades. Every single Mirialer stepped forward and saluted her, paying their respect to Layela, then exiting.

By the time she was alone again, the sun neared its zenith. Layela felt numb to the core. They had finally all accepted her as their Keeper.

They had all said goodbye to her.

She only had one duty left to perform as Keeper.

She only had to lay Mirial to rest.

CHAPTER 4

THE DESSICATE PASSED through the private Stollar tunnels without being challenged. They were expensive to get through and well worth the money. Lots of upper end smuggling operations used these tunnels, but you had to secure a good profit to afford it.

Avienne's fingers twitched on her panel. She wanted to flip a knife, but had promised Patros she would no longer do so on the bridge after the Kalrat system incident. Bloody temperamental space storms. That had hardly been her fault. Still, it had taken a while to get his bleeding under control, so she had agreed. That scar looked pretty cute on his face, though. Toughened up his otherwise smooth blue features.

She checked the systems again. Everything was fine, of course. She was starting to get on her own nerves, so she jumped up.

"Jaru!" Avienne bellowed, and the computer analyst practically jumped out of his chair.

"Captain!"

"Please brief us on the detention facility."

"Aye, Captain! Let's see…it's small and not very well guarded. Basic contingent. Independent hires, not actual soldiers, guard it. They house all sorts of criminals there, ranging from apple thieves to crimes that'll make your hair fall out."

"Stealing apples is pretty serious stuff on certain planets," Litras offered.

"Thank you, Litras. Jaru, anything else that'll help us out?"

Jaru scanned the details quickly, both hands tapping on the panel. He shook his head. "There isn't much in there, to be honest. It doesn't look like a place many people have ever bothered talking much about. Not very interesting or big enough. Nothing even on the smuggling boards, so they mustn't have captured many smugglers."

Avienne turned to face Litras. "How did you find out about Rose? No games, Litras. I'd still like to think of you as a breathing friend by the time this is over."

Litras' lips twitched into a grin, but she thought better of it and nodded instead. "I've been trying to find Rose and Ardice since they left." She held up her hand at the protest forming on Avienne's lips. "I was careful. I used an old Fated Link and focused on Rose only, saying I needed her for information on a lost relative of mine." She shrugged. "It's a common request on ether networks. Lots of us lost relatives when Solaria freaked out. Again."

"What's this Fated Link? I thought I knew every underground network in Solarian space."

"This one's different." Litras hesitated for a moment. "It's a network formed by ether races to help us mobilize faster. We'd lost it when Mirial had faded twenty years ago, but re-ignited it soon after Mirial's comeback. It's about as good as it gets. As long as you can connect into the telepathic network, you can pretty much scour the galaxy in instants."

Avienne sat down by Litras and leaned forward, glad to have something to take her attention off the few remaining hours before they could get to Rose. If not more. "Fated? You called it the Fated Link. What's it fated to do?"

Litras shot a look at Patros. Avienne followed Litras' glance, and Patros blushed. "Fated," he said, "is how ether creatures refer to themselves. Sounds better than 'creature,' really." He tried to smile but it came out twisted with embarrassment.

Avienne spared him and turned back to Litras. "Fated for what? Why?"

She shrugged. "Fated by Mirial. For something. I mean, Mirial practically keeps us tethered. There must be a reason for that, right? A reason we're dependent on her. We just don't know what, but ether creatures have always called themselves Fated, since Mirial's birth."

Avienne leaned back into her seat and stretched. "How long ago was that? Her birth?"

"Some Fated know. Some are as old as she is. But you don't see them much, and they don't play with us youngsters."

"Right." Avienne stared at the ceiling of the ship. She didn't want to ask, but she did anyway. "So what happens when Mirial stops? What happens when she runs out of gas? What happens to the Fated when Mirial vanishes?"

"Theoretically," Litras said, "things pick up when the new First Star takes over ether production. We barely notice a change, except in a higher influx of ether, which will be healthier for us."

"You said once," Avienne said, looking at her, "that a Seeder had visited your village and that you thought they were getting something for the new First Star." She turned to Patros. "What about your people, Patros? Did they visit you?"

Deep blue eyes met hers. "Not that I'm aware of. And there aren't many of us left, so I'd probably be aware of it."

"What does that mean for your people?"

He shrugged, but his downward look emphasized the worry clutching his limbs.

"Blood and bones. Why can't anything ever be simple?"

Silence accompanied the rest of the journey to Olte.

***

The detention centre rose on the horizon like a pimple on the land. It was small and round, with no windows. Olte didn't boast an atmosphere, but rather a series of bubbled domes connected to each other through various tunnels and walkways. Olte's gravity registered below usual Solarian thresholds, but Solaria didn't want to invest more into its little mining community. They mined titanium and oralium, which were the true worth of Olte. Oralium was one of only two known digestible metals, and a delicacy in Solaria.

From what Jaru had found out, the detention centre was used for criminals of all ranges, but mostly for drunken and disorderly conduct. In a desolate, dull place like Olte, stimulants and inhibitors were very popular.

Avienne thanked her luck that the detention centre wasn't directly attached to the community of domes. That would mean easier entry, but also a more difficult escape.

"I don't like this plan at all," Patros said.

Avienne corrected their course and slowed the shuttle. "If you have a better one, go ahead."

"We're just going to walk in there? That's the plan?"

"No," Gobran voiced from the back. "Avienne and I are just going to walk in there. You get to stay on standby in case we need our asses saved."

Avienne grinned. "See? The old blind man gets it, and he's not nearly as concerned as you are." She turned back. "No offence, Gobran."

"None taken, Captain."

"What if they put up a resistance?" Patros said as the shuttle received the okay flag to enter the landing area. Avienne navigated it in easily, letting the computer do most of the work.

"If they put up a resistance…" she landed the shuttle and turned to face him. "Then you come rescue us, remember?" She leaned in and kissed him hard. He kissed back but looked just as discouraged once she disengaged.

"It'll be just like on Trillium, three years ago!" Avienne said as she helped Gobran up. She was posing as his helper, so he would play along.

"On Trillium," Patros said. "Isn't that when we lost three shuttles and all of our guns, and made mortal enemies powerful enough to kill us if ever we get too close to their 22.4 quadrants of Solarian space again?"

"That'd be the one," Avienne winked at him. "Stay out of sight. We'll be back." Patros shot her one more pleading look before sliding down in the seat.

Avienne opened the door and stepped out, careful to account for the lessened gravity by taking small steps. She helped Gobran down and closed the door again. Guards didn't come to meet them, which told her that the security was really lax.

Gobran leaned on her as they slightly bounced towards the reception window. She caught their reflection in a ship's hull. He looked old and frail, and she doubted it required much acting on his part to look even more frail. She couldn't remember when her eyes had developed such bags. And were those some white hairs in her red? She'd have to fix that.

"Good afternoon," an automated attendant said, the voice gratingly pleasant. "Welcome to the Olte detention centre. Please state the purpose of your visit."

Gobran spoke up, his voice more wheezy than usual. "I believe my niece is being held here." Avienne kept her features straight. They were taking a chance. Rose and Gobran were about the same age, but they assumed Rose hadn't aged as badly as Gobran. No one would believe they were siblings, so they went for the better lie.

"Please state the name of your niece."

That was tricky. They'd debated that, and had come up with the best answer they could. Gobran coughed as though upset.

Avienne tried to soothe him and turned to the attendant. The lie slipped from her lips, and she hoped fervently that it sounded truthful.

"She probably gave you a fake ID," Avienne said, trying to keep her voice low as though not to upset Gobran. "She's been missing for a while. Stole from the family. We want to bring her to justice on her home planet."

"Please state home planet?"

"Thalos III. Your detainee is a member of the Thalonian royal family."

A pause in the system. When the attendant spoke again, it was a different voice, and one with inflection. They'd been passed on to a live attendant, which could be good or bad. But it certainly wasn't anything they hadn't anticipated.

"Thalonian royalty wear transponders for easy identification of bodies. There were no transponders on any detainees."

Avienne tried to keep her features neutral. "She would have removed it to avoid detection."

A pause again. "Please wait a moment."

Avienne squeezed Gobran's arm encouragingly. This was good. The tentative peace that had settled over Solaria and the Thalos system had been tenuous at best, especially in the past three years. If Solaria lost Thalos, they lost a major part of their trading network on a still-developing quadrant that included Mirial. Not that Solaria cared about Mirial now, but it would be a blow to Solaria's dwindling power, all the same. They were so busy fighting off insurrections on most of their fringe worlds—worlds that sympathized with their ether creature population—that they couldn't afford another major blow. Their military was already stretched too thin.

Which meant they'd do anything to maintain alliances with Thalos III. Avienne had banked on that.

A door opened on the left, the metallic wall sliding into itself to reveal the warden and two guards. The warden nodded at Gobran and smiled deeply at Avienne. Maybe she didn't have to worry about her hair, after all.

"Thank you for helping us," Avienne said in a grateful but harsh tone, as though it was expected. The warden's smile grew a bit colder.

"Of course, Lady…"

"Maid Lucha," she responded. The maid titles weren't bad on Thalos III. It usually meant you had access to vast information, and therefore treated with respect and well rewarded for loyalty. "And this is Baron Orlas."

The warden bowed deeper, even though it was not necessary to bow to a baron. "Welcome to Olte, Baron." He bowed slightly to Avienne, obviously not certain what her title entailed. "Maid. I am Warden Jos, in charge of this complex."

"My niece, Warden. We have come a long way to find her and bring her back where she belongs."

"Of course, Baron. But we would need some way to identify her, to spare you from having to walk the length of the detention centre." Gobran nodded towards Avienne. She pulled out her comm unit and showed him a picture on it. This was a gamble. As far as they knew, Rose's identity had never been recorded in Solarian databases. Jaru had looked long and hard to make sure, using every known facial recognition software program. But still, if he had missed even one database that this warden had access to, which identified Rose as being from Mirial, it would be their undoing.

The warden looked at the picture. "It's about ten years old," Avienne said. "We have been looking for a long time."

The warden nodded. "She is here. But she is not well." Avienne's heart dropped. She had to force her features to remain neutral. Gobran saved her by speaking first.

"She must be brought to justice, whatever her state of health."

The warden bowed again. "Of course, Baron. First, we will of course formally record your arrival and request, so that Solaria may properly take care of your relatives in the future."

"We expect quick service, Warden," Avienne said. "The journey has been long and the baron has important business to return to."

The warden bowed stiffly and led them into the back. She followed him through the metal door and into a side room, where they were seated. The warden apologized as he scanned their ID. Avienne wasn't worried, there. Jaru had implanted transponders on them with Thalonian signals, and he had hacked the detention centre's system to add their ID. The centre only connected with the Solarian database once a week, at most, so their deception wouldn't be detected for at least a few more days, when they were safely away.

Avienne sat in silence, keeping her posture straight, as she imagined a Maid of Thalos III would do. She knew they were proud with unwelcoming features, usually. It required a bit more acting skill than usual—she leaned more towards fun and flirtatious. But this way, she could hide her worry more easily. What had he meant, Rose was not well?

They waited and waited. Avienne resisted the urge to look at her comm unit. Fidgeting would not do, Jaru had warned her sternly. She never realized how much she fidgeted until she was told she could no longer fidget.

Finally the warden came in. "Maid, Baron," he said, without a hint of sarcasm or dissension that would let them know their deception had failed. "Your IDs have checked out. We'll be pleased to release unnamed detainee 1243 in your custody."

"I should hope so, Warden," Gobran said, his voice gaining strength. Avienne stopped herself from looking at him. He was enjoying this. Avienne decided to stray on the side of information gathering.

"Out of curiosity, Warden, how did you find her?"

The warden started to shrug before thinking better of it and just answered. "She was found in a shuttle nearby. When rescue ships were sent, she was raving and quite mad. I'm afraid she may not know who you are."

Gobran filled the silence that Avienne's grief let linger. "Thalonian justice requires only bodies, Warden. Not minds."

The warden bowed. "Very well. We shall deliver her to your shuttle. She was sedated, so your journey should be peaceful."

Avienne and Gobran stood. "Thank you, Warden." Avienne said. "We shall make sure to communicate of your cooperation to your superiors."

"Thank you, Maid."

Avienne helped Gobran walked back to the shuttle. They were already loading Rose, passed out and still in cuffs. Patros, wearing the slave markings of Thalos III, helped them load Rose onboard. He looked up and caught Avienne's eye for just a moment, but it was enough to let her know all that she needed to.

She took a deep breath and walked to the shuttle with Gobran.

***

The *Dessicate* boasted a single, sparse first aid kit that Avienne had finally purchased after that incident when she'd cut Patros' forehead open. She still blamed the space storms, certainly not her knife throwing ability. For the first time, Avienne wished she had taken her brother's offer of a better ship. *Stupid sentimental love of this old bucket!*

Litras, who seemed to have a better grasp of medicine than any of them, leaned over Rose. Avienne didn't need a medical degree to see that Rose was in bad shape. She had lost a lot of weight. Her skin stretched across her cheekbones, and her eyes twitched under bulging eyelids despite the sedatives.

Her skin looked gray in the light of the old ship. Her lips moved with half-formed words that dribbled into incomprehension.

Remembering the strong, vibrant woman who had taken her niece, the brilliance of her engineering mind and the dedication to her home planet and its ruling family, Avienne felt completely useless. This couldn't be Rose. Should she have looked harder for them, and sooner?

What about Ardice? Where was the child, now ten years of age? Layela had been younger when she had been left to her own devices, but Layela also had a streetwise twin, Yoma. Ardice was alone and had no one else to lean on, or to trust. No one to help her in the difficult vastness of the universe.

Avienne tried not to envision the worst, but her tired mind showed her visions that made her head spin.

"Is there anything we can do, Litras?"

Litras squinted her eyes as she placed her uncovered hand on Rose's forehead, letting her ether flow directly into Rose and affect her in whatever way Kilita could. Berganda could trigger memories with their telepathy and they could heal themselves and others. Kilita, as far as Avienne could tell, triggered ether in whatever form it existed. And some telepathy, too. Slonts like Patros could see and manipulate the molecules that composed objects.

"I think someone used ether on her." Litras said. "A strong dose. I'm not sure, but I don't think it's an ability I've ever seen."

"What kind of ability? What do you mean?" Avienne leaned closer to Rose.

"It scrambled her mind, or at least heavily interrupted her neural pathways."

Patros stood near the entryway of the quarter they were using as a temporary medical facility. "I've heard of some Fated who could do that, but those are in legends from long ago. They were said to have vanished centuries ago, when Solaria began its expansion. The Fated were unable to reproduce at the rate of humans, and not as aggressive about acquiring land."

"Well, could they be back?" Avienne looked from Patros to Litras. "Now that Mirial is almost done? How freaked out are the Fated?"

"Very." Patros simply said. Avienne was surprised he had never talked to her about it.

"It could be our lives," Litras answered.

They both remained silent as Rose twitched. Avienne sighed. "Well, could they have hunted Ardice down? Her connection to Mirial might show to some people, right? And I thought Mirialers were immune to ether creatures, anyway?"

"Still think I can read your mind?" Litras flashed her a quick grin before holding her hands up defensively. "Some Fated, the older races, the ones that were around when Mirial was created, would have a different relationship with the ether. I guess some of them could have tracked down Ardice, and they could affect Mirialers, too." Litras paused. "You weren't always around, you know."

"Fine, we'll worry about that later." Avienne was growing impatient. "Right now, we have Ardice to worry about. She's likely to be with those psychopaths who did this to Rose, right?"

"Unless Rose got her away first, then yes."

"All right, so we need to talk to Rose. Is there any way to wake her up?"

"We could," Litras said. "But her neural pathways are still compromised. She'll be at best an incomprehensible fool, and at worst a dangerous one."

Patros stepped forward. "We could try to remove the blast of ether. That might cleanse her neural pathways."

Avienne looked hopefully at him. "Can you do that?"

He looked hesitant. "I think so. I can manipulate elements, and that's what people are made of, too. Ether is harder to control, but I can still manipulate things around it and move it around, just like I killed cells around your brother's wound to save him." She was nodding vigorously now. This seemed like a good plan. Best plan they'd had all month about anything. "But I might just kill her. This is her brain we're talking about."

Avienne stopped nodding and looked at the fallen Rose. She remembered the determination the woman had when she took Ardice away. She remembered her warmth, her caring, her willingness to sacrifice everything for people and a world she might never get to see again.

"She would want this," Avienne whispered. "She would want us to find Ardice. She gave up everything for her."

Patros nodded and removed his gloves, which he wore mostly out of habit. Avienne kissed him gently on the lips. "Be careful. Don't kill yourself for this."

"I won't." He smiled at her.

Then he placed his hand on Rose, whose whimpers turned to a single high-pitched scream and then to silence.

Patros furrowed his brow as his concentration deepened, beads of sweat streaking down the side of his face.

Avienne watched and waited, flipping a knife restlessly in her hand, keeping a tight grip on it nonetheless and not letting it fly. Just in case they encountered more space storms outside the hull. Within the ship raged enough storms already.

CHAPTER 5

THE DESTINY II cleared the atmosphere of Mirial, the last to leave a streak in the doomed sky. The populace of Mirial had boarded their other two fleet ships, *Victorious* and *Lady Mirial.* The two ships were still well below capacity, the population being so sparse. Only a small crew manned the flagship, enough to take *Destiny II* to their new world.

In the belly of the ship slept a traveller's freighter—big enough to be a one-family home, but fast enough to avoid most ships and detection. As soon as the new sun produced ether and Layela was freed from its grasp, they intended to board it and bid farewell to *Destiny II.* The hunt for Ardice could then start in earnest.

The ship picked up speed and angled up as they prepared to pierce the atmosphere of Mirial for a final time. The artificial gravity and inertial dampers kicked in, and the ship stabilized. Layela sat near the captain's chair, watching the atmosphere caress the hull of the ship in a final farewell.

The ship lumbered towards the tunnel, the planet growing as small as its distant sun. She had become Keeper following Mirial's darkest days, and had stayed even as the days grew darker.

And now, she meant to put the final nail in Mirial's coffin, despite the star's support over the years. Despite her need for Layela.

The Keeper forced herself to keep looking at the great star, trying to bid farewell, but her heart had already leapt into the future, to her next goal, hopes ignited even as she looked at the withered, dying star.

Ardice. She would see her soon. She would hold her soon.

She clutched the back of Ardin's chair and tried to steady her breath.

***

Layela and Ardin stood on the bridge of the *Destiny II*, the wisps of the green tunnel fading as they exited. Layela's breath caught in her throat. Ten years ago, when they had found this place, new stars were igniting in the sky around them. The purple hues of the nebula that housed the nursery were accented by the ship's viewing screen, allowing them a glimpse of what might otherwise be invisible to their eyes.

No single star stood out from the others. The ship rumbled and Layela looked up, where pillars of dust streamed past the *Destiny II* in great numbers and at great speed, pebbles and mountain-sized rocks dragged into a single shaft and then compressed. Dust raged, but no pellet hit any of Mirial's ships, dancing around the hulls on their journey to the centre. The dance stopped and for a moment the space before them lay silent, until fusion burst into a great light, forcing the screen to dim and the crew to look away. The heat warmed Layela's skin and streamed within her. Ether stronger than Mirial's flooded and smothered her.

I'll always be with you, Yoma's voice echoed in her memories. Layela closed her eyes and gasped for air. The warmth dissipated and she sensed the hand of Mirial lifted from her shoulders. Layela could no longer reach out to tap the ether, could no longer feel that constant comforting presence of something greater than her. She couldn't feel any ether creatures in the area, and trying to reach out to Elsa seemed as impossible as lifting this ship with her bare hands.

All of the little graces that had filled her life without her even realizing were gone. Her body ached, as old wounds long kept in check began to complain under the canopy of a regular life. Layela reached out toward Loran, to find her friend and spread the healing her way, but she couldn't do that any more than she could reach out to Yoma.

She felt trapped in her own body, like she had lost wings she'd always taken for granted. Her heart hammered in her chest and she focused on her breathing. Each endless breath filled her lungs to their perfect size. It was as much air as she needed to live. She only needed air, not ether, to live. Just like she didn't need the ether to find Ardice.

She was free.

She opened her eyes and look at Ardin.

"Your eyes…" he said, and she didn't let him finish. She reached up to kiss him fully. Her ether, now gone, no longer fought with the darkness in his chest. She hoped that would be gone, too. She ran her hand along his chest, feeling nothing fighting her. He did not flinch at her touch or pull back. She let herself be held by him for the first time in a decade, losing herself in his strong arms, his warmth coating the emptiness where ether had been, his fingers electric against the small of her back

The ship rocked and Ardin gently broke free of her embrace. He kept his eyes locked on hers as he spoke, his breath catching on the first syllables.

"What's happening?" he asked Brosten, his second-in-command.

Brosten examined reports flowing in. Layela turned to the view screen and peered at the star. It was purple, its edges darker and fuzzier. And expanding.

"Ardin…" She didn't finish the thought. The sky was filled with brightness and they all looked away as the ship jostled.

"YOU MUST GO!" The Seeder's scream echoed all around them and the *Destiny II* was propelled back, too quickly for its inertial dampers to compensate. The crew was thrown forward and then back, the ship twirling out of control until it entered the tunnel and the green light absorbed them.

Layela managed to hold on to a station, and Ardin grabbed his chair, but not all of the crew was so lucky. By instinct, Layela tried to pull on Mirial, but there was nothing there.

Blinding light penetrated the enveloping green of the tunnel. The ship decelerated.

"Engines on full! Get us out of here, back to Mirial, now!"

Ardin jumped on tactical and Brosten on navigation. Layela opened a side panel where emergency supplies were kept and began tending to the fallen crew. Loran, loyal Loran who had insisted on staying by her side as long as she was still the Keeper, had fallen awkwardly, her prosthetic leg at a bad angle even though it was still connected.

She moved her and tended to a cut on Loran's arm.

"What happened?" Loran asked.

"We don't know yet. We're still escaping." The *Destiny II* rumbled around them. Layela met Loran's eyes, which were wide as they peered into hers.

"Keeper…"

"It's just Layela now, Loran." She finished bandaging the wound. "I have to go help the others."

She stood to go help the fallen helmsman, bleeding from a gash on his hairline. The engines cut out into silence, the throbbing light of the tunnel giving the bridge an underwater quality.

"Why did we stop?" Layela asked as she closed the gash with skin-tape.

"We didn't," Ardin said, sitting down at navigation. "The tunnel's tugging us along, back towards Mirial."

Layela stood and placed a hand on the chair behind him. "Back to Mirial," she repeated, the words mealy in her mouth, accompanied by a splash of acid.

Ardin turned his head sideways, just enough to catch her eye. He raised an eyebrow slightly.

"I don't know. I really don't know, Ardin. Everything seemed to be working, and then…"

"Your eyes…can you connect to Mirial at all?"

Layela reached out, willing the First Star to grace her with warmth. She closed her eyes and concentrated, her mind tumbling in a thousand different prayers, hopes and aspirations. She imagined the caress of Mirial on her cheek, let it drift there for a few moments, but knew it was wishful thinking.

This is what everyone else must feel, she realized. The emptiness of ether, filling the void of belief with imagined perceptions. Or maybe they felt it more? Maybe she, who had basked in full ether so long, no longer sensed a lesser connection.

She opened her eyes. Ardin looked at her eyes and then turned back to his console, pulling up readout after readout.

He had seen the lack of ether in Layela's eyes.

Layela let her hand drift to Ardin's back. There was no pain, no counter ether. His shoulders tensed and then relaxed. Whatever powers Mirial had blessed her with were now gone.

But what of Mirial herself?

***

The space around Mirial was littered with ships that had come to bid the star farewell, the star's glow steadily gleaming on their hulls. Hoast watched them all from his screen, trying to analyze and identify every ship.

He could only identify half of them, if that. Some models he'd never seen before. Others were achingly familiar from his youth; the ships of ether races living beyond the borders of Solaria. Solarian ships were definitely out in high numbers, their models easy to find and purchase on the open market, or steal.

He sucked in his breath as he spotted the Ralis ship. Their flagship, all crooked and banged up dark metal. The Ralis were not renowned for their ships, but the ether creatures feared and respected them. Solaria hadn't mingled with them since the Ether Wars, rare proof that Solaria could learn from its mistakes.

Hoast hissed. His ship turned towards the flag ship, the controls locking into place. His hands fell uselessly to his side.

"Are we there yet?" The small whisper was washed out by the whooshing sound of the shuttle being swallowed by the large ship's shuttle bay.

Hoast turned and looked deep into the eyes of his friend, one night blue and the other sea green. "We're here." He almost asked her if anything was different, but her eyes were the same.

Mysterious and shining, tears shielding tired eyes. Infinity caught in an iris.

***

Layela's hand was still on Ardin's back when the ship shuddered and the tunnel opened to Mirial.

"Report on the sun's core. Is it stable?" Ardin demanded. The screen immediately shifted to a close up of the sun, cycling through various views to look at its emissions, thermo-nuclear reactions, fusion outputs...Everything seemed in place. Mirial was as they had left her—weakened, but still there.

Ardin turned to face Layela. "Can you see if the ether is still streaming from her?"

Layela reached out to Mirial, squinting to see beyond the layers of weak light. Nothing. She closed her eyes and tried to feel the ether instead, feel the strength of Mirial flow from its centre, near her, through her. She imagined warmth, but quickly realized it was her proximity to Ardin. She dropped her hand to his back, unable to feel the dark ether within him, either.

He met her gaze as she opened her eyes. Her hand drifted to the side of his face. He took her hand and kissed the small of her wrist.

"The question remains: What do we do now?" His eyes flitted over hers.

Layela looked back to the view screen, which now offered them a panning view of the solar system. Red highlights showed the multiple ships still in the region, awaiting salvation or destruction. They would get neither this day.

"We should address them." The words tumbled from Layela's mouth before she thought them through. "Someone should tell them what happened."

"What did happen?" Ardin asked, looking inquiringly at Layela.

"I honestly don't know." She paused. "But I think it's safe to say that the ether creatures no longer need to fear or celebrate a new First Star."

***

Layela paused, glanced towards Ardin. He nodded, barely, or she imagined it. But she returned the gesture and turned back to the view screen, imagining all of the ether creatures looking back, wishing she could reach out and let them be comforted by Mirial's ether.

"I don't know how, but we will find a way to rejuvenate the First Star." Layela's voice trembled. "We'll reconnect with the Seeders and we'll find a way to save Mirial or rebuild a new one. No one will suffer because of this. We will find a way." Ardin reached out and interlaced his fingers in hers, his hand steady and sure. Mirial never filled her with as much strength and courage as this simple act did.

Biolt switched off the view screen. They waited, the ships as silent as the space around them. A light flashed on the console.

"One of the ships is contacting us, the *Star's Barrow*."

Layela nodded. "Let's hear what they have to say."

"Keeper of Mirial," a deep baritone resonated over the speakers. "I am Marlus of the Ralis Parliament. Our race is long-lived and we believe we may be able to detect some answers on the writing of the ancient temple, if you are willing to grant us access."

Layela turned to face Ardin, but it was Loran's eyes that caught her attention. She had pulled herself up on a chair and clung to it, her knuckles white. Her pale brown eyes brimmed with hope and longing, staring towards the screen where the planet Mirial continued on its quiet orbit.

"Of course," Layela said without looking away as Loran met her eyes. "We'll allow you access to the sacred temple, although you must understand that it's in transport and not currently in one piece."

"As long as the etchings are preserved, that is all we need."

"They are."

"Thank you, Keeper."

A slight click indicated the loss of connection. Loran gave Layela a grateful smile, and the ex-Keeper of Mirial turned back towards the planet on which she had spent almost half her life, wondering if she had just sacrificed the rest of it by granting this request.

CHAPTER 6

LAYELA HESITATED IN the shuttle bay, running her fingers on the smooth surface of a dark gray ship. She still preferred shuttles to space ships, even though they were more crammed and uncomfortable. She had always travelled through space in cramped quarters growing up, sneaking aboard ships with her sister, or making use of a stolen shuttle. It was a quick, efficient way to travel, but only for small distances. Anything outside a solar system, and a small one at that, required a much bigger ship with better propulsion.

Ardin walked through the door of the shuttle bay, grinning when he saw her and quickly closing the gap between them. He swept her in his arms and kissed her deeply. Her breath caught in her throat—it had been a long time since they could be so close.

He pulled his lips away, but kept her close. His eyes gleamed as he spoke. "We could go to the *Lady Mirial,* or we could just stay here a while."

Layela leaned into him and indulged in one more kiss. She broke free and let her fingers linger on his neck for a few extra stolen moments before pulling the door to the shuttle open. "Let's go!"

Ardin sighed but hopped in after her, taking the pilot's seat. He turned to grin at her as she settled in the co-pilot's seat. "We could just keep busy while we head to the ship."

"I'm sure no one will be paying attention to this shuttle, Ardin.

We'll just have every view screen, heat sensor, and probably weapon aimed at us as we travel."

His grin widened. "That's my girl!"

She laughed and hit him on the arm. He winked and activated the traction under the shuttle, speaking to the controls as they jerked into movement.

"Open channel to bridge."

A light flicked red on the panel. Ardin said, "This is D-2 Shuttle 1. We're ready for departure."

Brosten's voice boomed in the shuttle, making Layela jump. "D-2 Shuttle 1, you're cleared for departure. Head to decompression chamber 2."

"Aye. And Brosten, keep us in your sights. We don't know who all of the ships out there belong to, or what mood they're in."

"Wouldn't let you out of our sight, Captain. We'll be ready for anything."

Ardin switched off the channel as they reached the decompression chamber and the oxygen whooshed out around them, the shuttle running through its checks and cross checks to ensure its seals were holding.

"What's the plan?" Ardin turned to her as the lights dimmed around them, signalling that the bay doors would open shortly into the vacuum of space.

"I don't know," Layela whispered. The situation was so surreal her mind struggled to grasp its implications. "I guess we'll find out what happens at the temple."

He reached over and grabbed her hand. "That's not what I mean, Layela. I mean, what's the plan for us?" He paused and hesitated before asking the next question, his words spoken low, as though he feared they might shatter them both. "Your connection to Mirial is broken, right?"

Layela closed her eyes and tried to reach out to the great star, but was met with silence. No, not silence. Emptiness. This emptiness frightened her more deeply than she had ever believed it could. Not that she had given much thought to what would happen when her own connection to Mirial faded. She had only been concerned with Ardice, her future, their freedom.

She opened her eyes and looked into Ardin's. His eyes were riddled with fear and anxiety, tenderness and vulnerability. She leaned over the middle controls, the armrest pressing against her ribs as she planted a soft kiss on his lips. She then whispered in his ear.

"The connection is broken."

He squeezed her hand and leaned back into his seat. The shuttle bay door opened and he expertly navigated the shuttle out towards the *Lady Mirial,* which waited nearby.

***

The captain of the *Lady Mirial,* Erlin Gray, waited for them in the shuttle bay. He had been military before the Great Darkness more than thirty years ago, and had lived in exile for those twenty years. His work as a mercenary for different causes made him a strong soldier and ally. He'd proven an asset to Mirial since his return about seven years ago.

His graying hair and the lines defining his eyes indicated an age his posture denied. Ardin had always said it was a mark of experience, not just passing time.

"Keeper, Captain Malavant," he nodded to each in turn, and they followed him down the corridor to the next shuttle bay. "I've placed guards around the temple." He paused before the door of the second shuttle bay, the biggest one, where it had been agreed upon the building of the *Lady Mirial* that the temple would be placed for transportation.

"Do we know that we can trust them?" He looked from Ardin to Layela.

"They need Mirial to survive, Captain," Layela answered. She had never been very close to Captain Gray, although she respected and trusted him. He did not invite close relationships, and seemed only interested in his duty. Which was fine with Layela. Enough people expected her to play an important role in their lives. One fewer person asking something more of her worked out great.

He nodded curtly. "We'll keep an eye on them, regardless."

"I'd expect no less." She gave him a grudging smile, which he returned with another nod. Layela shared a quick grin with Ardin. The captain opened the door and Layela stepped in, trying hard not to let her jaw hang open.

The temple had been cut into large pieces, sixteen in all, crisscrossing the cuts lengthwise and height wise to respect the temple's asymmetric architecture. The front roof had been one piece, but the back had no roof, giving direct access to Mirial's rays. The three front pillars, each representing a Fate and each taller than twenty metres, counted each for a piece. The other twelve pieces consisted of the four corners, the walls and what could be brought of the floor.

They had not reassembled the temple on the ship. It was in various pieces, held in place by giant cables which hooked directly into the floor of the bay. Large cushioned tarps had been placed between the cables and the temple, to stop any rubbing from damaging the refinished stone.

At Layela's insistence, they had also brought a few of the massive oak trees, long dead and petrified, but as much a part of the temple as its stone. If not more so. The oak trees reflected Mirial herself. They mirrored her strength and her weaknesses. They were in a corner, planted in large buckets of soil, held up by cables with as much care as the stone. The soil was from Mirial. Layela resisted the urge to run her hand through it and let the damp soil coat her skin, inject her with the trapped ether, embrace her as Mirial once had.

Layela crossed her arms and tucked her hands under them. They continued walking towards the "entrance" of the temple, marked by the columns of the Three Fates. Their long, carved robes fell to the ground, sculpted so well they looked like they might rustle at any moment. The chiselled, statuesque pillars had been placed according to tradition, with one facing forward, one sideways and one back.

A chill ran through Layela at the Mirialers' insistence to preserve, even during a simple transport, the image and traditions of Mirial. She glanced across the room to where Selenor fussed over every detail. Traditionally, there were no temple attendants. The First Star kept to herself and the Keepers were enough to deal with the almost inexistent upkeep.

Selenor was the only architect remaining from before the Great Darkness. He had restored the palace to Layela's specifications and, from Layela's understanding, he already had drafts for the new palace.

The head architect spotted her and waved, turning to speak to a few of his apprentices, who scurried quickly to get to work. Layela smiled as he approached. Letting him reinstate the Architects Guild and take on apprentices had definitely been one of Layela's best moves. That and reinstating the shipyards, although that was more Ardin's doing.

"Keeper," he said, enfolding both her extended hands in greeting.

His hands were large and soft. "What will we do, Keeper?"

No other Mirialer had asked Layela this question, although she could see it burning in their eyes when they crossed paths. They were terrified and hopeful all at once. Afraid that they might never know a warm, safe home again, and hopeful that Layela could somehow bring Mirial back. No one else asked, but Selenor knew her well by now, and lacked social inhibitions.

"I'm not sure yet." She saw no point in lying. "I hope the Ralis will bring answers for us."

Selenor nodded slowly, placing his hands behind his back. She knew that look well. She had seen him looking at the palace and temple that way, sometimes from dawn to dusk. He wasn't lost in thoughts as he might seem, but rather he was allowing every detail his eyes captured to forge a plan in his mind. After a few days, he would finally jot everything down perfectly, without need for any alterations. Layela had always suspected that he only jotted them down for the benefit of his apprentices, so that they could benefit from his thoughts and learn.

"What are you thinking about, old friend?" Layela asked gently. Sensing the depth of the conversation, Ardin strolled towards the temple, examining some of the apprentices' work. Layela loved him all the more for it.

"What do we know of the Ralis?" He kept his head lowered as she answered, moving his feet slightly and cocking his head towards her, no longer facing her. His hearing had been going, although he never complained. Layela had asked Avienne to bring back an implant or anything that might be of use. They'd never get him off-planet to get the help he needed, this she knew. This was the first time he had even flown off Mirial.

She leaned in just a bit, so that he wouldn't notice her gesture but would hear her better, while keeping her voice low. "We don't know much, to be honest. They're an ancient ether race. Their lore extends as far back as the beginnings of Mirial, some say. But they're reclusive and keep to themselves, mostly. I don't even think they have a home world, anymore. They live on their ships, as far as anyone knows."

Selenor nodded, then shifted and stared back towards the temple. "Can you not read the writings on the temple yourself, Keeper?"

Layela stared at the piece he looked at, the single hardest chunk of the temple to restore and remove. It was the back of the altar, filled with markings from when Mirial was created, so fragile and brittle that a strong brush stroke would sweep away details. Selenor had handled all of the finer work himself, not trusting anyone else. It had taken him three years to restore that section, and materials so specific it had driven Avienne crazy trying to find them.

Well, crazier, I suppose.

The markings were small, carefully etched, yet laid out in no discernible pattern or order. They were instructions to Mirial, Layela knew this much, but could not interpret them herself, or really discern one set of instructions from another.

She sighed. "I don't think so, Selenor." She walked towards the wall, passed by the covered altar, and stood before the markings. Inscriptions and sharp lines graced the rock. Circles defied the hard material, along with different indentations: lines and triangles and symbols whose meanings she couldn't even begin to guess at. The symbols were messy, ignoring any type of line structure or left to right writing. They just existed in the space they needed to exist in, sometimes overlapping with each other, one set of symbols gobbling a less prominent one. Perhaps later instructions? Perhaps refined ones?

"I don't think these were all made at the same time," Selenor said from where he stood, a bit back from her.

"What do you mean?" She kept her focus on the wall.

"I cleaned and sealed each one of those myself, Keeper. You can see it yourself. Some chisel hits are deeper, some finer, some go on top of one another. And some had flecks of paint left in the cracks, showing this was originally a coloured fresco." He paused. "I couldn't save the paint, but I recorded everything so that historians could try and rebuild what it might have looked like when it was first created."

Layela ran a hand on the wall, her fingers catching on nicks her eyes couldn't see. She closed her eyes and let her finger follow a slight crevasse, into a curve, only to dip into a deeply chiselled symbol.

"Why would they add anything to it?" she mused. "Why would the original etchings change?"

Selenor approached the question with intensity and interest. "I think, Keeper, that the situation changed and so did the instructions."

"You mean like adding to an instruction manual?"

"Precisely!" Selenor exclaimed, as though he'd long been bottling up his theory. "Take this, for example." He leaned over some of the markings on the far right. "I don't think this is that old. Not old at all. I don't recall them from when I was a boy, and what I thought was paint could have easily been blood, not yet washed— little rain had graced Mirial for a long time." He let his words sink in before continuing. "Your mother," he lowered his head in respect, "encouraged young architects to study the temple closely." He paused. "Your mother was a wise woman, much like yourself, and perhaps glimpsed a strong possibility of this future."

Layela didn't respond, examining the etchings instead. She had worked on this piece, but hadn't realized it was more recent, perhaps even etched by her mother. She ran her hand on them, hoping to somehow feel her mother—to imagine her hands bleeding her sacred blood as she forced the stone to dictate a likely future and save her people. Save her daughter.

She let her fingers linger on the Three Fates, and then within the sun itself, the rays etched outward until so fine they vanished into older markings. As though her mother had lost the strength to express how grandiose the new First Star would be. Could have been.

If her mother had been the one to etch this. Layela tried to imagine the woman as she had been described to her so often: so much like Layela yet so different, with features as strong but with softness in her movements that Layela didn't seem to possess. She tried to peer into the mind and heart of her mother, to understand how she had felt, her dreams and aspirations. To connect with her through stone and flecks of sealed blood.

But she felt nothing, save the cold rock.

She stepped back and looked at it from further away, standing beside Selenor.

"I wish we knew more of Mirial's history," she whispered.

"Gresko Listan was the last historian of Mirial. Without him…"

Layela felt a pang of grief. Gresko had dedicated his life to Mirial, and had died for her.

"I miss him," Layela said. Ten years had failed to dull certain wounds.

"Keeper." Captain Gray walked up to them, and Ardin joined them. Layela blinked and faced him. "Your guards have arrived on board. And the Ralis have dispatched their shuttle. They'll be here shortly."

"Thank you, Captain." Layela exchanged a quick look with Ardin. "I thought I'd instructed Loran to stay on *Destiny II*."

Ardin shrugged. "She takes her duty seriously, Layela."

She raised an eyebrow. "And you had nothing to do with this."

He shot a grin her way. "Who am I to go against the will of the Keeper?"

Layela almost swatted him but restrained herself. Captain Gray and Selenor were deep in conversation, but glanced their way often.

Ardin said, "I wonder if anyone else has noticed your eyes."

Layela had no doubt they had. Every Mirialer and ether creature had, or would shortly, and they would either worry for Mirial or question her authority.

But now was not the time for her to step away from Mirial. She needed to ensure that the ether was strong, and if she could use her role to bring them all together, with or without Mirial's blessing, then she would do so.

She turned back to stare at the wall, hoping it would reveal the secrets she desperately needed.

CHAPTER 7

PATROS' HANDS DROPPED away. Rose lay still, her face drooping out of twisted agony. Patros' features were drawn, his skin a weird, sickly shade of blue. Like a polluted river at dusk.

Avienne waited, staying close to him, afraid he might fall.

"Well?" she finally asked.

Patros opened his eyes, but it still took him a moment to speak. When he did, his voice was barely a whisper.

"It's not good."

"What?" Avienne looked from him to Rose and back again. "What do you mean, not good?"

When Patros didn't answer, Avienne grabbed his shoulders and turned him to face her. "What do you mean, Patros? How's Rose? Where's Ardice? Don't make me slap some sense into you!"

Patros managed a slight grin. "Just a bit dizzy, that's all." He took a deep breath. "Her mind is littered with ether. It's like they just blasted through her, without care for what they were doing." He hesitated. "I'm not sure what to do. I can't help her. I'm not sure anyone can."

Avienne let go of his arms. "Someone can. Someone who's better at reaching minds than you are." It hit her like a refreshing rain. She grinned at Patros. "The Berganda. Layela used to rely on Josmere, a Berganda, to see her dream visions. They can be gentler with minds.

They know more about navigating them."

She stopped, realizing she was trying a bit too hard to convince Patros this was an answer. Blood and bones, she just needed something to strive for, some idea of what to do next. They needed to help Rose, of course, but Ardice was somewhere out there and might be in dire need of their help. They needed to know what Rose knew, and they needed to know it now.

To his credit, Patros just nodded. "That's a great idea."

Avienne grinned. A bit of colour re-appeared in Patros' cheeks. Good. One less person to worry about.

"Well, what are we waiting for?" she said, heading to the door. "Let's go find us some Berganda!"

***

Galka threw the warden's body down, enjoying the effects of the lower gravity. The body bounced several times before she stomped it with her magnetized boot. She crouched and listened intently over the sound of machinery and the irregular hiss of oxygen being pumped in the room.

She wrinkled her nose. She hated oxygen. Of all the useless gases, this was the worst. She could take it for a while, using the gases stored in her back hump as a supplement, but still, what a waste.

She heard nothing and stood up, kicking the body as she walked over it.

Useless.

Oxygen-based creatures were ridiculously weak, even though most didn't seem to know it. The only reason they existed was to fill the void the Fated couldn't fill. Oxygen-based creatures believed in quantity over quality. They were parasites at best, a virus at worse. Galka leaned towards virus.

She stretched to her full height, tall by most standards, and revelled in the strength of her muscles, sinews tightening and fighting the drift of the weaker gravity. Even with oxygen impairing her system, she could face whatever came her way. She flexed her arm, watching her yellow scales ripple over the muscle. She wanted to break into a run and snap the neck of every guard she encountered. Taking a deep breath, she lowered her head and let her muscles relax. Maybe her stimulants were getting to her. She hadn't slept in a long time, sent on a mission to get here while the caretaker still lived.

But someone had collected her first. It didn't take a genius to figure out who they were—a red-headed woman and a blind old man. The Keeper's smuggling force had found the caretaker first.

Galka struggled with her emotions as she walked back towards her ship, not once encountering resistance. On one hand, she would have enjoyed killing every guard here, and disappointment pulsed in the unspent energy of her muscles. On the other hand, she now had something to hunt. And she loved nothing more than a good hunt.

She slipped into her ship, a small one-person craft with deceptive amounts of firepower. Glotch rarely traveled together and didn't generally play well with others, except for their annual battleground gatherings. But that was just for the sake of the children, and Galka was no longer a child. She traveled alone.

Her people were mercenary, like the Kilita, except much more powerful. The Kilita were weak with their need for "understanding" and even "love." Galka scoffed. *As if anyone could ever love anything that ugly!*

She settled in her seat, specially modified to allow room for her hump. Not all of her people used their humps to store gas, but they were foolish. To breathe in only oxygen weakened the system. To never leave their home world, which was as rancid as the gas that now filled her ship, weakened the spirit.

She did not hurry to depart, part of her hoping the warden's body would be found and the alarm sounded, and she would have to fight her way out. Her hand shook on the steering column of the ship. Her hands, free from those forsaken Solarian gloves, gripped until her finger scales parted from one another.

Take a sedative before you get yourself killed. The kind voice rang in her mind. She closed her eyes and nodded, although no one could see her. She struck her gauntlet in the designated pattern, and a small pin injected directly into her bloodstream. Just a bit, enough to take the edge off. She could take another accelerant later. She would need it.

Think.

Galka leaned back against her seat and closed her eyes. She reached out through the Fated Link. She wasn't very good at it, but she could get by and find those who were better. She connected with some Fated who specialized in seeking. For a small fee, of course.

The instructions were easy to provide, since Galka knew exactly what to tell the Fated to find. The smuggler travelled with a Slont.

Not many Slonts travelled off their home planet, and certainly not many would be in Solarian space.

She settled the deal with the seekers. They were expensive but well worth it, and her employers had deep pockets.

Her grip tightened on the sides of her chair as the seekers dragged her along their hunt. They were incredibly fast. As far as Galka understood it, the Fated Link travelled in waves between each individual connected to ether. Some were open to inquiries and even visits within their minds, but most were closed to everything but specific events. The ether responded to the desires of the individual and alerted them of queries of interest.

That's how Galka had always viewed it, but she didn't know if she was right. She didn't care, either. As long as it got the job done, she'd continue using it.

Suddenly a light flared in the network. Everything else faded away, and there was the signature of the Slont, ridiculously blue, a pulsing light in the dark sky. He had used ether recently, probably to save the oxygen-sucking caretaker. Some Fated puzzled her just as much as her brethren.

I need to track him. She passed the request along to the seekers, who set up a tether to the Slont. She could find him wherever they decided to head next. It would cost her employers more, but they would appreciate the results enough to forget the bill.

She opened her eyes, queasiness settling in the pit of her stomach. If she concentrated, she could see the line leading straight to her prey. She licked her lips and pulled hard on the controls. The alarm hadn't sounded yet; the guards' incompetence squashed her appetite for battle. The Fated Link pulsed in the back of her mind, the flow of information exploding. So they now knew that the new First Star would not be their salvation. Galka didn't care, not right now.

She had interesting and immediate prey to find. The caretaker hadn't been meant to survive. No trail was meant to be left. But there she was, and the Mirialers had already found her.

She would kill them all before they followed the trail to its bitter, unavoidable end.

***

The Kilita jerked up, her wide eyes looking towards the emptiness of space displayed on the view screen. No, not towards, but *beyond.*

Her mouth seemed to chew on some bitter words, but no sound came out until a heavy sob broke free and she fell to her knees, weeping. Patros moaned and lowered his head on his control station. Avienne looked from them to Jaru, who looked just as confused as she felt. Gobran perked up in his seat, but waited patiently for someone to tell him what was happening. Or he perceived something they didn't.

Avienne slipped out of her seat and headed to Patros. She placed her hand on his back and knelt beside him. He wasn't sobbing like Litras, but he seemed even more shaken now, his skin flushing dark blue and then turning pale.

"Patros," Avienne whispered, ignoring Litras. She tried to keep her voice steady and professional, but so many fears danced in her mind that they latched on to her words, also. "What's wrong? Tell me what's wrong, please."

He drew a deep breath, his back rising under her hand. He let his chair swivel to face her, placing his hands on his knees, their faces close. She didn't like the look in his eyes. She'd seen it before, mostly in Solarian slave camps. It was the look of someone who'd given up. Who had fought one battle too many and just couldn't fathom fighting another.

She placed her hands on his cheeks and forced him to focus on her.

"Tell me what's wrong," she asked, her voice losing its power, her mind assembling possibilities that would make the two ether creatures on her bridge collapse into grief. "Tell me what happened to Mirial." Her heart accelerated and she desperately tried to keep herself in check. She wanted to both hug him and hit him.

"Mirial is fine." He focused on her finally, blinking grief from his eyes. Avienne swallowed in relief.

"Then what is it?"

Litras spoke from across the bridge, her voice grainy with grief. "It's the new First Star. It's dead. Gone."

Avienne leaned to look at her around Patros. Her hand had fallen to grab hold of Patros' hand, and she didn't want to let go. Not just yet.

"What does that mean?"

This time, Patros whispered an answer. "It means we'll continue to rely on Mirial for now, but Mirial is already dying. She won't live long enough to keep providing ether, not long enough for the Seeders to create another First Star. We can't tell if the Seeders even survived the blast." His voice pitched up, his eyes grew wide and his grip on her hand tightened. "Avienne, we can't survive without the ether. We're already struggling with what little Mirial provides. We can't go on like this for long! We thought that if we held on long enough, the new First Star would save us, but now…"

He lowered his head and closed his eyes, his breathing shallow. Avienne brought his hands to her lips and kissed them. Then she hit him hard on the side of the face. He fell backwards off his chair and looked at her, stunned.

She stood and looked at Litras. "You want in, too?"

The Kilita shook her head, a slow grin spreading across her lips.

"Now you listen to me." She spoke louder than was strictly needed, with only four other souls on the bridge. "Mirial is not dead, and Layela is working right now, I'm sure, at healing her. No one's going to just let you ether—Fated—die. And certainly no one on my ship, blood and bones! While the others are worrying about that, we're worrying about finding Ardice and nothing else, understood? I don't think it's a coincidence that she vanished right before the new First Star was supposed to become active, so wrap your little ether-ridden minds around that." She took a deep breath. Patros remained on the floor, looking up at her with wide eyes.

"And another thing!" she exclaimed. "No one is going to just give up, understood? We have come too far and done too much to just give up now because a bloody star exploded! Any questions?"

They all stared at her. Gobran was the one who broke the silence.

"How do we know that Layela and Ardin are safe and looking for an answer? They were supposed to be at the birth of the First Star."

Avienne almost snapped at Gobran, but reeled herself in. She didn't mind laying it on thick with Patros and Litras, but her first officer—her blind, old first officer—always received a bit more respect from her.

"We know because we trust them to get out of tight situations. And we can't go check right now, because Layela and Ardin would kick all of our arses until bone stuck through our backsides if they learned that we abandoned what might be a trail to their daughter, to come check up on them. That's how we know, Gobran."

"Fair enough," Gobran whispered.

"All right, any other questions?" She whirled around and looked at everyone in turn. "No, great! Then let's get going." She offered her hand to Patros, who hesitated a split second before taking it. She pulled him up.

"Get us to the Berganda, now."

He nodded, his eyes alert again. "Aye, Captain." He sat down without another word, his back stiff, either from anger or pain, Avienne wasn't sure.

Better anger or pain than just bloody giving up.

Avienne sat in her chair and gave a withering glance to Litras, who turned around and pretended to look at readings, though her station wasn't even active.

Smart woman. If Avienne wasn't mad before, she was now. And petrified something had indeed happened to Layela and Ardin. Any long-range communication would take days to reach them from here, and anything would be intercepted. On their network, or the Fated one.

"Litras," Avienne kept her voice level. The Kilita turned to look at her. "Keep an ear or whatever on the Fated Link. Lots of ether creatures, Fated, sorry, headed to Mirial to bid farewell to it. If something happened to Layela, I'm sure something will be said."

Litras nodded and turned back to her station. They entered the tunnel and sat in silence as the tachyonic shields closed around them.

CHAPTER 8

LORAN WALKED IN ahead of the Ralis delegation, entering the temple shuttle bay with a quick glance to the great monument before focusing on Layela.

"No one could ever accuse her of not being focused on her duty," Ardin said beside her, while Loran was still out of earshot. Loran wore her dark blue uniform with the green symbol of Mirial—flowers and plants encroaching on a bright, full sun. It mimicked some aspects of the traditional uniforms from before the Great Darkness, but Loran had added her own touches. Wider pant legs, for example, allowed ample space for her artificial legs and hid some of the awkward movements of the prosthetics.

Loran quickly closed the gap between them.

"Keeper," she said, meeting and holding Layela's gaze. She was making clear that it didn't matter what Layela said, or what colour her eyes were, or even if the ether courted her anymore or not. As far as Loran was concerned, Layela was the Keeper and no one was telling her different.

"Captain," Layela answered, returning the formal title. Loran nodded and moved to her side, to take her place in full view of the proceedings. A few other guards entered and took their places without question or hesitation.

Layela turned toward the door. Captain Gray came to stand beside her, sharing a slight smile with Loran. Layela tried to hide her surprise, and her happiness at knowing Loran wasn't alone. That she had carved out a piece of Mirial for herself, too.

The door opened and two more of Loran's guards walked in. Behind them followed creatures that could only be the Ralis. They were tall and very slender, their arms reaching up into their necks with barely a pause for shoulders, their oval-shaped heads seeming too large for their petite forms. They wore long, orange robes, hiding their legs. Their eyes were inset, surrounded by a dark purple colour which looked like blood streams just beneath their slightly translucent skin. The purple spread out in the rest of their face, but not as concentrated as right around the eyes. Their irises picked up the same dark hues, reflecting the purple of the veins.

Their silver hair streamed down past their elbows. Layela found it impossible to tell their gender, or if they even had any.

She had heard that the older ether races resembled humans less and less. The Ralis definitely leaned further away from humanity, and closer to the Seeders. She wondered if the Seeders used to be an ether race, or were still.

The procession stopped, and all eyes focused on Layela. She took a step forward and allowed herself a moment to gather her wits. *They're just people, too.*

"Welcome aboard the *Lady Mirial*. Welcome to the Temple of Mirial, though its grandeur may be harder to perceive at this moment." She paused, but the Ralis just stood there, unmoving. *All right, stick to business, then.* "We hope that, with your help, we may be able to come to a quick and peaceful solution and ensure a strong and sustainable flow of ether for all ether races."

She stopped and let her arms fall to her side, only realizing then the grand gesturing she had been doing. Ardin would tease her about that later, she was certain.

One of the Ralis took a step forward, the slight billowing of its robes being the only indication that a leg existed somewhere underneath the garment.

"Keeper of Mirial," the voice boomed louder than she'd anticipated, and its deep baritone suggested that it was a male. "I am First among the Ralis Parliament. We thank you for allowing us to visit the Temple of Mirial. We, too, hope for a quick and sustainable solution."

Layela let a few moments pass to ensure he wasn't about to speak again.

"First among the Ralis," she used his title, since he hadn't offered her any other identifier, such as a name, "how would you like to proceed?"

"If you will give us a few moments to explore the temple, we will study the inscriptions."

"Of course. Please have a look. We will be near if you need us."

The Ralis moved in unison towards the section of wall Layela had been exploring a few moments before. Ardin moved closer to her. "That went well."

Layela watched them stare at the inscriptions. Selenor strayed near, waiting to catch a bit of the conversation, but the Ralis remained quiet and still.

"I hope it did," she answered to Ardin absent-mindedly. "I hope it did."

***

Captain Erlin Gray sat on the bridge, flipping through technical reports and schematics. The *Lady Mirial* was a fine ship, and he was proud to be her captain. Every time he looked at her schematics or plans for her future upgrades, he couldn't help but be impressed.

Ardin Malavant certainly had taken after his father when it came to ships. Erlin had looked up to Captain Malavant before the fall of Mirial, and part of him always would. He had been the best: captain of the great fleet of Mirial, an engineer and architect, master of the queen's own shipyards… and he had made it all seem easy.

Erlin did not regret his decision to come back to Mirial, though he wished the Keeper had dedicated more resources to building an army. It might be too late now, but Mirial's obvious vulnerabilities always worried him. Stronger than ever before hardly meant as strong as the planet could be. He had fought in enough random wars and guerrilla conflicts to know that a strong military could be the difference between freedom and slavery.

Loran supported the Keeper in her decisions to choose a more peaceful path for Mirial, but Erlin had long accepted Loran's blind loyalty to the Keeper. It was one of her most endearing traits, and she had many.

Erlin stood and stretched his back. The bridge was quiet, most of the crew asleep. According to the clock, it was almost midnight Mirial time. One of Erlin's main concerns had been the new planet's rotations. Would the days have been similar in length to Mirial's, or much longer? Loran had laughed at his worry, but she was much younger. She didn't appreciate a good night's sleep, as he did.

His communicator beeped. He looked down at the name and smiled, and stepped aside to take the call in his office, just off the bridge.

"Captain Gray here," he answered, in case this was official business.

"Captain Gray." Loran paused a moment. "Can you talk?"

"I'm in my office, alone." He sat down in the padded chair and rested his feet on his desk. He made sure the door was locked. His crew didn't need to see their captain practically lounging. "Where are you?"

The sigh came so clearly across the airways that he could imagine her hot breath on his neck. "We're still at the temple. The Ralis have barely moved, and Layela seems intent on staying with them until they do. She looks about ready to fall over. It's been a long day."

"It was a long day for you, too."

She didn't answer directly, and he almost regretted speaking those words. Almost. Her loyalty to the Keeper represented one of her most endearing traits, but it was also the main point of disagreement in their relationship.

"They've started moving around, so I'm guessing we'll be able to leave soon."

A break, and he jumped in. "Let me know when. I can meet you in my quarters." When she hesitated, he added: "The Keeper's quarters will be right next door. I made sure of that."

He imagined the smile gracing her lips. "I'll see you soon."

"See you soon."

The line went dead. Erlin stood and stretched again. He needed coffee, and a walk would wake him up a bit. He pulled down on his jacket to work out the wrinkles and unlocked his door.

The scene on the bridge took him by surprise.

Three large, dark-suited soldiers had guns trained on his crew. His first officer turned to look at him, betraying his arrival. Erlin jumped into action, and in the split second it took for the invaders to turn, he hit the lock. The blast struck the door as it closed, but it was built solidly and would hold. For a while, anyway.

He could hit the alarm and warn everyone on the ship, but he guessed the stealth attack was meant to take them all by surprise, with minimal loss of life. If he rang the alarm, panic would set in, more shots would be fired, and more people would die. And the Keeper probably wouldn't escape.

Loran is starting to rub off on me, he thought as he opened the communication line to her, choosing his words carefully. If there was one thing he could count on, it was that Loran wouldn't risk her life to save his.

Not as long as the Keeper needed her, first.

***

The Ralis had moved, but not much. They had shifted sideways, turned as though to confer with one another, and then returned to staring at the wall. Loran sighed. This might very well be the dullest event to have graced her life this far.

Her comm unit buzzed and she looked at the incoming call—it was Erlin again. She turned to hide her flush and smile and answered in a whisper. "Are you that impatient?"

Her warm skin turned cold with his answer: "Loran, I don't have much time, so listen very carefully."

She heard gun shots in the background. Energy weapons, blasts not strong enough to break through the reinforced hull, but enough to do major damage to something like Erlin's office door. Loran knew what they were, but still she found herself asking, "Are those gun shots?"

Erlin's voice came back softly. Sensing his urgency for privacy, Loran fitted her earpiece and clicked it on. No one else would hear what he said. His voice came in a rush, yet still calm and controlled. This frightened Loran most of all.

"There are soldiers on the bridge. They've taken control. I'm not sure where they're from—no discernible markings. There's no doubt they're coming for the Keeper. Get Layela out of here and back to the *Destiny II.* We just don't have the manpower to take back this ship, not right now." He paused and repeated. "Get her out of here, Loran."

"I will," Loran whispered back. She wanted to say so much more to him, words and emotions tumbling in her head and heart, but the line went dead.

Loran placed her comm unit back on her belt but kept the earpiece in, in case he should call back. She pushed thoughts of him to the side as she planned her next move, fighting hard against nausea and dizziness. *Erlin.* He would be fine. He was a veteran of many wars. He would find a way to survive, without her help.

She turned to gauge the rest of the room, fighting to control her breathing. Everything had changed for her, but nothing had changed around her.

The Ralis hadn't moved, still exploring the mural. They might not be a part of this, but she couldn't take the chance. She looked at her guards, looking bored where they were around the room, a few looking like they were sleeping on their feet.

She couldn't risk alerting them. Erlin was right. The more gracefully they extricated the Keeper, the better. Loran took a step towards the Keeper, her legs stiff from standing still for so long. The nerves connected directly to the prosthetics screamed in protest, but she barely paid them mind.

Layela didn't even notice her until she stood right beside her, making her jump. The Keeper offered an apologetic smile, those new, strange blue eyes of hers rimmed with fatigue. Loran looked towards the Ralis as she spoke, keeping her voice steady and low.

"Keeper, do you trust me?" She couldn't risk describing everything to her, and she wasn't disappointed. Layela's whole posture changed as she became more alert, her hand reaching out to touch Ardin, who turned to look at Loran.

"I trust you," Layela whispered, not looking at her, either. She kept her eyes on the Ralis.

"Follow me," she said, heading as calmly as possible towards the door. Selenor saw them and walked towards them, accelerating his pace to catch up with them. "Keeper?" he asked as he came closer. "I believe we may be close to a resolution."

Loran wanted to hit him, but stopped when Layela did. The Keeper's face betrayed no emotions as she addressed him. "Ardin and I need to verify a quick fact, something we believe the Ralis will appreciate, as a thank you for their efforts here today." A smile graced her lips. "We'll be back momentarily. They won't even notice our departure."

Selenor never saw the lie, easily accepting the words that flowed from Layela's lips. Loran suddenly realized how much Layela had changed over the past decade. But that wasn't her business, not now. Now, she had to get her to safety.

Layela hesitated half a second, and Loran feared she would ask

Selenor to join them, which would be a dead giveaway. But the Keeper stopped herself and simply nodded at him before turning back to Loran. Her features were set hard.

Loran opened the door to the shuttle bay. The way was clear, so she turned towards the next one, where the shuttles were kept. She had barely taken a step when the door opened and black-clad soldiers stepped out. Loran registered what they looked like, focusing on the important. They were of average height and heavily built, and they carried enough firepower for a small army.

Helmets hid their eyes, but the lifting of their weapons sealed their intentions. "Run!" Loran shouted as she threw a flash bomb in their midst. She hoped it would confuse their sensors just long enough for her to get the Keeper around the corner. Of course, how quickly they could escape was another matter.

She turned as the light engulfed the corridor, followed by heat. Shots rang out around them, and Loran was hit in the leg. She almost fell, but caught herself and turned the corner. Ardin and Layela had armed themselves, each with personal guns. Useful, but not the best against fully armed militants. Loran pulled her sub-energy rifle free from its holster on her back.

"How do we get off this ship?" Loran asked, starting to run with them, the sounds of pursuit coming from the other corridor.

Ardin was leading the way, and Loran had to trust that he was leading them towards an escape. He had designed the ship, after all.

They entered a room and he punched in a code on the panel beside it. A metal siding slid down over the door.

"This is one of the safety rooms aboard this ship," Ardin said, crossing the room to the empty wall facing the door. "We have them on each of Mirial's ships, for occasions such as this. Officers know about them, so let's hope they have the time to make use of them."

"What exactly do these do?" Layela asked, running a hand on the metal plate. Loran wondered if she was looking for a latch that only trained hands could find. She was aware of Layela's past as a thief, even though she didn't think the Keeper had maintained those particular skills.

"It's now hidden from the corridor by false wall, which will block most scanning equipment, it's sound proof, and…" he paused as he pushed on a section of the wall, which looked no different to Loran. A small access pad slid out, perfectly parallel to the floor. Ardin pressed a combination in it, and the wall slid open. "It's loaded with weapons."

Loran could have kissed him. There were blasters and personal guns, energy weapons—and not low grade, either. More flash, smoke, and pulse bombs than she could count…all brand new and shiny.

"How did you get these?" Layela asked, then shook her head. "Never mind. Avienne, right?"

Ardin grinned. "She 'found' them. Thought we could use them more than she could. Although I'm pretty sure she kept some."

He selected a gun and a rifle, handing the same to Layela. Loran grabbed a few reloads for her rifle and some pulse grenades. Those would damage the ship some, but they would also take down the invaders.

"What's the plan?" Layela asked as she checked her weapons over. "Do we take back the bridge?"

"No," Loran said right away. "Erl… Captain Gray said the bridge is compromised. Our main duty right now is getting you off this ship, Keeper."

Layela's eyes narrowed and Loran braced herself for an argument. Ardin saved them both form one by activating his comm unit. "*Destiny II*. This is Ardin. Come in." They waited, but no answer came. He tried again, but still no answer came.

"All right, so they're jamming signals, possibly also within the ship, now."

Loran nodded. "And they seem to have secured the shuttle bay where our shuttles are," Loran said. "They're probably coming from the Ralis ship."

"I really thought…" Layela started, then shook her head and pursed her lips.

"All right, so we need a way to get off this ship before they can find us." Ardin continued. "There are escape pods generously strewn around the ship, but they don't have much manoeuvring capacity. We don't know what's happening out there, so we should get a shuttle, or something with some escape velocity, anyway." He paused, gauging his options. "The foreward shuttle bay might not be compromised. It's small, but should have a few shuttles lying about. Or we can retake ours. They might have abandoned the shuttle bay to hunt us."

"The children," Layela suddenly said. "This ship has the temple, but almost two hundred citizens on board, too. We can't just abandon them!"

Loran placed a hand on Layela's arm. "We have to. For now. From what Erlin said, they weren't shooting anyone, just gathering them up. We can come back for them once we know a bit more about what's going on."

Layela seemed to want to protest again, but just nodded and focused on her weapons.

"How far are we from the forward shuttle bay?"

Ardin shrugged. "About half a kilometer. We don't have a lot of options for corridors, however, so if we're spotted we'll be easy to trap."

Loran nodded. "Can we see where they are now?"

"Not easily, from here."

Loran turned to Layela. "Can you see where they are with the ether?" Hope filtered into her voice and coated each word. Layela just shook her head and looked down. "I don't even know why they'd want me. The connection with Mirial was broken when the new star began igniting."

"It might not be you they want," Loran said. "But you're still Keeper of Mirial, and it's still important to Mirial's survival that you go on. No one else can figure this out but you, and you're still our leader, Keeper."

Layela didn't meet her eyes, so Loran turned to Ardin. He offered her a grateful smile.

"So, what'll it be? We're gambling either way." Loran checked her weapons, wishing her leg wasn't shorting out where the shot had hit her. At least it was a low energy weapon, meant to stun more than kill. But it had played havoc with the electronics. She was glad she'd never bothered with the higher end models. They were so dependent on electronics that a blast like this would have rendered it completely useless. At least her leg could still function without the electronic controls. She would simply be less graceful.

"I vote we head back to our shuttle, via a different route. We can go down one floor and use access panels to come up near one of our shuttles. They'll expect that less than our heading to the fore shuttle bay."

"Sounds like a plan to me! Is there another way out?"

Ardin grinned, pushing aside a table to reveal an access panel. "Straight down we go," he said, opening it up.

Loran nodded and headed down first, keeping her weapon trained on the space in front of her.

CHAPTER 9

THE FLOOR BELOW them seemed perfectly normal except for the empty corridors. These were the living quarters for Mirialers, built to be practical and comfortable, with shared spaces in case of a long stay. They hadn't been certain if the new planet would be immediately hospitable, so planning for a few years had made sense. The *Lady Mirial* and *Victorious* held all of Mirial's people, giving them plenty of living space. The two ships had been designed to easily tether to each other across various space bridges, allowing Mirialers to visit back and forth without having to worry about the logistics of shuttles.

This floor didn't hold many personal apartments, designed instead to be a public space. To their left stood the entrance to the gardens, filled with flowers and crops that would help sustain the population. A play structure adorned the nearby space, near a large space window recycled from one of Mirial's old ships, which had been lying uselessly in a shipyard in one of the old cities.

A few food kiosks were spread around the grounds. Mirialers had been assigned work at different sections of the public areas, to ensure a fair division of labour and regular maintenance. But no one currently manned any station, no children played in the sand, and the gardens were empty of admirers. And Mirialers loved their gardens. The song of the cicadas was the only sound of admiration flowing from every part of the garden.

Layela bit her lower lip. The children would love this space. She had designed it herself, with them in mind. She hoped Loran hadn't lied to protect her. She hoped that the invaders would be good to the Mirialers, or at least wouldn't hurt them. She had always meant to leave them, there was no doubt, but not like this. Not imprisoned and scared.

She crouched and followed Ardin down a path, keeping low beside some shrubbery. Ardin stopped and indicated the space window with a quick motion of his head. She turned to look, and it took her a moment to figure out what he was trying to point out. The ships were still all dispersed, so an organized attack wasn't in the works. Not out there, anyway. She hoped *Destiny II* was near, or that they would respond quickly when their shuttle emerged.

Ardin ran and Layela followed, Loran not far behind, her leg clumsy where it had been shot. Layela kept close in case her captain of the guards faltered, but made certain not to let her concern show.

If Layela had been tracking their progress correctly, the temple was just above the gardens, and the in-use shuttle bay would be above them soon. Ardin turned them down a short corridor with a large eating area. Picnic tables were strewn generously around tall trees, fountains, and flower beds. The fountains gushed sprays of light and projections of water instead of actually using water, which was too precious a commodity on a spaceship to waste on decoration. But the effect was just as beautiful and amazing, the soft glow charmingly reflected by the moisture on the nearby plants.

Another space window, large and unsupported by extra beams, graced the entire back of the grounds. From this side, they could see the edge of Mirial, the sun's weak glow barely reaching them. Layela wondered again how they could possibly manage to reignite the fading star. If they could do it at all.

She'd worry about it later. Right now, something else tugged at her attention. She turned and realized the insects had stopped singing.

She placed a hand on Ardin's arm and mouthed the word "cicadas." He looked confused for a second but then clued in. The three fell into a crouch.

Loran motioned for them to keep moving, quickly. They did, as quietly as they could, until they reached the far wall of the grounds. Ardin shot a grin Layela's way, pointing at the access panel on the wall. He pushed aside branches of a bush that hid most of it, and opened it. Loran motioned for them to move. Ardin nodded and headed in first, gun in hand. Layela was about to follow when Loran hissed. Black-clad soldiers were entering the grounds. They hadn't been spotted yet, but that would change within seconds.

Loran pulled out a grenade and clutched it to her chest. She nodded to Layela to get in. Her eyes—wild, yet controlled—darted from Layela to the soldiers. Layela took a moment to reach over and squeeze Loran's shoulder. Her captain reached up and squeezed her hand back.

A silent farewell.

***

Layela vanished in the access port and Loran felt as though she could breathe again. The Keeper knew exactly what Loran was planning, and she also had known that no arguments would change her mind.

As she reached down and closed the access panel, she was spotted by a soldier. Another bullet penetrated her already wounded leg, electro pulses energizing every ligament and tendon tied to the prosthetics. She turned off some of the sensors, making the leg more difficult to control but less painful. Escape wasn't likely, but at least she could distract enough of them to buy time for Layela and Ardin's escape.

Flexing her muscles as best she could without exposing too much of herself, she threw the pulse grenade in their midst. She covered her head. The deck shook. Trees fell and dust billowed up. Two fountains were hit and their light jets went wild.

Loran hoped the soldiers' helmets couldn't quickly compensate for light. She stood up and ran across the grounds, using her broken leg to push her forward, and her good one to get her speed. Several shots fired near her, but she was too quick for them. Losing two legs had to come with some kind of advantage, and Loran's advantage was speed.

She vaulted over a lined of cedar bushes and swerved through the gardens, silencing the cicadas again. She kept her gun trained up, but the soldiers travelled in groups and didn't leave many guards in areas that were already covered. Loran hoped that it meant they were the sort of small force which could win only through surprise.

She threw herself through a door at the end, praying no soldier waited for her. The door closed behind her and she swept the large kitchen through her gun sights, but no one was there. Her breath came ragged, but she had no time to catch it. The soldiers had taken the bait, and they were already pounding at the door.

Loran jogged to the other end of the kitchen and crawled onto the conveyor belt. It was a tight squeeze for her and she was fairly small, so she hoped her broader pursuers wouldn't fit. If they even thought to look for her in here. There were several paths of escape from the kitchen, and she hoped they'd first look at the more obvious doors.

The conveyor belt turned and she pushed into the dried food stores. She stood and squeezed herself in between two large packs of grain, to catch her breath and figure out her next move.

Her duty to the Keeper was done. Maybe she could find a way to save Erlin, now.

***

The blast resonated through the walls and Layela clung to the ladder. Ardin's eyes were wide as he looked down.

"Where's Loran?" he asked, and for a second Layela feared he would come down on top of her.

"You know where she is, Ardin. She's buying us time." Layela met his eyes. "Let's make sure her sacrifice isn't going to waste."

"We can't just abandon her, Layela!"

Layela grip tightened on the rungs. "You said it yourself—she takes her duty seriously." She caught his eyes, willing him to keep moving. "She's smart and fast, Ardin. She'll make it. Or we'll come back for her. We both know that."

Ardin frowned. "We'll come back for her." He looked back up and continued ascending. She followed him, guilt numbing her fingers, the air of the shaft suddenly seeming heavier in Layela's lungs.

"We're here," Ardin whispered. "I'll open it up and see, but we may need to move fast."

Layela nodded and steadied her breath, her knuckles white.

Ardin opened the access panel, shifting it noiselessly sideways. Strong light from the shuttle bay poured in. Layela felt extremely exposed, but she followed Ardin up.

She barely had time to register her surroundings before Ardin grabbed her arm and dragged her behind a nearby control station. Crouching beside him, she pulled her gun free. He motioned left and she nodded. He leaned in for a quick kiss and stood, keeping low to the ground as he ran to their shuttle. Layela kept close to him while trying to keep an eye on everything around her.

Ardin reached the shuttle and practically threw Layela in as the door slid open. He jumped in after her and closed the door, lying on the floor beside her, just behind the pilot's seat.

Layela took a second to catch her breath before turning to him and whispering. "That was too easy, wasn't it?"

Ardin shrugged. "When you think about it, they don't really need any security here."

"Why not?"

"Because we have to open that exterior door to get out. The second we do that, they know where we are. And their ship is nearby, so they can easily take us out."

Layela stared at him a few moments before speaking, trying hard to control the volume of her voice. "If you knew that all along, then why are we here?"

"Because it's the only shot we have." He sighed and looked up at the ceiling, shifting to get more comfortable. The shuttle was only illuminated by its standby light and a few other indicators. The viewing screen was off, which turned it into a giant dark patch. No light from the bay could infiltrate.

"Loran is still back there," Layela said, not sure what else to say, an apology dangling from her words.

"And so are Selenor, Captain Gray, and a bunch of Mirialiers." He glanced at her sideways, as though acknowledging the unspoken apology for leaving Loran behind. "But Loran's right—we have to get you out of here. They lured you here first to get the temple and you at the same time. We should have sensed a trap." He offered her an apologetic smile. "I guess we were all eager to find a solution."

"We were." Layela sighed. "Ardin, I'm not even connected to Mirial anymore. I mean, I'm not even its Keeper anymore. Not really. What if we just told them? What if we just negotiated for everyone else's well-being?"

He let a few moments slide by before answering. "Layela, how many armed invaders come on board just to negotiate and admit they're wrong and work together hand in hand?"

Layela struck out at him, then bit back a curse when her hand hit his weapon instead. Ardin took her wounded hand and brought it to his lips.

"All right, so I'm feeling hopeful. It's just that this morning we were about to head off on our own adventure, and now everything's just so annoyingly wrong."

Ardin squeezed her hand gently before releasing it. "I know. But can you leave now, knowing the ether creatures will probably die?"

"Of course not. You know that. Josmere's children, Patros, so many other friends we've made over time." She paused. "Stupid friends."

Ardin chuckled. "Are you ready for this?"

"For what, our death run?"

"We can assume they won't blow up a ship with you on it. They need you."

"You're a fan of that assumption?"

"Yup."

She rolled over him and kissed him hard.

"Then let's go."

CHAPTER 10

ARDIN ACTIVATED THE shuttle, pushing buttons quickly and efficiently, one light popping up after another, the engines powering on, the view screen activating... Layela gasped. In the shuttle bay, right in front of their shuttle, was the young Zoorsa she had encountered on Mirial.

He shouldn't be here. Only Mirialers had been allowed on board. Unless... unless he had been with the invading forces! How many ether creatures had she welcomed in her home, and how many now betrayed her?

He held up his hand as though trying to tell her something.

"Blood and bones, he'd better be careful!" Ardin said as he pulled the shuttle up, breaking it from the traction system. The Zoorsa vanished from their view as they headed for the exit.

"Can you take the controls?" Ardin asked, and Layela switched her station to primary. She pulled on the controls and held her steady.

"Where am I going?"

"Go past the first blast doors—I'll see if I can override them." Ardin typed madly on the controls, his access screen flashing red.

"Blood and bones, they've blocked us out! Every system is shutting me out."

"Take back the controls and let me do that," Layela said, turning on her access screen. Ardin gave her an inquisitive look. "My sister taught me never to leave things to chance." She shrugged. "Old habits die hard, I suppose."

She entered a query string and let it run for a few moments, waiting for the hopeful results. "I planted a break program in the Mirial computer systems, with Jaru's help. It'll duplicate every time something else is created from it, like a ship's database."

"You put a virus in our computer system?"

Layela frowned. "Well, I was planning for various eventualities, okay?" The string identified access codes, flashing them in front of her. Layela pressed several of them to see if they would work.

One caught on and, as her sister would have put it, "jimmied the lock from within itself."

"Ready when you are. I can trip the first blast doors and open the outside doors."

"Perfect. But just close the first blast doors."

Layela glanced at him. "Won't it work better if we get out, too? Or are we just going to sit here."

Ardin shot her a grin, making him look ten years younger. "I have my failsafes too, I'll have you know! Ready?"

"I don't actually know what you're planning, but sure, I'm ready to lower the first blast doors."

"Do it."

Layela tripped the doors and the shuttle bay blared with alarms and lights. She hoped the Zoorsa had moved out of the way.

"Harness," she said, pulling her own across her chest and waist, making sure it was well secured. Ardin did the same before grabbing hold of the weapons control. Alarms flashed on the console.

"Shuttles are firing up behind us, Ardin. They're getting ready to follow." She turned to look at him. "What's this failsafe again?"

"This," he said, and fired a rocket straight for the doors. The blast knocked them back, the harness biting into Layela's flesh. Then the oxygen escaped, dragging the shuttle forward, slamming them back into their seats.

Ardin took advantage of the suction and let it carry them clear of the ship before turning the shuttle to follow the curve of the *Lady Mirial*. He kept them uncomfortably close to the hull, where the long-range sensors were weakest.

"That's your failsafe?"

"Well, no. If the shuttle bay door is blasted, a secondary titanium door seals the shuttle bay completely. It's not a good feature and it's dangerous in extreme situations, but I wasn't aware of it until it was already in place. Captain Gray and I had agreed it would be the next modification we made on the ship, but then the Seeders came."

Layela leaned back in her seat and allowed herself to breathe for a moment. "So they can't pursue us, then?"

"Nope!"

She glanced at the warning on her screen. "Okay, what about those, then?" At least fifteen small fighter ships were coming into firing range. Ardin swore and pulled the ship away from the hull. "I don't know where they came from, but we can't risk the *Lady Mirial.*"

Layela pulled up a map. "*Destiny II* is to the port side, 45 degrees."

"Can you handle weapons?"

"On it." Layela activated the two side lasers, plus the three remaining rockets. It wasn't a lot, and the shuttle had no shields.

One of the fighter ships came near, its long and sleek design warping their targeting system. Layela hit the lasers in a wide spread and managed to damage it enough for it to drop back.

"We're outside their jamming system now." Ardin flicked the shuttle comm unit, which turned green. Layela could have screamed with joy, except she needed to target the next attack ship. She fired as Ardin jerked on the controls to avoid an incoming ray-cannon hit. Layela's shot went wild. She flipped open the comm unit as her weapons recharged.

"This is Layela Delamores, onboard *Destiny II's* shuttle 1. We are currently under attack and require assistance. *Destiny II,* do you copy?"

"On our way, Keeper," Brosten's voice came in loud and clear. Ardin and Layela exchanged a relieved smile. The *Destiny II* loomed in front of them, closing in fast. They would be in weapons range soon.

The shuttle's own weapon indicators finally reached maximum. Where had Avienne found such antiquated weapons? Three ships were getting too close for comfort. She set her lasers on widespread and sent them flying again, although this time the incoming ships anticipated the move. But they didn't anticipate her sending the three rockets close on the tail of the laser, hitting the ships as they tried to escape. Two ships were down, the third damaged and sputtering oxygen.

"We have more incoming." Ardin announced. "Blood and bones, everyone's incoming!"

Layela looked up from her targeting screen to the view screen. Ardin was right. Every ship in the area was congregating near them, the usual backdrop of space almost entirely covered by the incoming ships.

"One of them is coming between us and the *Destiny II,*" Ardin reported. "They're boxing us in!"

"I'm out of rockets, Ardin. And we have limited power left for those lasers." Other fighter ships joined the fray, appearing on all sides, so close Layela could have reached out the window to touch them.

"Who ever heard of a traffic jam in space?" Ardin mumbled as he kept the shuttle steady. He looked apologetically towards Layela. "They're herding us straight for that large ship." The ship rumbled and Ardin cursed. "They're going to push us if they have to. That big ship is the *Sun's Barrow.* That's the Ralis parliamentarian flagship."

Layela nodded and they both sat in silence. "What if we charge them?" Ardin said suddenly.

"And leave Ardice without parents? No. We'll figure this out. Together."

Ardin reached across and grabbed her hand. She clutched it like it was the last oxygen tank left in the world.

***

Captain Gray was a proud man, but honest enough with himself to know that he feared death. Once, in a battlefield on a world far away from Mirial, he had ascended a hill, dragging a large laser fusion launcher. He was strong, so he had been given a duty usually left for animals. When he reached the top, he almost toppled backwards at what he saw. Large creatures, spiderlike and metallic, but alive enough to scream, bleed and die, were attacking an entire contingent of his militia.

They were ether creatures. Too gigantic to be anything else. They were given the weapons to deal with them, and would get money when, or rather if, they returned. They had never been told about the venom the creatures spat for kilometres, showering them with acid so coarse it ate through the toughest armour.

They hadn't fallen back as the acid showered them. It hit one of his comrades straight on the head and splashed Erlin's arm. He had been lucky—the canon protected him, mostly. He dropped it, the great tube sizzling uselessly, but the acid didn't penetrate it all the way. He didn't even think about setting it up and firing it at the creatures to help his battalion. Instead, he had dug until his hands were raw and his nails were filled with that world's disgusting purple earth, and he had burrowed under the protection of the cannon.

His comrade took a long time to die, his head melting under the helmet, his features grotesquely deformed, his screams turning to moans and harsh breathing as his skin vanished.

Ever since then, he had not fooled himself into thinking he was a brave man. He was a cautious man, now, and he reminded himself about the price of battle as they hauled him before the First among the Ralis.

Captain Gray lowered his head slightly as a show of respect. He did not need to antagonize the man who held half of Mirial's population hostage. Including himself.

"Captain Gray." Erlin found the voice much more grating this time. Probably due to the smugness dripping from it. "We are pleased you could join us."

Erlin bit his tongue. *Remember your duty.* He waited, keeping his head level and his features neutral.

"We seem to be missing an item of some importance, and we had hoped you could give it to us."

He took his cue. "I might be able to, but we would need to negotiate releasing some of the hostages."

A grating sound, like a misfiring engine, escaped the Ralis' mouth, accompanied by a convulsion of his body. *Great. Not only do they laugh at my request—their laugh is obnoxious, too.*

"Captain, let me make myself clear." The Ralis did not move, did not blink, but Erlin felt a fundamental shift in the creature, as though he was just beginning to take the discussion seriously. "We of the Ralis Parliament control your little minds. Well, regular minds, like these simpletons." He waved towards the black-clad soldiers: silent, loyal, standing guard all around him. He still didn't know what, or who, they were. He feared he would eventually find out.

"Mirialers are 'protected' by ether from our powers. Mostly." He paused and stepped aside. Erlin couldn't stop the gasp that escaped his mouth, or ignore the sudden faintness he felt. Selenor, the dedicated temple keeper, lay on his side, his eyes rolling back in his head so far that half of his visible eye was the tendon that held it in place.

His mouth foamed, his hands twitched, his entire body convulsed. Sounds broke free of his twitching lips, but no words came out. Erlin doubted the temple keeper would ever speak again.

The First among the Ralis continued from the side, to let Erlin stare at Selenor. Erlin forced himself to look away and soothe his features. He swallowed bile and doubted he managed to hide his disgust, rage and fear. "This protection stops us from controlling your mind, but we can scramble it well, if we have to scour it for the information we need."

The Ralis took a step forward and it took everything in Erlin's power to hold his ground. He thought of Loran—beautiful, young, vivacious, loyal Loran, who had given up two legs to save Mirial. Loran, who had helped rally Mirialers against the usurpers, ten years ago. Loran, who still managed to perform her duty and perform it well, despite her constant pain.

Loran, whom he now desperately hoped had escaped this wretched vessel.

He held his ground and waited for the blow. What he received instead was a simple question.

"Where is the sacred knife from the altar?"

He was glad he had no answer to give. He was glad that he wouldn't have to discover how loyal he was to Mirial, and how strong he truly was.

The Ralis took a step forward. And, for the last time in his life, Captain Erlin Gray held his ground.

***

The screams resonated across the air ducts. At first Loran wasn't certain who they belonged to, but then a groan mixed in and alerted her to the screamer's identity.

"Erlin!" Her cry came out choked, brittle. She grabbed her weapon and dropped all caution and fear for her safety. The Keeper was safe. Now Loran needed to take care of her own.

She tried to follow the screams, but they were diffused in the duct system, ethereal and poignantly real all at once. She kept running, her lungs aching, the screams becoming louder. And yet more faint.

The habitats! He had to be with all the other Mirialers, in the habitat rings. Where they must be keeping everyone else. Were they making an example of him?

She ran headfirst through the doors leading to the playing courts. She burst into the first games room, uncaring for her own safety, spotting several Mirialers kept in check by armed guards. She used her legs to her advantage and kicked two soldiers down and turned her gun on the third. Orange blood splattered her as the soldier fell, silent.

Another soldier tackled her and she fell hard, kicking up, her hit wild. Her gun went flying, and she kicked out again, connecting with a knee with a satisfying crunch. Two more soldiers came and she struggled, her fighting spirits dying down as she noticed Erlin was no longer screaming.

The soldiers hauled her up onto her feet, ever silent and efficient, her hands held tightly behind her backs. The Hundreds of eyes looked at her, so many she knew, and others she didn't. One soldier walked towards her, removing his helmet to show he was Kilita.

"Where's Erlin," she spat out, pulled on the hands holding her and managed a step before she was yanked back. The Kilita did not mock her, or hit her, as she would have expected. In his eyes, she found sympathy.

"Dead, if you're lucky."

She looked around wildly but couldn't see him. Dead? Where? Was there still time to see him, to hold him? To say she loved him, for him to know that he wasn't alone?

"Where is he?" she repeated, her words caught in an angry sob. She pulled forward again, but her damaged leg gave out, and she fell to one knee. "Please," she whispered, looking up into the wounded orange eyes of the Kilita.

"He's at the temple. And it's too late for him." He paused and indicated to his men that they put her with the rest of the Mirialers. "I'm sorry," he added, but Loran barely heard him as she knelt down doubled over, trying not to be sick. She placed both hands on the floor. Mirialers sat around her but no hands reached out to touch her, as though they understood her need to be alone.

Alone, her hands on the floor separating her from the man she loved. The only man she had ever loved. She closed her eyes and lowered her head, tears pooling on the ground between her open palms. She had never understood how the ether worked, and she had never really felt it. But she had seen Layela wield it, and had seen the good it could do. Mirial had been home to her, not just a mythical system.

In that instant, for the first time in her life, Loran Natwar prayed to Mirial. She prayed that Elrin died with as much peace and dignity as was allowed him, and that Mirial would take his spirit swiftly in her care. And that she be allowed to see him again, whenever her own time came.

She didn't feel a great presence or overwhelming warmth. But when she lifted her head, Loran felt at peace. Her tears were dry when she opened her eyes and looked at the Mirialers around her. Some were frightened, but most seemed accepting of their fate, as though they had never really dared hope that the universe had more in store for them than more pain and loss.

Loran stood, favouring her leg. Guns were cocked behind her, and she turned around with her arms held away from her. She looked at the Kilita, who still had his helmet off.

"My name is Loran Natwar, Captain of the Guards of the Keeper of Mirial. I wish to speak to your leaders about releasing the innocents here."

The Kilita shook his head. "It won't do you any good. Not now. Just keep low and stay out of trouble. There will still be a place for all of you on Mirial after this."

He put his helmet back on and walked out of the room, his shoulders slouched, as though the weight of so many lives was more than he'd ever desired to bear.

CHAPTER 11

A VIENNE STOPPED IN front of Patros' door. When she'd first met him, he had been given this room, a small, regular crew room on one of the few functional floors. One of the two functional floors, to be exact, with (some) heat, (flickering) lights and (clanky) elevator access. Well, more or less on that last one.

She offered him his pick once he'd officially joined her crew, but he'd always stayed there, in that little room, saying it was plenty for him. They'd never broached the idea of him moving into her quarters. They were casual lovers at best, although if pressed to say so, she'd admit he was also her best friend.

It seems there were many subjects they had never broached.

Avienne started walking again, slowly, feeling as though each step ripped a piece of time from her. A word unspoken, a thought left unsaid, a hope unrealized… She didn't know what was happening on Mirial, she didn't know why the new First Star had failed to ignite, and she didn't know if her brother and Layela were okay.

But, still, every time her worry for them spiked, which had been often in the last day, her thoughts turned to Patros. Loyal Patros.

She hit the chime on his door. A few moments passed, and Avienne debated turning around and leaving. The door opened and Patros looked surprised to see her.

"What, no barging in without announcing yourself?"

Avienne looked for signs of aging. She had never asked Patros how old he was, but knew his people were long-lived. She had never asked, because it had never mattered. And it still didn't.

The blue skin was still as tight as it had ever been. Her own eyes had slight crow's feet on them from too much laughter, but his were still line-free, even though he had shared so much of that laughter over the past decade.

"Avienne, are you all right?" She met his eyes, even the concern in them failing to reveal the passage of time, as though even their time together had failed to be stamped permanently on his features.

"Why didn't you tell me the Seeders hadn't visited your people?" she blurted out, standing just far away enough that he couldn't take her in his arms and hold her. She didn't want to be held right now. She wanted to scream, kick, bite. But not be held.

He looked startled, but then had the decency to look abashed. "I didn't know that it mattered, really."

Her hands curled into fists at her side. "Why wouldn't it matter, you idiot? It's okay if you're wiped from the face of the universe? Are all ether creatures so bloody accepting?" She was mad now, the words tumbling from her lips like poison, and she didn't care. "Oh, I'm sorry, I meant the Fated. Are you fated to just sit back and watch yourselves be destroyed? Is that your whole philosophy on life? Oh well, we've had a good run, guess it's time to lie down and die."

Patros didn't take the bait, and for a moment, Avienne thought she was seeing the wisdom and age in him. It didn't matter. She was still mad at him.

"I didn't think it mattered," he whispered, "because I didn't know if it meant we would just perish. There's really no history or lore indicating what will happen to any of the Fated, either those who were visited or those who weren't."

He paused. "Life means a lot to us, Avienne. We've been put through a lot for the past few decades. Some Fated think it was a test to make sure those remaining among us are the strongest—strong enough to survive losing the First Star. Others, well, others just don't know which battles are worth fighting anymore, that's all."

Avienne felt deflated. She had hoped for a good blow out, some screaming, and maybe some fun after. His measured approach hurt more than she believed it could. She just didn't believe him when he said they didn't know what would happen. What else *could* happen? Their races were dependent on the ether. When Mirial had spent twenty years hidden in a nebula allowing very little ether to escape, entire races had been wiped from the face of the universe. Still more, like the Berganda, had almost been destroyed, too. A hard blow to forget.

She narrowed her eyes but said nothing more. He was finally taken aback and stumbled out: "Do you… do you want to come in?"

She shook her head. "You're an idiot."

She walked back toward the bridge and didn't look back, satisfied not to hear his door close while she was still visible.

Let him gawk and wonder. Idiot. Now she was stuck trying to figure out a way to save him again, since he apparently refused to do so himself.

***

Elsa danced in the gardens, one green foot in front of the next, tiptoes followed by sole, arms curling up. The plants around her swayed to her pace, turning to face her as though she were the sun. She could feel them all, their simple needs, some yearning, some hope.

Her mind wandered, not like her sisters' minds wandered. Since having been forced out of her own skin a decade ago, Elsa had become something entirely different than her green-blooded sisters. She heard their chatter in the background of her mind but did not participate. She didn't understand them, and they didn't understand her. But they trusted her, and it was that trust that sent her running to a garden escape.

They would panic, if they knew. For years, Elsa had blocked other ether creatures from reaching them, spreading a protective field over her sisters, and their children, and their children's children.

Her limbs were energized by the chatter, the panic, the fearful undertone to it all, riding the winds as effortlessly as a symphony would fill the air. She intertwined her body around every grief-ridden cry and song of fear, letting the screams in her mind create the dance her body executed.

The ground sang underneath her, having been a faithful companion for the past few years. With great effort, Elsa had managed to bring more ether, had even infused the ground with it so that they could safely and easily seed.

Elsa's steps increased their tempo, her mind breaking away from her body, reaching far to find Mother Layela, riding the cries of fear all the way to Mirial. So many were around Mirial, now. So many had gone to bid farewell to the First Star, not realizing their farewells would be sadly misdirected.

She couldn't tell her sisters that the new First Star had failed. Shivers sprouted at the root of her leafy hair as a song of farewell traveled the length of the ether. The Shroplak, a short-lived race, had been hanging by a thread, surviving on hope of a new, strong First Star and a regular flow of ether that would secure their survival and prosperity. The song was answered by silence, and then grief. Crushing grief, which Elsa clutched to, its weight slowing her dance. She ignored where her limbs jotted and concentrated only on reaching Mirial.

And Mother Layela, whom she hadn't been able to sense since the new First Star's destruction. It was as though she had just vanished, swept away by the destructive tides of the star.

Elsa clung to the belief that Mother Layela still lived. It was more than belief, really. The Berganda knew. A part of Elsa could still sense, far away, the impression of Layela, who had cared for them since birth. Death would have bought Layela a fixed place in the firmament of Mirial, and Elsa had long ago learned how to see those souls. She could not see Layela among them.

The plants around her dissolved into stars, the ground into space, and suddenly the weak sun of Mirial stood before her. Elsa reached out to the great star, warmth filling her. She used to speak to the star, even though it rarely answered. Sometimes Yoma, Layela's sister, would appear and shoo her back to her skin, scolding her gently for further breaking her mind. If Elsa did as asked, Yoma would send a dream of the Berganda's mother, Josmere. At least, that's what Elsa imagined happened.

She wasn't sure.

She wasn't really sure of anything, anymore.

Mirial spread out below her, in a scale she knew was impossible. The white, small star flickered near, but so did the planet, which was no longer round but distorted. Was she actually over Mirial, or simply imagining it, her mind fuelled by hope and fear?

The space around her was riddled with ships. Their hulls stretched beyond her sight, expanding away from the planet like rays. Elsa shook her head and gasped, thrown back in her body, having tripped on a root as she danced without paying attention.

She had trampled some of the plants, something she had never before done. Guilt blossoming, Elsa knelt and soothed the flowers. She cupped a marigold in her palm and lowered her head, her hair blocking her vision. She tried to focus all of her energies and mind into healing the wounded plant, but part of her, the part of her that still seemed linked to Mirial, constantly echoed one word in her mind. *Help.*

***

Gilane Kat, captain of Mirial's *Victorious,* stood on the bridge, staring at the mess in Mirial's space. Communications had been scrambled, so she couldn't contact *Destiny II* or *Lady Mirial.* But what she could determine perturbed her. *Lady Mirial* seemed to be in a bind, with the Ralis delegation probably behind it. The shuttle with the Keeper was being escorted to the Ralis' flagship.

Destiny II was blocked by *Star's Barrow,* and several nasty ships surrounded her as well. Brosten was a good first-in-command, but Gilane feared he didn't have the military know-how to take them down and rescue the Keeper.

Gilane did, of this she had no doubt. She looked at the scene before her, painted in the poor light of Mirial, and she could spot weaknesses in their plans. But no one seemed to be taking advantage of them. They were either terrified or lacked the knowledge.

She liked to believe the latter. Most of the other ships were manned by ether creatures. Losing the Keeper would serve them ill, unless they were in league with the Ralis.

"What are the chances that we have some allies out there, still?" Gilane asked of no one in particular. Before anyone else answered, she did. "I imagine we have a few. Maybe enough."

She sprung back towards her seat and sat down on the comfortable leather. With a few quick touches she brought up her control screen and checked their weapons schematics. They were better armed than the *Lady Mirial,* and better armoured, too.

But they were also carrying more passengers, and more innocent Mirialers. Gilane let out a long breath. Mirialers were brought up with a staunch belief in two things: Mirial, and its Keeper. She had to believe that everyone below understood that and would support her decision if they knew what she knew. There simply wasn't any time to evacuate the ship, and the Ralis probably counted on the civilian on board this ship to stay her weapons.

Time to prove them wrong.

Gilane hit the alarm, which warned all passengers that troubled waters were ahead, metaphorically speaking, and they should stow away loose items and strap themselves in. They had rehearsed this, and had been through enough battles to understand the importance of protocol. The importance of following orders.

Her bridge crew quickly set itself up for battle. Their screen shifted from observational to a splash of colour showing heat signatures, x-rays and other warnings for defensive or attack systems.

"All decks report ready for battle, Captain." A shiver shrank Gilane's spine before warmth extended her limbs. Of course they were ready for battle. Did they have any other choice?

Gilane took a deep breath, ready to spring into action. This would only work if others jumped in. There were too many fighter ships, and she didn't know if others would take her lead and take them down before they took her down.

This was either going to be the shortest, most costly battle in Mirial's long history, or it would be the battle that saved them all.

She leaned back in her chair and tapped her screen, highlighting a section of her map. The Keeper's shuttle was surrounded by attack ships, so the chances of taking out the ships without destroying the shuttle itself were remote. But she was willing to bet that if they attacked *Sun's Barrow*, it would confuse the Ralis' allies and spring Mirial's allies into action. She was willing to bet a lot on it, in fact.

She highlighted the port side of *Sun's Barrow*. No time to figure out if it was their weakest spot—it was the most accessible, so it would have to do. The trajectory appeared on the main view screen. Time to find out just how many allies would favour Mirial today.

"Move us in. And prepare to fire with everything we've got."

***

Ardin analyzed map after map of the ships surrounding them, trying to find an escape route, but nothing seemed even remotely worth risking. Layela sat silent beside him, staring out the viewing screen, watching the maw of the *Sun's Barrow* approach as the ship opened its shuttle bay. They certainly were making it clear where they expected them to go.

He took a deep, stale breath. For having grown up on a ship, he wasn't used to recycled air anymore. He found it stifling, and the shuttle claustrophobic. Layela's words still bothered him. That she was no longer Keeper simply because her connection with Mirial had been severed. Who else could step up as Keeper, if not her? If she underestimated her worth to the Ralis now, she could do something stupid that would endanger her.

He glanced at her. She had aged, of course, since they'd first met, almost half of their lives ago. But she was much more beautiful, too. Her eyes had deepened with wisdom. Her hair was still dark, and her face was shaded by its shadows. She reached up with one long finger and pressed a button on her console, changing the view screen again.

He knew her well enough by now to know her constant flipping was more to do something, anything, and that she wasn't actually looking for anything specific. She was waiting, hoping inspiration would strike. Waiting on the surface only. Her mind would be buzzing with possibilities, missed or otherwise.

"Ardin?" She turned to him, a question pressed in the line of her lips. "What will they do to you?"

Ardin tried to pull together some fake bravado, but Layela knew him enough to see right through it, so he changed tactics and shrugged. "Depends on what they want from you."

Layela nodded, each nod slower than the last. "I think…"

Sun's Barrow suddenly shifted, as though sliding sideways to starboard. Both Layela and Ardin watched the ship accelerate sideways and tilt down. Ardin saw yellow gas escaping the ship's hull, some blue flames licking at it before being extinguished by the vacuum of space.

"Is that the *Victorious*?" Layela asked, pointing further left. Ardin recognized her immediately. The ship was using its full but limited capacity to turn on a dime in order to swing back and fire some more at *Sun's Barrow*, hitting her at angles that wouldn't send her flying into Ardin and Layela. The large ship corrected its course, having been caught off guard. Ardin grabbed the controls and pushed forward on them.

"Drop whatever weapons we have left on those fighter ships!"

Layela moved into action right away, targeting lasers on the nearby ships. Ardin pulled the shuttle dangerously close to the *Sun's Barrow*, navigating its hull in the hopes to avoid becoming an easy target for multiple weapons. With any luck, those fighter ships wouldn't fire, either. If fear of hurting the Keeper wasn't enough, then fear of damaging their flagship might tip the scale in their favour.

"More incoming from port side," Layela said. "Fighter ships, unknown class."

"Hang on," Ardin pushed the shuttle down, in between some weapon turrets. The shuttle shook as all turrets fired at once.

"They've hit the *Victorious*. She's drifting." The worry in Layela's voice filled the shuttle.

"The other fighter ships are coming up on the port side." Layela said.

Her view screen beeped with alarms. "More ships, right in front of us!" She looked at Ardin with wide eyes. "They're firing!"

"Blood and bones!" Ardin pulled the shuttle down, nearer the hull still, proximity alarms ringing through the shuttle.

"The shots cleared us." Layela said, pulling up data from the back sensors. She laughed. "They're not firing at us—they're firing at our pursuers!"

Ardin joined her in laughter and pulled the ship away from the hull. The incoming ships were clearing a path for them within their formation, while maintaining fire on their pursuers. *Sun's Barrow* opened fire, but they aimed for the ships further from their shuttle.

They crossed the ships of their rescuers. Ardin barely recognized any of them. Most of them were from lands he had never visited. Some bore symbols similar to Mirial's, others looked so different he didn't quite understand how they even worked. One was a series of five cubes connected by cylinders. Another was a sphere with no sign of weapons, but energy gathered around its hull, flowing wildly, until it grew in pink-hued intensity and concentrated in the front to fire on its target. A few he did recognize, but not well enough to name their race or world.

But still, none were allies he knew personally. They were saving them simply based on their belief that Layela, the Keeper of Mirial, was on board.

One freighter fired all its weapons before being hit by a blast, its engine imploding within the ship, sending a fireball within its broken hull and cracking it in two.

"There!" Layela suddenly screamed. "There's the *Destiny II!*"

Brosten had maintained position, but he was now moving in. The front bay was open, ready to swallow the shuttle. It wouldn't be a soft landing, but they'd implemented several emergency systems to handle potential crash landings.

"Hang on," Ardin said. "We're going in."

He pushed them forward, as fast as they could go, trying to ignore the warning signs flashing on Layela's screen that listed all of the attackers behind them, trying not to glance at Mirial, either her planet or her dwindling sun, concentrating on keeping the shuttle level. The *Destiny II* wasn't moving fast, but fast enough with the shuttle speeding towards it.

They'd be testing the emergency systems to their fullest.

A plasma beam shot across their path, but Ardin called the *Sun's Barrow's* bluff and kept pushing ahead, not giving up any speed. Layela's fingers were turning white from clutching her chair, her eyes locked on the growing size of the entrance. Their entire viewport was being engulfed by the majesty of Mirial's flagship, her hull reflecting some of the battle and some of Mirial's weak light. The lit bay glowed in space, beckoning them to safety.

Just a few more kilometres... Another plasma beam shot out, hitting the side of the *Destiny II*. The ship buckled, its entire hull streaked with blue lightning. The perimeter diffusers were working, but not fast enough.

"We have no shields!" Layela said, clutching her screen now. The electric blue snakes fighting against *Destiny's* hull reflected in her wide eyes.

"Too late!" Ardin cut the engines, veering just enough to clear the hull and enter the bay. A blue snake sliced across the entry and lashed at the shuttle's nose, overloading their consoles.

The metal hull of the shuttle sparked with energy, shorting all of their systems. Computers and lights both went out. The soft hiss of the life support system stopped, just as they cleared the entrance to the shuttle bay. The exterior door closed and the compression door opened, but not quite fast enough. Ardin grabbed Layela's head and practically slammed her into the dash as the top of the shuttle buckled. It partly sheared off, ripping metal grinding in their ears.

The shuttle hit the ground hard once, the safety harness biting Ardin's thighs and chest, jerking him back up against the seat. His arm extended in front of Layela, poor protection now that the view screen and top of the shuttle were gone.

Before the shuttle could bounce again, cushions deployed from the floor. Layers of heat resistant and shock absorbent textiles filled with air in time to catch them on their second hit. It had been meant for shuttles that were still in one piece with their crews well-protected. The shuttle rolled once, catching fabric in the gap. It blew in, stopping the ship mid-roll. Ardin hit his belt hard, the breath knocked out of him, and his arm dropped. They were stuck sideways, Ardin leaning hard on the coarse fabric, Layela held in place by her safety harness.

Layela reached over and grabbed his hand. The shuttle was dark, the fabric blocking the only exit point. Layela squeezed his hand.

He gave out a low chuckle, pleased that his ribs didn't hurt. "I do believe the emergency systems could use a bit of work, still."

She laughed softly, cut short by a jolt as the ship settled.

"We need to get to that bridge," Ardin said. He unstrapped himself and fell awkwardly on the cushion.

"My way, then," Layela said, opening the door on her side and grabbing hold of the shuttle's hull before undoing her belt. Her legs flipped down and almost hit him in the head. Ardin grabbed them and pushed her up, following closely. The ship jostled again.

He jumped down, as did Layela. The cushion caught them and they slid off of it, running towards the lift.

It was the slowest lift ride of his entire life.

CHAPTER 12

CAPTAIN GILANE KAT sat at tactical control. The weapons master clutched a broken leg in the middle of the bridge. The entire crew had been ordered to strap in, and Gilane hoped not too many of the civilians were wounded. Not that she had much time to dedicate to worrying about their safety.

Sun's Barrow had multiple plasma cannons, and they didn't seem to mind firing them all at once. Gilane couldn't even calculate the size of their energy grid. It wasn't any technology Mirial had ever been privy to. A grid like that would change the spacefaring world, she had no doubt.

It'd be a bit more exciting it if wasn't being used against us!

Their own energy grid was faring fairly well, but all of their power was going toward maintaining life support on the civilian decks and protecting their hull from the plasma cannons. The new defences could only deflect so much.

Meanwhile, *Destiny II* buckled under even heavier hits. They wanted her disabled and helpless, and neither of Mirial's other ships seemed in a position to help.

But at least they knew they weren't fighting this battle alone.

She opened every channel to every ship—every frequency, every code, leaving the sound file fully open for translation and manipulation if necessary. She didn't care what happened to her words—she needed them heard and understood.

"This is Captain Kat of the *Victorious*." Lights flashed on her console, showing the feed being picked up across space, by allies, enemies, and ships that had yet to make a move.

"The Keeper of Mirial is safely aboard *Destiny II*. The plasma cannons are damaging her hull, and Mirial's Keeper might be captured again." She swallowed bile. "She is working to find a way to save Mirial and all those who depend on her. But she needs time." She paused, took a deep breath, closed her eyes. "I need your help stopping the plasma hits while they make their escape. By any means necessary."

She ended the transmission, not expecting any words as answer. But an answer she did receive. Smaller fighter vessels of multiple design and configurations practically swarmed *Destiny II*, placing themselves between Mirial's flagship and the much larger and better equipped *Sun's Barrow*.

The Ralis' fighter ships and their allies tried to break down the wall, slamming their manned fighters into the blockade of ships. But as one allied ship fell, another appeared. The swarm followed *Destiny II* as she reached for the tunnel.

"Captain Kat," Captain Malavant's voice sounded on Mirial's channel. He sounded tired, maybe wounded. But he was alive.

"Captain Malavant," she answered.

"We'll regroup on the other side of the tunnel."

Gilane paused, looking to Mirial. The sun peeked around the swarm, its white core so small and weak she could hardly believe it was the same sun under which she had been born, been married, introduced her first children to Mirial…It hardly seemed possible to save, now.

"Captain Kat?"

Gilane surprised herself with her next question, her words soft in her ears. "Can Mirial still be saved, Ardin?"

There was a pause. The Keeper answered in his stead. "Of course it can be saved. We just need time to find a way."

"Of course, Keeper." She paused. "Time is a truant commodity right now. We'll follow you in."

"See you on the other side." The connection closed. The *Destiny II* entered the tunnel. *Victorious'* computers tracked her progress and scrolled updates across the screen.

The Keeper wasn't safe yet, and she never would be, as long as the Ralis hunted her. They were too well armed, too well defended. Mirial's fleet and allies had almost been destroyed in lazy, unfocused attacks, and still the *Sun's Barrow* didn't show any scratches or damage. Her energy grid seemed unaffected by the battle, her pacing easily maintained, her weapons just as potent.

Gilane stared at the sun, so dim in the skies of her youth. Ships limped around her, others floated uselessly. She turned the view screen to watch the *Destiny II*. The *Sun's Barrow* was already gaining on them, passing the *Lady Mirial* as though one of Mirial's finest proved no challenge.

Gilane charged the weapons, pushing her power grid until warnings flashed across her screen. All she needed was one good hit with an energy weapon.

One good hit, and Mirial could be saved.

***

Layela wanted to scream, but the crew was under enough strain without having to worry that their Keeper had gone insane. She brought up detail after detail of the impromptu fleet that had risen to their defence. They were disorganized, some ships slamming into their own allies. But most were armed, and they were intent on winning time for *Destiny II*'s escape.

For my escape, Layela corrected herself. All of these ships, trying to save a Keeper who couldn't even call upon Mirial to help them. She tried again and again to reach out to the First Star, but she might as well have been trying to flick the attacking ships out of the sky. Neither scenario seemed likely to happen without massive assistance.

Ardin had given up glancing her way. He hadn't asked if she could help, but she had seen the plea in his eyes.

"Defensive shields down. Tachyon shields up," Brosten reported.

"Get us in there fast," Ardin snapped, looking as though he might lunge at the helmsman and take over himself. He jumped up from his seat, but forced himself back down, entering command strings into his screen.

"We're clear, and we're in!" Brosten reported, shouting in relief.

"Where's the *Victorious*?" Ardin asked.

"Another ship is approaching entry." Brosten hissed. "It's the *Sun's Barrow,* Captain. No sign of the *Victorious.*"

"The *Sun's Barrow* is calling for us to surrender now."

"Tell them they can suck our rejected air!"

"Aye, Captain," Brosten said, though he didn't activate the comm. Not having a viewing screen was infuriating Layela further, but the sight of the tachyon tunnels would only result in massive seizures in all non-ether creatures. They were slaves to their instruments.

The ship danced on the tachyons. Ardin clutched the side of his chair and looked at Layela, his eyes wide. Tachyon tunnels had only two states: stable, and very unstable. Layela brought up the readings. A major shift could mean they'd be squished to a one-dimensional state. A quick but unpleasant way to go.

"Someone's firing near the *Sun's Barrow!* They're hitting the tunnel entrance." Layela tried to interpret the readings, but Ardin beat her to it. "It's the *Victorious*. She's trying to collapse the tunnel before *Sun's Barrow* makes it through!"

"Gilane!" He screamed into the open line. "What are you doing? We're still in here!"

Gilane's voice was disturbingly calm. "Biolt made adjustments to the tachyon shields, and they should protect you." She paused. "I'm sorry, Keeper, but I don't think you can save Mirial. I saw your eyes. You're no longer connected with her, and you can be free. Isn't that what you've always wanted?"

Layela's heart dropped. She stood and moved beside Ardin. "Gilane, we'll find a way to save Mirial. We have to. So many depend on this. If you do this, we might not be able to come back!"

"If Mirial wants to be saved by you, she'll find a way to help you do it," Gilane answered.

"She's firing again. Tunnel is buckling! The *Sun's Barrow* is withdrawing."

"Biolt! What improvements? I don't care, activate them now! Do what you have to do!"

"Already done. Hang on!" The engineer's grainy voice was engulfed by the sound of tachyons breaking free and surfing over their hull, screeching against the shields. Layela held on to the back of Ardin's chair, managing to stay upright as the shields latched on to the highest concentration of tachyons and dragged them with it. The *Destiny II* moaned from deep within her belly, skidding sideways, her energy grid flickering as all power diverted to the shields.

The crew was tossed sideways, barely held down by their safety harnesses. The velocity of the ship far exceeded any safe speed.

Layela wanted to reach out to grab Ardin's hand, but the mere metre between them seemed like an eternity as the blood rushed to her head and darkness collapsed her vision.

The ship screeched and then decelerated. The great clamps that kept the tachyon flow stable were no longer enough to keep them trapped and they escaped to float in the vacuum of space.

Layela's head rang still with the screams of the tachyons. The whole ship spun, or her head did; she wasn't sure. She gripped the edge of her seat and gulped down breaths, fighting the nausea and dizziness. She tried to give Ardin a convincing smile. As convincing as his was, anyway.

They both turned to the chief engineer, the fastest recuperating crewmember.

Biolt looked down at the results, nodding and muttering. "The shields held." She could barely hear him over the ringing in her ears. "A few improvements for future usage, but I think this one is a success."

"What about the tunnel?" Layela asked in a whisper, then repeated it louder when no one answered.

Brosten hit a couple of keys before letting his hands fall on his lap. He turned to face her, his dark eyes lined with tired sorrow. "The tunnel is gone, Keeper."

Layela closed her eyes.

Without the tunnels, they couldn't reach Mirial. Not within their lifetimes, anyway. Gilane had bought them escape, but at what price? Layela's stomach turned and she feared she might throw up. Ardin's hand found hers and she held it tight, letting him ground her.

Mirial was out of reach now. Most Mirialers were still there, at the mercy of the Ralis, and she was in no position to help them. And the First Star still refused to speak to her.

She was no longer Keeper of Mirial. Since the day she had first learned of Mirial, she had dreamed of being free and with her loved ones.

And now that she had all of space and time to find her daughter and live her own life, all that she wanted was to run back into the fray and save Mirial, no matter the cost to herself.

Even if it meant never seeing her daughter again.

CHAPTER 13

ELSA BERGANDA STOOD on a branch of the great oak tree, her hair mixing with the green leaves, the wisps of wind striking her naked body. The bark under her feet grounded her, made her want to melt into the tree and merge with its majesty. She closed her eyes and focused on the feel of it below her, blocking every one of her sisters out, hoarding the moment for herself.

Just to be this tree, and nothing else. Grounded, rooted in one place, unaware of anything more than the sun above and the ground below, reaching for both at once while only being able to expand finitely.

Tears hugged the contours of her face and she turned and leaned against the tree, the bark scratching her skin. She wanted to just be here, now, just this one moment doing this one thing, but already the universe broke down her defences, one by one, indifferent to the weak mind that crumpled under its vast weight.

Rise gentle flower, rise with the rain,
Rise my love, dare to bloom again,
Shine like the sun, like the light of day,
Shine, shine forever, always with me stay.

Her voice cracked as she sang the familiar song Mother Layela had sung to them, what felt like a lifetime ago. She expended her arms and hugged the tree, getting as close to the bark as she could, letting its ether embrace her back.

She longed for the simple days of Mirial. This moon had welcomed and served them well, its inhabitants indifferent to the Berganda population flourishing in their wilderness, but Elsa missed the days when one walled garden, the white palace in the distance, and her sisters made up her world. When it had seemed nothing could undo their happiness. When she had truly believed that Mother Layela could protect them from anything.

A soft breeze pushed the leaves gently against her back, casting shadows and hiding her. For a moment, Elsa felt herself drift away, extended from her body. She became the tree, felt every root digging deep, cutting through rocks to find nutrition and water. Her limbs extended to branches, and she reached high, her leaves greedily absorbing the sunlight.

Her skin became bark and her hair leaves, her blood turned to sap and her feet to roots. For an instant, Elsa vanished, her consciousness pursuing her desires deep within the core of the tree.

A prick pierced her skin and Elsa squeezed her eyes, unwilling to let go of the tree. Another strike, this one harder, like a needle jabbing her tender green skin. She pressed the back of her head against the tree, bidding it farewell for now.

Elsa took a deep breath, opened her eyes, and turned to see the usual orange sky turn electric blue. Downpours of energy struck the fragile atmosphere and plummeted straight down to the moon. She opened up her mind to hear the usual chatter of her sisters, no fear lacing their thoughts.

They couldn't see it, which meant it was something laced with ether, falling in the sky around her. Elsa walked forward as far as she safely could on the branch and looked up, the sky breached with what looked like tiny falling stars. Except they weren't, because they left no trail and they didn't break down in the atmosphere. They just seemed to go straight through the moon as though it didn't exist at all.

Elsa couldn't stop watching the downpour around her, the sky whistling as the pinpoints of blue and purple light sliced it. She wasn't sure what had caused it, but she knew it had something to do with Mirial.

The tree sighed below her, as though repeating her farewell.

Elsa suspected that it would soon be time for her to leave.

***

Hoast sat down quietly beside her. She wasn't scared—never was, really, not since he'd met her, anyway. Or since she'd met him, he supposed.

"Can you sense her?" he asked, his voice a croak. He hadn't wanted to ask, but had anyway. He felt like a bad friend and lowered his head on his knees, clutching his legs and closing his eyes. Ardice was his best friend, always had been, and always would be. He couldn't imagine life without her, and he felt so bad for hurting her.

"Why did you bring us here, Hoast?" Her whisper was laced with wonder, and some fear. Maybe she didn't trust him, anymore. That made him sadder and he shook his head, keeping his forehead on his knees.

His voice was muffled by his pants. "I thought we'd be safe after we lost Rose. They said we'd be safe, that your mom would be here, like, your real mom, and that we'd be okay…"

Her slender arms gathered him and she leaned on him.

"It's okay. We'll be okay."

Hoast shifted his head, looking around him. The room wasn't lit very well and was sparsely furnished with a bed and a sink. The entire room seemed built of metal, except the few beige synthetic blankets covering the bed.

"I thought we'd be safe," Hoast mumbled again.

Ardice tightened her grip on him and kept holding him until her breathing lengthened and her arms loosened. He'd met Ardice's mom on Mirial, he was certain, even though Ardice hadn't wanted to come. She had eyes like Ardice, and her cheekbones were pronounced like hers. Ardice was prettier, he thought, her face a bit softer and her hair a bit lighter.

Why would she give her up, though? Why send her away when she could care and provide for her? Rose always said her mom would come for her one day, but was that true? When? And why did she never make an effort to show up to anything?

When Hoast had met Ardice, she was very sick. A nasty virus from some world she'd never even been to. She was feverish, her skin pale and clammy, her hair plastered on her forehead. Her chest rattled for days, and he didn't even see her eyes until after being with her for a week.

That was the only time he'd ever heard Rose speak of home. She had mentioned nothing since then, but when Ardice lay in pain, so small, she had told her that her mother would come if things were dire, and that if she hadn't come it meant that Ardice could fight this herself.

Hoast gently shifted and took hold of Ardice before she hit the ground. She slept like a decompressed spaceship and didn't even stir when he picked her up and brought her to the bed. She was small for her age, and he was strong. He didn't know if all Zoorsa were strong—he couldn't remember knowing any.

He covered Ardice with the blanket and sat on the bed near her. If things were dire now, would her mother come? They said she could sense her mother. They said to let them know when her mother was near.

But Ardice sensed nothing except the usual vast breadth of the universe, which he feared someday would rip her away from him.

He wondered again and again why he'd brought her here. Even the promises made to him now seemed vague and sketchy. He knew better than to trust strangers—Rose had always warned them to take care of each other, and to trust very sparingly.

He didn't know if he could trust himself anymore.

CHAPTER 14

ARDIN HAD ALWAYS wanted to captain his own ship, since he was a young boy going on short space flights with his father, the great Captain Malavant. He had grown up on the bridge, had been bred to be the best captain he could be.

And, above all, to look out for his own. That definition, his own, used to only encompass the small crew of the *Destiny*. But it had grown to include Layela, and Ardice, and more Mirialers and ether creatures than he could count.

After the blast of dark ether, when he thought he would die, he had made peace with the fact that he would be remembered. He had been loved, had made a difference, had managed to mostly live by his rules, and was giving up his life for the person he loved above all else.

Except he hadn't died. He had been wounded badly, and had been unable to touch Layela without pain for years.

Ardin flipped through some ship schematics. Not schematics of the *Destiny II*, but those of the *Lady Mirial* and the *Victorious*. He ran through the crew and passenger list. Double-checked the security measures.

Layela had told him he could leave her. That he could find another family, somewhere, take to the stars again. He heard the despair in her voice as it escaped in his reply. "It's only ten years."

Ten long years.

He had thrown himself into building Mirial's fleet and some of her economy. With Avienne's help, they had smuggled top grade shuttles based on old Mirial designs, and the profits were used to bring back better materials. More weapons. More security.

Ten years they had planned for this. Layela had prepared the people, and he had been in charge of hardware.

He focused on the *Lady Mirial*. Loran was onboard. Layela had been right—Loran was smart, and she had some uncommon knowledge. Ardin had made sure she'd known it all. Her job was to keep Layela safe, and he had needed to make sure she succeeded.

She could buy time, this he knew, but not forever. And not with the enemies she might be facing. And they couldn't help her, or the Mirialers.

They were trapped here, with few allies, the dying ether creatures around them through the years would be a constant reminder of their failure.

He sighed and leaned back, rubbing the schematics from his eyes.

He never thought he'd wish they'd had more than ten years.

***

Layela wandered through the open space that would eventually become gardens in *Destiny II*, were it ever given the chance. Mimicking the original space of its namesake, the gardens were on the aft of the ship, with great windows that didn't reflect the light as the only thing standing between her and space.

Unlike the design of its predecessor, however, columns were strewn across the gardens to maintain structural integrity. The *Destiny* had suffered many blows by the time Layela had met her, but she held on to her beauty. *Had* held on to her beauty. Sometimes, her predecessor and *Destiny II* were so much alike that Layela forgot they weren't the same ship. That the *Destiny* had burnt up in the atmosphere above Mirial fifteen years ago, leaving a trail of grief in its wake.

Layela sat on one of the few metal benches, not yet adorned with the stone that would eventually cover it. Space spanned before her and engulfed most of her vision. From where they were, expulsed from a tunnel that no longer existed, she could see a few larger stars, solar systems so close but still too far to reach without a tunnel. There were other ones in the area, of course, space being littered by them following Solaria's failed expansion in this area. The plans had fallen through only because of Solaria's own weak economy and leadership. World after world was conquered or turned into allies, only to be left rioting and rebelling as Solaria continued to expand, leaving only poorly trained troops behind. Solaria's heydays were long gone now. Their borders had shrunk back to the Thalonian system, and they barely managed to maintain that alliance.

Ether creatures had fled their borders as Solaria turned its attention on its few remaining worlds and vowed to cleanse them. The purge had been bloody but short; the ether creatures had been aided by their own networks and will to survive. With Solaria so much smaller now, there were many worlds they could inhabit, many worlds that welcomed anyone not bowing to Solaria.

Still, now the question remained: where should *Destiny II* go? Mirial fought a war far away without them, and they had no way of returning or helping. Layela gazed into the distance, her heart sighing for the old, broken planet and its palace.

She had been fine leaving it when it meant leaving a better legacy behind her. An exit that saw Loran and everyone else safe would have been fine. But now…leaving had felt wrong, and rushed, and against her will.

How long now before Mirial stopped providing the life-giving ether? How long before the ether creatures withered, one by one? Had some already passed away, clinging by a string to the hope of a new, strong First Star—a reality that could now never be?

She took a deep breath, staring at the sea of stars. Mirial might be one of them. She wasn't sure, didn't even know where in space she was looking, but she imagined it. A weak sun. Although, maybe not here. Here, it might still seem strong; the light captured here emanated years ago, possibly decades ago, when Mirial shone at its prime. Perhaps here, even, the ether would be stronger than near Mirial. Perhaps it was still infused in those rays of light, though she knew the ether travelled at much greater speeds than light.

The ether had already passed, but the light could shine on worlds faraway for generations after Mirial's passing. The First Star could be gone now, and Layela wouldn't even know.

She looked down at the metal floor, the dance of stars making her dizzy. It all seemed so…*useless*. She was so useless. Why would Mirial strip her of ether before the First Star had taken over? Or had it taken over briefly, before exploding?

Layela closed her eyes and imagined the graveyard of ships left behind—ships from worlds she hadn't even known existed, all lost because they believed she was worth saving.

"It's all so useless," she mumbled.

"I don't think it is," Ardin said, making her jump. He came around and joined her on the bench, looking out at the stars with her. "I don't think it's useless. I don't think any of this is useless."

A slow smile spread across her lips. "You don't even know what I'm thinking."

He shrugged. "I know that I can do this, now." He turned and took hold of her chin, gently kissing her lips. "I know I couldn't do that for ten years." He held her eyes captive. "I know I might not be able to do it for long, because I know there's still a battle to be fought, and I don't think you'll rest until you find a way to fight it, and end it the way you'd like it to end."

He looked at her for a moment longer before turning back to stare at the universe unfold before them.

Layela kept staring at his profile—the straight nose, the strong chin, the deep eyes and the eternal ponytail. The crows' feet on his eyes. The lines at his mouth. Time stamping his features with its passage. She had almost lost him a few times. When still connected to the ether, the faint ringing of bells would announce that his time was coming, probably before hers. She didn't know that, for sure. But now she would never hear those bells again, unless she found a way to reconnect with the ether. With Mirial, who had blessed them their meeting, and cursed them with a physical separation that had lasted ten years. Ten long years, without watching their daughter grow up, without being able to hold hands, flinching every time they stood near one another.

The ten longest years of her life, longer even than her childhood surviving on the streets.

"You would be happy," Layela whispered, turning back to the stars and their seeming immortality, "to live out your days with me and Ardice. To find a small house somewhere and maybe have another child or two, while there's still time." She paused, the blue flickers of a tunnel lighting in the distance, where a ship passed at speeds too great to see beyond the trail of tachyons.

A moment of silence filled the garden and the space beyond it.

"I like to think," Ardin's voice was soft but reached every corner of the garden, "that we can save Mirial and have that life, too, Layela. I don't think this is a moment of compromise."

Layela tried to smile, but grief weighed down her features. "And what if we can't, Ardin? What if we choose one and lose the other?"

This time, he didn't hesitate. "This goes against every instinct, Layela, but Ardice is fine. She's with Rose, and Rose will take care of her no matter what. Her connection with the ether probably broke at the same time, so Rose might even know the time has come and she might come and find us."

"How? We can't even get back."

"I don't know yet, but there has to be a way. There might be old tunnels we're not aware of, or maybe we can reactivate this one. I mean, we just survived a collapsing tunnel. That wouldn't have even been possible fifteen years ago. Surely there's a way to get back out there."

"And risk losing Ardice forever."

"And find a way back. If we can get there with a collapsed tunnel, we can find a way back again!"

She shook her head vehemently. "This is stupid. We can't get there to start with, and now we're arguing about coming back. We have no way to do this, Ardin!" She turned to face him, her voice growing louder. "We have no allies and no plan."

"We'll find Avienne. She can help us. Maybe there's something in the ship's archives that can help us form a plan on how to get back. How to re-ignite Mirial, even."

"There's nothing!" Layela jumped up and walked to the window. "I've looked at everything, Ardin. Ten years of looking, and nothing, except..." She placed her hand on the window, the cold reminding her of the stone, the tactile memory reigniting into the curves of the etching.

"Except what?" Ardin asked from right behind her. She didn't turn around to look at him, looking out towards the stars. She laughed. "I feel silly for mentioning it, but any tedious connection, right?"

"We're not swimming in clues."

"Right." She traced the etching with her finger on the window. "Selenor mentioned an etching of the Three Fates that he believed was much more recent than the others." She hesitated again. "As recent as my mother."

"What did it show?" The enthusiasm and hope in Ardin's voice made her turn around and face him.

"Not much, but maybe everything. The Three Fates surrounded Mirial and then stepped into her, as though re-igniting her from within."

Ardin nodded and then frowned. "The Three Fates actually exist?"

Layela shrugged. "I don't know. It's the one myth aside from Mirial that seems to be spread across every culture and world, so it's possible. Mirial exists, after all."

Ardin nodded and gazed out to the left, where Layela imagined Mirial must be. "We'll find a way back, Layela. If finding Three Fates is the way, then that's what we'll do."

"Really? Just like that?"

He didn't give her the grin she expected, quickly closing the space between them and putting his hands on her shoulders. "I can touch you again. I know that right now it feels like we've lost everything, but we haven't. We can still make this work, Layela." His voice cracked. "We have to find a way to make this work."

Layela grabbed him in her arms, realizing that he couldn't bear to choose between the Mirialers and the ether creatures, and their own daughter, and that he desperately needed to find a way to save them all.

Layela didn't hold any such illusions. And she needed to make sure he understood the importance of the ether creatures, even if it meant giving up their daughter, who would be fine without them. Unlike Josmere's daughters.

"Let's go see Elsa," she whispered in his ear. "Let's go find out if the Berganda see something we just can't."

He nodded, his breath warm on her neck. She closed her eyes, losing herself in his warmth, terrified that grief would swallow them both. She knew they couldn't save them all. But she was the one who kept seeing him look at the few pictures of their child. She was the one who had watched him throw himself into his work, trying to revitalize Mirial's economy so that they could fly in necessities, all while preparing the small escape fleet. He was the one who had planned the two ships that could connect with each other, so that families and communities wouldn't need to be separated if the planet couldn't welcome them just now.

Ardin was the one who believed in family, and he was the one willing to give his up to save Mirial, because he couldn't stand just sitting on the sidelines. Because he always clung to his belief that heroes still existed—but only if people were willing to step up to be one.

It doesn't matter, really, she wanted to say. *It doesn't matter, because we'll probably never make our way back, and Mirial will perish without us, and we'll watch the ether creatures wither, including our beloved Berganda, and we'll be helpless to do anything but raise our own child, as human as the rest of the world, as powerless to stop the death around us.*

Her love for Ardin and her fear of such a horrible future stilled her tongue.

She tried to capture this moment in her mind—the feel of his shoulder, the warmth of his arm, his breath rising and falling… To capture it all, in case this gift of time proved brief.

She hoped his desire to do the right thing would ward off regret, for both of them.

CHAPTER 15

THE DESSICATE RATTLED, now. Her entire hull rattled. Not a particular section of the ship, or the engine. The whole ship rattled endlessly as they traveled the overpriced tunnel. Avienne had tried to ignore it, at first, but it was getting hard. Especially when clanking added itself to the rhythm.

She disliked the clanking more, though the rattling would give even the most sturdy of heads a migraine. Jaru looked over chart after chart of schematics, but he was a systems analyst, not an engineer. Gobran hummed along with the rattling and couldn't see the nasty looks she shot his way.

His humming proved more annoying than the clanking, she decided. Definitely.

The lift door opened, which she saw but certainly didn't hear over the symphony of the *Dessicate*. Patros stepped on the bridge, taking in Avienne's annoyance, Jaru's confusion and Gobran's singing before exclaiming: "Is anyone else concerned about the fact that we sound like we're about to fall apart?"

Avienne felt a bit better at seeing his wide eyes.

"So you do have some survival instincts, then," she said, then had to repeat it louder so he could hear her.

He practically hopped closer to her, his face flushed blue. "This isn't a game, Avienne! We sound like we're about to be ripped apart."

Avienne turned to Gobran. "Are we there yet?"

Gobran's fingers ran on a static screen. She didn't know how it worked, but it certainly seemed to, which was all she cared about.

"Next exit."

"Ah. Thanks for that heads-up." Avienne turned to Patros, who was still looking at her with wide eyes. She didn't care to enlighten him at this particular point in time. It was nice to see him worried for his own life.

"Are you going to take the helm and take us out, Patros? Or do you want to risk having me do it." She leaned forward. "I'm feeling cheeky."

Patros rolled his eyes but took the helm. The ship jerked and almost sent her flying out of her chair. The rest of her crew, much more sensible than Avienne, were all strapped in.

Patros turned, still glaring. "Sorry, Captain."

"No worries," Avienne said, forcing her grip to loosen on her armrests. "I like a bit of jostling."

Patros turned back to his station, but not quickly enough to hide the smile forming on his lips. Avienne leaned back as he lowered the tachyonic shields. The clanking stopped and the rattling lessened.

"Okay, so, the tachyon shields are the clankers, and we suppose the speed is the rattler? Wait, that makes no sense. What would we rattle on? We're in space! Best aerodynamic travel around."

Jaru piped up. "I think the rattling is the engines. Or the hull herself. Maybe a seam is starting to form?"

"Any way of detecting or fixing that before the ship rips apart? Just curious."

Gobran chuckled from where he ran his hands on his "screen."

"There should be," Jaru said, his fingers flying on his station. Avienne noticed two interfaces she hadn't seen before. It seemed that Jaru had been doing some deals of his own on the side. Good for him. And not all of it was linked to computers.

"Nice brewing machine and mug holder," Avienne said.

Jaru shot a grin her way. He had been the youngest crew member on the *Destiny*, aside from her and her brother, of course, and he still looked the same as he did years ago. He was in his fifties, maybe even closing in on his sixties, but he didn't look a day over forty.

All that caffeine must be pickling his insides.

"We're nearing the Berganda's home," Patros said, the anger completely gone from his voice. He was quick to forgive and, Avienne thought, maybe even quicker to forget. It was an important part of why he stayed, she was certain. "Should we bring the ship into the atmosphere, or just shuttle down?"

Avienne looked to Jaru. "Well? Can we tell if we're going to make it into the atmosphere? Or are we just going to rattle our little brains out?"

"Brains and skin," Gobran offered from where he sat. She shot a grin his way.

"I'm grinning, you silly old coot," she added for good measure.

"I'm seeing it!" he said, chuckling.

"I'm surrounded by insanity," Patros said, shaking his head as he brought them near the planet of Burnice, its moon so huge it was half the size of the planet. The two bodies played with each other's gravitational fields so badly that entire sections of the planet were on flood alert at all times, and high tide rose so quickly that it engulfed the careless within minutes—it was practically a state of emergency for the planet. And on a world that only housed distilleries, there were many careless vacationers.

Its moon, on the other hand, had become a haven of proper behaviour and sanctimony. Several cults had set up shop on the moon, trying to save the "poor" souls of Burnice. The Berganda, seen as innocents and basically children since they aged so slowly, had easily found a home there. Being the last of their race had practically melted the heart of the population. Not enough to invite them in their communities, but enough to give them land away from others where they could thrive. It had been ideal for all involved.

"Maybe we should hit the planet instead of the moon," Avienne muttered.

"Thinking about my offer?" Litras appeared beside her. Avienne jumped.

"Blood and bones, woman! Make some noise when you approach someone!"

"I did, but the ship is more noisy than I am."

"Make more noise then. Adapt. Survival of the fittest and noisiest. Especially if my jump involves a knife throw."

Litras shrugged and looked ahead at the growing moon. "If your fingers aren't too loose with drink, I suppose we might have something to worry about."

"Funny. We're going to the moon, not the planet. Patros, we're going to the moon, right?"

"We're certainly heading that way, yes." Patros said. "I'm still waiting on feedback on the whole landing thing. The crashing-of-the-ship thing is of concern at least to me, although apparently not to anyone else."

"Right. Jaru?"

The systems analyst's mumbles were swallowed by the rattling. Jaru shook his head before chugging a cup of coffee and placing it straight into the slot for the brewer. The scent of fresh coffee filled the bridge. Avienne wished she liked coffee, but she preferred her drinks to be the opposite of stimulants.

Avienne turned. "Gobran? Will we fall apart upon entering the atmosphere, or won't we? Isn't that covered in Shipfaring 101 or some such basic course?"

"Usually it would be easy," Gobran said. "But when most of the sensors are offline and the energy grid is limping along, it's a bit harder to tell. Even going out and looking at the ship might not reveal anything. A fully functional master computer might not be a bad thing, either. Just little improvements here and there."

"I sense sarcasm, old man," Avienne said, standing up. "All right, let's not risk the atmospheric entry, then."

"Really?" Patros called over his shoulder.

"Ah ha. Funny. Sometimes even I can take the safe route. Gear up, blue boy. You're coming with me, for that remark."

Patros turned and stood with a goofy smile. "At least you think you're funny," Avienne mumbled, not repeating when he cocked his head sideways to indicate he hadn't heard her. The ship really was making a lot of noise.

"I'd like to come too," Litras said, standing near Avienne.

"Oh, no. I'm not bringing you down there. You can hang out here until we bring us back a Berganda."

Litras shrugged. "All right. I'm flattered that you still trust me enough to leave me on board with your rattling ship and crew members."

Avienne cocked her head. "I'll throw you in the brig, then. Save me some trouble."

Litras held up both hands defensively and looked hurt. "No, I meant it! I'm flattered!"

"Really? You're pathetic. All right, try shutting off main propulsion, Jaru?" Within seconds the rattling ended. "That's better. This way, those of you who aren't already insane won't spontaneously become so. If that didn't wake Rose up, nothing will." She turned to face the Kilita.

"All right. You come with us, Litras. I don't know whether or not I can trust you, but I know that I'd rather keep an eye on you."

The Kilita beamed. "Great! I like ships, but I think I'm more of a ground-beneath-my-feet type of Fated."

Avienne shook her head. "Jaru, Gobran, the ship is yours. Contact us if you need anything. We'll be as fast as we can."

She would have preferred to bring Rose down to the planet, but as bad as the *Dessicate* was, it was still a more or less stable place for her to rest. Litras had suggested they leave her here and, sadly enough, the Kilita seemed to know the most about healing.

She hopped into the lift with Patros and Litras. She hoped adding a Berganda to the mix, potentially an insane one at that, wouldn't be the weight that tipped the sanity scale of her crew.

Like that matters at this point.

Avienne grinned all the way to the shuttle.

***

The rain had stopped falling, but Elsa still stood on the branch looking up at the sky, certain something else was coming their way, unable to peel her eyes away from the deep red sunset partially eclipsed by the planet. She loved the movement of this planet and its moon— always a dangerous dance, like a waltz gone mad and gigantic.

The ether bounced between the moon and the planet at this time of night. She was pretty certain she was responsible for that. She couldn't tell whether the ether was repelled by the planet or dragged from it, but she didn't care. They needed as much ether as they could find, especially if production from Mirial was likely to stop.

A trail of smoke broke away from the canopy above her and Elsa smiled. A ship was coming down! So few of them came to this moon, most preferring the party atmosphere on Burnice.

This was what she had been waiting for. Something sent to her from Mirial. She was certain the ship would come straight for their home. So certain that she scrambled down the tree and slipped her simple cotton robe back on, loving the way the fabric let the air dance on her skin.

She ran towards home, the grass tickling her bare feet, sending strings of excitement to her sisters.

It had been years since they'd had any visitors, and Elsa could use all the distraction she could get. Keeping herself grounded wasn't as easy as it had once been.

She slowed down, the excitement reflected from her sisters suddenly terrifying her.

I will have to leave. She was as certain of that as she was of her need for ether and of the new First Star's passing. The words played themselves over and over again in her mind, the weight crushing her until she fell to her knees in the tall grass.

She ran her fingers through the grass, the long stems plying and cooling her hands. She placed both hands on the ground and felt the ether flow to her and from her. Mirial was all around her still.

And Mirial was coming to take her away.

***

Galka pulled alongside the old ship that hovered above the moon of Burnice. Why the ship didn't get dragged down in the gravity well of the planet was a mystery. With its entire hull covered in rust, it wasn't a sight to behold. Flecks of rust floated off it into space, like spices floating in the surrounding space.

The ship had obviously been abandoned on a very damp planet for a few years before some unsuccessful smuggler appropriated it. That it was still functional spoke highly of either their luck or engineering skills. Galka guessed it was the former.

The oxygen dwellers inhabiting it wouldn't hear her enter, she was certain. So much corrosion meant that probably half its sensors were offline. The only aspects of the ship that gleamed in the sun were the gun turrets. The Malavant sister had apparently earned her reputation.

The ship's name was scratched off and had been repainted badly, in someone's poor handwriting, to *Dessicate*. Malavant's reputation was definitely earned.

Galka had watched a shuttle leave the ship a few minutes ago. The slont was definitely on it, his trail still ridiculously clear to her. But he wasn't of interest to her right now. She guessed the Malavant was on board with him, which saddened her a bit. She'd have enjoyed crushing the life out of her. The pleasure might be hers yet, if she could finish off her target first.

Target acquired. She sent the message off to her employers. The Ralis' pleasure filled the waves returning her way. She basked in it while her stomach turned.

She brought her shuttle close to the *Dessicate*, aiming for a port hole so that she knew she was on a floor with rooms. It was easier than having to cut through machinery. And much more subtle.

Once close enough to set off the highest proximity warnings, she deployed her boarding equipment. It was crude and reminded Galka of the suction mouth of a Glotch, but it did the trick. Her ship buckled as it grabbed hold of the larger one, and she turned off her engine and let herself drift along with it. The suction cup injected acid into the hull—enough to let her in, but not enough to allow the oxygen to escape and kill her in the process. With the condition of the hull, it wouldn't take long.

The yellow Glotch atmosphere danced near the rust, but it wouldn't create more rust, unlike the useless oxygen. The pure yellow gas killed most other creatures, but that's why only the strongest could live on their home planet. That's why her people had outlived so many other Fated.

She preferred not to suck in the weak oxygen, but she could survive on that, too. Her hump was swollen with Glotch gas, so she had some spare to allow her more speed.

Not that she would necessarily need more to kill a mostly brain-dead woman, but still, she wasn't paid to take a chance. Not on this part of the journey, anyway.

Galka leaned back and watched the acids melt the metal. She treated herself to a stimulant, imagining the drugs traveling her bloodstream like the acid travelled through the metal, stripping away everything that was useless and unnecessary.

In the case of the *Dessicate*, that meant stripping most of it away.

CHAPTER 16

BELLS TOLLED IN *the distance.*
    "Yoma?" Layela cried out for her sister, blood dripping all over the bridge leading to the temple of Mirial. Except it wasn't Yoma's blood, it was Layela's blood, she knew. She had lived through it and an old vision had become a memory.
    Yoma!
    The temple was gone now, a bridge leading to a void, her sister standing on the grounds that had once housed the most sacred structure in all of Mirial. Her eyes were sea green and set, determination painting fierceness in her features.
    Layela ran to her, but could not reach her. She was becoming further and further away the faster she ran, and she felt so tired… And the bells kept ringing!
    "Yoma!"
    "Layela!" Ardin's voice pierced through the dream and Layela's eyes flashed open, disoriented by the darkness when it had been so light but a few moments ago, confused her sister no longer stood in front of her, waiting for her.
    Ardin turned on the lights. He looked at her with thin, focused eyes. Her heart hammered in her ears and her breath eluded her. She looked around wildly, still looking for her sister even as the last threads of the dream released her mind.
    "Layela? You had a bad dream, Layela. You're safe now."

No longer used to having someone in bed with her anymore, she clung to him, fearing the darkness would return. Had it been a vision? Had she found her ether again in her anger? Had she doomed their happiness? She clung to Ardin, willing her breath to steady, her heart to slow down, her forehead to loosen. She lowered her head, focusing on her breathing and trying to lengthen each breath so that it was slower than the last.

The threads of the dream clung, still vivid. She could see her sister standing on the temple's old grounds, now empty. She saw the determination in her sister's eyes, and still felt as though she could reach out and touch her. She hadn't looked once at Layela. Not once.

Had she known she was there?

Of course not, silly. It was a dream. She tried to chide herself, but it didn't work. Goose bumps erupted all over her arms as she remembered how close she had been to Yoma. The strength in her features, the familiar sea green eyes…

She gulped in recycled air and turned to face Ardin.

"I think I just had a vision." She tried to keep her voice even. His eyes widened.

"How? You're not connected with Mirial, you said. And you haven't had a vision in years! Why now? How?" He stopped himself, his eyes darting down before focusing back on her. He took a deep breath. "Tell me about it."

Layela nodded and tried to recount it as faithfully as possible. Unlike dreams, visions didn't fade when she awoke, but capturing their ferocity with words proved near impossible. She injected it with her reactions and feelings, having learned long ago that they were as integral as the vision itself. Ardin only interrupted twice to ask for clarification.

When she finished, she reached out to Mirial, but it was like swimming up and being able to see the surface but not quite reach it. She was drowning in water, never having realized how much she had grown used to, perhaps even dependant, on air.

"You still can't reach Mirial, can you?" Ardin asked gently.

"Nothing." She was surprised to feel the tears well up to her eyes. She wiped them away, angry with herself. "Why is it that I've always wanted this, and now that I have it, I want anything but this?"

Ardin reached out for her and gathered her in his arms. He kissed the top of her head and held her. "This is stupid. I need more sleep or something."

"It's not stupid, Layela. Sometimes, we don't know what we want until we lose something." He took a deep breath. "And, sometimes, we want conflicting things so badly it makes our heart break. But we can't have everything, Layela. I wish we could, but we can't."

Layela held him back, sighing deeply as she held him. "You know, if we do find a way to return to Mirial, it might be at the cost of ever seeing Ardice again?"

A few breaths passed. "There was always a chance we would never see her again, Layela. Nothing's changed there. But maybe the future we had in mind for her isn't what will happen, too. Maybe she'll find us someday, on Mirial, and maybe she'll want to be a part of the culture." His voice dropped to a whisper. "We don't know her, and she doesn't know us. She'll always be our little girl, our firstborn, but we can't pretend to know where her heart will lead her. We don't even know if she'd want to be with us if we found her now. I mean, we did decide to let her go. Maybe she resents us."

"It wasn't us, Ardin. It was me. I decided to send her away."

Ardin pushed her away and held her at arms' length. "I was a useless sack of potatoes at that point. You did what you thought was best, which is all I can ask." He paused. "As my sister so gracefully put to me: don't go knocking up a girl if you don't trust her to do what's best for your kid."

Layela laughed. "I miss Avienne. I hope we find her soon. It'll be nice to shed her insanity on the situation."

"I've been sending out signals she would recognize. If she intercepts one of them, she'll know where we are, and she'll come meet us." He looked her up and down. "What do you…want to do until then?"

Layela smiled and leaned in for the kiss.

***

The land below them spread out in lush greens, hills peppered beneath forests and grasslands, lakes shining in the red glow of sunset.

"This is beautiful," Litras exclaimed, leaning forward from the back seat to try and see it from all angles. Avienne let herself be swept up in Litras' enthusiasm.

"It's a perfect place for the Berganda. They're really thriving. Several generations are already living down there. We try to visit what, once a year?"

"Thereabouts," Patros said from the co-pilot seat. He shot a grin her way. He loved this land, too, and loved the Berganda as much as she did.

"Several generations?" Litras asked. "That's fertile ether. How have they kept the ground that fertile for the last ten years?"

Avienne frowned. "I don't know. Does it matter? Maybe it doesn't need to be that strong to allow them to seed." Avienne knew better, but she felt better for the lie. It was an annoyingly good question. How did they manage to maintain such fertile ground if Mirial was dwindling? Entire races were said to have already vanished, yet the Berganda continued to thrive. Avienne pushed the mystery from her mind. She had enough to worry about, and she was just grateful for the Berganda's persistent survival.

"Is that it?" Litras leaned forward further, her head between Patros and Avienne. Avienne had to admit that she was impressed. Few people could spot the Berganda settlement from the air. Or the ground, for that matter. The Berganda were content sleeping in trees and on the ground, having built only a few houses from plants that had already linked with them.

In time, all of the plants around them would become more conscious from living with the Berganda. But that would take several more generations, or so they all assumed.

"Get back there and buckle your seatbelt," Avienne told Litras, who grudgingly did so but still craned her neck to stare out the side window. The woman was a danger to herself.

Avienne turned the shuttle and navigated away from the settlement, using the strongest airjets to bring them down while cutting off all other engines. She didn't want to pollute more than necessary. Not here, where the Berganda lived off the land.

Usually she came in one of Mirial's new shuttles, which you could eat off of even after atmospheric entry. They ran on water and recycled air, and were so sustainable and trail-less that smugglers gobbled them up like candy. But she had sold her last one just last week and hadn't returned to Mirial to get more stock. Not until she had answers for Layela and Ardin.

The shuttle landed with a thud.

"Let's go!" Avienne said, hopping into the back of the shuttle and pushing on the latch. The hinges creaked but barely moved. Avienne swore and started shoving the latch. The bloody thing barely budged, even though she threw all of her weight into it.

"The shuttles are doing as well as the ship," Litras deadpanned.

"At least they don't rattle," Patros offered.

"Would you two smart asses shut up and give me a hand?"

Litras stood and pushed on the door, sending it flying up on its hinges as though it weighed nothing. Avienne and Patros exchanged a look. "Well, at least she's useful for something." Avienne shrugged.

"I think we should be careful," Patros muttered as he followed her out of the shuttle. Litras was already walking to the settlement, turning back and waving at them with a big goofy grin on her face. Avienne waved back and then caught Patros' look of warning.

"Careful. Right." Litras tripped on something and went down before picking herself back up, laughing. Avienne cocked her head sideways. "She is kind of adorable, in a freaky abnormal sort of way."

"That's what I think of you," Patros said as they followed Litras.

"Ah, you think I'm adorable!" She turned and kissed him on the cheek before continuing on, leaving Patros to his goofy grin. Litras suddenly stopped and lowered her head, standing so still that she blended in with the trees.

"Litras?" Avienne asked as they approached. Litras held up her hand to quiet them, cocking her head sideways and squinting her eyes in concentration. Avienne looked to Patros, but he seemed just as confused as she was.

Litras' eyes flew open. "It's the Keeper!" she exclaimed.

"What?" Avienne took a step forward and grabbed Litras' shoulders, slouching to look her in the eye. She tried to force her voice to stay calm, making it grave when she spoke. "What do you mean, Litras?"

Litras focused on Patros. "Didn't you hear?"

"What? Hear what?" Patros sounded confused and concerned all at once. Avienne didn't turn to look at him, focusing on Litras instead and abandoning all pretence of calmness.

"What is it, Litras? Blood and bones, tell me now or you'll be a bloodied pulp on the ground!"

This time, Litras did focus on her. "There was just a message on the Fated Link. Some ancient ether race called for the Keeper to be found. Said she was somewhere along the tunnel from Mirial and should be found and brought safely back." She frowned. "But they said the tunnel was down, so another means would be necessary to bring her back. And that she was necessary for their survival, and basically had shirked her duties. It's not a very warm tone, really."

Avienne squeezed Litras' shoulders until the Kilita winced. "That means Layela is somewherehere in this quadrant! And my useless brother probably in tow with her!" She let go of Litras and hugged Patros. Then she pushed him off and stared at him.

"Why didn't you hear the message?"

"Someone was distracting me!"

"Oh, good point." Avienne exhaled deeply, feeling stress shed from her like grime in the rain. A smile came easily to her lips.

"First things first," Avienne said. Litras and Patros followed her as she walked between the trees, the dark forest not oppressive but rather welcoming, as though it recognized friend from foe and greeted the former.

The Berganda emerged from the forest around them, shadows taking on green tones as they stepped into the fading light. Most were wearing simple dresses; some were just naked and seemed not to care that Patros was in their midst. The Slont didn't know where to direct his gaze, and seemed to settle for staring intently at a spot on the ground.

Most of them knew them and they came to share a greeting, a hug, a giggle… Avienne laughed with them and hugged as many as she could. How many could there now be? At least a thousand, she guessed, and was exhausted but happy by the time the Berganda backed up a bit and gave them room. Patros' blush was so deep his skin practically glowed blue. Avienne nudged him playfully.

A hush fell over the Berganda. They were always silent, practically, the youngest ones used to communicating telepathically with one another. Some didn't even know how to form words, and Avienne always enjoyed teaching them to swear. Not that she would have time this trip.

The first generation of Berganda, Josmere's daughters, were getting old in Berganda years now, and some had already withered and passed, much to Avienne's sadness. There were no graves to mark their passing, their bodies absorbed back into the earth from which their daughters had bloomed.

A deeper hush fell on the Berganda now and they stopped pacing and shifting, moving aside to make way for the oldest amongst them, Elsa. Avienne observed her as she approached. Elsa had always been a bit different than her sisters, but the scars inflicted on her mind ten years ago had left her apart from all of them. Physically she was the same, but she held herself differently. Usually she seemed playful and lost, dancing in the distance to a symphony only she could hear. Now, she was the complete opposite, standing gravely and still amongst them, her features set and hard.

"Mother Layela needs us," she simply said, her words perfectly spoken, her whisper carrying across the forest as though it were the wind.

Avienne nodded. "Layela needs us, and Ardice, too." Elsa's eyes widened a bit. Avienne had always wondering how the Berganda felt about Ardice. Layela had been their mother first, but after Ardice's birth, well, things had changed. The Berganda had paid a hefty price.

But Avienne sincerely believed that the Berganda would come through for Ardice, simply because she was Layela's child, and they loved Layela. Especially Elsa, firstborn amongst them.

With her cotton dress outlined by the red setting sun and her features now cast in shadows, Avienne could have sworn Josmere stood before her.

"You look so much like your mother," she said. A ripple of what she hoped was pleasure travelled through the Berganda.

"Will you tell me stories about her?" Elsa asked, her voice suddenly small and young. Elsa might be old for a Berganda, but she would always be a child to Avienne.

"Of course. I'll tell you whatever stories I have, sweetheart. But after I bring you right back. I just need you to unlock Rose's mind."

Elsa lowered her head a bit and Avienne thought she saw tears running down the perfectly smooth cheeks. "No you won't. I'm leaving with you. You'll need me. Mirial told me you'd need me, raining colours from the sky."

"The tachyons," Litras said, wonder lacing her words. "The tachyons would have travelled far and fast, once released from the tunnel. She must have been able to see them."

"They were full of ether," Elsa said, as though it was a sufficient explanation.

"You're the one filled this land with ether," Litras said, taking a step towards Elsa. Avienne stayed back. She had no reason to believe the Kilita would harm the Berganda. "You're the one who did this." She reached up and offered her two hands, which Elsa took. Litras' whisper was hoarse. "It's so beautiful."

Elsa smiled then, a full smile, and Avienne felt as though she were seeing the Berganda for the first time—young and unsure, old and wise, all at once.

"So beautiful," Litras repeated, her voice hoarse, and Avienne wished she could, for just one moment, see the world through their eyes.

CHAPTER 17

JARU CHECKED ROSE'S pressure and wiped down her forehead. They didn't have anything resembling saline solution to keep her hydrated, so he moistened her lips and let drips fall into her mouth. She was definitely getting worse. They'd done their best to keep her clean and hydrated, but without proper training and supplies, there was little they could do.

He felt uncomfortable around the sick and dying. He always had, which was why he preferred working with computers. People in general made him uncomfortable, unless they were familiar faces. He'd never quite fit in when he was a child, and became more and more withdrawn, until experts had deemed he was gifted by Mirial and should be allowed to blossom.

He had been encouraged to try painting, writing, ship design and any other art form that would help him tap into his gifts. He had wanted to be a ship designer, but he had difficulty with the three-dimensionality of design. It wasn't until he found coding that he understood everything clearly. The code danced with mathematical perfection, and his mind grabbed the possibilities and multiplied them in an instant, giving his mind thousands of possibilities until he'd distilled them down to one, which proved the perfect answer. Usually.

He loved that. And he'd loved the *Destiny*, and Captain Malavant and then Captain Calin. And now he loved the *Dessicate,* and working for the new Captain Malavant—though he'd always believed he'd one day work for Ardin, not his unconventional sister. It didn't matter to him. They were both fast on their feet and he enjoyed their company and even their conversation.

It was the slow ones who threw him off. Those who didn't follow a reference quickly or understand logic. That was why he rarely left the ship. Why would he? Everything he needed was right here.

"How is she?" Gobran's voice boomed on Jaru's comm unit. He jumped, his heart racing. Maybe he did need to cut down on the caffeine a bit. Maybe he would, another day.

"She's the same. Maybe going downhill a bit."

"Did you check her temperature?"

Jaru touched her face briefly. "Um, she doesn't seem any hotter."

"We have a thermometer at least. You can check with that."

Jaru pulled out the thermometer and stared at it. It was an old clunky thing, probably an antique someone had tossed aside. Sometimes, Jaru questioned the decision-making skills of their captain.

"Do you need help?" Gobran's voice boomed again.

"No. No, I'm fine. I can do this. Where should I stick it?"

Even over the comm unit, he heard Gobran's sigh. "I'm on my way. Stay there—I'll need your eyes to read the useless thing. Transferring bridge control to your leadcom."

"Okay! I'll be here." Jaru was more relieved than he could express.

Sick people were the slowest of all. They didn't mean to be, he understood. And when he contracted the flu, he too became slow and useless, and he could barely stand himself. It was something he'd learned to accept. He would never be a great humanitarian. Which was why, he imagined, he fit in so nicely with Avienne's crew.

A strange stench caught his attention—something acrid permeaing the room. He turned to the door just as a blow came down, hitting him on the side of the head and sending him flying.

***

Galka felt dissatisfied. The woman was unconscious, and it looked like if she were just left alone for another day, she would pass on her own. Her employers had greatly overpaid her, and for what? A dissatisfying journey coming to a poor anti-climactic end.

She pumped relaxants to still her growing nerves. She was annoyed with herself, with her employers, and with the woman for being such poor sport. The entire crew lay crumpled at her feet, and she could just stomp on the man's head before leaving and be done with it.

Poor, poor sport.

She heard a noise from the hall and withdrew into the back of the room, behind a half wall. A man shuffled in.

"Jaru?" he asked, his hands reaching out to grab the side of the woman's bed.

Great.

She'd only get to take out an old, blind and feeble man.

***

Gobran had visited many worlds in his youth, always enthusiastically seeking old maps or creating new ones. He'd always wanted to discover a new world and be known for that. A true explorer.

He had always stood out in Mirial for that desire. Mirialers were notorious for their desire to stay on the planet of their birth. But not Gobran. He had wanted to travel the stars, and he had, to some degree. But then his daughter had been born and he had been exiled, and time swept away his youth and left him trapped in an old man's body.

But one world Gobran did have the chance to visit was the Glotch homeworld. He'd had to wear layers of protective clothing, but he had been twenty years old and wanted an adventure to talk about. He'd gotten more than that, in the end.

He'd never forgotten the stench of the Glotch.

Gobran reached out for Rose, feeling her hand. It was warm. She still lived.

The Glotch were hired by others sometimes, and it was never for anything good. Even Solaria had integrated a few in their army, recognizing their special talents for destruction and killing.

Jaru hadn't answered him, and he had to accept the high probability that the systems engineer was already dead. His heart ached. He forced himself to focus on saving Rose and the precious knowledge trapped in her mind. He reached to his belt and let his hand linger there, as though thinking. But he was now within easy reach of his small pistol, grateful Avienne had insisted he learn how to use it and carry it on his body at all times. That was one of her rules. They were never to be unarmed. Too many unfavourable folk out there, ourselves included, she always said.

It seemed his paranoid captain had been right to be cautious.

He stayed still, listening for any hint of the Glotch. The stench of it was everywhere, permeating the entire room. He couldn't locate it that way, but he just needed one clear shot and he could make a run for it.

Gobran felt the side of the bed with his foot for tre release. He found a pedal and hit it, pleased to hear the bed clunk and not lower or eject Rose. If he was right, he'd just released the latch to the floor. If he was right and lucky, there would be wheels under the bed. He was too old to carry the woman, but he might be able to wheel her.

A small sound followed the unlatching of the bed, and Gobran didn't hesitate. He jerked the weapon free, and pulled the trigger. A guttural scream, and he knew it was indeed a Glotch and a female. He didn't linger to find out if the Glotch was dead or just wounded. He started pulling on the bed, dragging it towards the door. The bed was heavier than he'd anticipated, and he had to put the pistol away and grab the siding with both arms to move it. He ran it through the door, banging it against the sides, and locked the door behind him. A shot hit the door, and he thought he could hear melting metal. He couldn't smell it over the stench of Glotch, but his ears were sharp and he was fairly certain the door wouldn't hold long.

Hegrunting as he pulled the bed down the corridor. "Security protocol 333," he shouted, almost out of breath. The computer didn't answer. The voice controls were probably down. He heard a grunt and banging down the hall. The Glotch wasn't even bothering to be quiet, probably understanding her advantage. Gobran's sweaty hand slipped on the bed, but he still managed to keep a grip on it.

The air shifted slightly and he mapped out the ship in his mind. He was at another corridor, and he veered left. The one thing still fully functional on this ship were the escape pods, present on all active decks. Again, a paranoid captain, and one who actually cared about the well-being of her crew, could come in handy.

A shot rang out and hit the bed, almost ripping it from his grasp. Gobran held onto it, his fingers raw from dragging it. He pulled it into the next corridor, grunting, hoping Rose hadn't been hit.

He then turned right, praying he wasn't forgetting the map in his panic to escape. He'd memorized the schematics over and over again. He hated being dependent, and Avienne expected him to pull his own weight.

His hand hit a door and he could have wept with joy. He opened it and pushed the bed in, using his full weight to propel it. The room was small and he had to scoot around the bed, but he managed to lock the door.

A bang echoed on the door, followed by another scream. The Glotch was certainly under stimulants, too. That would make her even more unpredictable and dangerous.

Gobran's hands slipped with sweat as he opened the door to the pod. Escape pods were cramped and uncomfortable, but they were safer than staying here with a crazed Glotch. The *Dessicate* had limited internal defences, relying almost exclusively on her crew. And right now her crew was running. Captain Malavant could come back up and deal with the Glotch herself, if that was her fancy. His main mission was getting Rose out of here, which was the only way he could protect her.

He grabbed Rose by the shoulders. "Sorry," he mumbled, and then he pulled hard, letting his weight pull her down. She crumpled over him and they both landed into the pod. Gobran hissed as he landed on some of the controls. He'd have bruises for weeks.

He dragged the rest of Rose in, made sure she'd cleared the entrance, and hit the emergency release button. The pod's doors slid shut and the entire thing rattled as he buckled Rose in and did the same for him. The pod eased out, and they were on their way.

Gobran allowed himself a breath of relief. He reached down, finding controls that had been adapted for his lack of sight. Again, he loved his paranoid captain.

The pods were simple enough, able to project a distress beacon for light years. But he didn't activate it, choosing to run silent instead. He didn't know how the Glotch had come onboard, or what she intended to do with the ship, and he had no intention of giving her an easy target.

He plugged in two simple command strings: run silent and head to Captain Avienne's shuttle.

He hoped he wasn't bringing an army down on her.

***

Galka injected a relaxant before her heart burst with adrenaline. An old man! An old, blind man had managed to escape her. Galka ran back to her ship.

He was probably running silent, but she could find him easily enough. He would head towards the Slont, she was certain. She slowed down a bit, allowing herself to enjoy the moment. That would be perfect, really. It would give her more targets, and some targets of interest, like Avienne Malavant.

She could kill the Rose woman in front of them before killing them. Rob them of hope, first. Let them embrace the futility of their journey.

Yes. And she would cut that old man's legs off for having outrun her. Then she'd let him die there.

-report-

Galka scowled. Her employer had horrible timing and seemed to enjoy interrupting her most satisfying daydreams.

She reported back before they pestered her again. They were also not very patient.

-under control. Target located on moon. In pursuit.-

A pause, and she knew they were going through her memory files. She should never had agreed to that implant, but it gave her so many more job options and really increased her pay scale. It was worth it for that alone, but wasn't very useful when missions weren't quite as successful as she'd hoped.

Like this one.

She reached her ship and untethered it, oxygen flying out of the rusty ship as its protective systems failed. She hardly cared. Her job wasn't to spare the ship.

- backup is on the way. Accept assistance or contract will be terminated.-

The background noise of her employers stopped, meaning they'd found something else to occupy their time. Probably finding her "assistance."

Galka growled and pulled hard on the controls. She'd show them how little assistance she needed. Maybe they could pick up the mess she'd leave behind.

She grinned at that thought.

CHAPTER 18

THE DESTINY II exited the tunnel, the majestic world of Burnice silently hanging in space before them. Layela had never been to this system, but she had considered coming to work in the distilleries when she was twelve. The money was good for anyone who could keep their heads on their shoulders. But Yoma had talked her out of it, saying the atmosphere and lack of plants would kill her. Layela hadn't disagreed and they'd started thieving shortly after.

But she could have made the moon her home. Even from here she could see the familiar hues of oxygen lining its surface. The Berganda loved it, and Avienne always spoke of how much they thrived there, generation after generation seeding in the soft ground.

Layela wished she had come to visit them before today. But leaving Mirial, even on an informal visit, had seemed like such a chore, and so much had needed doing over the last decade.

But still, Layela had missed them, especially Elsa. They were her daughters in a way, too, and she had missed so much of their short lives. The loss of Ardice had been somewhat tempered by knowing that the Berganda were safe. Safe and happy, and on a world that wouldn't stifle them, away from the dwindling Solarian Empire.

At least some of her children she would see again. She had heard the names of the few who had passed, mostly of old age, and she had wept for each of them.

"Approaching the moon of Burnice," Brosten reported.

"Are there any other ships in the area?" Ardin asked.

"A few, mostly trading ships. No recorded ships from Mirial."

Ardin nodded.

"Would Avienne even have her transponder on?" Layela asked, partly out of curiosity, partly out of hope.

Ardin grinned. "Probably not. That girl can't make anything easy for me!"

"There are several ships coming around the planet now," Brosten said, his voice picking up speed. "They're all ships unknown to our database. There are three of them, and they look pretty serious."

"What's their heading?" Ardin asked calmly.

"The moon, Captain."

"Are our transponders off?"

"Since leaving Mirial."

"Good. Let's run her silent and follow them."

Layela stared at him. "What if they're after the Berganda? They're known allies." She paused. "Would they even be after us? I mean, how could the Ralis send a message here? With the tunnel collapsed, not even a message pod could make it through."

"I'm not sure, but I wouldn't discount anyone as an enemy at this point." Ardin said, not looking up some his console. "And, unless I'm mistaken… got it!"

He pressed a button and a ship was magnified onto the view screen. The *Dessicate* loomed in all its rusty glory.

Layela stood. "Avienne's here. How did you know?"

"She can't stay out of trouble. And we leave signals for each other. Things you need to know to look for. Old habits die hard."

"The ships are heading near the *Dessicate,* but their heading is a bit off for the ship itself," Brosten reported. "They're either preparing to attack, or they're overlooking her."

Ardin frowned at his view screen. "If Avienne's here, that means she might have received word of what happened on Mirial and might be trying to get the Berganda out. She's either not on board or the ship's disabled. Or they're not enemy ships at all." He held his breath then released it slowly. "The *Dessicate* isn't doing anything. Wait and bait is hardly Avienne's style."

Ardin leaned back in his chair. "Let's head closer to be near *Dessicate* if they prove hostile. Can we take three of those ships?

Biolt, what other improvements have you made?"

The old engineer guffawed. "Not enough to take on three full-fledged warships, which is what those things look like to me."

Ardin met Layela's eyes. "We can't let the Berganda get hurt," she whispered. Ardin nodded.

"Well, let's find out what they want! Brosten, take us in."

"Aye, Captain."

Layela strapped herself in, waiting for the battle to begin. She wondered why Mirial hadn't sent her a vision she could actually use.

***

Avienne flipped a knife impatiently, the blade catching the fading red light.

"Why can't this sun ever actually set?" she mumbled. Her nose itched. This planet was beautiful, but it morphed pollen into one of her biggest enemies. She hadn't even thought to take something against its slobbery effects.

"It doesn't, here. Part of the charm of this land for the Berganda," Patros offered.

"Thank you for answering my whiny rhetorical question, Patros."

"You're welcome."

Avienne gave him a half grin. He was seated, wearing comfortable but practical clothing, his shirt loose around his shoulders, not bothering to hide his identity as an ether creature. Nor had he for a long time. They were careful on certain worlds, of course, but overall they didn't face the same problems they had in Solaria.

A refreshing change.

"Do you see what they see?" Avienne asked, jerking her chin towards Elsa and Litras, who were whispering to each other as they got ready, sharing moments of excitement and graveness, the two acting like siblings separated at birth.

Patros looked at them and for a moment. Longing flitted across his features. Then he shrugged and gave her a weak smile.

"I don't think all Fated see things the same, kind of like all of your eyesight isn't the same."

Avienne looked back at the two women and sniffled. She wished she could interrupt them and drag them away, but she could feel the weight of their discussion from where she stood. This wasn't something she was meant to participate in, which annoyed and awed her.

"We can get corrective surgery easily enough, though," Avienne threw the comment out in the air and wished she could reclaim it immediately. "I'm sorry, Patros, I didn't mean...blood and bones, even I know that sounded pretty bitchy."

Patros laughed mirthlessly. "I don't disagree. I guess some Fated are older than others. And the older your race gets, the more attuned you become to the ether. You see it and sense it more, and even things like constantly listening to the Fated Link without having to shut it off becomes easier. I can't interact with it like Litras can. It's so distracting. And I can't send messages over it, either. I'm not sure how. Not everyone can, I don't think, or I'd have heard from my people."

Avienne sat down beside him. He shuffled over a bit to make room for her on the rock. She leaned forward to see as much of him as she could.

"You miss them, don't you?"

Patros flushed just a shade. Avienne saw a lie forming in his eyes and on his lips, but then he dropped it. "I do. I mean, we're longer lived than a lot of Fated, and so we miss less quickly, and love less quickly." He shot a look her way and she smiled. It had taken him a while to give in to her advances. Give in fully, anyway.

"Would you like to go visit them once we've reunited Ardice with her parents? And figured out the whole First Star thing? And possibly had a nap?"

Patros looked towards Elsa and Litras, the two women now laughing. Even the other Berganda gave them space. *Guess we're not the only ones left out.*

"Yes, I would, but it's quite far, Avienne. The tunnels don't go all the way there, so we would have months of spacefaring once we cleared the nearest tunnel. And that's at the other end of the Solarian Empire."

Avienne whistled. "Wow. Whatever possessed you to leave?"

He shrugged. "I was bored, I guess. I never quite fit in. I miss them, but I always thought I'd go back there to die, not to live."

Avienne leaned her head on his shoulder. "Well, you and me, Patros. We'll make the journey after all this, even if it takes us a few years to get back."

He held his breath for a few moments and she allowed herself to smile. Even her nose was giving her a break and she could breathe normally. A breeze ruffled the green leaves, creating a rustling symphony to which the light danced in the forest.

She didn't feel the need to flip a knife, didn't feel the need to tell everyone to pack up so they could go, go, go…

She sighed, content. Maybe she should go off-ship more often. It seemed to do her some good. Well, the right worlds did her some good. Others just left her running for her life, or running for someone else's.

"What does your home planet look like?" Avienne asked.

"It's beautiful," Patros exclaimed, awe dripping into his voice and energy into his limbs. Avienne sat up to look at him. "The buildings there are made of pure elements—gold, silver, titanium…nothing is synthetic. Windows are diamond, and clothing is pure cotton. There are touch centres, where you can go and just commune with elements. We touch them and it's like the universe spans around us, all of its working revealed in the atoms. I wish you could see it!"

Avienne smiled. "I wish I could, too, Patros. But at least I can see your homeworld."

His smile lessened. "Are you sure, Avienne? It's a long way for you. It might take at least two years to reach it, and another two to return, plus time spent there…in your lifetime, that's a lot for you to give up."

Avienne felt a bit less rested now. "Patros, I will hit you if that's what it takes to convince you! I know what five years is worth to me, and I know what ten is worth, and what twenty is worth… and I know that I want to spend those with you. You're stupid and unable to take a simple offer, but I still like you and I think I owe you by now."

Patros broke out into a full grin. "I don't know that you owe me anything, Avienne Malavant, but I'm happy to follow you wherever you'd like to go, and if that's my homeworld, so be it."

Avienne laughed. "All right, but you do the navigation." She pushed him playfully. "Enough of this sappy stuff. Let's go check out the engines on the shuttle. That thing's as old and well maintained as the *Dessicate*. We won't be much use to anyone if we can't even clear the moon's atmosphere!"

She jumped up and Patros followed suit. "Aye, Captain." She nudged him again, and this time he almost fell down.

"Let's go!"

Avienne glanced one more time at Litras and Elsa. She'd come get them after the checks were done.

If Elsa was right and she wasn't coming back, then they would have a long time to chat.

***

Patros wanted to whoop with joy, but restrained himself. He feared he might curse every good thing that was happening to him. Plus, the Berganda struck him as skittish, and he didn't want to frighten them all away. Although he did wish they'd all wear clothes.

Avienne turned, continuing to walk backwards, her eyebrow raised. "What are you blushing at, lover?" she asked, her voice dripping with suggestion. A crazy grin broke out on his face and he didn't even bother hiding it. Of all the gifts he'd ever been given by Mirial, Avienne Malavant was the craziest and most beautiful one.

The wind gently carried wisps of her hair across her face, the rest cascading down, made even more red with the sunset. Her green eyes shone in the half light, and the high grass danced around them, casting deep auburn shadows like a sea of magma.

He wanted to drag her to the ground, but movement caught his eyes and his heart dropped. Avienne saw the shift in his face and pulled out a knife, throwing it as she turned, striking the incoming Glotch in the chest. The knife bounced off the Glotch's armour. Without missing a beat, the Glotch raised her weapon and fired, her eyes glowing yellow.

Patros froze, watching the scene unfold before him, a spectator to the horror unfolding before him. Avienne leapt out of the way but the shot caught her firing arm. She went down screaming, managing to stay on her knees. She pulled her gun free with her good arm and fired several shots at the approaching Glotch, but they either hit armor or missed completely. The gun clicked, out of bullets. She looked at it and then tossed it aside, standing back up to face the Glotch. Crimson flowed down the wounded arm, impossibly red in the light of this sun. Her hair plastered into the pouring blood.

The Glotch didn't even look at Patros. She reached Avienne and smiled, her teeth capped by metal spikes. "I destroyed your little crew," the Glotch said, her entire face twitching.

Patros, no longer frozen, ran towards the Glotch screaming. He pulled his gloves free and struck her hard. He was strong for his size, and she hadn't expected it. He didn't place his hands on her skin, since Fated had little effect on each other. Instead he went for her armour, a complex mix of para-aramid synthetic fibres and titanium. He grabbed the atoms before she could push him off, and superheated them, making them move so fast her fireproof vest melted and bonded with her skin. The Glotch screamed and pushed him off, but the vest still melted and seared her skin, trapping her in the fabric.

Screams from the Glotch resonated until she closed her eyes and her features drooped. She collapsed to her knees, a loose grin on her face.

"Nice." Avienne's voice dropped to a tone Patros had never heard. It sent shivers down his spine. "You killed my crew?" Her voice was not as strong as it should be. She grabbed Patros' gun from his belt and pointed it straight at the Glotch's forehead. The Glotch didn't seem to register it, her eyes mellow, stinking of burning flesh and the rotten eggs of Glotch gas.

Avienne fired and the Glotch flew back, yellow blood weighing down the grass.

"I guess that's that," Avienne said, and slumped to the grass. Patros barely caught her before she collapsed completely, her arm still bleeding way more than he thought humans should be able to.

In the distance he saw some people running towards them. He would have recognized the Kilita's orange glow anywhere.

"Help!" he screamed. Litras managed to pick up speed and practically slid the rest of the way. "Avienne's been shot in the arm," he said, feeling useless. Litras cast a glance at the Glotch, but didn't ask, concentrating on Avienne.

The captain's features were drawn and pale, but at least she still breathed.

"Don't worry," Litras said, putting a comforting hand on Patros' arm. "Her time has not yet come."

Elsa joined them and knelt by Avienne. Without hesitation or preamble, she placed her hand on the wounded arm. Avienne jerked a bit.

"Hold her still," Litras told Patros. His instincts to protect Avienne fought with him, but his mind told him some pain was necessary to heal the arm. He held down Avienne by the shoulders. Her eyes slit open and a weak grin found its way to her mouth.

"Always want to be on top, don't you?" she mumbled, before her face crumpled in pain and she bit back a scream. A few seconds later her features relaxed and she seemed fast asleep.

"She'll be fine," Elsa said, pulling her hands away, which were covered in blood, staining her green skin brown.

"Thank you," Patros said, pushing a strand of hair from Avienne's face.

"Where's the Glotch?" Litras asked.

"Avienne shot her in the head, and I melted her armour straight onto her skin."

Litras nodded slowly. Patros looked up from Avienne's face, and realized their wounded attacker was gone. Elsa stood and looked wide-eyed at the Kilita.

"Get your sisters to come together and stay together," Litras said, a smile spreading on her lips. "And get Avienne to safety with them. I have some hunting to do."

CHAPTER 19

THE THREE WARSHIPS passed right by the *Dessicate,* ignoring the wreck. His sister's ship didn't react, which meant Avienne was definitely not on board. She was entirely too trigger-happy to play dead in space.

The ships were forming a line near the moon's atmosphere, and Ardin wasn't sure if they were planning on entering or sending in attack ships of their own. He didn't intend to find out.

Ardin opened the comm unit, a red light flashing above the view screen alerting all crew members that a channel was open. "This is Captain Malavant of the *Destiny II.* Please state your intentions."

"Two of the ships have stopped their approach," Brosten reported. "The third one is continuing to the moon." His voice became strained. "The first two ships have changed course and are now heading our way."

"Weapons and shield at the ready, Biolt."

"Done," the engineer reported.

"Are their shields up?" Ardin asked, turning towards the engineer.

"Impossible to tell. If they are, they're no type I've ever encountered. Their weapons are out, however. Lots of them."

Ardin brought up the image of the two incoming warships. They were a sleek design, almost egg-shaped and pearlized. The guns had been pearlized to match the hull, but they were impossible to miss. And Biolt was right. There were lots of them. The hulls were almost entirely covered with plasma cannons and other weapons he couldn't identify.

"That's a bit of overkill," Layela said from tactical.

"What are our options?" Ardin asked as he pulled up nearby maps. There wasn't much to work with in this area. No meteors, no old mines, not even drifting ships. Well, except for his sister's, but he wasn't about to involve her ship in a battle. Not unless she brought it in herself. The gravity wells weren't of tactical interest, and he doubted the *Destiny II* had an advantage defensively or offensively.

"They're hailing us," Brosten reported. Ardin clicked on the comm unit.

"This is Laurorian warship Troshil," the voice came across as mechanical—probably a bad translation device. "You will surrender the Keeper of Mirial to us and leave peacefully."

Ardin closed the communications channel. He didn't even bother looking at Layela or his crew. The only one who might argue for that plan was Layela herself, and that was just because she wanted everyone else to be safe. Well, he was captain of this ship, and he would decide their course of action.

"Let's hope they're intent enough on getting you back alive that they'll hold back," Ardin said, not turning to see Layela's face. He could imagine it well enough.

"Weapons armed and ready," Layela said and this time Ardin did turn. She raised her chin and looked at him defiantly. "We won't save Mirial unless we make it on our own terms."

That's my girl, he thought.

"Brosten, bring us to flank the portside ship. Biolt, concentrate energy shields on that side. Layela, fire everything we've got as we pass by. Aim for their weapons only. Let's see if we can cost them some assault power."

Destiny II responded immediately, gliding into action as though she were a skater on perfect ice. Ardin kept an eye on every movement their ship made, and the enemies' ships made. If a hole existed in their defences, he would find it.

They skirted the ship on the port side, Brosten bringing them close and Layela's aim true. By the time they finished crossing the ship, half the plasma weapons were down. Brosten brought them around, to hit the same side again.

Another successful pass, and most of the plasma cannons were black marks on the side of the pearlized ship.

"Why aren't they firing?" Ardin asked, looking at the readings. Brosten brought them around for another pass. "Why aren't they fighting back?"

"They don't want to take a chance at harming me?" Layela offered as she targeted the next weapons. The only weapons left were those of unknown make and purpose.

The second ship started moving away from the one they were targeting. *Why wouldn't they fire back? Why would they leave all of their weapons out for us to target without using any of them?* Ardin brought a close up of one of the weapons turrets. The ship was perfect aside from those ugly weapons. Even the pearlization was a bit off, so the weapons would stand out more. Why create such a perfect ship and taint it with such ugly, off-coloured weapons?

Ardin suspected it was an ether race ship, since Solarian models followed certain patterns and technologies. Most of the ether races, especially the older ones, were like Mirial herself—they liked things that were pleasing to the eye. Even the *Destiny II* could pull in her weapons, leaving a flawless exterior to be admired.

These weapons were more like acne marks—you could try to blend them in, but even that blending somehow always drew the eye. The other ship was moving away from the first one, now that it was substantially damaged.

"Brosten, pull us back! Cease fire!" he ordered as Layela fired another round. Her shots were true and hit several weapons, but this time the hull cracked, having sustained enough damage. For a split second, as Brosten pulled them away, it looked like an egg splitting in two. But then gases ignited and the whole thing blew, sweeping the *Destiny II* in a greenish tide.

Ardin clung to his chair as the ship shook, feeling the safety harness cutting where the shuttle's had hurt him earlier. The ship moaned and groaned, tilted sideways and then grew silent. The lights flickered out. A few seconds later, the emergency lights came on.

"Biolt?" Ardin whispered, trying to bring back his view screen. He glanced back at Layela, but she was trying to do the same with her own.

"It was a trap!" Brosten said indignantly from the pilot's seat. "They set a trap for us!"

"Some people just don't play nice," Ardin said, looking at his engineer again. "Biolt? Status?"

"It's like a spider web, almost. Or goo? The ship is ensconced in a cocoon. It's taken down our shields and clogged our engines, blocked any exit points. We're basically trapped in our own ship and unable to move."

"How do we break it?" Ardin asked. "There are still more of these ships out there."

"One of them, actually. If I'm guessing right," Biolt said, "the second one that came forward has the same mechanism. The one that stayed behind must be the lead ship."

"That's the one we need to take out, then," Layela said, joining Ardin.

"Yes," the old engineer said. "But how we're going to do that is beyond me. I didn't foresee this particular scenario when I designed the tactical capabilities of the ship."

"But Avienne might have," Layela pressed. "You had her review the schematics, and she made improvements. Maybe if we look at what she did to the ship, we'll come up with an idea?"

"That's a possibility," Ardin said.

Biolt sighed. "I'll have a look. I'm diverting emergency power to all of your units as well. It'll use our life support faster, but I'm only pumping into the bridge and adjoining rooms." Biolt let out a dry laugh.

"We're going to get real comfy until we figure out a way out of here or they come and get us. I vote for the former."

The bridge lit up as stations came back on. Layela squeezed Ardin's shoulder gently and went back to tactical control, her blue eyes lit up by the screen. Ardin stared at those eyes for a few moments before concentrating on his screen.

He knew *Destiny II*'s basic functionality, but hadn't run any simulations with her. He suddenly felt very foolish to have let his guard down; for believing they would make a clean escape from Mirial once the new First Star had ignited. But then, hadn't they all thought that?

CHAPTER 20

JARU'S HEAD FELT like it had been split open, leaving his jaw hanging. He brought his hand up and touched his face. It still seemed intact, although swollen. He was pretty sure a few of his teeth were missing. He didn't want to even try moving his jaw. That he still had a jaw was good enough for him.

He opened his eyes, groaned, and shut them again, taking deep breaths. He could stand the light a bit more when he reopened them.

He was disoriented, couldn't think of where he was, his usually quick mind smothered by confusion. He was in a small room… Rose's room. Of course!

Someone had attacked him from behind. The bed was gone, so someone had taken Rose. Gobran? The old man had been coming to meet him. Jaru stood, groaning. He had to find him. What if he was in trouble? How well could he defend himself? Even if the blindness wasn't an issue, his age might be.

Jaru took a careful step forward, his head still ringing but more anchored as adrenaline rushed his mind. He looked around as quickly as he could without making the room spin, and saw that he was alone. *Good.*

He pulled his pistol free. He was a poor shot, but the captain had made him practice enough that he was fairly certain he could at least hit the right target.

That might be enough.

Jaru reached the door and stepped through. The thing was broken off its hinges and half-melted. That led him to believe that Gobran had at least managed to escape temporarily, hopefully with Rose.

Jaru took in the state of the corridor, the blackened marks showing where shots had been fired. He followed the trail, keeping his gun trained. His hand shook slightly and his mouth was dry.

He wanted to call out for Gobran, but feared he might give away his position and the old man's, as well. So he kept walking, one foot in front of the other, listening intently for a noise, any noise. The ship was quiet, especially for the *Dessicate*.

He followed the burn marks into another corridor, carefully turning pistol first, his heart dropping when he saw that he was alone. The door to the pod room had been blasted open. Jaru peeked in. The pod was gone, and Rose's bed was broken and mangled in a corner, as though it had been attacked by a wild animal.

He felt relief. Gobran had escaped. Gobran and Rose, it looked like.

His relief turned short-lived when he realized the enemy might still be on board with him. Why hadn't they come back to finish him off, after Gobran had escaped? Jaru needed to reach the bridge and make sure they still had control of the ship. Avienne would be returning soon, and he had to warn her if this was a trap.

The light turned red when he tried to activate the lift. The power grid still seemed active, so why wasn't the lift working? He could take the stairs, but they were rickety and dizziness still inhabited the edges of his mind. He pressed the lift button again, and it turned red again.

Jaru suddenly remembered that Gobran had transferred bridge control to his leadcom. He would have slapped his forehead, but didn't want to further injure himself. He was slow. Too slow for his own good. He needed to clear his mind and set a plan.

The leadcom chirped to life as he activated it, the flat tablet instantly lit with warnings. Jaru leaned back against the wall of the ship. The *Dessicate's* hull had been breached, and most of its floors had lost oxygen flow. He was lucky he still had anything to breathe.

He suddenly started taking in all of the little details he had missed, his mind still recovering from the blow. The frost lining the lift door, where space existed beyond it. The silence of the closed vents, the lack of flow of oxygen. He turned and looked at the walls, and then up, towards the vents. Frost had started forming on them. Jaru pulled up all of the readings he could get, and none of them were promising.

The *Dessicate* was an old ship, and space should have reclaimed her long ago. Now that space had gained access, it didn't look like it intended to let go.

***

Galka could barely move her body. The relaxant and her combined injuries turned her limbs to lead. She wasn't even sure how she was moving, or why she still was. She couldn't remember where she was. All she could see was the red hair of the woman who had shot her. Her world became that red hair, dancing in the breeze, some covered in blood.

She could see the world beyond it, but wisps of it still came and fractured her vision, the world a mosaic of hair and trees. She turned left, moving faster and faster, stimulants dripping into her blood and accelerating her heart, which pounded in her ears and head. She could only hear the pounding, and the drip of stimulants, even though she knew it was impossible to hear the drugs filtering into her system.

Glotch gas started pumping into her blood, too, her hump shrinking. It was the weirdest feeling. She always kept it so full that she'd never thought it would actually deflate like old skin.

She moved faster, her body animated by the stimulants and proper atmosphere. But Galka felt nothing, as though she were merely a passenger in her own body.

Maybe she was. Just drifting along, not able to formulate thoughts. Trees danced around her, leaves falling from high above, and the eternal hair… Everything was red. Everything was that hair. Even the leaves were red, the bark was red, the Berganda in front of her were red… They didn't see her and she crouched, waiting for something.

She thought she should feel pain, but she felt euphoric instead.

Just relax. It's all right to nap. The voice came in her mind again, and for a fraction of a second, Galka understood. They had taken over her body, her broken little body, and they would push it for as long as it would go. Sometimes they would walk their soldiers home, if the investment in improvements were so high or secret as to be worth recouping some of their costs and technology. But not in her case. Galka Glotch was expendable. Galka Glotch had always been disposable.

Another shot of stimulants and the euphoria was wiped away, sweeping her consciousness with it. She tumbled up into the sky, following the red haired demon who had cost Galka her life, and danced with her into the stars, all the way to Mirial.

***

The pod was approaching the shuttle, and its chute deployed for a softer landing. They struck the ground fairly hard, Gobran gasping as the breath blew out of him. Stars exploded in front of his eyes, his optical nerves still operational enough to react to the spasms sent through his nervous system.

Gobran took a deep breath and reached over to feel Rose's arm. As far as he could tell with his numb hands, she was still alive. He reached over to the controls. He could send out a short burst message now, only detectable from very close. The shuttle was near, but Avienne might not be.

He hoped she was close enough to hear his call, and to come get him. For one of the first times since losing his eyesight, Gobran had to admit that he felt completely lost. And terrified.

***

Patros crouched near a tree, using the tall grass to his advantage. Avienne was still unconscious, but colour was returning to her face and the deep wound on her arm seemed fully healed. The Berganda were around him, he knew. He could see Elsa, who had positioned herself to be visible to him. But the rest had vanished quietly into the woods and trees.

Litras was off somewhere, hunting… Patros wasn't sure what she was hunting. That Glotch was shot in the head. He didn't know much about their physiology, but in most races that was a dealbreaker with life.

"Avienne, do you copy? Patros? Litras? Anyone? This is Gobran. Please respond." Patros' comm unit chirped to life. The old man sounded tired—or terrified.

Patros grabbed it immediately, lowered the volume and whispered as clearly as he could into it. "Gobran! Where are you? We thought you were dead!"

"Not quite yet," Gobran wheezed and laughed. "I'm in a pod near the shuttle, with Rose. We could use some help."

"I'm on my way," Patros said, turning his comm unit off. A hand grabbed his arm before he could stand.

"We're on our way," Avienne said as she pulled herself up.

Patros knew better than to argue with her. "Litras is hunting the Glotch and the Berganda are in hiding. We'll have to be careful."

"Didn't I shoot that annoying swamp sucker in the head?" Avienne asked. She examined her arm and flexed it.

"Your aim is apparently just that poor," Patros deadpanned, to be rewarded with a hit. She was definitely feeling better.

Elsa appeared beside them. "Quiet. The Glotch isn't far!"

"You're tracking her?" Avienne asked, still testing her arm.

Elsa nodded. "Litras is tracking her with my help. She's getting ready to take her down."

"Great. Is the way to our shuttle clear? Gobran needs our help there."

Elsa cocked her head and her eyes lost focus as she mapped out the land in her mind, or so Avienne imagined she was doing. "I believe so. Be careful, though."

"We will be, I promise. You too."

Elsa nodded and blended back into the forest, vanishing completely. Avienne kept to a crouch as she ran through the tall grass. The light had dimmed a bit more, but they could still see.

Patros followed her quietly, wishing for once that her hair wasn't quite so vividly red.

***

Galka had lost a piece of herself, she understood. She had felt it float away, so far away, fast and free and fleeing towards Mirial. Or she thought she had lost it. For all she knew she had imagined it, a stimulant-induced hallucination. And the missing chunk of her head probably wasn't helping her think clearly.

She was hunting, she knew. She looked everywhere, to every tree, every branch, every blade of grass. She looked near and far, her head no longer hers to control. Her limbs were slack beside her, her torso uselessly moulded with the fabric of her armour, melted and bonded to her flesh. She couldn't feel the pain, and so didn't care. And it was her eyes and ability to move that seemed to matter right now.

She turned left and spotted red hair in the dwindling sun. Not like the red hair part of her had pursued into the sun, but real hair, crouched low to the ground, running out of the forest.

The girl is leaving. She is heading somewhere important.

She didn't know if the thought was hers or someone else's but she followed it regardless. One clumpy foot after the other followed the girl, trying to keep her in sight.

Then the plasma hits rained from the sky, chunks of earth following the girl as she ran faster, no longer hiding. Galka watched her, unable to tear herself away, understanding that, if she did, she might be safe.

And that was the last thing she wanted.

***

"We can burn it off!" Biolt exclaimed, jumping up from his station. "I think, anyway." Layela looked up, blinked the readings from her eyes and focused on the engineer.

"We can or we can't?" Ardin asked.

"We can, I'm pretty sure. Our weapons were slightly modified to be able to basically leak out their energy cells. Space has been kindly freezing that goo, so chances are it'll snap and break when overheated."

"Or it'll just turn back to goo," Layela offered.

"Yes, it might. And it'll leave most of our weapons destroyed, and maybe even a hole in our hull. Though I think it's solid enough to take it."

Layela looked at her station, her heart dropping. "Ardin, they're firing on the moon."

Ardin joined her at her station and looked at the readings. They were firing near the Berganda's home, perhaps into a concentration of them. The Berganda weren't warm-blooded and so were difficult to read with their systems. She hoped the same applied to the Laurenon ship's systems.

"They're going to kill them," she whispered, using a numb finger to bring up the damage. They were certainly intent on killing something down there.

"Do it, Biolt. But keep enough weapons if you can to take down that warship. Now that we know who the lead is, we'll just attack them directly and hope that the other mine ship can't be triggered without our help."

"Aye, Captain," Biolt said.

"I think we're safe from the mine ship," Brosten added as Biolt worked with Layela to leak the energy cells straight onto the goo.

"What do you mean?" Ardin asked him. Layela listened with half an ear.

"From what I've analyzed of the gas, the ship has to be under such pressure that adding a trigger device powerful enough to ignite the attack would be almost impossible. The ships would become ridiculously unstable. I'm guessing they count on enemy fire. I'm assuming that other mine ship will work as a shield for the main warship. We'll have to find a way to get around it, or render it useless."

"Let's hope we move faster than they can," Ardin said, looking up at Layela.

"We're ready." She read the reports over and over again, and dismissed all of the warnings. The Berganda would be slaughtered down there, and probably Avienne, too. If the *Dessicate* hadn't moved, Ardin's sister was either dead or on the planet.

Ardin looked at each of his crew members. A small crew, Brosten and Biolt both willing to go off world for a bit and then bring back the *Destiny II* after Ardice had been found and Layela and Ardin had started their new lives.

A small, but loyal and efficient crew.

"Let's do it," he said, sitting down. "Prepare to move, and stop that warship. We'll do whatever we have to do to make it happen."

"Unleashing half the energy cells," Layela reported. The ship buckled and shook. Her hull cracked under the acid being released.

"Hull holding," Biolt reported.

The hull cracked again and Layela looked at her readings. "The net is reacting, but not enough. I need to unleash more, but we might compromise our hull if I do that."

"Biolt, any way to solidify that hull?" Ardin asked.

"We've done everything we could, Captain."

Layela bit her lower lip. They would be no use to the Berganda if they couldn't fire any weapons or move once freed from the net.

"What if we just activate the engines?" Layela asked, looking up. "We've weakened the net. What if, while the weapon fluids are still eating away at it, if we turn on our engines, fire all weapons, open every flap and unleash the side engines? It might be enough to push the rest of the net off of us. It's worth a try at least, right?"

Ardin looked down, as though turning the idea over in his mind. He looked to Brosten and Biolt, but they both nodded.

"Worth a shot," Biolt said. "Ready when you are."

Ardin shot Layela a grin. She returned it before turning her attention to her station.

"All stations ready to cause mayhem?"

"Aye!" All three reported at once.

"Do it," Ardin ordered, and the ship groaned as they activated everything at once. The net screeched and strained against the assault. The *Destiny II* started turning sideways and rolling, jerked around by its own engines.

Layela wanted to will the net off of them herself, stand outside the ship and pull it off with her own bare hands.

Mirial had claimed enough from the Berganda already, and she refused to let her have more.

CHAPTER 21

AVIENNE FULL-OUT RAN towards the pod, screaming at Patros to keep up. He wasn't far behind her, but the shots were coming fast and furious, chunks of earth flying all around them. She was grateful that the assaulting weapons were best used in outer space and seemed to lose potency in the atmosphere. But that would be a better blessing if they were in a shuttle.

"Gobran!" She screamed as she neared the pod, hitting all buttons of her comm unit. "Open the door! Open the door! Open the door!" she screamed over and over again, pounding the ground with her feet, hoping she wouldn't trip on a hidden root. The metallic chute covering the pod buckled in as the hatch opened.

"Patros, grab them!" she shouted as she ran past the pod, grabbing the chute and pulling it out of the way. She turned back when a shot rang out not far from the shuttle, making the pod. Gobran flew out of the pod, landing hard on his knees. Patros ignored him and reached in, throwing Rose over his shoulders. Avienne shielded Gobran as another blast struck close, her face seared by the heat, rocks snapping her skin.

"Come on." She pulled him up and kept a strong hold on his arm. Patrosran towards the shuttle, Rose's weight not slowing him down. Gobran moved as quickly as he could, but Avienne mostly dragged him.

Patros reached the shuttle first and opened the door, throwing

Rose inside as he leapt over the pilot seat. Avienne pushed Gobran in and jumped to join them, but large hands closed around her waist and slammed her back into a wall, knocking the breath out of her lungs. Disoriented, Avienne looked down at the two thick arms that squeezed her and stole her breath. The Glotch!

She reached up her sleeve and pulled a knife free, embedding it hard into the arm. Instead of loosening, the grip tightened. *If being shot in the head didn't slow her down…*

Avienne kicked back, but might as well have been hitting cement. The pain in her abdomen spread to her arms and legs, and her head began to spin.

Like I'll let you crush the life out of me, Avienne thought. With numb fingers, she grabbed for a hand grenade and activated it. She reached up and stuck it to the back of the Glotch's armour, melted but still magnetic enough to hold it in place.

The Glotch's thick body wouldn't be enough to save her, but it might be enough to protect the shuttle. Her vision was growing blurry, but the shuttle door was still open, and she could see Patros firing the engines. When he looked back and spotted her, she waved him away weakly. She wanted to tell him to take off, when another blast hit near. The ground jostled and Avienne landed on her feet, managing one step towards the shuttle before collapsing on her knees. Patros grabbed her and yanked her in ungracefully. Adrenaline jostled her and she shook feeling back into her limbs. Another hit nearby almost knocked the shuttle over. Avienne jumped up and closed the hatch. The Glotch was still struggling to get up, her face a wreck beyond repair, covered in so much blood that Avienne couldn't make out any features.

"All right, well, that was fun," Avienne called out. "No point wasting another bullet on that thing."

She joined Patros at the controls. The side of the shuttle buckled as something exploded, throwing a large object against the side of the craft.

"Oh yeah, the grenade …Shields up!" She screamed just as another blast struck close, warnings blaring on the consoles.

"Get us up, now!" Avienne screamed, hitting the engines to life. They sputtered but kicked in, and she pulled up, not caring this time if she left generations of contaminants on the ground. Cleaning the land would take time, but the blasts from that ship would kill them all in no time at all.

"Gobran, what about the *Dessicate?* Is she still space worthy?"

"As much as before," Gobran wheezed. "The Glotch was coming for us. I had to get Rose out of there, and the pod was the only way I could think of doing it."

"You did good," Avienne said. "Now we have to get back on board and get that ship to stop shooting the ground!"

She pushed the shuttle hard, the hull rattling as it hit the atmosphere. Nobody complained, even though Avienne feared her teeth might rattle out of her skull. They cleared the atmosphere and finally saw the warship. It was huge, shaped like an egg.

And its weapons were now trained on them.

"Blood and bones!" Avienne screamed as she manoeuvered the ship sideways. She'd expected some fire to be diverted her way, but not all of it! The sky around them glowed, but their aim wasn't true, their instruments probably thwarted by the proximity of the atmosphere and the shuttle's small size.

Warships were rarely built to take on ships smaller than themselves.

The *Dessicate* limped along in the distance, nearing the atmosphere herself.

"Gobran, what about Jaru? Is he still on board?"

Gobran was slow to answer. "I believe he encountered the Glotch before I did."

Avienne swore. "Blood and bones, I'm glad I shot her in the head. Prepare for entry into the *Dessicate.* Patros, open up the shuttle bay doors and throw her shields up as soon as we're in."

Patros looked at her. "What?" she asked, flying erratically to avoid another hit. "Get that door open!" Avienne skirted near the *Dessicate* and then behind her. "Once we're in we can activate her shields and put up a good fight!"

"She's decompressed." Patros blurted out. "Most of the ship is completely decompressed. She's dead in space, Avienne."

Avienne slowed the shuttle, looking at the great beast. Her hull was rusty and Avienne had done a crappy job of maintaining her, but she had been her ship, and hers alone.

And she had been their best chance of survival. She leaned back into her chair, her mind blanking.

"Blood and bones, I loved that rusty bucket of space junk," she said to no one in particular.

***

Jaru ran strings of calculations in his mind, ignoring the pain in his head. He wished he had a cup of coffee, something warm to soothe him and tease his mind awake. As it was, he used the complexity of the situation as his stimulant, running scenario after scenario on the leadcom.

The *Dessicate's* shields weren't responding, nor was any part of tactical. The controls were probably frozen by now. The engines retained more heat and looked like they might start if he activated them. That wouldn't last long. If his calculations were correct, and he was certain they were, another ten minutes and they wouldn't start any longer, and his life support systems would fail shortly after that.

And escape was impossible. The one reachable escape pod had been used, and Jaru was glad it had been. He assumed Gobran hadn't known he was lying there, and so had saved the one person he could locate, who also happened to be the one person who could locate Ardice.

Jaru hesitated to call Avienne's shuttle. He'd listened in on everything, but hadn't interjected. He also knew the *Destiny II* was breaking free of its web, but that would take another few minutes. Quite a few minutes, actually. Too many, if he were to do something before time caught up with him.

Time always catches up. He had loved his life, traveling from world to world while never having to actually set foot on any of them and face so many people. He had tasted exotic foods, encountered amazing programs, and had broken into systems around the universe. And his name was everywhere. Well, sort of. Jarial was marked in systems he had encountered along the way, a stamp for himself and for others to find. He had left a mystery behind, a code only for those good enough to break the most complex systems.

There was no final answer to the puzzle he had left behind. Just a series of more complicated algorithms strewn across systems, all bearing his name. The puzzle itself was enough, and would be enough for someone else to find and decipher.

He let himself daydream for a moment, imagining a young genius following his mark across systems, finding all of them until he stumbled on the notes Jaru had left in Mirial's systems, all over their computers. He had known it was the one place that would somehow always survive, because his home world always did. And always would.

Beyond this day, too. He thought about contacting Avienne again.

To tell her farewell, and thank her for everything. To let her know how much he had enjoyed the journey, and had never worried about the destination, because that had never mattered to him. The world was a series of puzzles, and that had been good enough for him.

But he didn't want human contact just now. He didn't want to hear the grief in her voice, or the regret in Gobran's. He didn't want his final moments to be marked by people, no matter how much he loved them.

He wanted to go out alone, accompanied by nothing but this final puzzle.

***

"The *Dessicate* is powering up!" Patros exclaimed, sitting straight in his seat. Avienne brought up the readings on her own screen.

"Blood and bones, Jaru must still be alive!" She turned and squeezed Gobran's knee, and the old man's face crumpled into sorrow and relief. Avienne opened the comm unit.

"Jaru, this is Avienne! You're alive! We'll figure out a way to get you out of there. Do you have tactical? Can you fire on that warship? You can take them out, right?"

No reply came, and Avienne's stomach began to slide down.

"Jaru?"

The great ship shuddered and began chugging along. Avienne briefly wondered if the rattling was better or worse with half of it decompressed.

"Is he doing what I think he's doing?" Avienne asked, turning to Patros. Her stomach was now in her toes. Patros didn't answer, closing his eyes instead, his hands still on the controls.

"No, no, no, no!" Avienne screamed before re-opening the comm channel. "Jaru, pull back! That's an order! Pull back now!"

The *Dessicate* continued on its silent journey. When the warship hit her with its massive weapons, chunks of the hull ripped straight off. Patros pulled the shuttle back to a safe distance.

"What are you doing! Don't pull us back—we're going forward! We can stop him. He won't run us over. We just have to get in front of him!"

Patros didn't try to stop her, to his credit, as she started pushing the shuttle forward. The shuttle was too slow to catch up to her ship, and she knew it. She dodged the craft around a piece of rusted metal and let go of the controls, curling her fists on her lap.

The second ship was pulling away, as though to interfere with the *Dessicate,* but they weren't fast enough. Avienne watched, refusing to peel her eyes away. She could see the other warship now, twice the *Dessicate*'s size. Her ship was hurt but moving at full speed, her engines still protected by her large hull.

The warship tried to move aside, but the *Dessicate* plunged straight into her without pause, catching the front of the warship. Avienne hated the silence of space. She wanted to hear her ship's final cries. She wanted to scream along with her as her carcass crumpled and ripped the other ship in two halves.

She wanted to cry when the ship started falling towards the atmosphere, too close to avoid its pull. The other warship followed her in, a streak of light setting the upper atmosphere ablaze as they caught fire and burned their final journey away.

The shuttle was quiet. Avienne wanted to reach over to hold Patros and be held by him. She wanted to tell Gobran that everything was going to be okay.

But first, she had a final duty to perform for Jaru and the *Dessicate.* One final duty as they plunged to their resting place.

She opened the comm and took a deep breath to steady her voice.

***

Ardin and Layela stood hand in hand on the bridge. Layela didn't even bother wiping the tears anymore, letting them trickle down her face. Avienne's final pleas had travelled their channel, too, and they knew Jaru was gone.

Plucked from the sky like so many great sailors before him.

"Avienne just opened all hailing frequencies," Brosten whispered.

"Open ours," Ardin said back, still clutching Layela's hand.

Avienne's voice flowed unsteadily over the airwaves, gaining in strength as she sang on. She sang the *Dessicate* and Jaru home, in one of the oldest songs known to Mirial. She sang it without restraint, pouring her grief into it. Patros and Gobran's voices came through, joining her.

And the *Destiny II* joined in, too. Singing word by word, line by line, as they all grieved the loss of another Mirialer, lost on a planet far away; for a body never to find its way back home again, only his soul traveling back to the welcoming sun of Mirial.

When they were done, silence smothered the bridge.

Then Avienne's voice chimed up. "I'm tired and in dire need of a bath. *Destiny II,* requesting permission to board."

Ardin turned to Biolt. "Can we open a shuttle bay yet?"

He nodded. "We're almost free. They can come in safely."

"Permission granted."

Avienne drew in a deep breath. "One more thing. We have one badly wounded on board." She paused and exhaled. "It's Rose, Ardin. And no, I don't know what happened to Ardice. That's what I was trying to find out."

Ardin swallowed hard and squeezed Layela's hand. Dread danced up his throat.

He swallowed hard and whispered the final words: "Welcome home, sailor."

CHAPTER 22

L ITRAS FOUND THE Glotch in the field where the shuttle had been. Well, what remained of the Glotch. She had been blown to several pieces by the cannons of her allies.

Maybe not her allies. Litras suspected the Glotch had been controlled in those final moments. In her experience, few people who were shot in the head ever got up again, unless the shot was really off... or they had extra motivators. She doubted Avienne's shot had been that bad, but she was willing to believe in the extra motivators. The Glotch race had been a mess since signing that treaty with Solaria. Half of them were enlisted for continuous battle, and the other half were so high on stimulants they might as well not even exist. The worst were the ones who were both enlisted *and* on stimulants, which Litras suspected had been the case for this one.

What a waste of life. Litras had seen death, but hated that so many of the Fated suffered like this Glotch, as though their lives didn't matter or meant so little.

Litras looked up, watching flaming debris fall into the atmosphere. Another ship falling into unfamiliar skies.

***

Layela practically jumped in the shuttle as soon as the door opened. She shimmied behind Gobran and reached for Rose.

"Hello to you, too," Avienne said, jumping out to hug her tired-looking brother. She didn't even bother joking about how old he looked. She was sure she looked way older than he did, today.

Ardin squeezed her in a huge hug. "I'm so sorry, Avienne," he whispered in her ear. Avienne freed herself from him and quickly wiped the tears from her eyes. "Don't you start getting mushy on me, Ardin." Her brother smiled at her and reached over to give Patros a hug. "Definitely getting mushy," Avienne mumbled, reaching into the shuttle to help Gobran.

"I'm sorry," he wheezed into her ear. "I really thought Jaru was gone already, had I known…"

Avienne gently chided him. "Had you known, you would have tried to save him. And then all three of you would all be dead. And probably us, too. Don't go down that path, old man."

He nodded and let go of her to stand on his own. Ardin reached for him. "It's good to see you again, Gobran." Gobran hugged him and then pulled away. "So much like your father, Ardin Malavant. If I didn't know better, I'd swear you were him."

Ardin beamed and Avienne muttered, "Did you hug our father often, Gobran? He never struck me as the huggy type."

Ardin stuck out his tongue quickly at her and Gobran held his peace. The siblings turned back towards the shuttle.

"How is she?" Ardin asked.

Layela shook her head. "She's alive, but not well. We need to get her to the medical quarters and get her some nutrients." She turned to face Avienne, who almost recoiled at the sight of her eyes. Layela had two blue eyes when first they'd met. It was hardly a reason to step back from her now.

However, it did answer her question about whether or not she was still connected to Mirial.

"We don't know what happened to her," Avienne said. "We found her like that, in a prison. We were bringing her here to get Elsa's help. We'll need to go get her. And Litras."

"The Kilita?" Ardin asked, surprised.

"The one and only. It's been a fun ride, Ardin."

"All right." Ardin looked to Layela. He took her aside and whispered to her, and she shook her head, obviously agitated. Ardin sighed and gave his sister an apologetic smile. "Avienne, are you up for one more journey? We can go get them together." He looked inside her old shuttle. "Maybe we'll use one of our shuttles instead."

"Sounds comfy," Avienne said. "All right. Patros, Gobran, you wait here. We won't be long, and I'm sure they could use your help here, right?" She lifted an eyebrow at Ardin. He contacted Brosten and told him two crewmembers were meeting him on the bridge. After a quick trip to the medical quarters.

"We'll take care of her, and maybe Elsa can tell us where Ardice is," Ardin said gently to Layela, who looked about to bust a seam. Avienne couldn't blame her. Everything they'd done so far had been to secure a safe future for Ardice. They'd always accepted that they wouldn't know where she was, but they at least expected her to be with Rose.

"What happened to you, anyway?" Avienne asked as the siblings walked towards the shuttle, much more gleaming and impressive than her own.

"I'll tell you on the way." Ardin replied.

Avienne nodded and followed his gaze across to where Layela and Patros moved Rose onto a gurney, Gobran helping to steady it. Layela and Ardin's gazes crossed for an instant, and Avienne wanted to cry. She turned and entered the shuttle before she could run and hug them both. Losing Jaru and her ship had not done any good for her psyche, apparently.

Blood and bones. Litras is right. I need to start drinking again.

***

Elsa waited for the Malavants by the edge of the forest, knowing they would be back for her. She watched them walk towards her in silence. From where she stood, in the shadow of the forest, she could see how tired they were. They weren't even joking with each other. Behind her, some chunks of forest had been blasted away. If not for the lush condition of the land, she was certain everything would have gone up in a blaze already.

Her home would be fine, she kept telling herself. Her sisters would live out wonderful lives here, as would her children, as would their children and all of the future generations of Berganda. The moon of Burnice would be their forever home now.

Litras appeared beside her, like a shadow detaching itself from the forest.

"Are you worried?" Litras asked, her voice low. She seemed to understand Elsa's desire to not draw attention to herself, even if she didn't seem to understand her need for quiet, as well.

"I am," Elsa whispered. "What if my sisters encounter dangers they can't fight? What if this world decides it doesn't want them anymore? Should we bring them with us? Should I tell them I won't return? I love them so, Litras. I fear for them so."

"I know," the Kilita said. "You're certain we won't be returning?"

Elsa nodded. "I am. Sometimes Mirial tells me things, to soothe me, and she told me to bid farewell." She gave Litras a wry smile. "I may look young, but I am very old for a Berganda. My seeding years are long past, and my life is drawing to an end."

"So much wisdom for such a short life." Litras shook her head. "I wonder about the wisdom of Mirial, sometimes."

Elsa didn't answer. The truth was, she didn't wonder. What was the point of wasting precious time thinking about why her life was so short when those of other races were so long, when her life was already short to begin with? It would be compounding an already sad condition.

Elsa stuck her foot deep into the earth, the soil welcoming her and coating her with warmth. The land would protect her sisters, and Mirial would be strong once more for them. Even though she would no longer be here to cultivate the ether for them, there was plenty of it to last them. And she would just have to make sure that Mirial would be strong again for a good, long time.

Litras extended a hand to her. The Malavants were nearing the forest. "Are you ready, Elsa Berganda?"

Elsa smiled. She liked the Kilita. She understood Elsa in a way no one had in a long time. Not since she had lost herself in Mirial.

She placed her hand in hers and let the Kilita lead her towards the Malavants.

It wasn't until she was safely in the shuttle, strapped in and looking out the screen at her shrinking world, that she sent waves of farewell to her sisters. Farewell, and love, and hope, and belief in them. The Berganda responded with grief and love, and a farewell so strong Elsa feared her heart might burst. She reached out and took Litras' hand, who held hers without question.

Elsa closed her eyes and basked in the love of her sisters. The Kilita grounded her, and waves of soothing ether warmed her through their connection.

She had never felt so loved, and so alone.

And so frightened and excited. She was going back to Mirial, land of her birth. She would die there, as her mother had. Except that she would not seed any more children, which she did not regret.

She would instead make sure her sisters and daughters had enough ether to see generations of Berganda, for as long as a First Star existed.

***

Layela gently washed Rose's face with a soft cloth; the engineer's skin was ashen. Her breath rattled in her chest, and she had not stirred once. Layela had hooked her up to ensure she would receive nutrition, and she ran a course of antibiotics into her system, but if the damage was as deep as Avienne suspected, Layela feared Rose might be beyond help.

Layela sat with Rose, not knowing what else to do. She held the old woman's hand, which was much smaller and frailer than when she had last seen her, whisking away Ardice at her request.

Rose Delamores. A woman who shared no blood with her, but who shared her last name. A woman who might as well be family, having given up her own future to raise Layela's child.

Ten years. It should have been only ten years. The last few days had been longer than all of those years combined, and now Layela didn't think she'd ever be able to breathe properly again.

"Rose?" Layela whispered, leaning forward. She expected nothing but still felt disappointed when nothing happened. "Rose," she said again. "I'm sorry I asked so much of you, Rose. I really am. I don't even know the dreams you sacrificed for us."

And now I might never know.

"But I know you did the best you could, and that you raised Ardice the best you could." Layela stopped talking, feeling foolish. Rose's mind might be completely gone, if what Avienne said was true. Elsa could find out, when she arrived. Just as Josmere had once helped Layela see her visions, Elsa could unlock Rose's mind and heal it.

And then Rose could tell them what had happened to her little girl. Layela closed her eyes and lowered her forehead to Rose's arm. It wasn't supposed to be like this. Ardice was supposed to be safe, and they were supposed to be a family. Layela could not have given her up to save Mirial if she hadn't believed that Ardice would be safe, in the end. That was all that mattered.

She had gotten used to the idea of being a bedtime story, an imaginary mother she could never live up to in real life. As long as

Ardice was safe, she wouldn't have minded being only that—a story enhanced by the imaginings of a little girl.

Ardice would be ten now. Ten. She remembered what Yoma looked like at that age—like a lamppost. She wondered if Ardice looked like Yoma. She wondered if she would recognize her. She wondered if her eyes were now only one colour as well, and if that colour was green, or blue. She hoped she liked what she saw in the mirror. She hoped her little girl had enough to eat, and friends to keep her warm at night, and hope to keep her moving forward.

Layela fell asleep imagining Ardice.

But it was Yoma who greeted her in her dreams.

CHAPTER 23

Y OMA," LAYELA SAID, *taking a step towards her sister. But Yoma did not see her, and Layela felt compelled to stay, as though her legs had grown roots that reached to the very heart of Mirial.*

Layela looked around, the bleak landscape of Mirial surrounding them. The palace shone in the sunrise.

The sunrise… it was strong again! Mirial rose as a full, yellow sun, and the ground below her exploded in flowers. Trees jutted from the ground, grass sprouted, multi-coloured blooms covered the land as far as she could see. Oranges, yellows, blue and purples… the flowers seemed alive, dancing in the sunrays.

Layela smiled, but when she turned to Yoma the smile faded. Yoma was gone. The knife was planted neatly into the ground where the temple should have been. The Three Fates surrounded it, their stone robes steady in the rising storm, the sun swallowed by dark clouds.

"Yoma?"

Layela still could not walk forward, trapped in Mirial. "Yoma!" She screamed and screamed her name over and over again, but Yoma was gone.

Layela was jerked awake when the door to the room opened. The threads of the vision clinging to her still, she blinked at the sight of a Berganda walking through the doors.

"Josmere?" she asked, knowing it couldn't be. She gathered the woman into her arms and held her tightly.

"It's Elsa, Mother Layela," the small whisper came for her ears only. Layela broke the embrace and looked at her closely. "Of course." She tried to smile. "You look so like her, Elsa." She let go of her, wishing she could wipe the grief from Elsa's features.

"Another vision?" Ardin asked, coming to stand beside her. She nodded.

"Ah. We're doing that again, then?" Avienne said, walking in with Litras. Layela gave her a weak smile. Avienne looked at her with guarded excitement. "So, you can connect to Mirial again?"

Layela looked away from the expectation. "It seems more that Mirial is connecting to me. Maybe she still needs me."

Avienne returned a grim smile. She then turned and indicated the engineer with a sharp movement of her head. "How's Rose?"

"Same, I guess," Layela said.

"What vision did Mirial send you?" Litras asked, her voice full of wonder. Layela felt disoriented from her vision, and being peppered with questions wasn't helping. Ardin came to her rescue. "We'll worry about that later. First, Elsa, can you see if you can help Rose?"

Elsa nodded. She met Layela's gaze. "I can, but I want everyone but Litras to leave the room."

Layela was surprised. Elsa had never taken a stand like that. But, then again, she hadn't seen her for ten years, receiving news only from Avienne whenever the smuggler returned to Mirial to reload her stock and drop off supplies.

Elsa met her eyes, the Berganda's unwavering. She reminded Layela so much of Josmere that a slow smile spread across her face. "Your mother would be so proud of you, Elsa," she blurted out. The Berganda looked down at Rose and flushed green.

Layela left the room, Avienne and Ardin not far behind.

They all stopped just outside the door, not one of them intending to go anywhere until they had the answers they so desperately sought.

***

Elsa reached down and brushed hair away from the engineer's drawn features. Her fingers tingled at the slight contact.

"Someone used ether on her," she said.

Litras nodded. "We're not sure which race, but they attacked her mind. She's trapped in there, I think."

Elsa held on to the side of Rose's bed, not sure what to do. She seemed so frail, and Elsa understood better than anyone else how easy losing a mind could be. And how damaging.

"You can do it," Litras said. Elsa wasn't sure why she'd asked the Kilita to stay. She didn't know her, really, but felt a strong kinship with her. Maybe they were both wanderers. Maybe they had both been badly broken at one point, and sensed that in each other.

"Thank you," Elsa said. Litras looked at her questioningly. "For being here. For staying. I just… I just didn't want to be alone to do this."

Litras nodded and smiled, a few sharp teeth poking through. Elsa giggled and looked back down to Rose.

Elsa had been ripped out of her body and brought back to it so many times that she sometimes didn't understand where she was, or who she was anymore. Or if she were even alive, and not just a strange imagining from Mirial. If anyone could bring Rose back, she could.

She first reached for Rose's belly, pushing up her shirt to touch her skin. Elsa poured healing energy into her, so that her mind would have a healthy vessel to return to. Once satisfied, Elsa moved beside her head. She seemed more peaceful, now that her body was no longer in pain. She seemed like she could just be sleeping.

"What if she doesn't want to come back, Litras?" Her voice was a whisper, her eyes wide. The song of Mirial called to her in the distance. Maybe she would join Rose, instead of forcing Rose to join her. The engineer had always been so kind. She was certain she would be welcome.

Litras took hold of Elsa's hand, squeezing it, forcing her to focus. "There's a child lost out there, Elsa. A child who might be able to save Mirial."

Elsa shook her head. "What if Mother Layela can do that by herself? What if Ardice could still be free and happy?"

Litras squeezed a bit harder. "Whoever did this to Rose is probably the one who has Ardice. Do you really believe they would take care of Ardice? That they would love her, and keep her…" Litras paused. "As a mother would?"

Elsa felt the familiar grief choke her breath. "Elsa," Litras continued. "Layela loves you, just like she loves Ardice. She just had to learn to let you both go. For your own good."

Elsa didn't argue. She knew the arguments by heart, had run them in her mind herself, had screamed them at Mirial. But, in the end, all that she could truly cling to was the fact that when Ardice arrived, Elsa was forgotten. Elsa had lost children too, and she understood Layela deeply for that, but they had never been able to bond through that grief. It had torn a wedge between them, and Layela didn't even seem aware of it.

"Elsa?" Litras asked, snapping the Berganda back. "I think Rose would like to come back. She could see all of the improvements that were made to this ship."

Elsa smiled at that. She remembered watching Rose tinker with the various part of the ship, never satisfied until they were perfect. Elsa had heard of some of the improvements from Avienne. She had no idea really what Avienne was talking about, but Rose would. And that would make her so happy.

"You're right," Elsa said, smiling. "She would love to see those."

She reached with her free hand for Rose's head, but kept her other hand in the Kilita's. Elsa feared that if she found Rose, and Rose was happy, she might decide not to return.

And she still had so much to do, for her sisters, and for herself.

***

Rose stood near the window, watching Ardice play. She laughed and laughed, butting the ball around with her tiny feet. Sometimes, Rose swore the ball was butted back at Ardice, but she washed the memory away and just kept smiling.

Her sister called her from the dining room table, and Rose joined her.

"Tea?" she asked, and Rose smiled gratefully. Ardice sat with them, looking beautiful in her gown. Tonight she would be presented to the court of Mirial. Rose took her hand and smiled. Ardice smiled back, with those mysterious eyes that had always held deep secrets.

"Ardice! It's lunch time!" Rose called out, and Ardice ran in, pulling off her boots and leaving them in the hallway. Rose helped her with her coat. She still had a hard time with the zipper.

"Your coat is getting too little," Rose said. "How about we go to the market tomorrow and get you a brand new one?"

"Yellow!" Ardice shouted happily. She turned, danced, and turned back as she hugged her new jacket. Rose shook her head. She didn't think anyone ever looked good in yellow, but Ardice loved it.

A knock at the door, and Rose stood up, leaving her tea. It must be Ardice, come home from school. But why would she knock?

Rose opened the door, and her wide smile disappeared when she saw a Berganda standing there instead of the little girl.

"Where's Ardice?" she cried, pushing aside the Berganda. "Where's Ardice!"

"Here!" Several screams echoed around the house, and there was Ardice, waving as she played with the ball, and there she was, smiling as she drank tea with Rose's sister, and there she hugged her yellow coat.

"Oh good," Rose said, and returned to drinking tea.

Except the Berganda didn't vanish. She walked into the house and joined them at the table. Where had that fourth chair come from? That was ridiculous. Why would there be four chairs here? They were only three. Only ever three, and no one else.

"Rose?" the Berganda asked, and Rose tried to ignore her.

"I have to go coat shopping with Ardice!" Rose exclaimed, taking little giggling Ardice by the hand and heading for the door.

"Rose, sit down," the Berganda said, more forcefully this time. Rose found herself sitting.

"I didn't want to sit down," she marvelled. She wanted to go to the palace of Mirial and present Ardice to her mother. She wanted to show her how well she'd done. How she'd helped save Mirial. She wanted to see how lush and beautiful Mirial would now be, covered with Mirial's strong rays and multi-coloured flowers.

"Rose," the Berganda said again, snapping her back. Rose looked at her, insulted. Why was she here? Why was there a fourth chair at her table?

"Rose, do you remember me?" the Berganda whispered.

"Why do I have four chairs?" Rose muttered. The Berganda reached across and touched her. Rose jumped up so sharply that she knocked over her chair. She felt so… real. Her arm was cold where the Berganda had touched her.

Rose looked with alarm at Ardice and her sister, still chattering at the table. "They're not real, Rose," the Berganda said. "None of this is real. They're hopes and memories, intertwined. I'm so sorry, Rose. What you've created here is beautiful, but you can't stay here."

Rose picked up her chair. Why did she have to pick up her chair? Why was there a lump in her throat, now? Ardice looked so beautiful, and…

"Where's Ardice?" Rose cried. "Ardice!" She ran outside, where the ball lay abandoned. "Ardice!"

She stormed back inside and pulled the Berganda to her feet, slamming her against the wall. "Where is Ardice?"

The Berganda remained calm. "That's the question we need your help to answer," she said. And the walls of Rose's home started to shimmer and vanish. Rose felt lightheaded, and she clutched to the Berganda to keep herself from collapsing.

She held on as she was swept up in a tornado of wind and memories, words and laughter riding the winds around her, tugging at memories too vague to revisit. She clung to the Berganda, and the Berganda held her back, and they turned together in the tornado until she felt grounded again.

And thirsty.

She opened her eyes. Her mouth was so dry she could barely croak the word as she looked into a face that now proved so very familiar.

"Elsa?"

***

The door to the room opened and Litras stepped out, a big grin on her face. Layela leapt up and practically knocked her down to get into the room. Rose smiled weakly when she saw her. The engineer's white hair cascaded like a halo around her face. Layela crossed to the bed and took Rose's hand.

"How do you feel?" she asked.

"Better. A friend brought me back." Rose croaked.

Layela kissed Rose's forehead and moved to kneel beside Elsa, who sat in a chair, crumpled in on herself. Avienne brought Rose water, and held her head as she slowly drank, sputtering some. Avienne made some joke that made the engineer laugh hoarsely.

"Elsa, sweetheart, are you okay?" The Berganda's elbows were on her knees and her head in her hands. Her hair cascaded around her face. Her yellowing hair. Elsa didn't answer, so Layela stood up and crossed to the medical supplies. She always made sure to stock nutrients for Berganda, imagining someday a few would travel with them. The gardens would have helped them, too, but those would have taken some time to build. The nutrients would keep them healthy until then.

She knelt back beside Elsa.

"Elsa? I know you spent a lot of energy and I am grateful, but you need nutrients." Elsa shifted just enough so that she could peek through her hair.

"You have some?" Her voice was almost a squeak. Layela realised Elsa was crying.

169 | MARIE BILODEAU

"Of course I do. Hang on," she injected a dose into Elsa's thigh, the swoosh of air indicating the nutrients were running their course into her bloodstream. She would be better soon. Or she hoped she would be. Elsa was a bit older than Josmere had been when she had passed away, and some of her sisters had already passed away from old age. Their lifespan seemed much shorter than Josmere's generation seemed to have enjoyed, but maybe the renewed flow of ether would lengthen that, too.

She looked back. Avienne was still giving water to Rose, who seemed to be doing better now. A few pillows propped her up and she seemed able to drink on her own. She wanted to ask a thousand questions of Rose, but first she had to make sure Elsa was all right.

Little Elsa, born under the star of Mirial, daughter of her best friend; a wild, rebellious child who had been broken in an attempt to get to Layela. Little Elsa, who was old now, and would have lived a much more peaceful life had she never known Layela.

Layela pushed the rest of Elsa's hair out of the way. "Are you hurt?" She looked the Berganda up and down, wiping the tears away. Elsa had calmed, and seemed so tired now. She collapsed against Layela.

"There's room on the bed," Rose said, her voice already sounding stronger. Ardin came over and took Elsa gently in his arms, placing her beside Rose. Layela pulled a blanket out and placed it over Elsa. The ship wasn't nearly warm enough for a Berganda. Josmere had always huddled under blankets with Layela, trying to absorb what little heat she could. Elsa huddled near Rose, hiding under the blankets.

"Will she be all right?" Rose asked, running her hand on the little bit of hair that stuck out from under the blanket.

"I think so. She's exhausted," Layela said, hoping she was right. She focused on Rose, keeping her breath steady. The world seemed slower now. Layela wanted answers, but feared them so much it smothered her. She forced her fingers to loosen their grip on Rose's blanket. "What about you? I'm so glad to see you and I want to hear everything, but right now, we need to know what happened to Ardice."

Rose looked down, biting her lower lip. Layela wanted to shake answers from her, but let her compose herself, first.

"I'm not sure." She looked up, into Layela's eyes. "I'm really not!" She took a deep breath. "We lived with a young boy, an orphan. He showed up once when Ardice was really sick, when she was about six." Layela didn't interrupt, but the thought of her daughter being sick and her not being there made her heart ache. She placed a hand on the sleeping Berganda, feeling the rise and fall of her steady breaths. "He was such a nice young boy, an ether creature, and Ardice liked him so. They played and laughed together." She paused. "I just always felt so bad for her, stuck with an old lady in a small home on a remote planet. I had more than enough money to take care of two children for years, so I figured a sibling would be good for Ardice."

She didn't meet Layela's eyes, looking at her hands, which lay flat on the blanket.

"Rose?" Layela prompted. Rose might be awake, but she didn't seem quite all back. She would eventually be. Layela hoped.

Rose's voice seemed far away when she continued. "He grabbed my hand. I thought nothing of it. I'm from Mirial, and ether creatures rarely affect us, and he'd become like... like a son. But something happened. He looked up, and his eyes were different. I tried to take my hand away. Ardice was laughing somewhere. I screamed, I think."

She stopped, took a deep breath, and looked back up. "That's it. That's all I remember."

Avienne offered Rose more water. She looked from Ardin to Layela. "An ether creature might be easier to track. If they've headed anywhere in Solaria, then he'll probably be tagged somehow. We can just ask Jar..." she stopped and looked down.

"It's a good idea," Layela offered. "We'll look into it. Rose? Can you describe the boy for us?"

Rose handed the glass back to Avienne. "Yes. He's a race I'd never met before. A Zoorsa. His name is Hoast."

The world spun around Layela and she had to grab a hold of the bed for fear of falling.

"Layela?" Ardin was holding her up.

She thought her eyes might leap out of their sockets as she met his gaze. "I've met him."

Rose, Avienne and Ardin all chimed in at once: "What?"

"I met a young Zoorsa named Hoast, on Mirial, the day before the Seeders came. There were so many visiting ether creatures, I never even thought it was out of place... and I saw him, again!" She turned to face Ardin, cold sweat running down her back. "I saw him, Ardin. On the *Lady Mirial,* as we escaped! He was in the shuttle bay! He was right there!" She was growing hysterical and she knew it, but she didn't care, letting the sobs finally break her body.

"She was right on the ship, and we left her there." Her eyes grew smaller, wildness turning to tired sorrow. "Ardin, what did we do?"

He gathered her in his arms and kissed the top of her head. He didn't answer her question.

There was nothing he could say.

CHAPTER 24

THE HALLS OF the ship echoed with the clanking of a lone soldier's gun against the wall, probably bored with his station or simply too numb to realize he was even doing it. Loran tipped her head, stretched out her aching legs, and leaned back against the wall. There were few chairs and beds available in this communal room. Certainly very little privacy.

There were fifty-six Mirialers in this room, which meant other pockets of citizens were spread out within the belly of the ship. When Loran had first heard the clanking of the weapon, she had hoped for some sort of code. But the regularity of metal clinking on metal had only revealed rhythmic boredom.

Her legs hurt. The synthetics grated her shredded nerves. She refused to take them off in front of her captors, or other Mirialers. She didn't want them to see her as anything but the captain of Mirial's guards. She gazed around. Possibilities for escape weren't lacking, but taking the ship back without getting all the Mirialers on board killed was something she hadn't yet managed to figure out.

The clanging stopped and she looked to the door with interest, pushing herself back against the wall. The connections to her legs were frazzled and barely gave her nervous system enough information to properly control them, but it was enough for her to stand and look confident. By now, after two days of watching the ebbs and flows of the guards, she understood enough of their behavior to predict some of their movements. The guard outside only stopped tapping because his superior told him to.

The Kilita who seemed to lead them remained a mystery, but she was certain he bore sympathy for her people. He feared for his own—they were trapped in their own bodies by the Ralis, as far as she understood. Or the Ralis had destroyed their minds and simply hitched the Kilitas' will to their own.

Loran took a deep breath and focused on moving towards the door. Experience indicated that the soldier would be walking in with a couple of minutes. Her first step took her too far to the right, almost splitting her legs in two different directions. She frowned, pivoted on her right leg as she lifted her left, and let the right one navigate. One sharp, calculated step after another brought her close enough to the door to state her intent to hold a conversation, but not so close as to be perceived as a threat and get shot. Or so she hoped.

A few of the Mirialers looked up with interest, others with fear. She hadn't taken any of them in her confidence, hoping to spare some wrath her actions might incur. Not that she even knew what exactly her actions were going to be. Erlin had screamed his last more than a day ago. Layela's escape had secured a potential future for Mirial, but what of the Mirialers? What of the people who had been left behind and were held captive for unknown reasons?

Loran had been born off planet, only hearing of Mirial through legends and stories from her parents, and had always promised never to tell those stories to others. She hadn't understood why the stories were secret, as a child, but nor had she overly questioned it. She loved having a secret she shared with her parents and no one else.

They were stories of battles, of duty, of art and hope. They were stories of standing up for what was not necessarily right, but what was necessary. And of always maintaining what must be maintained.

As Loran waited for the door to open, marking the seconds with her breath, she realized that her parents hadn't wanted her to share the stories not only because they were of a world hunted by Solaria, but more importantly, because Solaria would fear what they might mean. What effect might stories of freedom and fighting for one's own family have on an empire built on fear and blackmail?

When the door opened, Loran didn't even think about her actions. She saw only the graying, smiling faces of her parents, who had believed in Mirial so fiercely and yet never had the chance to see her again.

She jumped on her right leg, using it as a pole vault to leap up and land square in the chest of the surprised Kilita, whose wide eyes betrayed his surprise. They both slammed down and Loran rolled off him into the corridor, turning around and preparing to strike him hard to avoid getting shot. But as she turned, she pulled back her punch, seeing it wasn't necessary. Three other Mirialers had followed her lead, and they had him secured.

A middle-aged palace gardener, Olrik, handed her an energy rifle. A dangerous weapon on or off ships. He smiled grimly and she nodded in return. The Kilita struggled to his knees, with two other weapons trained on him from unflinching Mirialers. Loran clutched her gun with pride. They had grown up on the same stories, too, and she should have known that they would move without hesitation.

Olrik met Loran's eyes. "It won't do you any good. Don't you think we tried?"

Loran didn't lower her eyes or let him see any hesitation. "Maybe we'll succeed, maybe we won't. But at least we'll go down fighting."

The Kilita shook his head. "You'll go down, all right. They know your greater weakness, and they'll exploit it. It's their strength." He looked at Loran again. "Try if you must, but remember that they'll win, in the end, and you'll never be the same."

She ignored him. "How many of you are on board? How many Ralis?"

The Kilita just shook his head. He might not even know, and getting the information out of him would take too long, of that she was certain.

"Tie him up and gag him. Leave him back there. Anyone who doesn't want to come can keep watch on him."

Olrik nodded and dragged the Kilita back into the room.

Loran listened carefully down the corridor. No one had come, even though she knew a guard was just around the corner.

Olrik stepped back out. "Most of us are coming. Just a few injured and elderly are staying behind." A flicker of concern shifted his features as he peered down the corridor.

"We'll go slowly," Loran whispered. "And we'll head to the secondary bridge. With any luck, they're not even aware it's there, and we can take over the ship, one system at a time."

Olrik nodded and stepped back in to tell the others. Loran stood in the corridor, clutching her weapon. No one came and no threatening messages blasted over the intercom. And they'd made plenty of noise escaping. Either the guards were horribly incompetent, or didn't care, or the Kilita was right: the Ralis had something so horrible on the Mirialers, something that would stop their fighting in their tracks so assuredly, that they required no more security than this.

***

The ship thumped once in a while, making Ardice jump. Hoast stared at her from the other side of the room, forcing himself not to get up to try and comfort her. She had never been on a ship before, despite her gram's—despite Rose's—obvious knowledge of their inner workings.

Hoast leaned his chin on his knees, tucking his feet as close to his body as possible, shuffling himself as low as he could behind his own legs. The heated floor made for a fairly comfortable seat, though he wished he and Ardice could just lay in bed and chat about this and that, and make up stories, just like they always used to do. He figured they'd never do that again. He lowered his forehead on his knees and hugged them tighter.

Another thump and Ardice gave out a low yelp. Hoast forced himself to look at her, but her wide eyes were staring at the door. Hoast followed her gaze, to where the door stood open.

They hadn't tried to open it, but it had definitely been understood that they wouldn't be able to get out. Their room was spacious and comfortable enough, except for Ardice's silence since crossing into Mirial's space.

Bring her out, the voice came to the Zoorsa's mind, unbidden and irresistible. He stood up before he'd even realized what had been asked. He wanted to fight it so much, but it had proven impossible before. Still, he tried. He forced himself not to take another step, his legs trembling under the weight of struggling wills. A fine sweat broke out on his forehead.

Ardice looked at him and he opened his mouth to tell her that he didn't want to do this, that he hadn't wanted to do any of it, that she was his friend above all else. But he said none of it. The urge to go outside and wander erased any other thoughts.

He smiled. "It's cramped in here. Do you want to go for a walk?"

Ardice turned her head a bit sideways, in a familiar gesture that indicated she was weighing the suggestion. He ached to hear her debate her ideas with him, like they used to do in their room, whispering so that Rose wouldn't hear them. Ardice had chatted about everything that fascinated her, mostly concerning her garden and the bugs she enlisted to help her grow the plants.

Inspiration struck Hoast. He forgot why he had stood up in the first place, but intended to make the most of the open door. "Hey, I heard there's a garden here. We could go check it out."

He smiled his easy smile, and Ardice considered for a moment longer before standing and nodding. She said nothing, still, but her eyes were more focused than they had been for days. She indicated with a quick motion of her chin that he should go first. He wanted to feel the warmth of her hand in his, and to laugh and chat, but she didn't seem up for it.

He grinned at her and walked, soon feeling her presence beside him.

A part of her still trusted him. He frowned. Why did he feel he couldn't trust himself?

The thought fluttered out of his mind as they continued walking, turning this way and that, along corridors lined with closed doors. They entered a large living area, filled with trees and benches and windows for peering at the stars.

Ardice stared at the dying star in the distance, her eyes so wide and filled with light that Hoast wanted to cry. When he spoke, it took him a moment to recognize his voice, which seemed distant and strange.

"Do you sense it?"

Ardice turned slightly, not quite looking at him, her eyes narrowing. Her voice came thinly. "What do you mean?"

"The star. Do you sense it?" Hoast drifted near, himself. He imagined he dreamed this. He imagined he would soon awake and tell Ardice about this dream, and they would laugh at it together.

You were looking at me like I was weird! And she would laugh, and laugh, and give him the look again before breaking into more laughter...

"I don't know what you're talking about." Her whisper snapped him back. He could see the lie in her eyes. He grew terrified of what that lie might mean for her.

This is for you, a soothing voice calmed his fears, a cool shower after a long, dry spell. Then the shower turned to rainstorms, and he saw ether flow from Mirial, weak and thin. He looked down and saw a string of it leading from the star to him, a soft glow that seemed so fragile that at any second it might break.

He felt himself drift back into his body and he reached down to touch the strange glow. His hand went through it.

This is for you, the voice still sounded in the back of his mind. Such a small string leading back to Mirial. A frail lifeline. A necessary shackle.

A hand gently took his and pulled it away from the glow which he could not unsee.

He forced his eyes up, catching Ardice's with his. She held his hand in both of hers.

"Do you see it, too?" he whispered, afraid that too loud a sound might shatter the fragile lifestring.

She nodded and her eyes flickered down to it before looking back to him. "What's happening, Hoast?" Her voice fluttered about in a way he had never before heard. But he'd never really known her to be afraid. Not brave, calm Ardice.

He wished he had something reassuring to say. But he could think of nothing except that lifeline. Nothing except its frailty and thinness.

"I don't know." He paused. "I'm scared, Ardice."

She held his hand tighter as she whispered, looking back towards the First Star, burning in the silent sky.

"Me, too."

***

Layela walked the length of the gardens, then stopped and walked back. She held the flower Hoast had given her when they'd first met. Was it meant to be a sign? If she had paid more attention to the gift when she still held the gift of ether, could she have sensed Ardice in the petals? Did he try to warn her, to get her help? Perhaps she had let her one chance to find her daughter escape. Did Mirial's urgent whisperings warn of Hoast and Ardice, and not of the impending tunnel?

How much else had she missed in her eagerness to escape the First Star?

The great window drew her reflection amongst the stars. Ardin had gone back to the bridge, grasping a faint hope that they could somehow make it back to Mirial.

Mirial. Where everything began and, it seemed, ended. With or without her.

She stopped and leaned against the window. Her ghost looked back at her, faint and washed out, almost non-existent. Something from another life, another world. Something that had never been meant to even exist.

"You picked the wrong battles to fight," she told her ghost and it echoed back word for word. Her childhood eyes, looking at her, were now so unfamiliar. She reached up and let her fingers glide on the edges of those strange, dark, blue eyes, so empty of life. So lost.

"What did you want? What kept you going?" she whispered.

A place to call home.

The answer came unbidden, laughing on the silent winds around her. Layela closed her eyes and lowered her forehead against her ghost. "A place to call home."

Layela had fought with everything she had, growing up, saving every penny, foregoing meals, to open up a flower shop. She had been eighteen, just the legal age on their current planet, Collar. She had been so young and full of hope—hope that her sister would settle down with her, hope that flowers would sell on the desolate landscape of Collar. Hope that she would succeed, and never have to worry again, never have to go *without.*

But she had been wrong. She had thought that all she needed was food, a roof over her head, a purpose to get her up in the mornings. But she needed more than that. She needed her family close to her, too. She had let go of her dream once, for her sister, who was trying to save her from a dark fate. But, in the end, Yoma had left her, and so had Josmere. And now, Ardice.

No.

She had let Ardice go, thinking there could be a better future for her. But what future, away from her family, from her home?

All of her carefully constructed justifications crumbled in her memories. She had wanted a family and a home, but under her own conditions. When that hadn't been possible, she had given up first her family, and now her home, in an effort to find a perfect one.

"You picked the wrong battles," Layela whispered. She had let go of Mirial, without first making sure that her daughter was safe. And now, with Mirial still the First Star, she didn't even know if the great silent star had let go of her innocent daughter, as well.

Layela had deserted Mirial, and so Mirial had deserted her.

Could she really just desert me?

Layela looked back up, for a second seeing green eyes reflected back at her. But then Yoma was gone, and there was only Layela's own pale reflection in the glass.

She wanted to be free of Mirial, but she needed her now more than ever. She would take it all back, now, if it meant being safe with Ardice. Mirial would be her home. She would let go of one dream to make sure another, more important one, existed.

"But how do I get back?"

Her reflection stared back at her, as silent and free from answers as Layela herself.

CHAPTER 25

WHAT IF WE use our tachyon shields as some sort of propulsion device?" Avienne glanced at her brother.

Ardin shook his head. "They won't maintain for that long, and I don't think they'd surf like we do on the tunnels."

"Okay, then we figure out how to make them stronger and more surfy."

Ardin sighed. "And how are we supposed to do that? We have limited knowledge, expertise, and parts on board."

Avienne shrugged. "We can get the knowledge easily enough. And we might be able to get parts from junk ships. Even the *Dessicate*. She might as well be good for something."

"But we don't have the tools required for major off-ship repairs, which we'd need to do to modify the mechanisms. And we don't have the crew. Would you send Gobran out to do the work?" He turned around and stormed towards the sealed coffee jug. That stuff was so old it might even have been too stale for Jaru. Avienne swallowed hard and leaned back against her chair.

"You're right, Ardin. We should just wait and see what happens. Why even bother discussing solutions when someone is bound to come looking for us. You know, Ardice will probably be fine." His spine seemed to turn to steel and he didn't turn around to face her.

She pressed on. "How do we even know she's on Mirial, Ardin? So Layela saw a Zoorsa on the *Lady Mirial*, and it might very well be this Hoast kid. That doesn't necessarily mean Ardice is there, does it? Maybe we should start looking elsewhere."

Her brother seemed to decompress, his spine slacking as he exhaled. He turned around, his eyes narrow with grief. "I let her go, Avienne. I let her go, and now I can't help her."

Avienne leaned forward again, wishing she didn't feel as though years of traveling down different paths hadn't left so many empty spaces between her and her brother. She didn't know this Ardin as well. She didn't know how he grieved anymore, or how he coped. But she had known, once, and that would have to do.

"You didn't let her go, Ardin. Layela and I did, in difficult circumstances, doing the best we believed was possible."

"It doesn't matter. She's my little girl, and I've never even really ever held her."

Whatever distance she'd felt from him shattered with the grief gluing his words together. She stood up and gathered him in her arms, as though he were just a boy still, just her brother needing to be comforted.

His body shook with sobs, years of grief wracking his limbs. Avienne held him as strongly as she could and let herself become lost in his grief, allowing it to pour from him and mix with hers.

She held him even after he stopped, remembering a time when all they had was each other, and grateful they now had so many more people in their lives. So many more people who could help make a greater difference than the Malavant siblings could, alone.

He finally stood again and she let go of him. He grinned weakly at her, his face blotchy. She returned the grin, the distance between them washed away.

"So, where to, then?" Avienne asked.

"Mirial," Ardin answered, looking back down at the quadrant map. The only thing it really told them, unfortunately, was that traveling to Mirial without a tunnel would be an impossible journey, at least within their limited lifetimes. Avienne fought her weariness and frustration. The whole thing was a mess.

"You sure she's there?" she asked, zooming the map out to encompass all known and charted space. Which proved so very small. The universe was vast, with so many unknown worlds and species that at times it seemed impossible to discover it all. And it was, with their current technology. How do you discover the world when your only quick means of travel are tunnels that require time and money to build and, once crumpled into disrepair, could only be put back together with the same amount of time and money all over again? Mirial's tunnel had been rebuilt once, when Solaria had believed it could become a strong trading partner, and perhaps a good world to conquer. But lack of resources and a population that held back instead of striving had long ago lost Solaria's interest.

And they wouldn't regain it now. Mirial was a mere dying stain in the night sky, the ether races had mostly abandoned Solarian space, and Solaria itself felt the edges of its empire straining from its expansion. They couldn't help. They wouldn't help. If Ardice was on Mirial, she might as well be buried and out of reach.

And if not? If she wasn't on Mirial? Could they find a lost child in a world of black market slave traders and poor census data, where vanishing was both art and science?

"Layela's sure," Ardin answered, startling Avienne. He met her eyes. "I'm sure, because Layela's sure."

Avienne hesitated before speaking. "Layela doesn't have her connection with Mirial anymore, Ardin. How does she know?"

She hated herself for asking, but was relieved to see the steady certainty in her brother's eyes.

"It makes sense, in a way," he said, absent-mindedly zooming the map in on Mirial. "Layela loses connection, but someone wanting to gain connection with Mirial makes sure they have the sole person who could maybe connect with Mirial. The fact that the tunnel collapsed seems an inconvenience, that's all."

Avienne nodded. "Okay, I'll bite. Say this is true. Say that this is the Ralis' evil plan. What I want to know is: how did they even know about Ardice? And how did they find her? I scoured Solaria and its borders for her, Ardin. Rose was good at hiding."

Ardin stared intently at the map before answering in a rush. "They weren't alone. They had the Zoorsa with them."

"Okay, so he betrayed them?"

Ardin shook his head. "That seems unlikely. Rose seemed to think of him as a son, and then he changed drastically. If he did betray them, it might not have been under his own volition."

Avienne's limbs tingled with worry and excitement. Ardin was right. Why would he have betrayed them?

"On the *Lady Mirial*," Ardin spoke slowly, fielding his thoughts.

"We were under attack by ether creatures. They were the guards, and they turned on us, but not in a passionate way. They were just doing it, because someone told them to. Almost like they weren't acting of their own volition."

"Okay, so someone was controlling them, and could have controlled the Zoorsa?"

"The Ralis are an old race. Some books say they could even rule the other races if they wanted. Layela and I had assumed that meant they could rule them politically, but what if…"

Ardin and Avienne both reached for the comm unit at the same time.

"Patros, Litras, report now." Avienne's voice was tense.

The Kilita's rough voice boomed. "Litras here. What can I do for you?"

"Is Patros with you?"

"No. Is something wrong?"

Avienne closed the connection with her and opened a ship-wide signal. "Patros, come in."

The seconds that followed were so tense Avienne thought her own spine would crack under the pressure. But the comm remained silent.

"We need to find him. Now." Ardin said.

"Why would they still want to attack us? Why would it matter? We can't get to Ardice!" Avienne swore as she secured her knives and guns. She wanted nothing more than to hurl them across the room. Why were they after them? And why Patros?

"We'll find him, Avienne. And then we'll figure it out."

Avienne grabbed Ardin by the shoulders and squeezed hard. "I lost Jaru and the *Dessicate*. They won't get anything else from us today, understood?"

Ardin nodded. "We'll find a way to restrain him."

She held him a moment longer and then nodded, satisfied.

"How do we find him? Where would he go?" Ardin asked, not rubbing his upper arms, to his credit. "The engine room? The bridge? We can put the ship on lockdown."

"That'd stop us from getting to him more easily, too, and alert whichever rat-skinning bastard has control over him. No, I've a better idea."

She grabbed the comm unit and got Litras back.

"You just closed the line on me," Litras said, sounding hurt.

"We need your help, sailor," Avienne said. "We think someone's controlling Patros. We need to find him. Now."

Seconds dripped by in silence. "I have him. He's on the ship."

"Where?"

"I don't know. Somewhere to my left. It's not exactly a map. I'll meet you on the second deck, forward section, and we'll go from there."

"Third deck," Ardin said before shutting the line.

"What's there?" Avienne asked as she and Ardin jogged towards their meeting point.

"Some social quarters, aft engineering, and the gardens." Ardin swallowed bitterly after the last. He activated his comm and Avienne saw he was trying to contact Layela.

No answer came.

Avienne wanted to say something comforting, like that she might be asleep, but she felt stupid for even thinking it. Of course Layela would be in the gardens, and of course they wanted something that she had. It was the story of her life, really. From the flower shop to Mirial. Always in the right place, but always at the wrong time.

Ardin broke into a full run and she held her tongue, using her precious breath to keep up instead, cursing the size of the ship and its long expansive corridors with every step.

***

Patros couldn't remember waking up or getting dressed. Much less walking here, to the empty gardens, staring at the Keeper from the safety of a pillar. Why was he even here?

The knife.

Yes. Of course. The knife. He walked towards her with renewed purpose. He needed to know where the knife was. That was all. A simple question, a simple answer, and he could go back to sleep in the comfort of his cabin. Maybe Avienne would have the time to join him.

She would. She would have the time to join him. In fact, he suddenly thought, she was there right now, waiting for him to find out this very simple fact first before he could join her. One simple question.

The knife.

***

Litras stood in the corridor ahead, Ardin screaming at her in between breaths: "Which way!"

To her credit, the Kilita didn't waste time on questions, responding only to the siblings' worry. "This way!"

She turned left into a nearby corridor and they followed, feet trampling heavily on the metallic decks. Avienne's lungs hurt but she pressed on, keeping up with Ardin's fuelled limbs. If anything had happened to Patros, she would, she would…she didn't know what she would do, but it would be memorable.

"Bridge to Captain Malavant," Brosten's voice managed to pierce through their breaths.

Ardin practically shouted into the unit attached to his wrist. "Not now!"

Brosten answered as though he hadn't heard Ardin's reply, which would have amused Avienne under different circumstances. "We're being approached, sir. Multiple ships, not all makes known. The known makes, however, indicate that a small fleet of ether ships are heading straight for us."

Ardin glanced back at her. "What are the chances they just want to take the tunnel to Mirial?"

Avienne gave a bitter laugh. Ardin spoke in his unit. "Brosten, Avienne's coming back up. She'll be acting captain until I get there."

"No way, Ardin." She grabbed his arm and pulled him to a stop. Litras kept jogging up ahead. "You go, I'll go after Patros."

"I'll take care of it."

Avienne pressed harder on his arm. "Ardin, if you're pulling some heroic shit, hoping to spare me from having to shoot my own lover, then spare me. He won't be the first lover I'll have shot. I know what my duty is."

Ardin shook his arm free, rubbing it with his hand this time. "I know you do. But it's Layela, Avienne, and I need to find her. I promise I'll do everything I can for Patros." He grinned. "I think his chances of survival are quite frankly better with me, anyway!"

Avienne laughed. "You are a terrible shot!" She sobered. "You'll be all right?"

He nodded. "I'll find a way to make sure we all are. Take care of the ship."

"Blood and bones, I'll break so much of you, Ardin Malavant, if you just lied to me."

"I've no doubt," he said as he ran after Litras, who had vanished down another corridor. She watched him until he also vanished, twitching to go after him. Once he was out of sight, she pushed herself to turn and run the other way, towards the bridge and the incoming fleet.

***

Layela jumped and wheeled around. A small smile crossed her lips. "Patros, you startled me." Her smile lost some of its intensity. "What's wrong?"

Her comm unit beeped. She reached to grab it from her belt, where she preferred to keep it. Before she could open it and answer, Patros reached for it. She was so surprised that she didn't try to stop him. This was Avienne's Patros, the only man who had ever kept Avienne's interest for a decade.

He took the unit and crushed it easily, letting it drop to the ground.

Layela's heart raced and she tried to take deep, normal breaths. "Patros, will you please tell me what's wrong? Perhaps you can walk me back to the bridge as we speak?"

She tried to remain nonchalant and welcoming, but as soon as she took a step towards the door, he stepped in her way. She stopped. She had no weapons on her and knew the Slont's strength was much greater than her own. His speed bested hers easily, too. And, without the protection of Mirial, he could choose to damage her with his own ether. Mirialers were naturally better guarded against the flow of ether, but they could still be wounded. Incapacitated, at least.

Patros smiled mirthlessly, his body depicting an emotion that his eyes did not reflect.

"Where's the knife?" he asked, his voice too flat again for the curve of his lips.

"What knife?" Layela asked, her mind numb as she analyzed every possible means of escape and came up with nothing.

"Mirial's knife."

Layela's brow furrowed. "Mirial's knife? Oh! You mean the sacrificial knife?"

Patros' smile widened, but the emotion again failed to reach his eyes. Anyone who didn't know the warmth of the Slont might mistake this for fatigue, but Layela had seen Patros tired beyond reason, and still manage a genuine smile.

She shrugged. "I left it with the temple on the *Lady Mirial.*"

His face became slack and he spoke with an inflection that defied his usual accent, wielding a single word that cut through Layela's remaining calm: "Lies."

She took a step back, matched by his wider gait which closed the gap between them. She tried to gather her remaining courage and invoke her Keeper training. "Patros," she said gravely, "I'm not lying. I left it there. Where else would it be? And why are you so interested in it?" She tried to make herself taller, failing beside the greater height of the Slont. "Regardless, Patros, the knife does not concern you."

His face grew slack, his mouth moving seemingly without using the muscle surrounding it, letting the cheeks move awkwardly a split second after the lips had moved. "The knife is the possession of Mirial, Keeper. You are no longer Mirial, and you must return it to us, where it belongs."

"Who are you? Do you have my daughter?"

She bit her lip, wishing she had not spoken the words. Had she revealed too much? There were so many players, so many possibilities, that she just didn't know anymore. All that she knew was that she wanted it to be over, and she wanted her family.

Patros stood limp before her, moments of silence stretching into minutes before his slack jaw formed words again, his eyes still without animation.

"We have her. You can see her if you give us the knife."

Layela's fear fluttered with hope before smothering her again. The knife had cut generations of women in her family, some to their eternal rest, in an attempt to control connections with Mirial. Ardice was on the *Lady Mirial.* She was more than certain, now, replacing instinct with knowledge.

"First among the Ralis," she ventured, regaining some of her posture. "I would be pleased to negotiate with you the terms of release for my daughter, but first you must assure me she'll remain safe."

"What of your people? What of the ether creatures?" The words came quickly, and dripped with anger that were not reflected in Patros' features. "You care for nothing, Keeper of Mirial, shirking sacred duties for a simple pay-off of a few years. Your lifespan is too short to understand or care, but you have disappointed nonetheless. We will not provide anything except passage. You may come to Mirial and give us the knife, and bring it to your daughter."

Layela's spine turned to ice, which crystallized her thoughts and her words. "You want me to kill my daughter?"

Something flickered in Patros' eyes. She wasn't certain if it was fear or disgust, or maybe contempt. She didn't know if the thoughts his eyes mirrored were mocking her.

"No." The answer was guttural, and something else flickered in the eyes. Fear, anger...Patros was fighting to be free.

"Patros, no. I need a moment more, please." She felt ridiculous for asking, but she stepped forward and grabbed his arms, looking at the still slack jaw, the muscles around it twitching for control.

"Why do you want the knife?" She screamed at that mouth. "Why do you want the knife!?"

The word broke free as the muscles snapped back into place. Patros suddenly went limp and Layela rushed to catch him. The doors flew open and Ardin screamed her name.

"I'm okay! Patros needs help," she replied, letting his last word blanket her heart and mind.

Freedom.

CHAPTER 26

BROSTEN, WHAT DO they want?" Avienne barked as soon as she stepped on the bridge. The first officer didn't turn to look at her, focusing on the screen instead. It was peppered with approaching ships.

"We believe they want the Keeper, plain and simple. The Ralis want the Keeper and they've convinced the ether races to help them out."

Avienne took over tactical, refusing to take the captain's chair.

"Can you charm them out of it?"

The bearded, staunch man raised an eyebrow.

"Right," Avienne said, focusing back on her console and the flow of information. Cross-referencing the ship's databank with Solaria's brought up relatively few hits, considering how many ships faced them. *Jaru could have accessed more databanks by hacking them.* She ignored the pang. Her fingers glided over her console, initiating the energy shields and shutting down non-essential systems. The hull showed damage already, and half the weapons were missing. She quickly scanned status reports, grinning as she looked up at Biolt. "Did you really leak out the energy cells? That's a desperate move, at best!"

He didn't return the grin, his skin pale and clammy. Avienne had forgotten how little space faring experience Mirialers actually possessed, and even less battle experience in space. The metre in her mind calculating chances of survival suddenly shrank.

"Well, let's do this politely. Open all communication channels."

She hopped over to the captain's chair and pushed the final button to let her voice travel unimpeded in space.

"This is Avienne Malavant of the *Destiny II*. Please state your intentions." She turned off her outgoing channel before mumbling, "and please do so without firing on us." The silence stretched into minutes.

She stood and took the three long strides back to tactical. The ships were still approaching, but at least they were slowing down. She couldn't see any remotely familiar attack pattern, just a lot of ships practically layering each other. Unless they were planning on going classic cavalry on them, hardly a necessity in the multiple dimensions of space, Avienne began to suspect they had no clue what they were supposed to do.

She glanced to navigation, where Patros should be sitting. Gobran stood stiffly, his hand cupping the electro-reader that allowed him to "see" the action.

"Gobran, tell me you can tell me something about these ships? Maybe their intentions? You've studied maps. You knew about the Seeders. Come on, old man, impress me again."

Gobran chuckled. "You would be surprised with how little is known of the universe, Avienne. I could guess about the tunnels because I studied maps, but ships, their makes and their people? Sorry—that I can't help you with."

He exhaled slowly and turned to face her, removing his hand from the electro-reader. "I can tell you one thing, Captain," he said, his voice softer, as though he thought only he and Avienne were in the room. Avienne was certain he knew better, so she came closer and knelt in front of him, giving him her hands so he knew she was there. He took them before she'd touched his. She smiled.

"I can tell you something, Avienne, about feeling like you've lost it all." Avienne squeezed his hands gently and swallowed hard. "They've lost Mirial, for all intents. Layela might have lost her chance to know her daughter and freedom, but these people have lost everything. The hope of a new, healthy First Star is gone. Mirial is dying, and with her death, their death will follow. I imagine it's like losing sight and your only child in one day." Avienne forced herself to study the familiar scars on his face. "It would be like being washed in despair, like there's no chance of anything making sense ever again. Like death wouldn't matter, and would in fact be welcome."

He squeezed her hands again and lowered his head closer to hers, whispering the rest, as though it were too important to share with anyone else. "But then, someone tells you to get up. Someone tells you there will be light again, even if it's a light you've never known. Someone pulls you off the ground, and drags you to someplace you can call home again. And you follow them, because it's all you have, and you desperately want to believe that there might still be a place for you in this world."

His face was a mere inch from hers, and she kissed his forehead as she stood. "Sometimes, you help me see, old man."

He chuckled again and she sat back down in the captain's chair. She heard the lift door open, but ignored it, pressing the comm line open again. She took a deep breath.

"This is Avienne Malavant of the *Destiny II* again." She looked toward Gobran as she spoke, and he looked right back at her. "Mirial isn't lost yet, but we need to get to her to save her. To save everyone. We don't know how to do that yet, but you might. Help us reach Mirial again and revive the First Star." She stopped, debated adding a line about them helping themselves by helping the *Destiny II*, but she'd already laid it on pretty thick. She closed the line.

"Lovely. You're a veritable poet now," Ardin said at her side, grinning.

"Thanks! I'm trying a new approach. Plead first, shoot later."

"Nice. It's good to see you expanding your skill set."

She stood and searched Ardin's face. "He's fine. Just resting," Ardin said. "Layela will keep an eye on him."

Avienne hopped out of the chair and this time reached tactical in two giant leaps. "Good! Now we can deal with these ships." She glanced down at the warning lights flashing on her console.

"Well, screw pleading. They're moving into attack formation!"

The lift opened again and Elsa leaped onto the bridge, twirling perfectly on her green tiptoes, her loose cotton gown fluttering around her thighs. She started singing in a loud soprano: "Get the Keeper! Get the knife! Get the Keeper! Save Mirial!"

"Elsa, what's wrong with you, girl?" Avienne said. She was tempted to hit the Berganda. Litras nonchalantly stepped between the two of them, gently grasping Elsa's shoulders to cease the twirls.

"I hear it too, Elsa. Try and block it."

Elsa smiled expansively and tilted her head to the side. "Why block the pretty music, Litras? I was just warning Ardin and Avienne of the danger!"

Elsa broke the grip and danced more gently around the bridge, just humming the tune. Litras turned to Ardin and Avienne.

"Well, that's the main message. They're after Layela. After that knife."

"Care to clarify who 'they' are?"

Litras gave her a toothy grin. "The Ralis, of course! They're strong. They can control some of the ether creatures, which is how they got to Patros." Avienne hated herself for letting the worry show on her face. Litras held up both hands. "He's fine. He'll be fine, now. I blocked the Fated Link from him. They can't get to him anymore."

"Great," Ardin piped up. "But what about you and Elsa? How do we know you both won't turn against us, too?"

Elsa shrugged. "Some Fated have different abilities than others. Elsa and I will be fine." She glanced at Elsa. "Well, we won't turn on you, anyway."

Avienne turned back to tactica. Whatever hesitation their attackers had experienced before, it had certainly evaporated. The ships were near, now, approaching in perfect formation. *Destiny II* would be hard-pressed to fight her way out, and the fastest ships could outrun her. The ships approached in layers, but with enough dexterity that each ship could fire deadly weapons, at the same time, so that a continuous stream of weapons would strike *Destiny II*.

Their shields would fall fast, and their already damaged hull would quickly follow.

"Litras," Avienne said without looking up. "You said you blocked the Fated Link from affecting Patros. Do you think you could do the same for those ships out there? If they're responding to the Ralis' message, you should be able to stop it, right?"

When Litras didn't answer, Avienne looked up to see her shaking her head. "That'd be nice, but no. I can't. The Ralis aren't strong enough to control all of them. They just made the request. Right now, it's all up to them and how desperate they are." She paused, looking to Ardin. "Maybe Layela can stop it?"

"Layela doesn't have ether anymore," Ardin spoke a bit too quickly and harshly. Avienne raised an eyebrow at him, but he didn't look her way.

"I didn't mean use the ether. She's still the Keeper. Maybe their loyalty to her would be enough."

Ardin did look at Avienne then. And his face reflected the same incredulity she felt. Layela had never sought their loyalty or favoured them.

It might prove to be a mistake with a hefty price tag.

***

With Patros' long and steady breaths as background music, Layela left the room. The newer door systems were quiet as a whisper. She could no longer hear his breath, but hoped he had not awakened.

Her legs ached to run, her feet wanting to clop down on the ground, but she forced herself to walk at a reasonable pace. With each step, the same word shouted in her mind.

Freedom.

Layela had forced herself to believe she wanted something more noble. Saving the ether creatures, Mirial, those who probably still considered themselves her people... She wanted those things, of course, but what she truly ached for was freedom. Her family's freedom. Leading a life that wasn't dictated by a silent star. A *star!* A giant ball of gas with the sole purpose of burning until fully consumed.

Not even with a purpose. Just... an existence. Nothing more. Just a thing that chemical reactions and physics had assembled by chance; a thing that only allowed for life due to its length of existence and its constant heat-producing fusion.

That's all Mirial is, Layela tried to force herself to believe as she turned a corner. That's all it'll ever be. A giant chemical reaction. That's it.

But Yoma... Layela ignored the emptiness she had felt since Mirial had deserted her. She tried to ignore the loneliness of missing her sister, a spirit who had always been present, thanks to Mirial's grace. Not, not grace. Maybe it had something to do with Yoma herself. Maybe she had been the catalyst, and not Mirial. Maybe a piece of Yoma was still within her, infusing her with dreams and hopeful visions. Maybe every legend was just that, a story, and Mirial was nothing more than a conduit for what existed naturally in people. Maybe the ether creatures would suffer but not perish.

Like Josmere. Layela stopped outside her door, her fragile arguments crumbling around her. Of course the Fated would suffer. They had before. The Berganda were almost wiped out the last time Mirial couldn't sustain them, and other races were said to have gone extinct. Whatever Mirial really was—and Layela simply had never managed to find out—she produced the right ether to help the creatures, across a vast landscape.

Freedom.

Layela sighed and opened the door to the gardens. Light ignited across the room, illuminating the sparse contents. Stars spread around the room through the great windows. She had cherished such dreams for this place, envisioning multi-coloured blooms living in a carefully constructed harmony not before seen in Solaria or beyond. A masterpiece she had planned for years, to distract herself from the dying planet around her.

She crossed to the back of the room, where supplies were kept. Inside a small cabinet, carefully labelled vials contained hundreds of seeds from across so many worlds. Two hundred and thirty-four worlds, to be exact. She had counted and recounted them. She'd figured out how to pair plants to account for different atmospheres, so that the plants could support themselves by generating what their neighbours breathed. The room itself would be maintained with oxygen, and she'd carefully maintain their growth so that the balance would always be perfect.

She picked up a vial labelled "Ardice" and turned it around slowly, watching the thirty seeds roll on the synthetic glass. She didn't know the name of this plant. It was a soft pink with small petals that grew until they shed, leaving newer petals in their stead. It never stopped blooming as far as Layela could tell, always offering more beauty and oxygen. Sometimes, a different-coloured petal would appear for no reason. A purple or a blue instead of a pink. It would grow like the rest and fall off, leaving another purple or blue petal in its wake. And, eventually, the bloom was no longer pink at all, bearing rich jewel tones instead of baby pinks.

Ardice had been a great name for the plant. A wish and a desire.

She sighed and placed the vial back down. Maybe she would get the chance to grow all of these flowers, yet. And to see the jewel tones on Ardice.

Just because the path she'd hoped would prove easy now proved difficult, it might not mean that the outcome had to be any different. She reached beyond the vials and pulled out the knife, which she'd hidden there. It had been silly, but she'd wondered if slicing the earth with the ceremonial blade, as she had sliced her flesh on multiple occasions, would help the ground flourish.

The small symbol of Mirial on its wooden handle the only indication that there was anything special about the dull blade. The wood had absorbed the unwashed blood over time, and was now darker brown near the blade. Regardless of its appearance, Layela knew that time had not robbed the two-sided blade of its biting edge.

The ship alarm system sounded twice, indicating imminent attack. Layela turned towards the great windows and gasped at the number of ships that now faced them. A great freighter, at least three times the size of the *Destiny II*, flew near, exposing its sturdy centrifugal design. The guns peppered on its core forced Layela to re-evaluate her assessment of it as a freighter.

Layela covered the knife with a gardening glove and ran towards the bridge.

CHAPTER 27

LORAN LED HER band of Mirialers towards the heart of the ship. The secondary bridge, a fully functional command centre created as a backup for the main bridge, had been the Malavants' idea. They argued that had *Destiny* benefitted from a secondary bridge, some of her crew might have been saved. The argument hadn't taken much to convince the Mirialers, who had for the most part been planet-bound for more than twenty years. Innovations that aided the chance of surviving in space, it turned out, had been easy to champion.

Loran skirted the trees of the main habitat and signalled back for the others to do the same. She realized she didn't even have to signal. Although no longer spacefaring, the Mirialers were used to being under siege and going by unseen. Only their pride assured they embraced the world around them anew and didn't cower in a hole, deep underground.

Loran paused and listened intently. She couldn't hear any guards, not even any of the possessed Kilita. The hairs on the back of her neck stood straight up and she clutched her gun more tightly. She took a deep breath, glanced left and right, and ran across the expanse leading towards the gardens.

She reached the door and turned around, banging her back against the metal wall as she lifted her weapon's sight to look for enemies or traps. Save for the Mirialers, nothing else moved. She shifted her

197 | MARIE BILODEAU

weight slightly, debating which leg could handle the most, before signalling to Olrik, who had flanked the other side of the door.

The secondary bridge's access lay past the gardens, through a hidden access panel in its storage shed. The debate of hiding the secondary bridge or maintaining it open had been brief. Loran had tipped it herself, asking if all Mirialers would be faithful forever. It had been insulting to her people, but the few in the design room couldn't argue. What if the Keeper needed to escape? What if security was compromised on the main bridge?

The secondary bridge had been designed just off the gardens, where their Keeper spent most of her time. Of course, no one mentioned that Layela had no intention of staying as Keeper. No one had said that she would try to leave, towards the stars, and her freedom.

Even Loran, who followed Layela loyally and spent more of her days with her than anyone else, had no idea what the Keeper had been planning. But she had not been surprised, which both saddened and enlivened her.

She didn't dare to believe anything other than that Layela would come back to help them, or that she'd left them a way to save themselves. That she'd somehow foreseen the potential threat of discontented ether creatures and had done what she could to protect her people. Loran dared to believe in her Keeper, still, and refused to think that she had wasted almost two decades protecting someone who had always intended to turn tail and run.

Loran held up her gun and nodded to Olrik. She took a deep breath and pushed the release controls for the door. They slid open and she turned, her gun raised, one finger on the pulse attack, the other firmly on the blast trigger. She surveyed the terrain quickly and aimed her sights at the two people moving in the room.

An ether creature, the Slont who had greeted Layela on Mirial, stepped in front of a young girl. Loran lowered her weapon but kept her finger on the pulse trigger, just in case. She stepped towards them, waiting for the closing of the door before speaking to the youth.

"What are you doing here? Did you stow away on board?"

The Slont shook his head, but Loran's eyes were drawn to the young girl behind him. She had straight dark hair and high cheekbones, and wore simple clothing. But it was her wide eyes that drew Loran's attention and made her hold her breath.

An eye of night blue and one of sea green looked back at her, wide and frightened.

The eyes of the Keeper of Mirial.

***

The First among the Ralis tried to lift his arm, but found himself too weary to do so. He did not care, could manage without an arm for a while. But the fatigue in his body indicated an ageing beyond its thousands of Solarian years.

His people were old, and long-lived. Their histories were rich with details of this First Star, and its predecessor. The dying First Star's weak light begged for release. To be let out into the cosmos. Free, without being bound by chemical reactions so mundane and unnecessary they bordered on insult.

The First held the most years lived, the most history read, the most time spent observing Mirial. The First even knew the Seeders, who often visited the Ralis, both their races old with histories spanning greater lengths than any other in the universe. The older Fated did not often find common ground with the shorter-lived, newer Fated, who often acted more like humans than Fated. But still, they were Fated.

The First worried, sometimes. He did not possess a pump for his blood flow as so many of the newer Fated did, based on the creatures selected to keep this First Star. This Mirial. But he did possess a circulation system dependent on ether to keep vitality flowing through his limbs. That one arm now did not work, proved to be of concern.

What if freedom is not possible? They had waited for this moment, when Mirial would fall from grace and a new First Star would be seeded. Since the seeding of Mirial they had waited for this chance to free themselves fully from the shackles of a First Star, of *any* First Star.

When Mirial had vanished into its own defences for twenty years, many of the Fated suffered. But not all of them. Some began to thrive. Others vanished, but those that remained could suddenly survive more easily without ether. The new Fated Link, which the Ralis had helped to establish as a means to further their cause, would not have been possible even fifty years ago, with a strong First Star.

Because when the First Star was strong, no one was driven to survive. No Fated felt the need to reach out to others, to increase their strength by combining their knowledge and their ether. Not even the Ether Wars, fought by the younger Fated, had been motivation enough. It had required the Ralis. Without realizing it, they had managed to create a network that they now owned, one of the most amazing accomplishments in the history of the Fated. All with the weakest First Star the Ralis had ever known.

Living without a First Star had to be possible for the Fated. They could be free from the shackles of a distant Keeper. No one would weaken them again, and they could truly become an independent people. Independent, and free, and unafraid of losing contact with the First Star, and of being snuffed out as easily as a candle.

For generations, the Ralis had foreseen the eventual possibility. They had even tried to sway the Seeders away from creating a new First Star. But the Seeders, whose only remaining purpose was the First Star, could not see beyond their own beliefs. They were convinced that too many Fated would die. That the great engine that formed the First Star was as necessary as oxygen on a Solarian ship.

It was change that they feared. Change, and uselessness. Eventually, something would happen to a First Star that would destroy them all. The more reliant they became on that First Star, the greater the damage would be. Best to do it now, when the First Star had performed so poorly, if at all, over the past forty years. Best to do it now, and strike while the iron was already been burning their flesh. They had the girl, and just needed the knife, Mirial's crude control point.

The Seeders didn't understand what seemed so simple to the Ralis, and to other older Fated: the First Star served as a shackle to the Fated, and would for as long as they allowed it.

The First managed to move his arm slightly.

If they didn't learn now, it would be too late for all of them.

If it wasn't too late already.

***

Loran tried to find the right words to greet the child, her grip on her gun loosening as gasps sounded behind her. She ignored them and tightened her grip again.

The Kilita had said they would have something to hold them with. Something so horrible it would stop them in their escape.

If this was a trap, Loran did not intend to fall for it. First, she needed to make sure this was, indeed, the Keeper of Mirial.

She tried to think of something that would trap the child into revealing her origin. Something clever, she imagined. But the child had only been a baby last Loran had seen her, and so only one word came to mind.

"Ardice?" She whispered the name, afraid her voice would crack. Layela had named flowers after her and cared for them so tenderly. Without an incoming Keeper, she had told her people, a new Keeper would be selected for the new First Star. A new beginning, she called it, and Loran had never known if she meant it for Mirial or for herself.

It hadn't mattered. Loran would stay and serve the new Keeper, and continue to serve Mirial, in whatever form it survived.

The child's eyes widened further. "How do you know my name?" She sounded scared, but determined, too. Her little hands formed fists at her sides.

"I'm a friend of your mother's," Loran said, trying to find an undisputable tell on the child's origin. But there was nothing. She looked like Layela, was graced with the eyes of a Keeper, and even sounded a bit like Layela, but all of those things could be faked, if necessary.

And the Ralis were quite capable of faking those things, this girl, if they believed she would stop the Mirialers in their tracks. But *why?* If this was Ardice, why now?

"I don't have a mother," Ardice whispered, looking at her defiantly. Loran forced herself to keep looking at the child and not tell her everything about Layela, and how much she had loved her, and loved her still. If this wasn't Ardice, she didn't deserve to know. She didn't deserve to hear something so private to the Keeper.

She didn't have to speak—the Zoorsa spoke instead. "You do, Ardice. I've met her!" He turned to face her, ignoring the Mirialers. "She's the Keeper of Mirial. She even has eyes like you!"

Ardice glanced at Loran and then focused on the Zoorsa "What are you talking about?" She sounded annoyed, and a little bit frightened. Loran instinctively clutched the gun tighter and kept a close eye on the ether creature.

"She's the Keeper of Mirial, and you are too, now. It's what keeps the Fated alive!"

Ardice glanced up at Loran again. "I know that, Hoast. I don't know why you'd tell me about my mother now. Or bring me here! And why you would say these things…why are you acting so strange?"

Loran remembered the possessed Kilita and spoke up. "Do you think someone else might be controlling him, Ardice? The Ralis are powerful. They might have taken over his mind."

Ardice looked up at her and back to the Zoorsa. Her mouth

opened but she said nothing. She took a step back from Hoast, glanced to her left and right and, seeing no escape, stood stiffly apart from everyone.

"It doesn't matter, Ardice," Hoast said, dejectedly. "We're here now. We can make the best of this."

Ardice bit her lower lip, in a way that Loran had seen Layela do. The gesture looked so much like the Keeper's that Loran's heart leapt to her throat. She wanted to protect Ardice now, regardless of what happened to her. Regardless of whether she was the right heir or not.

The Ralis know your weakness and will exploit it. She shoved aside the Kilita's warning.

"Ardice, we can help you, but you have to trust us."

Ardice looked at her again, and then to Hoast.

"We can just have fun," Hoast said, cocking his head sideways and leaping towards Ardice, who yelped as he landed on her. Loran ran towards them, but they both vanished before she could reach them.

There was nothing left but air.

"What do we do?" Olrik asked, and Loran looked at him grimly, seeing the same hesitation she felt.

"We split up. Go after Ardice, and activate the secondary bridge."

"What if they hurt her while we're activate the secondary bridge? She might be the only one left to save Mirial!"

Loran felt the Ralis' trap tighten around all of them. They'd waltzed into it, regardless of the warnings. Nor could they escape it now. They had to continue to its bitter end.

The Ralis had known all along that no matter what obstacles stood in their path, Mirialers would always choose to try and save Mirial over themselves.

CHAPTER 28

ELSA STOPPED DANCING when a shrill pierced the entire bridge, slicing ear drums. Avienne clenched her jaw, pulling up schematics, trying to shout over the buzz. She could see Ardin doing the same before he jumped up and pushed Biolt aside to look at the engineering panel. The old engineer sat on the floor and covered his ears, his face a mix of concentration and agony.

The shrill didn't sound like any electronic buzzing she'd ever heard—its undertones didn't convey the metallic whine of machinery. If she didn't know any better, she'd swear it was organic.

Avienne looked back towards Litras. The Kilita stood protectively in front of the Berganda, sporting a wicked looking serrated blade. For a moment, Avienne was distracted, wondering how she'd kept such a weapon hidden on her body, until she realized what the Kilita's stance meant. Avienne pulled free two knives just as fighters just...*appeared.* Out of thin air, they seemed to ride the shriek, the sound vanishing as they materialized. Five of them, wearing armor and drawing weapons.

They were large and bulky, weapons directly infused into their skin where arms should be, their legs mechanical. Avienne didn't give herself time to figure out which part would be a head, but threw her knife at the chest area of the nearest creature. The knife bounced off the metal-reinforced chest.

"Sealing all stations!" Ardin shouted, and the stations around the bridge turned inactive. Only level 1 access codes would re-activate them now. A precaution against boarding enemies.

"Their heads! Cut off their heads!" Litras shouted. Avienne leapt over her station to avoid being shot.

"What are their heads!" Avienne shouted back, ducking to avoid being hit. She spotted Ardin, who narrowly avoided losing his own head.

Gobran shouted. Avienne turned to see one of those creatures knocking him down. Avienne jogged around the assailant facing her and threw herself against the one assaulting Gobran, the wind knocked out of her as she hit the metal straight on. She grabbed the two shoulders and pulled up the weapons.

"The left arm! That's their central system!"

Avienne pulled up her knees and wrestled the creature to the ground, pinning her right leg and the creature's right leg under its bulk. She pulled and screamed, twisting the weapon back until it snapped and the creature went limp. She rolled down and kicked it off her leg. Above her a weapon buzzed and she looked up into the energy cells of her assailant.

"Blood and bones!" She shouted, reaching for her weapons, too slowly. The weapon buzzed again but the creature fell sideways, revealing Ardin, armed, behind it. She took his offered hand and he pulled her up.

"They're all down," Litras said, kicking the last one.

"So is this man," Elsa said, hovering over Brosten, whose dead eyes stared their way. "He's gone to Mirial." She grinned up at Ardin. "He's happy."

Ardin knelt by his first officer and gently closed the man's eyes. He then glanced at Elsa as though to say something, but stood up instead and snapped at no one in particular. "What were those things? And how in the Forty Solarian Suns did they get on my ship!"

Avienne helped Gobran back up and examined his wounds. All superficial, but he still looked shaken, and was clutching her arms tightly. "Which man?" Gobran asked. Avienne whispered to him about Brosten and the scene on the bridge, Gobran nodding as he absorbed everything she told him.

"We drifted into a teleportation pocket," Litras said. "It's an old trick, though I haven't seen it in a long time. You set a field of space with and wait for a ship to pass through. The shrill reforms them, since that means enough gas is present to hold reconstitution."

"Does that make sense? Screams make weird people?" Avienne said as she unlocked tactical.

Litras grinned. "Well, I don't know the science, but I know how it works."

"And those ugly things were..."

"I'm not sure. Fated, but mangled ones. A race that adapted cybernetics to their detriment, I assume."

Avienne's head whipped up. "Will there be more on the ship?"

Ardin punched his comm unit. "All hands, report in."

He stared intently at the silent comm, letting seconds slide into a minute. "Of course," mumbled Avienne. She looked up to Biolt, who had pulled himself up to his chair and was running reports on the ship's systems.

"We have a problem."

"No kidding."

The engineer ignored her. "Some of our systems are disabled. Directly from engineering. I have backups running, but whoever is working on them seems intimately familiar with the workings of this ship, and it won't take them long to sabotage everything that's left."

"We know they have the *Lady Mirial*," Ardin said. "It's not impossible that they'd have pulled out schematics by now, and the Ralis could have sent the information through the Link."

He looked at Litras for confirmation. She nodded, her entire posture signaling combat readiness. Avienne was suddenly glad the Kilita had found them again.

Avienne finished loading her weapons and headed for the lift door. "Stay there, Ardin. It's my turn."

"No chance, Avienne. It's my ship!"

"Why don't you both go," Gobran said, his voice already regaining most of its strength. "You can keep an eye on each other. Now that the bridge is free, we can handle things up here. We'll make sure the bridge is tightly locked so no one else will gain access." Biolt nodded and then spoke his agreement for Gobran's sake.

Ardin glanced at Brosten, setting his jaw, then turned to face Litras. "Will more of these things show up?"

Litras shook her head. "One shot only. Whatever's on board now is all we'll get. Unless we hit another pocket."

"As impossible as it is to stay in one stationary place in the vastness of space," Gobran said, "we'll do our best to stay put."

"All right, so we might have more of these things around, and something's taking over engineering—presumably something smarter." Ardin sighed. "It'll slow us down, but lock down the ship, and change all security settings. If they have our schematics, which we should assume they do, then let's be unpredictable."

He glanced at Avienne, who grinned. "Unpredictable is my specialty. Reroute our security systems independently instead of as a whole. It's easy enough to integrate, just tough to undo. If they do know everything about this ship and come hunting, they'll still be stopped by each new section."

"So will you," Biolt said, raising an eyebrow at Ardin.

"Well, give us the codes, first, so we can get through more easily," Avienne said. "This ship will become like a puzzle for them—they'll have to force their way through, and we can gamble that they won't, because they don't want to accidentally injure Layela, which isn't something we're worried about." Ardin shot her a look and she held up her hands. "I meant forcing our way through. Not hurting Layela. We're worried about them hurting her, remember."

"The other advantage of sealing off the ship in sections," she continued, "is that we'll be able to track their progress, right?"

"As long as they don't cut off our main computer access," Biolt said, shrugging.

"Well, the computers are separate from engineering, just for such a contingency, so that'll buy us time." Ardin turned to Litras. "We'll need your help. There are too many of them and not enough of us."

"I'll help too." Elsa stepped up. Ardin was about to protest, but she cut him off. "I can track Mother Layela. Litras and I will make sure she's safe, while you focus on making sure the ship is safe."

Elsa's features were set. Ardin looked annoyed, but he nodded.

Avienne pulled up the schematics as she grabbed the guns and extra knives she kept under tactical. "We're going old school, then." Avienne jerked open a panel and pulled out old leadcom units.

"Why are those on my ship?" Ardin asked, lifting an eyebrow. Avienne grinned. "Because you gave your sister the ability to make whatever changes she saw fit, and she didn't bother putting all of her genius in the schematics. These are smuggling faves. Not dependent on a central server or ship systems, they're perfect for one-on-one, hard to hack communications. Heck, they use limited airwaves, even, that most people don't even pay attention to. They're boosted enough to make the length of the ship, but not much beyond that." She handed one to Biolt.

"Brings me back," the engineer said, immediately turning his on. He turned back to his panel. "All systems independently secured now. I'll feed you the codes through the leadcoms. Don't lose them."

Ardin spoke up. "Those ships out there are hovering, but they're not attacking. I'm guessing they don't want to risk Layela, so they're letting their little invasion force do the work."

"Let's go greet our guests, then," Avienne said. He practically jumped into the lift. Avienne, Litras and Elsa all followed, Ardin shouting his last orders as the lift doors closed.

"Keep the ship safe!"

***

Still disoriented by the shrill noise and unable to reach the bridge, Layela pulled out her gun and hid in an alcove while her ears recovered. The dizziness was passing and her recovering hearing indicated someone walked near. The steps were strange, too rhythmic and metallic to be any of the ship's crew.

She focused on lengthening her breath. *Thief's breaths.* She drew them out silently, greedily, letting her mind sharpen and her body energize. The creature walked by, not noticing her in the shadows of the alcove. Layela analyzed it—more metal than creature. Whatever this was, it had stopped being organic long ago.

The clunking of the creature disappeared into the distance. She glanced around the corner at the empty corridor. *Good.* Her first instinct was to reach the bridge and Ardin, but Patros and Rose weren't far and they would be practically helpless right now. She needed to reach them, first, and ensure their safety.

She instinctively reached for her comm, only to drop the useless, crushed unit. She braced herself and quietly headed down the corridor, her gun held at the ready.

***

"Here!" Elsa said, her voice lacking breath. Ardin pressed the emergency stop, and the lift jostled. Avienne and Litras held their weapons forward as the door opened. The corridor stood empty before them.

"Be careful out there," Avienne said. "If you can, get to Patros and Rose, too, just in case."

Litras showed all of her teeth in what could either be a snarl or a smile. "Don't worry. We won't let them get anyone else."

They slipped out and the door closed. She glanced at Ardin. He nodded and activated the lift, bringing them just above the boarding points. The lift doors opened again to another empty corridor. Ardin indicated the locked door with his chin. Avienne reached for her leadcom and pulled out the access code. She looked at Ardin who held his gun at the ready, nodding to her.

Keeping a firm grip on her gun, she punched in the code. The doors slid open and both siblings held up their guns. Two mechanical creatures roamed the corridor. Both guns fired at once, and the creatures crumpled to the floor.

"I betcha an electro-bomb would be great on these," Avienne mumbled as she kicked one aside.

"Not so great for ship systems, though," Ardin said, looking more closely at the other. "What do you think happened to them? This isn't anything normal."

Avienne shrugged, scanning down the corridor just in case. "Maybe something from the Ether Wars? I don't know. Anyway, they're easy enough to take down when you know they're controlled by the left arm."

Ardin stood back up, his eyes dark. "How do you think Litras knew that? Seems like pretty specialized info."

Avienne looked down at the leadcom. "That girl ain't normal. She knows stuff she shouldn't." *Including promises made to the Fates!* "I think maybe she gets a lot of info through the ether. I don't know. But, back to the present, engineering is right below us. They haven't left yet—they're probably trapped in the next section. What's our plan? We have no idea what's down there. Even *I* think a direct assault is nothing short of suicide."

Ardin cast a grin her way. "There aren't any crew members where they are, right?"

Avienne double-checked. "Shouldn't be, unless they wandered down there before we locked it down. And that's highly unlikely. They didn't land on our most stellar of decks."

"Well, we know Layela isn't there, unless Elsa is really off her mark, and chances are Patros and Rose are still in bed." He glanced at Avienne. "Are we willing to risk that for a threat?"

Avienne's eyebrow shot up. "I love a threat. What's the plan?"

"This way," Ardin said, grinning as they ran to the nearest shuttle bay.

***

Litras stayed low, trying to keep up with the lithe Berganda. Elsa looked back and smiled at her, as though they were doing nothing more than enjoying a walk in the park.

"She's this way!" Elsa exclaimed before taking off, her long legs far outstriding Litras.

"Not so fast!" Litras hissed, keeping her blade near, wishing the corridor was either more illuminated, or completely dark. Either would be better than these half-dancing shadows.

Elsa turned a corner and gasped. Litras pushed herself to go faster, her breath inflaming her lungs. Her heart dropped when she saw the metallic invader right before Elsa. Litras tried to slow time, to give herself a moment to jump high, avoid the ceiling, step in front of Elsa, but the shot was fired before her mind could grab a single possibility and manipulate it into reality.

The scream caught in Litras' throat, the energy shot engulfing Elsa before vanishing. The Berganda smiled back to Litras and then walked forward, spinning as she struck the creature, going through him. The creature collapsed, the gun clanking against the floor.

Elsa didn't stop or look back. She took another step, extending her legs wide and pushing herself up on the toes of her right foot, arching her arms up as she twirled again, a mixture of light and earthiness.

Litras wanted to dance with her, to forget everything this world still called for her to do. To just lose herself in the grace of Elsa's steps, to match with her spirit what her stumpy body could not, to lose herself in ecstasy beyond all sorrow.

Elsa accelerated her pace and the scent of earth permeated the corridor, as though a fresh rain had just fallen on fertile soil.

Litras wanted to exclaim at the beauty, the rhythm, the warmth of Mirial. She stepped towards the Berganda, gasping at the flow of ether and promise, tears biting her eyes.

She reached up, uncertain if she would join Elsa or stop her until her hands found the almost translucent arms. She forced the Berganda to stop, forcing her arms to retake their full physical form, to let go of where Mirial dwelt, and where the Berganda so desperately wanted to exist. Elsa did not fight her, but still Litras pulled on every inch of concentration and strength to call the Berganda back.

She wanted to scream at the sight of the reappearing leafy hair, the solidifying arm and slender fingers, the tired, wise eyes.

"Not yet," Litras whispered, gasping. "Not yet, Elsa."

The Berganda's voice still straddled both realms, a whisper and a bell all at once. "I'm old, Litras. I can feel Mirial calling me."

"Just hang on, will you? I can't lose you now—you've just shown me that I'm not alone. And that the third is here, too. Just wait, will you? Wait for me? We'll go together, to Mirial, when we're all ready."

Elsa weighed her words, then put one foot before the next, lifted the first and twirled gently down the corridor.

CHAPTER 29

ARDIN AND AVIENNE crouched by the security panel, trying to override the air vent controls. Avienne leaned against the wall, catching her breath, studying the three large canisters on the other side of the corridor. *Blood and bones, we still have to bring them all the way over here!*

"Why do you have so many bloody different canisters, anyway?" She closed her eyes and forced her breath out through her mouth. In the nose, out the mouth...

"In case different ether races traveled with us for a while. Layela felt it was important."

Avienne reopened her eyes. "Did she even tell them she bloody thought about their comfort once in a while."

Ardin looked up grimly and focused back on the leadcom. The panel was as closed as before.

"This isn't going to be much of a threat if we can't even get the gasses into the next section," Avienne mumbled. Ardin was practically punching the leadcom.

"How can anyone even use these outdated things!"

Avienne sighed. "Stop that. Look, we can't open the vents without giving them access, too. The point is, they don't know that."

Ardin glanced up from the leadcom. "Add a bluff to the threat?"

She shrugged. "Why not? Just because we could have done that before dragging these out here, and killing more of those weird things. I wasn't thinking I needed more exercise, but I'm feeling the burn a bit more than I should."

Ardin stood up and hit the comm unit to the next section. "This is Captain Ardin Malavant." Avienne flipped a knife, biting back on her instinct to shout out that there were *two* captain Malavants here, and their enemies were doomed. "We know of your malicious intent. We will flood the area with a complex gas unfit for life within two minutes unless you surrender."

He hit the comm unit again. Avienne looked at the gasses. "Two minutes? I like it. Decisive and deadly. But does that mean we have to drag these over here? We could detonate them. It'd take down the wall and not make a liar out of you."

"And take out half the ship?"

"You exaggerate. A third at most."

Ardin shook his head. "It's been two minutes. What do we do now?"

Avienne scrolled through her leadcom notices, where Biolt had been feeding regular information. "Well, they seem to have stopped damaging things. Maybe we just go in with guns firing?"

The shadows grew deep under Ardin's eyes. "They might surrender."

Avienne kept her gaze steady. "Maybe."

He pulled his gun free and they walked towards the door.

***

Patros struggled through the layers of synthetics jammed into every neuron of his brain. He pushed to the surface, his mouth dry and his skin tight. Stale air robbed him of full breaths and his chest hurt. A lot. Pain ripped him awake and he struggled to sit up, but something held him down.

His eyes snapped open, the dim light of the room revealing a strange creature standing on top of him, its knee on his throat, or not a knee, but a part of it—his mind couldn't digest the information his eyes were feeding him.

With of his dwindling strength, he struck sideways, but the creature didn't even seem to notice him, as though Patros were nothing but a piece of flooring. He tried to scream, but couldn't, tried to grab the creature and see what elements greeted him, but something prevented him from doing so. He kicked, his legs connecting with nothing. Tucking his feet down, he tried to push up, to gain some sort of footing or leverage, but the creature held fast. He might as well have had a building on him.

Part of him thought he must still be dreaming. Stars exploded in front of his eyes. His throat burned.

Avienne...

A blast pounded his ears and the creature slid off. It would have dragged him down had two strong arms not held him up.

"Avi..." He tried to choke out the name, looking back. But Layela's face greeted him instead, blue eyes lined with concern.

"Are you all right?"

Patros sat up, suddenly embarrassed. He looked down to make sure he was clothed. This wasn't even his room. Where was he? What... He flushed, looking at Layela.

"I tried to hurt you," he said, the memories coming like fog, or old wisps of fractured dreams. "I didn't want to, but I tried to hurt you!"

He felt ill. Because of the attack on his mind or his body, he wasn't sure. He tried to stand but almost fell over, Layela steadying him. He hated himself for having to lean on her.

"It's okay, Patros. It wasn't you. You fought them off."

He looked for a lie in her eyes, but found none. He could remember trying to regain control, to just move a hand under his own accord...

"What's happening?" he whispered as the door opened. Layela held him up with one hand and whipped her gun around with the other. Litras stepped in.

"We'd better head back to the bridge. We got all the invaders, the ones that rematerialized, anyway." She looked to Layela, and Patros saw different coloured flecks invading what should have been solid orange irises of the Kilita's eyes. He suddenly felt a chill, and Layela's hand tightened around his arm.

"I think it's time to face them."

***

The door slid open and they entered guns drawn. Engineering, more like the networking heart of the ship than an actual access to engines, appeared before them. The room wasn't that big, *Destiny II*'s design allowing for multiple smaller access points instead of one omnipotent one. To prevent what both Malavants couldn't help but note as a flaw in her predecessor's design.

It stank of rot and caramel. Avienne wrinkled her nose.

The room was squared off, panels and stations lining the walls. At its centre stood the control for the tachyon shields, an island of energized coils and throbbing buttons. Avienne loved it.

Ardin indicated the left hand of the island, and Avienne nodded, heading that way, gun still drawn. Ardin went to the right, and they both advanced slowly. Avienne spotted it first. A hand, on the ground, out of place. Translucent, with sparkling purple blood, the fingers flexed and unflexed in a slow rhythm. She hesitated for a second before turning the corner and seeing the full fallen creature.

She gasped. It couldn't have been more than a child. The Fated lay on its back, all shimmer and purple blood, not a strip of hair or clothing on her. Her eyes snapped open and Avienne jumped. The eyes were translucent as well, the purple blood throbbing behind the pupil.

Ardin joined her, not saying a word.

Avienne put her weapon away and crouched. She could see the heart slowing, the blood barely throbbing. The hand seemed to be reaching out further, as though melting into infinity. A thousand questions peppered Avienne's mind but nothing reached her lips. The Fated look to her and managed to smile without moving her lips.

"I stopped them," she whispered, her voice as grainy as her blood seemed. The Fated looked behind Avienne. The smuggler looked back and saw the damage that had been done to some of the units. And then she saw the open wires. She looked back to the Fated, the outstretched hand curled by her side, seared black and half melted.

"You stopped them, all right," Avienne said, and the creature smiled again before the blood stopped flowing. The sparkle in the blood vanished and the skin became opaque, as though a warm breath had been blown into a cold glass container.

Avienne wanted to do something, say something. She didn't even know her name or what kind of creature she was, only that she looked like a child and smelled of sugar. Avienne's stomach turned and she stood up and walked out for some fresh air.

Ardin joined her within a few minutes. He didn't ask.

"The damage isn't that bad. I managed to contact the others and we've reactivated sensors. Looks like Elsa and Litras took out most of the creatures. Layela will meet us back on the bridge."

Avienne nodded. Ardin started walking towards the lift, but she called after him. "What was that? I mean, that girl? What was she?"

Ardin walked back to her. "We've met one of them before. A rare Fated. They have a long name, but Mirialers call them Star Children. They can travel space, become one with it." He hesitated and looked down. "And they reproduce by osmosis. Just, just one at a time, I guess. A lone traveller, but one that could get in this ship easily, under the right control."

Avienne exhaled sharply to control her nausea. "You mean that was the last one?"

"The only one. There's always only the last one."

Avienne pushed herself from the wall, punched it sidelong and stormed off towards the bridge. "Let's go. I'm getting pretty pissed with these people. Blood and bones, they're about to encounter a world of hurt!"

CHAPTER 30

▌NEED TO SPEAK to them," Layela said, holding Ardin's gaze.

"Tell me you're not planning on playing martyr and giving yourself to them?" Avienne asked from tactical, her brow furrowed. "Because I'll have to hit you."

Ardin sighed and Layela raised a hand to stop him. "Nobody's giving anything up. Not today. But we need to get to Mirial, and we need to get there now. They might be able to help us."

"They tried to kill us," Avienne said, glancing towards Patros.

Layela shook her head. "The Ralis tried that. I don't think the ships out there are acting on much more than false promises and fear."

"Two powerful things," Litras offered.

"Then we'll offer them something better," Layela said, glancing at Ardin.

Ardin nodded and gave her a quick grin. "You're on," he whispered as he turned on the communications channels.

She took a deep breath. The First among the Ralis wanted the knife? For Ardice, she was willing to bring it. But on her terms, only.

"This is Layela Delamores, Keeper of Mirial," she did not stumble on the title as she would have once had, nor did she hesitate in using it. If not her, than who? Ardice? It had never been her intention to let that happen. Not then. Not now.

"Mirial and I need your help. We cannot reach the First Star, not with the fallen tunnel, but if you could help us rebuild, or re-initialize, we'll be able to reach it."

The airwaves remained silence, so she continued. They were afraid of losing everything. She could understand that.

"You have no reason to trust me, but believe me when I tell you: Mirial wants to save you. And I want to save you. But we need your help. I don't know what the Ralis are after, or why, but I do know that helping Mirial is my first priority."

The ships stared at her silently.

"They're not a receptive bunch," Avienne mumbled.

Elsa appeared beside Layela, making her jump a bit. The Berganda looked at her and whispered, "Tell them about Ardice. Tell them everything." Layela raised an eyebrow—she'd never discussed Ardice with Elsa. And she'd barely seen Elsa in the past decade. Layela reached up and passed the back of her hand on Elsa's cheek, the skin so smooth and hiding her age.

She nodded and turned back to the screen.

"I want to see you," she said. "I want to see you, and I want you to see me. And then I will tell you about Mirial's legacy."

Within moments, video feeds were coming up, until hundreds of faces filled the view screen—ether creatures from across the worlds, some with origins she couldn't even discern. Others had anatomy so different from her own that she couldn't tell if they were even alive. She tried not to stare at one that looked like a giant pile of mashed potatoes.

Ardin cleared his throat. "You're on." He stood near her. Elsa stayed beside her, too.

"I had a daughter, ten years ago," she said, reaching out to take Ardin's hand. "And I gave her up." Ardin squeezed her fingers. "I gave her up, because I didn't want her to be the next Keeper of Mirial. Because I had never wanted to be the Keeper of Mirial." The little faces in front of her shifted. Some looked uncomfortable. Some looked angry, others betrayed no thoughts. "I didn't want to be Keeper, and I felt that the only way to be free was to let the new star take over with a new Keeper, so that I could then find my daughter and be free."

She let go of Ardin's hand and held both her hands before her. "I'm sorry. I'm sorry I couldn't be the Keeper you needed, and I'm sorry I couldn't be the mother my daughter needed. I can't necessarily make things right, but I want to try. I need to try. And I can't do it without you."

A guttural voice sounded. She couldn't identify the speaker, there were too many video feeds. "The Ralis say that they can break the shackles of Mirial from us. How do we know you're not just a glorified jailer?"

"I'm not sure what the Ralis are speaking of, but I will find out. And no, I'm not a glorified jailer. If Mirial only provides shackles, then I'm a prisoner with you. I've already admitted I want to be free so badly that I was willing to give up ten years with my daughter."

Another voice, this one more effeminate. "They said they needed the knife. What if your daughter must die?"

She bit back her anger. "If an innocent child must die, any innocent child, whether mine or yours, then it's too high a price. We've all lost enough children."

One by one, the faces vanished from the screen, until only one remained, a long-haired Senari, which would be mistaken for human if not for the fully purple eyes. She spoke with a thick accent, dropping every second syllable.

"Then remember, Keeper, that by helping you, we put the lives of our children in your hands."

"I understand," Layela said. She wondered if she would have to betray their children to save her own.

***

The ship docked barely an hour later. Layela and Ardin were waiting to greet the Senari, who had been selected to represent the Fated. Layela was fairly certain the decision had been made to make the human Keeper more comfortable, which insulted and saddened Layela.

"Welcome aboard the *Destiny II*," Ardin said as soon as she crossed the threshold, her robes dancing around her ankles. "I am Captain Ardin Malavant. My crew will assist you with whatever help you need."

She nodded in acknowledgment. "I am Sirse of the Senari. We are here to assist you in whatever capacity we can, to help you return to Mirial."

"We appreciate your help, Sirse," Layela said, and Sirse lowered her head in greeting.

"Keeper."

"How shall we proceed?" Ardin asked. They still weren't certain why the Fated had asked to board the *Destiny II*, but having little choice, had agreed. Regardless of their peaceful demeanour right now, they were still vastly outnumbered.

"We can restart the tunnel, we believe, by jolting the mechanism into activity from this end. We have confirmation from the other end of the tunnel that the gate seems intact, and only the flow of tachyons was disrupted."

"From the other side of the tunnel?" Ardin asked, and Layela jumped in.

"The Fated who helped us escape the Ralis. Are they all right?"

Sirse lowered her head slightly. "They are. The Ralis seem to be in a holding pattern. They have captured the Mirial ships but have not made demands or threatened any of the remaining ships. Until someone attacks anew or negotiations begin, we fear not much will happen. They've decided to wait, for now. Especially as they've heard of your imminent return."

Layela wasn't certain if the Senari engaged in sarcasm, so she decided to take her words at face value. "Very well. How shall we get the flow of tachyons moving again?"

The purple eyes shifted slightly. "We shall detonate some ships to garner the energy and restart the mechanism."

"Some ships?" Ardin asked. "Which ships?"

Sirse looked at him, unblinking. Suddenly, she didn't seem human at all. "Whichever ones we can do without, yet which are loaded with enough weapons and a strong enough energy core. We'll worry about that."

"What about the mine ship?" Layela asked. "There's still one out there, and that's loaded with a fairly hefty explosive device."

"Mine ship?" The Senari glanced her way.

"The white ship sitting beside ours. We'll send the specs over," Ardin answered.

"Very well," she said. This time, she turned fully towards Layela. "Keeper, you know why the Ralis want the knife, do you not?"

Layela felt herself flush. "I'm not sure."

Sirse nodded, staring with her large, unblinking eyes. Layela felt a sweat break across her brow, and she heard the voice in her mind. *The blood will tighten the connection with Mirial. Mirial does not take gifts back, Keeper, although at times they become harder to see.*

Layela gasped and Ardin took a protective step in front of her. She reached for his arm. "It's all right." She looked at Sirse. "I don't need ether for you to be able to send me a message, though. That's you, not me."

"It's not. You need ether to receive a message of ether. Otherwise,

I would need to be in direct contact with your exposed skin. Why do you think they want the knife, Keeper?"

Waves of fatigue washed over Layela as she answered. "To establish the connection between Ardice and Mirial. They think they can control her."

Sirse lowered her head in acknowledgement, her eyes still trained on Layela. "And, if the Ralis believe they can control something, Keeper, it means that they can."

She took a step back. "We will await the schematics. You should know that the tunnel will in all likelihood fail after we jumpstart it. The chances of our channelling exactly the required energy into the mechanism are poor. We will probably fry the gates. And, without the gates, whoever proceeds down the tunnel will not return."

"We understand," Layela whispered. Ardin rested a hand on her lower back, but the heat of it couldn't keep the chill from her spine.

CHAPTER 31

AVIENNE WAITED NERVOUSLY in her quarters. This was ridiculous. So painfully ridiculous she wanted to scream. Space travel was only fun if you could *get* places. Without tunnels, no propulsion system would get you anywhere fast. To be trapped in the same star system forever… She sat down and lowered her head to her hands, watching her red hair fill her vision as it spilled forward.

It was her choice, and she had made it. She had always known she would make this choice. Leaving Ardin forever…she couldn't do it. Not all of the adventures in the universe were worth deserting her brother, though she feared being trapped. She'd make the best of it. Maybe a planet, if there still was a planet, could prove as much fun to explore as all of space. She doubted it, but she was willing to find out.

A knock came at her door and she stood. "Come in," she said, positioning herself against the wall. Gobran and Patros entered. Patros kept trying to catch her eyes to seek answers in them, but she refused to look at him directly. What Gobran was thinking was anybody's guess.

"Thanks for coming," she started, cringing at her own words. "Well, of course you came. I ordered you to." She grinned, and nobody returned a smile. "Well, let's sit down, shall we."

She'd set the chairs in a circle instead of facing them both, so that they were all equals. So that they were all in this together, and a very selfish part of her hoped they would be.

"We'll be re-activating the tunnel within the next few hours, thanks to the Fated," she said, forcing herself to remain seated and not fidget. "The *Destiny II* will go through, and a few others ships, as well." They were starting to smile, so before they could raise their hopes too high, she blurted out: "But we won't be able to come back."

"We won't?" Gobran asked. She looked to Patros, who revealed nothing of what he was thinking. She'd have to remember to suggest that he take up poker.

"The tunnel mechanism will more than likely fry out. And we're not exactly a priority on Solaria's list, plus they have plenty of other worries right now, so we probably won't see it back up in our lifetimes." She leaned back and let out a long breath. "Once we cross to Mirial, if we make it, we won't be coming back."

She looked at each of them in turn. "You've both served with me for the past few years, and I couldn't have asked for a better crew. *The Dessicate* was a fine ship, and may Jaru and she travel the stars forever." She swallowed hard. They deserved better. But right now, she was just worried about losing the rest of her crew, as well.

"I can't offer you much. If you who choose to come, you will be welcome to share in whatever future we find there." She looked to Patros, who was now looking down. She forced herself to keep speaking. "If you who decide to stay, I have monies spread here and there. Not a lot, but enough to keep you comfortable. I'll share all of my access codes with you, and it's yours to do with as you'd like. I won't be needing it anymore." She hadn't meant for the bitter note to slip into her last words.

"Do you have to go?" Patros whispered.

Avienne looked at him, dumbfounded. "Ardin is going. Of course I have to go." She softened, this time unable to keep the plea from her voice. Blood and bones, she was getting softer by the minute. "He might need my help, Patros. I can't abandon him."

Patros nodded. "Then I'm coming, too." Avienne was afraid the smile would split her face. This time, his expression was easy to read.

Her voice softened with the burden of the decision. "Patros, you'll never see your home again. You meant to go back there. And I meant to visit with you."

He shrugged. "I might make it back. I'll stay with you until the end, then I'll try and reach home. I might make it, I might not. It doesn't matter now." He gave her a gentle smile. "I'm coming with you. You were willing to give up years for me, to visit my home. I can't believe you'd think I would be willing to do any less for you!"

He winked at her and she smiled, her heart shedding the fear of losing him.

She turned to Gobran. "What about you, old man? One last ride home?"

Gobran chuckled, but Avienne wasn't certain if he was laughing or crying. "Home, Avienne Malavant. I don't know where that is, anymore. I fought for Mirial and I lost her and my family for twenty years. We lived in peace and I lost my daughter and my eyesight. I just don't know, anymore."

Avienne knelt before Gobran and took his hands in her own. "Home can be with us, Gobran. You'll always have a home with us."

He tipped his head sideways. "I never buried my daughter, you know." His whispers cut Avienne to pieces and she closed her eyes, forgetting everything else but Gobran. Sturdy, loyal Gobran. "By the time I made it back to Thalos IV, they had cleaned everything up. They'd thrown her in a communal grave. Just like that! Another unnamed traveler from a distant world come to lose her life on Thalos IV!" His voice grew more pointed, and he took a deep breath. When he spoke again, he had regained some control.

"I don't know where home is anymore, but I know that part of me will never find peace again. I've accepted that a long time ago. I gave everything to Mirial, once, and I used to hope I would one day be buried in her sacred soil. But not anymore. Now, I just want to be buried on Thalos IV, in an unnamed grave, so that my blood can mix with the same earth that absorbed my child."

"Gobran," she choked on his name. She opened her eyes and let the plea fall into her voice. "Don't do this. You don't have to come, but don't live your life just waiting for death. You mean so much to so many people. Don't let go now. You've fought for so long." She suddenly grew angry. "And, you know what? I won't have a second-in-command be so dramatic! I will allow for no martyrs! You can stay, but only if you have something to do. Only if you have plans to spend my money and spend it all and well! Blood and bones, old man, if you just go all pathetic on me and leave us like this, I swear I will tie you up and throw you into a closet until we reach Mirial, your wishes be damned!"

Gobran started wheezing and Avienne feared he was about to keel over until she realized he was laughing. She grinned. "That's better. Now, out with it. What are you going to do?"

He looked toward her. "I'm going to Thalos IV."

"Gobran…"

"Let me finish! Have some respect for your elders, daughter of Malavant." Avienne shot a grin towards Patros. "I'm going to go drain your accounts. And then I'll re-open a shop in a nice location. I'll specialize in maps of mythical beings, and spread stories of Mirial until the day I die. I'll have lived so well and expensively that they'll have to throw me in a common grave. A strange desire, but then we both win."

He paused and squeezed her hands. "Trust this old man. I won't go down without some fun. But I'm tired, and I don't want to face another fight. You always told me to be independent, Avienne. Now let me go and be independent." His voice softened. "I'm finally ready for that retirement."

Avienne stood and squeezed his hands one more time before letting go of them. "All right. That sounds like a wonderful plan. I'll make sure you get on board a reputable ship and they get you to your destination. And I'll give you everything you need. All of my accounts had best be drained, Gobran."

"Or what? You'll come from Mirial to beat me up? You'll rebuild the tunnel with the express purpose of scolding me."

"Oh no. Too much trouble. I'll just invent a new propulsion system to hunt you down."

He nodded and looked serious. "That, I'll believe. Avienne, there are no other tunnels from Mirial. If you're thinking there's another one like the Seeders' tunnel…it's not one I know of."

She shrugged. "Maybe I can visit the Seeders, then."

"Best not. Exploding stars can be nasty, and you'd head into radiation death or a black hole. If the tunnel even survived."

"Well, I'll figure something out." She reached down and hugged him. "Thanks for everything, old man."

He hugged her back but didn't say anything. She didn't need him to. She'd had enough goodbyes for one lifetime.

***

"I can't believe we're going back to Mirial," Elsa whispered, her eyes as vast as the stars in the surrounding sky.

Layela sat beside her, running a hand through the leaves of her hair. The Berganda were beautiful, and Josmere's daughters were strong, and so were their daughters, in turn.

"Elsa, I think you should go join your sisters, now. I think it's time to say goodbye."

Elsa didn't look at her with the hurt Layela had expected, but rather with tenderness. "Oh, Mother Layela, don't worry about me. I'll be fine. I want to go back to Mirial. Litras said she'd stay with me."

"There's no guarantee we'll make it. And we may lose Mirial, the planet and the sun. It might take a long time before we find a planet to land on again, if ever. You need the earth, Elsa."

Elsa looked back out to the stars, her voice taking on a serious tone she had never heard on the Berganda. At least not since before her mind had been ripped to shreds.

"Layela, I'm old. I know I don't seem so, at least not to you, but I can feel my skin shrivel around me as each day passes. I won't be here much longer, and I want to see Mirial with my own eyes at least once more before I pass." She turned to Layela and took her hand. "I want to die on the land where my mother died to give birth to me. If not on that planet, then by the sun it orbits. My sisters and nieces will stay here, safe. But I want to go home, with you, for however much longer I have."

Elsa reached up and wiped a tear from Layela's cheek. "Thank you," she whispered, and then looked back towards the stars. Layela stood up and kissed the Berganda gently on her head.

She didn't want to bury Elsa, or Ardice. Or any other children.

She had meant at least one thing she had told the Fated, and that was that enough children had already died.

***

Avienne double and triple-checked all weapons and shields, rerouting a few through different networks in case of another internal attack. If their engineering room had been destroyed, they would have been more useless than an empty oxygen tank in the middle of space.

The bridge was quiet, which she appreciated. Everyone hid somewhere in the decks below, weighing their future and their options. She groaned when the lift doors opened.

"I brought you a gift," Litras said, sporting her usual toothy grin. She handed Avienne another bottle of astium. Or maybe she'd stolen the first one from her quarters.

"No thanks," Avienne turned back toward her station. "It's been a while. Now might not be the best time to start again." She threw Litras a grin. "But, tell you what, if we make it out of there alive, I'll drink it in your honour."

Litras' grin broadened. "I'm coming with you! We can share it on Mirial."

"Are you? Great. Wonderful."

Litras grew quiet and Avienne turned to look at her. The grin was gone, her eyes looking deep into Avienne's, or beyond her. She was about to make a joke, but Litras narrowed her eyes a bit and stilled the smuggler's tongue.

"Not many people left that are like you, Avienne Malavant," Litras said, her voice hushed. "How much would you give up for your family? How much of yourself would you re-invent to save them?"

Avienne offered a crooked grin, growing more and more uncomfortable under the Kilita's stare. "I gave up drinking, Litras, which was my one escape." She cocked her head to the side. "Well, I guess Patros is a good replacement, now that I think about it."

Litras' face broke into a grin again. "I'm glad we'll get to travel together for a good long time yet, Avienne Malavant." She turned on her heel before Avienne could crack a joke. Litras exited as Ardin entered.

"Must she come?" Avienne said quickly, before the lift doors fully closed.

"She's useful enough in a fight, and knows a lot of stuff we don't. Those are pretty good assets, right now."

"Assets. Nice word. You running a business?"

He gave her a grin, then sobered up. "I'm sorry." He hesitated. "I mean, I'm sorry I couldn't understand your desire to live on a planet, so many years ago, Avienne. I'm sorry I'm about to trap you on one."

Avienne shrugged. "It's all past, Ardin. I'm not so great at staying put, so we'll have to make sure we can get back. I know Ardice is already there, but I'll need to get away from the loving trio that will be you, Layela and Ardice. Too much for a smuggler to take."

Ardin almost cracked a smile, but he pulled her in a hug instead. She hugged him back without hesitation, Litras' words echoing in her mind.

How much would you give up for your family.

***

Gobran reached the shuttle two hours later with his few belongings in tow—a few pieces of clothing, the captain's chips containing all of her access codes, and a gun she insisted he carry. He walked as confidently as he could. He knew the layout of the *Destiny II,* but he didn't know the shuttle. He didn't know the race of Fated that would accompany him, but he was curious to learn more about them.

"We are ready to depart," a voice said to his left, and he was grateful for the simple indication of location. He hated people just taking his arm and dragging him around as though he couldn't muster an ounce of independence. The Mirialers were proud and respected and understood pride. They chose independence in all things, and so respected his need for it.

Avienne Malavant had been his main supporter, forcing him to stretch beyond where even he believed he could. He had learned to command a ship again. To feel the life of the great beast burst to life, to know when it suffered injury, when it needed a little bit more power or care. He had learned all of these things because he hadn't been allowed to stop. He hadn't been allowed to wallow.

And she was right again. Now was not the time to wallow, not after everything he'd seen and done. He could still do more. He could change the way people accessed and viewed maps. Who better to do so than a cartographer who had become blind at a later age? He could understand the challenges of sight and the intricacies of cartography?

He grew excited at the thought, but a noise caught his attention as he reached the shuttle. He felt the shift in the air that indicated the shuttle was near—a slight change in the movement of the air around him. And he also heard a slight movement to his right.

Avienne. They had already said as much of a goodbye as both intended to, but she had come to see him off. Without letting him know. Once, during a long stay in port, trapped by incompetent officers, she had spoken to him about how she had been made to say goodbye to Captain Calin, the man who had raised her, while in a shuttle bay. And he remembered her grief at losing her then second-in-command in a shuttle bay, years later. She had joked that all of the worse goodbyes were in shuttle bays because they were so gaudy and horribly decorated. They just oppressed the mood even further.

He had chuckled. But he now understood. Shuttle bays were for goodbyes, and Avienne wanted to be there for him without having to say goodbye. Gobran loved her even more for it. And he supported her in this last thing, as she had always supported him.

"Tell me, where do you hail from?" he asked jovially.

"The Stttsri Quadrant," the young male voice answered.

"Ah, I know that one well. Do you know the story of how the tunnel came to be built leading to your homeworld? It's actually quite a funny little tale…" he became engrossed in telling it as he entered the shuttle and heard the door shut behind him. The shuttle was smooth and only a slight change in the internal compression alerted him that they'd exited the shuttle bay.

The young pilot was now telling a story of his own, but Gobran barely listened. He imagined Avienne singing for him as she had for so many others. Singing the song he was now certain he would never hear again, as he left Mirial behind forever.

The same song he had sung to the *Destiny* as she burnt in the atmosphere of Mirial, almost two decades ago.

You imagine too much, old man, he chided himself, and yet he hummed the tune as his nostalgia battled his excitement.

Welcome home, sailor.

CHAPTER 32

S EVERAL OF THE ships would be joining them, the final journey to Mirial as necessary for them as it seemed to be for Layela and Ardin. They were coming to support them in the inevitable battle, or so they had put it.

Their plan had been disclosed as little as possible over the Fated Link, for fear of the Ralis listening in. They might be too late, regardless, since they'd enquired on the state of the bridge mechanism on the other end. But, of course, the hope was that the Ralis expected them to bring the knife, and they wouldn't expect full out resistance.

Layela stared at the small fleet that would accompany them. Ships hovered around *Destiny II*, about twenty in all. Some were small, others barely noticeable with their strange opalescent hulls. One was three times the size of her ship, and she hoped it would put up as good a fight.

"Litras?"

"Yes, Keeper?" Litras perked up from where she sat on the bridge. Everyone on the ship seemed to be here, now. She guessed no one wanted to miss the action. That, and everybody would be needed once people started firing at them on the other side. An inevitable outcome to any of their outings, it seemed!

"Won't the Ralis just be able to take over the fleet? We'll be right beside them. Won't they be strong enough to just take everyone over, then?"

229 | MARIE BILODEAU

"Incoming message," Avienne said. "They're ready to jumpstart the tunnel. Counting down thirty Solarian seconds."

"Well, this is it," Ardin said from the captain's chair, his gaze locked on the tunnel in front of him. "Raise tachyon shields. This might be a bumpy ride, so brace yourselves." Everyone on the bridge tightened their safety harnesses and clutched their stations.

"Fifteen seconds," Avienne counted down. "Tachyon shields are up."

"Litras?"

A light drew their eyes towards the tunnel. Where the mine ship had floated, only a remaining explosion lingered. The light had dissipated quickly, as space robbed the fire of its necessary oxygen, leaving behind a slew of debris. Several tubular ships in the blast radius captured the energy at their glowing cores before redirecting it towards a ship that was harnessed to the bridge mechanism. The ship glowed red and the gate soon did as well.

"Now we see," Avienne said to no one in particular. The tachyon gates didn't do anything at first, but then the blue energy indicators came on, glowing bright against the red ship. The ship detached itself and manoeuvred away as the gate began accelerating particles into tachyon particles. Within moments, a full tunnel flickered to life, its blue hues a welcome sight against the dark backdrop.

Layela would have cheered if her stomach weren't in knots. Everyone on the bridge leaned forward as Ardin gave the command that sealed their fate.

"Patros, take us in. Let's head back to Mirial."

"Aye, Captain." The ship headed steadily towards the tunnel, the great visors closing over the viewing port to protect the non-Fated on the bridge.

Avienne coordinated with the other ships, to prevent them from colliding in the tunnel.

"Litras?" Layela asked one last time as the *Destiny II* began shaking and groaning.

"It's not smooth, but it's stable," Avienne reported. Layela gritted her teeth and looked to the Kilita.

"I guess we'll just have to find a way," she said.

Layela clutched her seat, not finding much comfort in either Avienne's words or the Kilita's.

***

Captain Kat of the *Victorious* sat alone on the bridge, stubbornly adhering to a duty that no longer demanded anything of her. Sheathed in darkness in an attempt to save energy, the bridge still glowed from various warning lights, all designed to get attention from a crew that might not be manning that particular station. She could see them all from her peripheral vision, but ignored them. She knew what they meant.

The red light on the right indicated no engine power. The one below it, on the tactical station, marked the damage to the hull. And the others, all of the others on the left, indicated engineering failures to the decks, life support systems, and the energy cells. She was musing that they should just develop a giant light that indicated "your ship is dead," when a new light flashed on tactical and grabbed her attention. It flashed blue, meaning something had changed in the space around them, not in the ship itself.

She hopped off her chair and brought up the information on tactical, the view screen flickering as the data filed by. The translator unit from sensor codes to basic language seemed busted now, too. But she could at least make out the coordinates.

She activated the main view screen, hoping it still worked. The light filled the dark bridge until the brightness adjusted, leaving Gilane with floating spots blocking her vision.

She blinked them away and gasped. The tunnel flashed blue before her! But she'd made sure the tachyons were disrupted. How had they jumpstarted the tachyon flow?

That doesn't matter! She scolded herself for lacking focus. It didn't matter *how* it had been done. What mattered was *who*.

If it was the Ralis, it might mean that they'd managed to capture the Keeper and were bringing her back. If it was the Keeper, that meant she'd be arriving here, and would be counting on some help. They couldn't have gotten very far along the tunnel before it had collapsed. A few exits, at most, meaning they were near. And so they'd be arriving shortly.

It didn't matter why they were coming back, how they'd managed it, or what exactly would be spilling out of the tunnel. The Keeper was involved in some way, and that was all Captain Kat needed to know.

She took stock of her ship. She had some weapons left, but almost no propulsion. That would make aiming nearly impossible. But she could help, and they would help, and today her ship would earn its name: *Victorious.*

She switched on full ship communications. "This is Captain Kat. The tunnel has just been reactivated. It's unclear at this time who activated it, and who's returning to Mirial, but I believe it's safe to assume the Keeper is involved." She took a deep breath. "All hands to battle stations. Prepare to fight, for Mirial."

She turned off the comm. She wasn't certain how her words were received by the civilians who dwelt on the dying ship, but she could imagine how any Mirialer would take it.

Once upon a time, they would have fought by themselves, their stubborn pride forcing them to stand alone against any enemy of Mirial's. But now, with a crippled ship, a boarded ship and one missing ship, Captain Kat wasn't fool enough to believe they could win the day alone.

Her crew appeared on the bridge, filing out from the lift with varying levels of enthusiasm, but each with purpose marking their every movement.

"Open communications to all ships," she ordered. She took a deep breath and prepared her words.

After years of stubborn independence, it was time for Mirial to ask for help.

***

The First among the Ralis had regained most of his arm's movement. A huge victory for his freedom. He stood, pleased and worried. Time had taught him many lessons, and the main one he clung to now was that desires led to downfalls. Without any desires, there could be no failures. No fear, no worry, just steady movement toward an undetermined and unimportant goal. All flesh vanished, eventually. The ultimate goal and unavoidable end.

But he desired something; he had limited time to see his goal achieved. To desire and not accomplish would lead to discontentment, and a difficult passing, without peace.

They were so close now that he could only focus on the potential failure. He could brace himself, but not his people. They all expected victory now. He hoped today would not teach them a harsh lesson.

The ship's communications flared to life.

"This is captain Gilane Kat of Mirial's *Victorious*. As you can see, the tunnel is now reactivated. I'm not sure who activated it, or why, but it's safe to say the Keeper is involved, and will need our help." There was a pause, a hesitation. The Mirialers were a broken people, and he could hear in her voice that this captain knew it. But her desire was so strong that she chose to ignore it. "Our ship is wounded. We can't do this without you. For Mirial, help us save the Keeper."

The line broke. The First walked towards the large windows that adorned the *Sun's Barrow*. The Mirialers were on a useless chase on the *Lady Mirial*. The child was in the Ralis' control, even though she failed to realize it. The younger Fated could easily be controlled, but the First hoped their own desires would lead them in the right direction, rather than forcing the Ralis to resort to mind control. Only the Kilita deserved this treatment, and only because one among them had defiled the order of the universe.

He sighed, the flesh around him sagging and heavy. They all wanted the same thing, in the end. The Mirialers, the Keeper, the child, the Fated and the Ralis, they all wanted the exact same thing.

If only they possessed enough wisdom to see that.

CHAPTER 33

THE SHIP JOSTLED for what felt like hours before Avienne announced: "We're coming to the end. Mirial is up ahead."

"Can you tell what's waiting for us?" Ardin asked, leaning forward.

Avienne looked for any signal on any channel, or maybe some shift in the edge of the tunnel indicating radiation increases, but nothing came up. Her sensors only went as far as the tachyons, relying on their patterns to indicate shifts, so they couldn't see anything past the last gate. "Nope! No indication whatsoever. We're flying blind." Avienne automatically looked up to Gobran's station, but looked back down, feeling silly. He would have chuckled though, she was certain.

"As soon as we exit, I want our energy shields up and our weapons ready to fire, understood?"

"Clearly!" Avienne had managed to repair a few weapons with Biolt's help, but hardly enough to win a war. Still, she breathed a sigh of relief when more than half of the weapons popped from the hull without difficulty. The other half wouldn't be going anywhere without some serious dry-dock repairs.

The ship grumbled from deep within its core and the hull began to clatter and shake. "Biolt?" Ardin asked the chief engineer.

"The tunnel is starting to falter. Two of the junction gates are failing. We should make it."

"Should…?" Avienne grumbled along with the ship, almost

hitting her head on her station as the ship bucked left and then right.

"We're almost at the end, but the tunnel is starting to fail!"

"Punch the engines," Ardin screamed. "Get us out of here *now!*"

Avienne reconnected two other weapons to extra energy sources, trying to finish reconfiguring the entire weapons grid. It would give them fewer weapons, but more energy per weapon. She swore as the clanking ship resulted in her missing the correct key combination. Her fingers glided on the keys, trying to regain precious lost seconds.

The ship jolted sideways and down, its artificial gravity systems failing for a few seconds. The air was forced out of Avienne's lungs as the belt pulled her back against her seat. The ship restabilized with a great clunk that reverberated across the hull.

"We're almost out!" Patros shouted, fear tinting his voice. Avienne grinned. *Bet he regrets agreeing to come with me, now.*

"Tachyon shields holding," Biolt said, "but the tunnel is failing. We need to get out!"

"Avienne!" Ardin shouted, and Avienne fired their rear cannons at full power. It would waste some of their attack capacity, but it would also get them out a few seconds earlier.

The ship jostled and their velocity decreased as they spun out of the tunnel sideways, with Patros trying to stabilize them despite the cling of tachyons on their shields. Their stabilizing engines were being fried by the change in velocity.

Avienne's attention was drawn back to her console. Emergency signals flared up. "Two of the Fated ships were torn apart at exit, and—blood and bones!" She fought the urge to duck as the *Sun's Barrow* flew right over them, missing them by barely a kilometre—the centimetres of the spacefaring world.

"Three other Fated ships made it." Ardin said from the captain's chair. "Let's find our allies! Biolt, Patros, stabilize us. Avienne, are we ready to shoot stuff?"

"I'm always ready to shoot stuff!" Avienne shouted back. "We're getting quick messages from several ships that they're ready to help us. What should I shoot first? The big ship? Or the hundreds of tiny ships facing off with us?" She switched the view screen to show the Fated ships under the Ralis' control, which had assumed a formation resembling the one they'd faced outside of Burnice.

"Sirse," Ardin called over the comm, "is this the only formation the Fated know?"

Her voice rang as clearly as if she stood beside them. "It's a formation sent to us by the Ralis. The Fated don't really have any mixed battle formation."

"Prepare for our orders," Ardin said. "Okay, so they're always using this formation. It's good, but it's not infallible. What do we know about our last encounter?"

"There are a heck of a lot more of them than us," Avienne said, " but they're poor shots. And they're counting on a straight-on attack so they don't shoot each other in the back."

"So we approach from five different quadrants quickly enough to avoid ridiculous amounts of fire, and we shoot with all we have? Do we even have enough weapons? Sirse?"

A strangled gurgle pierced the system. "Sirse?" Ardin asked again, looking at the comm unit as though he could see right through it.

"Captain Malavant," the voice came back crisp. Avienne would have sighed with relief had it not sounded so flat. "You will give us the ceremonial knife and you will be allowed to live. There will even be a place for you on Mirial, once this is all over."

Ardin sat back in his chair and turned off the comm.

The Fated ships surrounded them now, and the *Lady Mirial* and *Victorious*, the only two ships potentially not manned by Fated, limped in space and didn't respond to any call.

Avienne sighed and sat back, offering Patros a smile as he looked back at her.

"Guess I don't get to shoot anything."

***

Layela's stomach leapt to her throat and iron filled her mouth. Her tongue grew numb and she could feel sweat trickling down the sides of her face. She closed her eyes and took a deep, steadying breath, Sirse's voice slicing her mind into dizziness.

"Give us the ceremonial knife and you will be allowed to live. There will even be a place for you on Mirial once this is all over."

Layela took another deep breath and re-opened her eyes. Litras knelt before her.

"It's the Ralis. They're drawing everything they can to control the Fated. They're an old race. They can have such powers."

Litras put a steadying hand on Layela's arm, warmth comforting her. The nausea and dizziness vanished, leaving her drained. "Can you stop them? You helped Patros," Layela whispered as Sirse's voice boomed again in the background, the same words spoken at the same clip. Layela tried not to think about how helpless the confident Fated must feel.

"I can't," Litras said. "My control of ether is limited in this realm." She stared at Layela. "It's the ether that's hurting you. It's battering you down to get you to speak to it again."

Layela frowned. "That makes no sense. I'm not Keeper anymore. I'm nothing to Mirial."

Litras shrugged. "Then why do they want the knife so badly, if only your daughter can communicate with Mirial now?" She stood up and went back to her chair, strapping herself in.

The noise on the bridge faded to the background as Layela took a deep breath. Avienne, Ardin and Biolt were throwing ideas at each other, each sounding more desperate than the last, but Layela focused within, instead. Why was she feeling so ill?

She pulled the knife out of her boot and looked down at it. Why were they fighting so hard to gain this knife? What possible value could it hold for them... *Ardice.* They needed the knife to pass down the ether. They needed Ardice to bleed for Mirial before she could fully tap into it, just as Layela had done, and her sister had, before her.

Which meant Ardice had not automatically become Keeper of Mirial. Which also meant...

She stood and moved beside Ardin. The conversation on the bridge stopped as all eyes turned to Layela.

"I want to talk to her. To them all," she said. Ardin opened his mouth in protest, but then bit his words and indicated that the channel was open.

"Sirse. I know you're not doing this under your own control. And I'm sorry you've been trapped. First Among the Ralis, hear me. You can't fight us using the Fated. And you can't have the knife. You can't keep Ardice, either. What you can have, is me, and this." She swiped the blade finely across her palm, biting deep into the flesh, the shudder of pain replaced by one of ecstasy as Mirial flooded in her again, as greedy for her as Layela was. The bond sealed deep within her was easily reforged and Mirial infused her with ether.

Layela could see the wisps of ether, thousands of them, flowing from the *Sun's Barrow* to every ship, even the *Destiny II,* though a protective barrier protected each of the Fated.

237 | MARIE BILODEAU

Layela held up her palm and squeezed it into a fist, her blood trickling down her arm and onto the floor of the ship, igniting ether as it touched the air.

She grasped the ether and hurled it around the *Sun's Barrow*, shearing each of those threads so easily she wanted to shout and cry. Her hand began to tremble and she lowered it, letting her eyes take in the details of space before her. The weak glow of Mirial did not impact the ether dancing throughout the system, as though the large concentration of Fated had somehow sealed some of it in place instead of traveling through the universe.

She smiled as she heard Sirse's voice. "I… Thank you, Keeper. What shall we do next?"

She looked at Ardin, and knew from the pain in his eyes that her own were one of blue and one green again. "It was me or Ardice, Ardin. I think that fate was sealed when the new First Star was destroyed."

He took her hand in his and kissed it, meeting her gaze unflinchingly. "What now?"

Avienne reported, "Some of the Fated ships are moving up, weapons armed. I don't think they're friendly!"

"I thought you'd broken the Ralis' control over them?" Ardin asked as he looked down at his screen, releasing her hand.

"I did!" Layela said, sitting back down and buckling herself in.

"The Ralis promised them freedom from the First Star," Litras said. "A lot of them will buy into that."

"Freedom?" Avienne said, her hands gliding over her station. "It's not like Mirial hunts them down or anything." She looked up to Layela and raised an eyebrow. "Wait. Or do you?"

"Of course not," Layela said, eliciting a grin from the redhead. "But I guess they fear what happened before. That the ether will vanish again and take them with it." She watched the ether dancing around the solar system, escaping Mirial at a much less impressive quantity than before.

"Litras, is that even possible? Could they survive without Mirial? Could they really be free?"

Could I still be free? She was willing to take on the mantle of being Keeper a thousand times to keep her daughter and her family safe, but if the chance still existed of shedding it, she certainly wasn't about to let it slide by.

Litras shrugged. "I don't know. I don't think so. A lot of them would die, although some would probably adapt, survive. But at what cost?"

Layela nodded. Mirial was a fact for now, and rescuing most of the Fated hinged on her survival. Untested theories didn't matter. What mattered was getting to Ardice. Layela focused on the universe around her, on the *Lady Mirial* and the *Sun's Barrow*. She and Ardice and had shared a bond when Ardice was born. Ardice could tug on the ether, and Layela could protect her like no one else could. Those had been the most exhausting days of her life, but some of the most rewarding, as well. To have such a small being wholeheartedly depend on her had been terrifying and exhilarating.

Ten years had passed, but Ardice would probably still connect to the ether in the same way. Layela had never connected to the ether differently until she had come to Mirial, and Ardice was likely unaware of her potential. If the Ralis wanted the knife so badly, it meant that her true potential couldn't be reached without using it first.

Layela concentrated on that child. On her first cries. She remembered the tiny wrinkled fingers wrapping around her own, the small, barely opened eyes of blue and green, the little nose and a mouth that barely showed lips. She focused on Ardice's fear of the ether and how she used it as a security blanket at the same time.

Ardice's weight. So small, so fragile. And handing her over to Rose, that last kiss, the scent of the flowers she had named after her daughter—a tender, shy scent. One that required closeness to fully experience.

The heartbreak at watching the shuttle leave, with her daughter.

Ten years. Layela realized she was looking at the *Lady Mirial*. Near her aft section, in the civilian quarters, she could see Ardice. Not *see* her, but see a trail of energy. She tried to stand, but her safety belt pulled her back. "Ardin!" she said with stolen breath.

Ardin turned to her, worry in his eyes. "I see her, Ardin! Ardice! She's on the *Lady Mirial!*"

"How…" He was cut off by Avienne.

"Thirty-seven ships are in attack trajectory and accelerating. We should move, now."

Ardin tore his eyes away from Layela. "Sirse? We need to get on the *Lady Mirial*. We can dock with her if we get close enough. Can you cover us?"

"Of course." The three surviving Fated ships crossed in front of the

Destiny II. Sirse's voice boomed across the interspace communications system.

"This is Sirse of Senari. The Keeper has requested our help in securing Mirial's future. We shall give it. Whoever dares oppose the *Destiny II* shall feel our wrath. Allies are welcome."

"To the point," Avienne said. "I like that! But does that mean I don't get to shoot anything? I worked hard at getting these weapons back up, you know!"

Ardin shot her a smile. "Patros, turn us towards the *Lady Mirial.* Prepare to dock with her."

Avienne flipped Patros the schematics for the possible links with other Mirial ships.

"Aye, Captain," he said, turning around slightly to give a quick grin to Avienne.

"The Fated ships are meeting in battle." The mirth vanished from Avienne's voice. The ships, hundreds of them, of all sizes, shapes and makes, collided into each other, weapons blasting, shields glowing, explosions blooming.

Ardin leaned forward in his chair and passed his hands over his face. Layela feared for one moment that he would join the fray, unable to let others fight a battle for him. But the promise of seeing his daughter again held more pull than a battle. He kept his eyes fixed on the screen.

"Steady, Patros."

CHAPTER 34

L ORAN GRABBED THE Kilita by the front of his armour and amazed herself by pulling him up against the wall. "Tell me where they've taken her!" She breathed the words into his face, lingering centimetres from him. She didn't blink, didn't look away, keeping her sights on the orange eyes.

"I don't know," he said, his voice still tired. She banged him against the wall and let him fall, forcing him to look directly up to see her face.

"They took the Keeper's child, snatched her right out of our hands. You said they'd have our biggest weakness and you were right. How did you know? Did you know they had her?"

The Kilita sighed. "No, I didn't. But I knew they'd have your biggest weakness, or they wouldn't have left you here, like this, with so little security." He looked up at her, his eyes rimmed black from fatigue. "Would you?"

Loran took a step back, to leave him room to sit up. Olrik kept his gun trained on him.

"Why are you able to speak, still? The rest of the guards seem…lost."

He looked at her. "A trap for someone else, of course. A weakness."

Loran almost asked for whom, but a more pressing question slipped her tongue. "Where would they have taken Ardice?"

The Kilita shrugged. "I don't know." He sighed. "Think about where you'd be most vulnerable. Where would be a greatest weakness.

Chances are, they're using her to trap someone, probably the Keeper. So where would they need her?"

Loran knew immediately. *The temple of Mirial.*

She nodded to Olrik and they both withdrew to the corridor, letting other Mirialers guard the Kilita.

"The temple," he said before she could suggest it. She nodded grimly. "If it's a trap for the Keeper, they might not be expecting us."

Loran nodded again. "I don't think so. They took her when we were about to reach the secondary bridge, right in front of us. So, they don't want us to access it. They're trying to distract us."

"They don't want us taking control of the ship? Can we take the chance that they won't hurt the Keeper's daughter?"

Loran sighed and ran a hand through her short hair. There were few on board the ship who knew about the secondary bridge, and fewer still who had the skills to pilot the ship. They'd dispatched the crew, so the Mirialers had limited resources.

"Whatever plan they have," Loran said, "it hinges on *Lady Mirial* not being manned. Why else destroy the crew and keep civilians alive? Why else let us know about Ardice?"

"Why would they need us, then?"

"They don't. But maybe they need us for Ardice. Something for her?"

Loran bit her lip. If Ardice was being played to become a new controllable Keeper, then…she suddenly feared that she understood all too well.

"They need Mirialers to bear witness to their new Keeper's awakening. They want us to witness Ardice becoming the Keeper, and protect her and take care of her, as they know we will."

"What about Lady Layela?"

"We need to get to that second bridge. Keep the Kilita here, and keep the Mirialers busy here."

"What about the Keeper's daughter?"

Loran checked her weapon as she replied. "She's safe for now. They need her. But if I'm guessing right, they need something from Layela, too. That's why nothing's been happening—they're waiting for her to return!"

"Stay here," Loran said, running down the hall back towards the gardens. If she was right, they needed Layela's death to pass on the ether to Ardice.

And Loran had every intention of fulfilling her duty by securing the safety of the Keeper.

***

Captain Gilane Kat watched the sky explode around her as Fated ships rammed into each other in a flurry to protect or destroy the Keeper. The *Destiny II* had fared better than the other Mirial ships, but she still limped along as she headed toward the *Lady Mirial*. Gilane watched with interest and a bit of disappointment.

Why would they protect the Mirialers aboard the *Lady Mirial* and leave her people to die a quiet death in space? Would salvation come, or would they be taken out by one of the ships? Gilane fired her weapon at an approaching ship, which veered off course.

Gilane had to believe the Keeper had a purpose. The *Lady Mirial* transported most of Mirial's artifacts. She probably needed something there. It was the source of their betrayal, as well. Perhaps she intended to stop the enemy directly?

A ship exploded nearby, the brightness of the blast forcing Gilane to avert her eyes. The *Destiny II* veered off course as the explosion rocked it. The ship seemed to have developed a list. Its engines were failing, and reaching its destination now seemed unlikely.

Gilane went through possible scenarios in her mind. She had helped the Keeper escape, before, but the chances of survival had been quite high. Now, the only way she could help was to use her ship as a battering ram—*a* manoeuver she feared neither she nor her people would survive for very long.

There were one hundred and three Mirialers onboard her ship. She was responsible for each of their lives, and had worked hard for the honour.

Mirialers were brought up to put Mirial above all else. To always choose the needs of the First Star above their own. The First Star cared for them all, and they, her people, cared for her in return.

In Gilane's lifetime, when the glory of Mirial had faltered and failed them, a shift had begun to occur in her people's perceptions of the star.

The Lady Kilasha, Lady Layela's mother, had chosen her twin daughters over the well-being of her people. Lady Layela, in turn, had chosen her daughter's freedom above Mirial's expectations.

Gilane firmly believed the Keeper's daughter still lived, although some believed that she had been destroyed and the Keeper could not bring herself to speak about her. But no mother who had lost children, like Gilane herself had, would recover as well as the Keeper had. No mother would look at reminders of her child with hope. Whatever had happened to the Keeper's daughter, it did not involve death.

If Layela Delamores could choose her daughter over the First Star, then so could Gilane Kat.

She sat back in her chair, clutched its arms, and watched *Destiny II* limp along.

***

Loran took a different route towards the garden, in case the Ralis were watching. According to the dejected Kilita, the Ralis were smart at calculating all of the potential moves and weaknesses of their opponents.

She peered around a wall. Two guards stood uselessly. Loran took a deep breath, clutched her gun and walked in front of them. They didn't move, didn't even turn to watch her. She turned the next corner and breathed in relief. They were basically abandoned husks, as she'd started to suspect. Just shells strewn about for show. She shivered, wondering who deserved such a horrible trap.

The garden doors easily slid open. She closed and secured them before heading to the back, into the small shed. She closed the door behind her and pulled some seeds off the shelf to reveal a small access pad. She punched in the code to the secondary bridge, counting down three seconds before the floor shifted under her. It lowered for at least two levels, and an entryway appeared. She stepped through it and gagged on the smell, knowing something was wrong before her eyes adjusted to the dim lighting. She reached sideways for the lights, but the switch had been destroyed. Loran held the gun before her and stayed perfectly still while her eyes adjusted.

The lift went back up behind her, and she regretted not stepping back onto it.

Outlines began to emerge in the darkness. The main command console in the centre of the room had been smashed, wiring and metal at jagged angles. The view screen flicked on with a view away from Mirial, into the darkest region of space.

The hairs raised on the back of her neck. What if the Ralis hadn't just left traps for the Mirialers? What if they'd left *specific* traps for some of them? The Ralis were old ether creatures and they might be able to affect even the Mirialers.

She brushed the thought aside and took a step forward, cursing as she kicked a piece of rubbish which grated across the ground.

If she was correct, Layela would try to board this ship. Loran's goal was to stop her from doing that, at any cost. But if the bridge was out of commission…

There was someone in the captain's chair. She trained her gun on the outline. Someone sat there, their head slightly back, she was certain. They hadn't moved, and she debated shooting first. But it might be one of her own, come to take refuge here.

"Who's there?" she hissed, taking one more step towards a secondary station where supplies were kept. Including a light. She rested the gun on her shoulder and reached in with her other hand. She fumbled around but found the torch finally, drew it up and turned it on, careful to slit her eyes and aim away from them.

Even at its dimmest level, the light proved effective. The person came into sharp relief, the features popping out against the darkness. The silent scream and open eyes were not so decayed that Loran couldn't easily identify Erlin Gray.

She dropped the light and screamed until she retched, her echoes pounding her skull into tears.

CHAPTER 35

WHAT'S THE PLAN?" Avienne asked as the ship slipped sideways. She clung to her station. "Can we even dock if we're listing so badly?"

"With difficulty," Biolt replied. "We didn't anticipate getting half our stabilizing engines destroyed by stray tachyons."

"Right," Ardin said. He glanced back at Layela. "Shuttle, then?"

Layela's features were set as she nodded.

"I'm coming too," Avienne said.

"Me too!" Patros said. Litras piped up as well.

Ardin was about to protest, but Avienne stepped in. "No. You'll need help, and the *Destiny II* will wait for us. Our battle is going to be onboard the *Lady Mirial,* and you know it as well as I do."

"She's right, Ardin," Layela said before he could protest. He sighed. "Biolt, can you keep out of harm's way? There isn't much else we can do, now. Just keep the ship safe, and we'll come back as soon as we can."

"Aye, Captain. We'll limp somewhere safe. Safer," he corrected himself.

"All right. Be careful."

The five of them piled into the lift and descended into the bowels of the great ship.

***

Elsa could hear the stars singing. She hadn't known that they could sing, but now she felt like she'd known it forever. It seemed so basic to the workings of the universe. As right as the hair on her head.

She swayed to their song a bit, leaning against the window in Rose's room. Rose still slept, but she'd be all right. Mostly, anyway. Elsa enjoyed her company, even if the engineer hadn't stirred all day. A fractured mind was something she understood and hardly feared, and it was nice to have company.

Elsa... the voice called to her, a song on a different wind. A song just for her! She recognized pieces of it, just like the day the fake Keeper threw her spirit from her body to draw Mother Layela back to Mirial. Elsa smiled. Mother Layela had come. She would always come.

Why would she doubt that?

Elsa... the voice grew more insistent, and Elsa danced to her own name. She danced out of the room and into the corridor, listening to that voice, that strange, familiar voice that drew her deeper into the ship, tugging at her spirit as strongly as the First Star herself.

She wanted to lose herself in that voice. To dance with it. To drown in it.

Elsa. The song stopped and so did Elsa.

She stood in the shuttle bay and turned just in time to smile as Mother Layela walked in.

***

Layela saw the Berganda standing in the shuttle bay, wide eyed and smiling, and she almost snapped at her. Litras stepped in front of her and greeted the Berganda by taking both her hands.

"I'll take care of her," she promised.

"Litras..." Layela began to say, but the ship jostled, struck. Layela almost lost her footing but managed to remain standing, unlike Avienne, who went down in a flurry of red hair and curses.

"She'll be safer with us," Litras offered. Layela sighed.

"Fine. Let's all pile in and get going. We need to stop the fighting."

She turned to Ardin, who stared at her quizzically. Before she could ask what his problem was, he said, "Layela, your eyes... they're both blue again."

Layela reached up for her eyes before she stopped herself. What would that show her, exactly. She pulled the knife out and looked at it, her drying blood smeared on it.

"We gotta go, blue eyes," Avienne said, pushing Layela and Ardin

247 | MARIE BILODEAU

into the shuttle. The siblings took over the command seats, and the four others piled in the back. Elsa snuggled on the floor of the small ship with her head on Layela's lap.

Why had her eyes turned back to blue?

"*Destiny II,* we're departing," Ardin said.

"Good luck, Captain." Biolt's voice answered.

"And to you. Remember to stay safe!"

She had channelled the ether as easily as if she and Mirial were still connected. But now…she looked outside as they cleared the ship and the stars surrounded them. Now, space looked riddled with ships and faraway stars, and not coated with ether.

She placed the blade on her palm, over the throbbing cut. Her breath caught in her throat and she removed the knife.

It had created a temporary connection, not a lasting one.

And Layela knew how to create a lasting one. She'd done it before. She needed to bleed in the altar at the temple of Mirial, waiting in the ship they were about to board.

Her breath caught in her throat, blocked by hope and fear.

CHAPTER 36

ARDICE HUDDLED IN a corner by a great stone, looking at Hoast, who sat with his head on his knees and his back to her. He rocked back and forth, mumbling to himself.

She didn't know what to tell him, anymore. He was scary, different, and mean. He'd tackled and hurt her, and brought her here. It had felt like a tornado. She couldn't breathe. She'd cried out but the wind had stolen her voice.

He had looked terrified and scrambled off of her. They'd been this way, since.

Hoast had always been her friend. Her only friend. She'd had Rose, of course, but Rose was an adult, not a friend. Hoast was a best friend. Exactly like she'd always wanted. Funny, loyal, and caring about stuff she cared about.

She had been sick when he'd come, and he had never left her side.

But now, someone was hurting him, and he was hurting her in turn. She didn't understand who or why, but she hoped they would stop. Or that she could stop them. Or Hoast. He was stronger than he thought. Maybe she should tell him that.

She pulled her legs out from under her, but they were numb from sitting for so long. She winced and stretched them out, trying to rub them back to life.

Hoast had stopped mumbling and shaking, which drew Ardice's attention. He looked towards the door of the big room they were in. Ardice couldn't see from where she sat. She wanted to crawl out and look, but she was too terrified. She heard the door close, and she pulled her legs back under her and pushed herself as far into the shadows as she could.

Hoast didn't look back towards her, but he stood as someone approached him. Someone tall and with orange robes. They spoke with a hollow quality in their voice.

"Are you scared?"

Hoast nodded and for a second Ardice thought he would look her way and betray her, but he didn't. She held her breath.

"Don't be. We'll be free, soon. But there's one coming who'll want to stop it from happening. She'll try to stop you from being well again." Hoast lowered his head and his shoulders began to shake. Ardice bit her lip.

"You can be well again and play with your friend, but first you have to stop the woman who will come. She'll have a knife, so you'll know she's bad."

Hoast asked something, but it was too soft for Ardice to hear. She could hear the rumbling answer. "No, you can do it. I won't be far and I'll help. You would be surprised at how much you can accomplish, when you have friends backing you."

Ardice sucked in her breath. He knew she was there, in the shadows. But he just turned around and left, the doors closing behind him.

Hoast eventually looked her way.

"I'm sorry, Ardice." He couldn't look her directly in the eyes and looked down towards her feet, which tingled with pain.

"You can be free from all the weird stuff happening to you?" Ardice whispered, testing out her legs.

He shrugged. "I think so. I guess so. But I don't think I can do it alone."

Ardice managed to walk, using the stone wall for support. She stood near Hoast, facing him.

"I'll help you."

***

Boarding the ship had seemed too easy. It had *been* too easy. Avienne was certain of that, and she flipped her knives nervously.

Patros looked even more nervous beside her, and he gestured pointedly to his scar.

Avienne shrugged and tugged the knives away.

"The temple is this way," Layela said. Shots rang by their heads. They scrambled, Ardin landing on the other side of the corridor from them, the shots keeping them separate. No one was approaching, but little space was given for firing back. Avienne swore, but was cut short as screams ripped the corridor.

"What the...is that Loran?" Layela asked, staring wide-eyed at Avienne. Avienne looked up to try and localize the sound. It was coming somewhere past the corridor where Ardin crouched.

"Ardin," she said as softly as she could, under the barrage of shots. She pointed down past him. "I think her screams are coming from there."

He cocked his head to listen, and then nodded. He looked to Layela.

"We can't leave her," Layela whispered.

Ardin nodded. "I'll go after her. You go after Ardice. Be careful!"

Avienne swore. Two minutes into this ship and they were already separating. "I don't like this!"

Her protest was cut short by a fresh volley of screams.

Ardin nodded and took out his gun, running in a crouch towards the other corridor. Avienne debated trying to fire a shot, but they were so consistent she'd only succeed in getting herself shot.

Patros grabbed her and dragged her the other way, away from her brother.

She hoped she swore loudly enough for every soul on the ship to hear her.

***

Litras kept Elsa close to her as she ran. The Berganda hummed to herself, but still kept up. She was not a child of battle, that one.

They turned a corner too quickly and hit two guards, hard. Litras pulled herself up and trained her gun on the man, but could not bring herself to shoot. The man stared back at her through his helmet, slack-jawed, with dead eyes.

"Risl?" she whispered.

Elsa stopped humming, staring intently at the Kilita. Layela and Avienne rounded the corner, weapons drawn.

"Litras, shoot him!" Avienne said, but Litras held up her hand.

"Don't. Please. It's...he's a friend. An old friend from back home."

"He doesn't look so good," Avienne said. "What's wrong with him?"

Litras bit her lower lip and brought her hand up to try and remove the helmet, but she couldn't. It was stuck on the skull, the bone and plastics fused through ether. Through Ralis ether.

Litras turned around and threw up. Avienne moved her feet a second too late to avoid splatter. The redhead cursed softly but didn't lose her temper.

"Can we do anything for him, Litras?" Layela asked, looking close into Risl's eyes.

"He was funny," was all Litras said, not able to say more. He liked to make her laugh for no good reason, making funny faces and trying to scare her in the dark. He'd even made her laugh when they'd buried her parents, silly boy. He was a third cousin, but everyone in Kilita was related closely. The pool was so shallow, and now…

"They took them all. My whole village." She looked to the second soldier, and whispered his name, confiding it to Mirial herself. "They took them all…" She didn't want to see them like this. What of her nephews and nieces? Her siblings, her cousins? Her uncles and aunts… there were too many to bear. Everyone she'd ever known. Everyone she'd left behind to keep them safe, more than a decade ago.

"Why would they do this?" Avienne asked, looking around the corridor for any other potential threats.

Litras' stomach settled and a cool wave washed over her. Cleansing, freeing. She looked into Risl's dead eyes as she spoke, confessing to someone who could no longer hear her. But infinitely easier than looking at the disbelief of the living.

"Because the Ralis asked me for a favour a long time ago, and I refused." Litras said, and continued before they could ask, focusing on Risl alone. He would have found a way to make her laugh, even now. But she couldn't see the humour in any of it.

"He wanted me to help vanquish Mirial."

Avienne swore.

"I refused, obviously," Litras said. "I had been sent to help Mirial, not impede her."

A pause. A stretched silence. "Who sent you, Litras?"

The Kilita smiled, the teeth scraping her gums. "I did. Generations ago, when Mirial was but a newborn star, I sent myself."

She remembered Risl's face when she'd confessed her dreams and beliefs to him. He hadn't laughed, then. He'd believed her, and her brother had believed her, too. Because Kilita didn't lie to each other. Kilita had too many other enemies to worry about, to make them amongst their own ranks.

But it wasn't to Risl that she spoke. She turned and faced them, her companions. Elsa stared at her with tenderness. Layela curiosity. Avienne stared everywhere but at Litras, keeping an eye on the expansive corridor.

"I'm a Fate, or rather a new incarnation of the Three Fates."

Avienne stopped searching and raised an eyebrow. "You're kidding, right?"

Litras grinned. "You promised to the Three Fates that you'd give up drinking if your brother was saved, a promise that you've staunchly kept despite my assurances that you didn't need to."

Litras turned to Layela. "I'm sorry for what was done to you by one of my own," Litras said. "There are different tribes, and no excuses. Every people has its vermin. That's why I didn't approach you until you needed me, Keeper of Mirial. I knew my form would prove difficult."

Layela's eyes widened and then narrowed. Avienne cut in. "Blood and bones, I *could* have been drinking all this time. So is that why you have an invisible ship, then?"

Litras smiled at her. "No! I stole that a long time ago. Experimental stuff. Being a Fate really gives you nothing except some insight into the world, how it works, and what needs to happen."

"That's it?" Layela asked, incredulous. "You're telling us you're one of the most mystical beings in all of the universe, and all that you can do is see things?"

The Kilita shrugged. "It's for the Keeper of Mirial to wield the ether. I can only offer advice, when I have it."

Layela grew frustrated. "What about the mural, then? What about what my mother etched in the wall, about the Three Fates re-igniting Mirial? Aren't you supposed to be the answer?"

Litras' shoulder dropped a bit. "I am only one, Keeper. Your mother was offered a vision of a possible future. But all Three Fates are needed to join with Mirial and boost the ether from within the First Star. All three."

Layela seemed deflated. "Three Fates."

"I'm sorry, Keeper, but I can only provide you with some wisdom. They will play on your worst fears," Litras whispered, forcing herself to look at Layela and not turn to Risl. "Whatever you fear the most, whatever your heart tries to desire most or least, they will know. And they will try to destroy you."

Layela nodded and let a few moments slip by before speaking. "If you're a Fate, tell me this: Can the Fated survive without Mirial? Do we even need the First Star?"

Litras looked towards where the star burned silently, beyond the walls of this ship. "Some would survive. Most wouldn't. The Ralis are hoping they're one of the ones that survive."

Layela looked down the corridor, where the temple's hall rested. "Is there any chance that the other two Fates will come?"

Litras offered Layela a smile. "They must be willing to give up a lot, Keeper. It often means never returning to this realm, this world. The individual's conviction must be strong enough to undertake the full change to a Fate and then, if they have any willpower left, sometimes they're allowed to return. But so rarely. It is not something one can do lightly."

"Why did you?" Litras glanced at Risl this time, but before she could even begin formulating an answer, Patros rounded the corner fast, ducking as shots grazed his head.

"Incoming!" he screamed, and the party retreated further into the corridor. Avienne returned shots and took cover in an entryway, as did Patros. Litras pulled Elsa into an entryway.

"Where's Layela?" Avienne screamed. "Blood and bones, I'm going to hurt her!" Litras watched the Keeper vanish around the corner as she held Elsa tight.

She hoped Layela Delamores cared about Mirial as much as she cared about her daughter.

CHAPTER 37

LAYELA LEFT THE others to fight off the attackers. Avienne and Patros could handle a few gun-wielding Kilita, and Litras could probably help, she imagined. She didn't allow her mind the space to debate whether the Kilita's claims were true or false, focusing instead on finding her daughter.

The knife was safely tucked in her boot, and she hoped she wouldn't need to use it. But if someone needed to bleed in that altar, it would be her, not Ardice. She clung to that as she reached the temple door.

She took a deep breath and pressed the access code.

The doors opened. Beyond, the pieces of the temple were just as they had been last she'd seen them. The doors closed behind Layela, the bright lights and wide open space making her feel exposed. She skirted the wall towards the rocky surface.

She wanted to whisper Ardice's name, but she had no idea where exactly she was. She reached the stone and stood, listening for any sound, any indication that she was here, hidden somewhere in the maze of rocks, waiting to be found and brought safely home...

Layela's heart ached to see her. She had held the grief and longing at bay for years, and now they crashed into her. Stepping safely away from the temple, she pulled the knife out of her boot.

She had found her once using ether, and she would do so again.

***

Ardice hid in the shadows, under some rocks, with Hoast. The lady looked nice enough at first, if a bit sweaty and jerky in her movements. But then she pulled out the knife and cut herself with it, and Ardice thought she might throw up.

She looked away and hid her face into Hoast's shoulder.

"We have to stop her," Hoast whispered into her hair. "Otherwise we'll never be free!"

Ardice nodded and pulled her head out of Hoast's shoulder. The woman was staring into the shadows, her eyes aglow with greens and blues, her dark hair casting dark shadows on her chiselled features.

When she spoke, Ardice couldn't hold back a yelp.

"Ardice?"

***

The ether was clear—her daughter was under the rocks. And she cried out! Layela contained her excitement and forced herself to take a step back. The girl was terrified, and rightly so. Layela couldn't force Ardice to come to her.

She slowed her breath to soothe her emotions. She had no right to ask Ardice to come to her. Not after giving her up, no matter how noble her intentions.

The shadows stirred and Layela tried not to take an eager step forward. She fought disappointment when the young Zoorsa stepped out of the shadows instead of Ardice. Layela forced a smile. "Hoast, wasn't it? It's great to see you again."

He looked at her sceptically, his steps hesitant. "Are you really the Keeper," he said, his eyes wide with... Layela couldn't quite read him. Fear?

She kept her smile. "I am. You know that—you saw me on Mirial." Something shifted in the young Zoorsa's smile and his eyes lost some glow. Layela forced herself to see the ether around her, but it was too late to break the Ralis' control over the Zoorsa. He ran towards her, screaming.

Layela tried to grab the boy by the shoulders to stop him, but he ran straight for her, grabbed the knife and struck it into his own chest before Layela could stop him.

"Noo!" Her cry was echoed by Ardice, who ran out of the shadows to watch her friend crumple in his own blood, the ceremonial blade sticking out of his chest.

"Ardice—" The name caught in Layela's throat as the hatred in the green and blue eyes was turned upon her.

"I didn't…" she tried to say, but knew there was nothing she could do or say to make this better. Her daughter thought Layela had killed her best friend. She hated her. She would always hate her.

The Ralis had known her greatest fear. And they had executed it beautifully.

***

Ardin followed the screams, which lead him uncomfortably far from Layela and Avienne. He met no resistance, and as soon as he reached the gardens, he knew where he was headed.

He stopped. Loran's screams still resonated around him, making it difficult to concentrate. Had they simply wanted to lure him away? Was this a trap? Did it even matter anymore? Had it already succeeded?

The screams spurred him into action and he activated the lift down, holding his weapon at the ready. As soon as the lift stopped, the screams stopped, as well. Loran knelt on the floor, looking away from him. He followed her gaze and suppressed every emotion he could at the sight of Erlin. His eyes were lolled back into his head, the warm room accelerating his decay.

Loran wasn't screaming. He doubted she had, for a while, she looked so fragile crumpled on the floor. They had used her to draw him away from Layela. He swallowed his bitterness. It didn't matter now. What was done was done, and Loran needed his help.

He jammed the lift open and stepped off. "Loran," he said. He repeated her name before she turned to him. He thought her eyes would be shallow and broken, but instead they shone with anger. "I couldn't get out," she said, her voice calm and even. "I couldn't get out, so I looked at him, instead. If the Ralis knew this was my worst fear, then I conquered it. I conquered it, and now I'll kill them for making me face it."

Ardin couldn't think of any words to say, so he just nodded. She stood awkwardly, her legs obviously bothering her. She used her rifle for support. He didn't offer help, and she didn't ask for any.

He followed her into the lift and they headed back up. Ardin hated the lack of resistance. Someone, anyone, should have been trying to stop them. It made it feel as though nothing they could do would matter.

***

The door opened and the First among the Ralis walked in. Layela wanted to take Ardice away from him, but her daughter's hatred stayed her hand and her tongue. She forced herself to remain standing and defiant. If she could only be an object of hatred for her daughter, she would at least show her one that wouldn't give in.

"She's just a child," Layela said, the accusation coating her words.

"She's your crutch," the Ralis said. Ardice stood quietly, the hatred lifted from her features. Layela furrowed her brow and gazed at the ether. It was everywhere, and she could discern none of it. Ardice looked blank, slack-jawed.

"She's fine," the First said, his voice echoing from within his own smug head. "She's just easier to reach into. And," he added, and Layela jumped as Hoast stood back up. "To use her own ether to form a perfect little puppet of a friend. An extension. The perfect manipulation."

Hoast grinned, his eyes still lolling, dead. Goose bumps erupted all over Layela and she swallowed a lifetime of screams.

"You could have just approached me, and left her out of this," Layela said, unable to peel her eyes away from Hoast, who went to sit by Ardice's feet.

"Do you know the legend of the Three Fates?" the Ralis asked. Layela didn't answer, frantic to come up with a plan that would see both her and Ardice survive the day. It was like trying to swim up a waterfall.

"It doesn't matter. You've heard variations. But basically, Keeper of Mirial, we wish to be free. All Fated, and yourself included." It waved towards Ardice. "Think about it. You craved freedom for your child so badly that you gave her up. For ten years. We of Ralis live for thousands of your years. And I, too, would give up some of my children to secure their freedom."

Layela laughed. "By give up, you mean kill, right? Because a lot of Fated might not survive without a First Star. I'm assuming that includes some of yours."

The Ralis lowered its head slightly, as though acknowledging.

"It's too large a price to pay," Layela whispered, forcing herself not to look at Ardice. "Too large a price to pay."

The Ralis rumbled. "We have one thing in common, it seems. Desires are what doom us all.

Layela bit back a retort as Ardice moved, dragging her eyes back to her daughter. Ardice grabbed the handle of the knife and pulled hard.

Without hesitation, Layela slammed ether into her own child, sending her, Hoast, and the knife flying.

She grabbed all of the ether available to her and slammed it into the Ralis, who vanished into a garbled scream. The illusion fluttered in Layela's ether. He hadn't even been there!

Where was he?

The hull shook and threw Layela against the temple. She reached over to her unconscious daughter, shielding her with her body. They slid agross stone and into the temple as the ship buckled under attacks.

"I'm so sorry, Ardice," Layela whispered. She held her tight and tried to keep her safe on the turbulent ship, but some part of her knew that it didn't matter anymore.

She had already dealt her the worst blow of all.

***

Avienne lost her footing when the ship buckled, falling right in the path of fire. She swore, but Patros pulled her beside him, narrowly avoiding bullets.

"They're not dancing like we are!" Avienne screamed to Litras.

"We'll need to kill them," Litras said, so matter-of-factly that Avienne hurt for her. Fate or not, no one should have had to make those calls for those they loved.

She pulled out a carbon grenade. It would take them out without killing them.

"You sure?" she asked, pulling the pin.

"Of course."

The voice was filled with certainty and calm. Not the Kilita she had grown fond of, in her own strange way.

"So that's what a Fate sounds like," she said as she threw the grenade.

***

Loran lost her footing with the first jostle, falling against a doorway with a snap. She slid to the ground, swearing in a way that would make even Avienne blush.

"I need to get there, Ardin!" she screamed. Her eyes filled with anger and tears as she tried to stand, but the connection to her left leg was severed.

He grabbed her arm and threw it over his shoulder, and started running again with her hobbling along beside him. The ship shook again, and some of the Kilita tumbled into the corridor.

Ardin let Loran go and pulled out his gun. The Kilita seemed to need a moment to orient themselves, but then they stood, aimed, and started firing.

Ardin dragged Loran around the corner.

"I'll hold them off," Loran said through her teeth. "Just promise me you'll make it hurt."

She glanced around the corner and fired a few shots before ducking back to safety.

"They haven't known pain until today," Ardin said. Gun in hand, he ran down the corridor, hoping he wasn't too late.

***

Captain Kat saw the *Sun's Barrow* begin her attack on the *Lady Mirial*. The assault would not destroy her, but the *Sun's Barrow* was definitely trying to get *Lady Mirial* to do something. She was already crippled, but they were doing some notable extra damage.

She jumped out of her chair and headed to tactical. The temple of Mirial was on that ship— the greatest, most important item in Mirial's history and culture. It had survived cataclysms, and it was meant to survive even Mirial's demise. But it wouldn't survive unless they stopped firing.

Gilane had no engine power left, and so little in weaponry it was a laughable offence. She might as well try and spit on the enemy ship.

There were one hundred and three Mirial souls on board that ship. And they might soon all be dead, if they weren't already. The reality of keeping her own people safe suddenly smothered her. She needed to escape—to save the few Mirialers left in the universe, she needed a way out.

And she had none.

But others had it. They had a way to help. She had asked for help before, and she would do it again. And again. As often as it took to save her people. Her pride as shattered as her ship, she reached for the comm unit.

***

Sirse did not like the Mirialer's voice. It reeked of defeat. But she understood the message. The Keeper needed help.

She didn't care that much for Mirial, but she knew they needed the Keeper, and the ether. And that her people, the Fated, needed—no, deserved—the chance to stand on their own.

The Ralis wanted to offer them freedom, and some fools had fallen for it.

They could have freedom. Maybe not from Mirial, not from the ether, but rather from the races who constantly tried to control her people.

If they were the Fated, then they need to take control of their fate.

And today, they would. She smiled and turned her ship towards the *Sun's Barrow.*

The Ralis did not expect this.

Sirse imagined the smell of the blood of her enemies.

***

The First Among the Ralis predicted the attack from the Fated two minutes before it occurred. He sat in his chair and debated what to do. They did not crave freedom, as he did. They had not had centuries to know the effects of ether, as he had.

Even with the Keeper stepping back to her post, it would not matter. Mirial was a doomed star, dwindling at a slower rate than they'd hoped. Without breaking the connection of the Keeper's daughter, he could not destroy the star. It was still protected by its people.

By its Keeper.

And without the knife, the key to it all, they could not finalize their plan.

But it didn't matter. Mirial was trapped, without help. The Keeper's daughter hated her. The one Fate that walked amongst them would die, alone, trapped in a mortal shell on a lonely world.

He still mused his desire for freedom when Sirse's ship rammed his own, the *Sun's Barrow* shining as bright as Mirial for a brief moment before breaking into hundreds of pieces.

CHAPTER 38

THE SHIP DANCED as though caught in a blast, and the Kilita stopped firing abruptly and fell to the ground, dead.

Avienne holstered her gun and stepped out. "Blood and bones, that was strange. What happened?"

Litras stepped beside her. "The First among the Ralis was destroyed by the Fated. They followed his instructions, but they chose freedom from *him*, instead." Litras grinned.

"Layela," Avienne said, but Litras grabbed her arm. "She needs a moment, still. Just a moment more. She'll become Keeper again, to help her daughter. You should know that."

"And Mirial? Can they build a new First Star?" She glanced to Patros. He never complained about dwindling ether, but his skin used to be bluer and his eyes less yellow.

The Kilita shrugged. "Most of the Seeders were killed, and it will take a while to build a star with the few that are left. Probably not for a few lifetimes."

"Blood and bones," Avienne said, flicking her last knife up. "That's not good enough, Litras. If you're a Fate, what can you do?"

"She can do nothing, no more than I," Elsa said stepping out of the shadows, placing one foot before the other and her arms out to her side as though she were about to curtsy.

"What do you mean…oh, blood and bones, another Fate?" Litras and Elsa exchanged a look.

"This one's an accident," Litras said. "She found songs older than Mirial and remembered." Litras glanced towards the room with the temple. "Sometimes only one walks. But there are never two without three," she said.

"But what's your purpose?" Patros asked, a hint of despair in his words. "Why are you here, if you can't help us?"

Litras looked to him. "We can only help if we are three, Patros. I'm sorry. Three, or nothing. There is another way to assure the Fated can survive longer, though it isn't a great way."

"What's that?" Avienne said, looking from Litras to Patros. "Out with it!"

"We can remove some of the strain on the star by taking back some of the loaned ether." Litras' gaze was steady. "Half less consumption of ether should do."

It took a moment for Avienne to realize what she was saying. *Loaned ether...* "You mean kill half of them. Half of the Fated." Her hand sought out Patros. He grabbed hers and held it tight.

"If it's the only way to save at least some of us..." he started, but Avienne cut him off.

"Shut up, Patros." Her eyes threw darts at Litras. "That's not good enough. I want a better solution. Something that'll work without so much death! Come on, Litras!"

Litras shrugged. "Half of them can be claimed. Just like that. It's easy, and it'll work. To ease the tension on the First Star, until a new one can be ignited."

Avienne's blood grew cold. "How does Mirial even choose?"

She shrugged again. "She doesn't. It's random. Maybe whoever's closest, whoever's best connected, I really don't know."

"There must be something we can do! This is stupid!"

Litras looked her straight in the eyes, and Avienne stilled. The Kilita's voice was thick like honey. "There is one other thing. The Three Fates can walk again. United, they are stronger. But the third does not yet walk."

"The third one...Layela?" Avienne asked. Litras kept her eyes steady. "Or Ardice." Avienne flipped a knife. "Layela or Ardice." She caught the knife. "Well, you can't have either one. My brother deserves both. A bit of happiness, blood and bones!"

The ship shook and Avienne almost lost her footing, glad she hadn't been flipping a knife at that moment.

"We have to go," Litras said, turning towards Elsa, who danced down a corridor. "We'll wait as long as we can."

Avienne nodded. The Kilita was leaving it all up to her, to decide whether to tell Layela—to sacrifice half of the ether creatures, or her brother's happiness.

"Blood and bones, I need a drink!"

***

Layela gently placed Ardice's hand on the floor, rolling her coat under her head to make her more comfortable. The *Sun's Barrow* was gone. Destroyed.

But Mirial still hurt so badly. The Fated outside were riled up for freedom, for a battle, and they drew on even more ether without realizing it.

The First Star caressed Layela urgently, as though crying for help before she buckled under her own weight.

Layela knelt near Hoast. His eyes were open, and he was breathing.

"Do you know what you are?" Layela asked him, now seeing clearly what she hadn't noted on their first encounter. That his ether was Ardice's ether. That he was linked to her, like a puppy on a leash.

Hoast nodded. "I think I've always known, because part of her has always known." He coughed blood and gave a half grin. "She won't let me die. Even hurt as she is, she won't let me go."

Layela placed her hand on the boy's forehead and brushed his hair aside. "Do you want to continue, Hoast, as your own person?"

Hoast smiled. "I could?"

Layela nodded and stood. Part of her selfishly just wanted Ardice to forgive her, and another part didn't want to bury one more child, even if that child had been created out of ether and loneliness.

Layela picked up the knife and stood before the altar. Her hand shook and she tried to steady it.

Just one cut, and some blood, and I can save Hoast. I can save Hoast.

A hand covered hers and steadied it. She recognized the warmth and smiled. "Yoma," she said. "You didn't leave me."

Of course not. But you left me. Not that I noticed or anything…

Layela bit back a laugh for fear of crying.

Mirial is your home, now. And mine.

She vanished, but Layela's hands had stopped shaking.

Yoma is my Hoast, Layela suddenly realized, and suddenly understood the vast strength of Ardice's connection with the ether. Layela could only conjure the spirit of her sister. Ardice had managed to create her own sibling.

Layela looked back towards Hoast and Ardice. Overwhelmed with pride, she couldn't wait to see how wonderful a Keeper Ardice would be. In time.

She smiled.

Without hesitation, she drew the knife across her palm and bled into the altar.

***

Avienne held Patros' hand. *Half of all ether creatures. Half of the Fated.* Half were willing to give up their lives, so that the other half could live longer, in the hopes of a new First Star. Unless Layela chose to follow Litras and Elsa, and become a Fate. A Fate to take care of the Fated.

Time slowed around her as she ran her hand up Patros' arm, up to his face, cupping his cheek with her palm. His warmth infused her whole hand. He looked as young as he had when they had met. He would always look this young, and would outlive her by years.

Or would he? Would Mirial rip his life away, leave him an empty shell?

We'll see. Litras had looked at her so strangely when she had spoken. Not at her, but through her. They would see...what? If Layela would come? Or was it not Layela, at all?

Memories began swirling around her, stealing her breath with their intensity, flashing strings of event into one coherent snake involving one person. *Litras.*

Litras, who always stayed near her. Litras, who had led her rescue on Thalos IV. Litras, who had involved Avienne in this again, even though she could have handled it herself. Litras, who had told her what needed to happen for the Three Fates to come back. Litras had never mentioned Layela's name, but rather Layela had been an assumption on Avienne's part.

Time stopped.

Patros' eyes were closed, his cheek resting against her hand, as though he wanted it to be the last thing he would ever feel.

"Do you remember how I saved you the first time we met?"

He smiled. "Of course."

She stood on the tips of her toes and whispered in his ear, his warm breath on her face. "I didn't save you then to lose you now."

Before he could say anything, she kneed him in the gut. He bent over with a whoosh of air, and she elbowed his back. He fell, unconscious.

She knelt beside him.

"Sorry, lover."

Time resumed as Ardin ran into the room. He looked at her, wide-eyed. "Is he okay?" He knelt beside her, concern lining his tired features, sweat on his brow and his hand on his gun. She tried to imagine his life without Layela. She tried to imagine him rebuilding himself after losing her.

"He'll be fine," she said, and they both stood.

"Go after Ardice and Layela, Ardin."

He shot her one more look and nodded, but she called out after him as he started running.

"Ardin!" He stopped and turned to look at her, frustration and concern highlighting every feature. She wanted to tell him she loved him, and his family. That she was proud of him and the choices he'd made. That he was still a hero to her, had always been. Always would be. But he would hate himself for letting her go later on, for having been made to choose between his blood family and his chosen one. She tried to think of something funny to say instead, so he would know, in retrospect, that she'd be fine. That she'd known what she'd been doing, and had embraced the choice.

"I have to go, Avienne," he said, about to turn.

She blurted out the first thing that came to mind: "Make the Malavants proud." It was stupid, and it was all she could think of saying. He grinned at her.

"Someone has to!"

He turned around and ran into the next corridor, followed by the echo of her laughter.

"Yeah, someone has to, all right." She grinned, blew one last kiss toward Patros, and turned back to find Litras.

It looked like she wouldn't be trapped on Mirial, after all.

EPILOGUE

PATROS STOOD ON the edge of the dock by the one-man cruise ship, and looked back to Layela.

"My sister never left me, Patros. A part of Avienne will always be with you, as Mirial is."

He gave her a thin smile. "Was it ever the same?"

Layela lowered her eyes. "Of course not." She looked back up. "But it helped during the darkest days."

He nodded and walked away, nothing left to say.

Maybe Layela was right. Maybe Avienne was still there, her laughter drifting in the rays of Mirial, enveloping the air around him.

Maybe.

He hoped she was right. Patros had no doubt that he would face many dark days ahead.

***

Ardin kissed Ardice on the forehead, and then Hoast. The bedtime routine had taken months to establish, but both children had taken a shining to it as long as it involved him telling them a story. He still couldn't believe his luck.

He had his daughter back: a smart, sassy and beautiful girl, who would one day steal the hearts of every Mirialer and Fated in this region of space. He had gained a son, as well, in Hoast. He knew where the boy had come from, and he didn't care. He was good to Ardice, and helped bridge the awkward silences with a joke or a story.

Months later, they were still all learning how to be a family. But it was getting better. Rose had been a big help in bringing them all together, even if she didn't quite fit all the logic into her head that she used to. She was family, too, and they all made do in their home.

Home.

Ardin stepped outside to enjoy the scent of fresh blooms on the evening breeze. He glanced towards the palace, where they had once lived. Layela had split the power when she returned. She would be the Keeper, and live by the temple and care for the plants of Mirial. But another would be the leader of Mirial. Layela had refused to take up the political mantle.

The people had selected another, instead. One who had been born off-planet, but always put Mirial ahead of her own needs, and who had given up both legs to the cause. Loran had never let Mirial down, and Ardin believed she never would.

Beyond the palace, the shipyards were nearly empty. With almost nowhere to go, the ships had fallen into slight disrepair. He had fixed up the *Destiny II* a bit, and sometimes Rose seemed to regain her old self and would work on the engine, but overall, Mirial's great fleet seemed a dream for another life.

So many things seemed meant for another life, now. And today, on Avienne's birthday, he was reminded of it more acutely than he had felt it since they had taken Mirial back. Layela stepped up beside him, and before he could think of it, he said: "I miss her."

Layela tried to give a smile, but it faded and her face flushed red. She whispered, "It should have been me, Ardin."

He placed his hand under her chin and forced her to look at him. "She knew what she was doing, Layela. She was too stubborn to consider any other way. She chose to do this, for us. For Patros." His voice dropped. "For me."

He gave her a half smile.

"Can you imagine the world with that woman as a Fate! The world doesn't know what it's in for!"

His laughter came out crooked and ill, and his smile fell with his eyes. Layela quickly closed the gap between then and held him close, well into the night.

***

Patros felt better than he had in the months since leaving Mirial. The freighter was as small as they came, but it would get him most of the way home. Maybe he'd find Gobran, first, and see if the old man still lived and had been true to his promise to Avienne.

"Avienne," he whispered. He missed the laughter. The insanity. The unpredictability. She had become his family. Avienne, Jaru, and Gobran. Jaru was gone, and Gobran probably would be soon, if not already. He missed them all. And because he no longer had them, he missed his home, a pain that wrapped his heart and his bones, and riddled his nightmares with desperate hopes and desires.

Parsecs still separated him from his home. In all of his months, he had only encountered the debris of one of the tunnel stabilizers, even though he followed their course. That meant he had many, many more months and years to go.

It would have been too far for Avienne to ever make it there with him.

Yet, every day, he felt a bit stronger. Despite his space travel, his skin tone was much better.

Mirial was recovering, he had little doubt.

"You did it, you crazy, beautiful woman."

Something made his spine shiver, a familiar touch on the back of his neck. He closed his eyes, afraid to lose the sensation, illusion or otherwise. He smiled when the familiar voice breathed into his ear.

"Hello, lover."

-THE END-

Layela &
Ardice